A DETECTIVE INSPEC

TO HUNT ᴬMAGPIE

NEW YORK TIMES #1 BESTSELLER **TONY LEE** WRITING AS

JACK GATLAND

Hooded Man MEDIA
INTERACTIVE ▪ PRODUCTION ▪ PUBLICATION

Published by Hooded Man Media.

First Edition: June 2021

PRAISE FOR JACK GATLAND

'This is one of those books that will keep you up past your bedtime, as each chapter lures you into reading just one more.'

'This book was excellent! A great plot which kept you guessing until the end.'

'Couldn't put it down, fast paced with twists and turns.'

'The story was captivating, good plot, twists you never saw and really likeable characters. Can't wait for the next one!'

'I got sucked into this book from the very first page, thoroughly enjoyed it, can't wait for the next one.'

'Totally addictive. Thoroughly recommend.'

'Moves at a fast pace and carries you along with it.'

'Just couldn't put this book down, from the first page to the last one it kept you wondering what would happen next.'

Before LETTER FROM THE DEAD...
There was

LIQUIDATE THE PROFITS

Learn the story of what *really* happened to DI Declan Walsh, while at Mile End!

An EXCLUSIVE PREQUEL, completely free to anyone who joins the Declan Walsh Reader's Club!

Join at bit.ly/jackgatlandVIP

Also by Jack Gatland

COVERT ACTION

COUNTER ATTACK

STEALTH STRIKE

DAMIAN LUCAS BOOKS

THE LIONHEART CURSE

STANDALONE BOOKS

THE BOARDROOM

For Mum, who inspired me to write.

For Tracy, who inspires me to write.

CONTENTS

PROLOGUE

THIRTY YEARS AFTER THE BOOKS HAD BEEN FIRST RELEASED, THE *Magpie* series of children's detective stories were almost forgotten in the contemporary book market. Set at the start of the nineties, the novels were simple and quick to follow; Agatha Christie for the pre-teen generation, a series of adventures with titles like *The Adventure of the Drowning Duchess, The Adventure of the Missing Prince* and *The Adventure of the Broken Clock,* all stories that showed how a small and clever team of teenage sleuths could defeat grown up criminals, with detective skills and good old fashioned *gumption*. More contemporary than their Enid Blyton related peers, the Magpie series however had one major difference to the others.

They were based on the *truth.*

The official story was as old as the novels themselves; that author Reginald Troughton had learned of the Magpies and their crime solving through a report in a local newspaper, and had written their adventures as stories, never expecting the interest that they would generate. In fact, he wrote seven novels in total involving the adventures of *Tommy, Luke, Tessa, Jane* and *Daniel,* and their group mascot and crime solving spaniel *Dexter the dog,* finishing when the Magpies themselves disbanded after a distinguished teenage crime solving career.

The books had sold on for a few years more, but in the same way that many other book franchises suffered, they were overtaken by new trends, new technology, and eventually faded into the realms of nostalgia.

But the *fans* never forgot them. And, as the years passed, and the Magpies moved on with their lives, the fans still supported them.

Well, some more than others.

Thomas Williams, or as he was known back then, *Tommy* wasn't a teenage sleuth anymore. Now he was in his mid-forties but still looked a good few years younger, his brown hair short and styled with the slightest hint of bottle-dye, a Ted Baker suit over a pale Eton shirt, his tan brogues shined to perfection and his stubble carefully curated. He looked like a cross between a television presenter and a self-help guru. Which, actually, were two of the many roles he'd played over the years.

Today however he was there, not as Thomas, but as Tommy once more. The fourth floor of Waterstones' Piccadilly branch had been converted from bookstore to event venue for the night, with folding chairs in rows facing a clearing at the front where a lectern had been hastily placed, a table to the side piled high with newly released editions of the Magpies books. Beside that a sign had been tacked onto the wall, the same poster that had been strategically positioned around the store; a photo of the Magpies in their prime, above a line of text that read

MEET THOMAS WILLIAMS - 'TOMMY' FROM THE MAGPIES - 7PM!

Thomas hated the photo; he hated that Daniel had got to sit beside Jane for it, while he had to place a brotherly arm around his 'cousin', Luke, who was being an absolute prick to him at the time.

Nothing changes.

He looked across the floor at the chairs from his hidden 'backstage' area, which was in actuality a small, closed off space made from repositioned bookshelves. It wasn't exactly a West End dressing room, but he'd had worse.

The audience was primarily female; it always was for these events. Thomas assumed it was the same for teenage heartthrobs when they attended events years later, but he had never been a heartthrob in any sense of the word, and these women only wanted him now because he was a reminder of their youth—

He stopped scanning the audience as he spied a lone woman in her forties in the fourth row, her blonde hair pulled back. Slim and still as stunningly attractive as she was as a teenager, Thomas grinned on seeing her, and straightened his jacket.

Ah, Jane. You couldn't stay away from me.

Now, Thomas Williams had an audience that he gave a *damn* about.

As the audience mumbled and muttered excitedly to each other, a small, stocky woman in her late thirties walked to the lectern, tapping the microphone on it to check that it was working, silencing the audience's conversations as they turned to face her with expectant gazes. When he'd arrived an hour earlier, she'd told Thomas her name, and he seemed to remember that she was the manager of one floor, but there were so many managers and store owners over the years, that in the end they all merged into one. He never remembered the names.

Well, only the pretty ones.

'Thank you everyone, for attending tonight,' she began, her face beaming with pride. 'When I was a girl, I loved the Magpie books. I'd even dream of one day solving cases with Tommy Williams, Luke Ashton, Tessa Martinez, Jane Taylor, Daniel McCarthy and Dexter the dog. Anyone else do that?'

There was a smattering of hands and a chuckle of approving laughter. Validated, the manager continued.

'One reason the books sold so well, apart from the excellent writing of Reginald Troughton, was that the five characters—'

'And the dog!' a voice called out. Thomas, listening, cringed. He had *hated* that bloody spaniel.

'And the dog, yes,' the manager replied. 'One reason the books sold so well was because unlike so many other 'teenage detective' stories, these were *true*, written by Troughton, based on notes and interviews given to him by the Magpies themselves.'

Thomas moved into position for his entrance, and the audience, seeing this, fidgeted with excitement as, unaware of this, the manager continued.

'And tonight we're very lucky to have with us one of the original Magpies, a man who has written new introductions for the upcoming reprints, celebrating the thirtieth anniversary of the group's first adventure,' she gushed. 'He's here today to sign them for you, but before we put him to work, let's hear it for 'Tommy' from the Magpies, Thomas Williams!'

As the audience applauded and cheered, Thomas walked to the lectern, waving to the crowd and nodding to the manager as she backed away to give him space. Now at the lectern, he gave a second brief wave to his adoring fans and then spoke, a prepared speech that he'd spoken at events around the world for over twenty years; one so well rehearsed that he could alter it on the fly.

'When my cousin Luke and I started the Magpies, it was to prove that our milkman wasn't a killer,' he explained. 'We couldn't even conceive the global phenomenon that it would become. But Reginald Troughton did. He believed the stories he would write about us would become famous. Would make *us* famous.'

He went to motion towards the back of the room, but paused, thrown for a moment.

There was a gap at the back of the crowd that shouldn't be there.

And a cryptic message he'd had earlier that day suddenly made sense.

'Uh... Unfortunately Reginald can't be with us today as he's suffering from a head cold in Scotland,' he continued on, recovering. 'But he sends his regards to all of you.'

He looked at Jane who, realising what he was about to do, started shaking her head.

'But that's not to say I'm the only celebrity here today,' Thomas smiled, pointing to her. 'I'd like to introduce to you another member of the Magpies, my good friend Jane Taylor!'

As the audience, surprised at such a person in their midst, looked to Jane and applauded, Thomas took a deep breath, grateful to her for the distraction.

Because Reginald Troughton wasn't in Scotland and didn't have a cold.

He was supposed to have appeared, out of nowhere, from the back of the audience. It was a 'surprise appearance' skit that he'd performed for years, and one that was as far from a 'surprise' as you could get these days.

So where the hell was he this time?

REGINALD TROUGHTON SAT IN THE OFFICE OF HIS APARTMENT IN Temple Inn, facing his desk and MacBook Pro with an air of frustrated irritation. He was on a deadline, and he was failing it. He remembered some kind of anecdote by Douglas Adams about *deadlines* and *whooshing noises,* but it didn't really help that as far as he was concerned, Adams was a hack who could write a novel in a week, while he, the great and lauded Reginald Troughton couldn't write a sodding children's book in a month.

His agent had called earlier that day, passive aggressively demanding the finished manuscript by the end of the week, or else the advance was being taken away. Reginald had taken the scolding before pointing out that *he only heard from her when she needed something,* and *where the hell was the auction for his adult thriller series she'd been promising.* However, as he'd already spent the pittance BadgerLock Publishing had sent him months earlier, and after Michael's funeral expenses, he didn't have the cash around to give back.

He would in a few days though, a windfall was coming his way; but that was his *retirement.* There was no way that he'd be using that to pay back Julia Clarke and her band of merry marketers, and this meant that he had to buckle down and finish the bloody thing, which meant he couldn't go to the Waterstones event.

Which was fine by him; now in his mid-sixties, he wasn't interested in fanboy totty anymore. Also, Thomas Williams was an insufferable bastard to be around, a little snivelling shit whose only income was milking people's nostalgia for pennies. He'd passed the message that he wasn't attending tonight down the line, but he'd left it vague in case he managed to actually make it.

He *hadn't*.

And now he was finishing up the 'lost' Magpie adventure, trying to work out how to say what he wanted to say without shitting the bed too much. It was supposed to be called *The Adventure of the Blacksmith's Apron*, and was possibly the most made up bollocks he had ever written, but halfway through he'd had a revelation. He was going to write the *truth*. And so the book had been re-titled *The Adventure of the Stolen Innocence*, and instead of some bullshit about a blacksmith in a Devonshire village, the book was now the truth about the bloody Magpies, why they'd been formed and, more importantly, why they'd ended. He knew it'd piss people off, but frankly he didn't care. The contract didn't state what the novel had to be about, and they didn't pay him enough to keep silent anymore.

There was the sound of a sudden *crack* in the other room, as if someone had thrown a stone at a window, breaking it, and Reginald rose wearily from the chair. The bloody teenagers were buggers for smashing windows in the Inns of Court—

He didn't finish the thought as, to his left, a man entered the doorway to the office. That was, it *looked* like a man because of the full-head latex mask of a bald man that the figure wore. The black clothing; a hoodie, gloves and cargo pants were shapeless and could have been of either sex, but the one thing that was obvious was the intention, shown by the brand new tyre iron that the bald man held in their left hand, likely the item that had made the glass cracking noise, as they'd forced entry through the glass in the front door.

Reginald swallowed nervously.

'So,' he whispered. 'Which one of you finally had the balls to face me?'

The 'bald man' didn't reply as they moved in, striking down hard with the tyre iron.

THE AUDIENCE LAUGHED AS THOMAS FINISHED READING ALOUD from the first of the books, *The Adventure Of The Rusty Crowbar*. He'd learned many years ago that they'd eat up anything he said, and it was easier to read books they knew by heart than to actively work on something original.

Looking up at them, he grinned.

'I think you all know what happens next,' he finished. The audience nodded and murmured in agreement, before applauding.

Of course they knew what happened next, he thought to himself, as the manager leaned past him, a little *too* close as she brushed his arm on her way to the microphone. *They've read everything a dozen times.*

'And now if you bring your purchased books to the signing table, Thomas will sign them for you,' she gushed with excitement, as the chairs were almost thrown to the side by the rush of hormonal women running to be first in line.

As Thomas closed the book on the lectern and walked

across the event space, gingerly picking his way to the table that had been set aside for his signing, a woman moved in front of him, effectively blocking his way. She was in her late thirties or early forties, scarily thin and with her hair scraped back into a bun, giving her the look of a stern governess a good decade older.

'Mister Williams, before you start, can I have a moment?' she asked.

'I have a signing,' Thomas smiled politely. 'I can write whatever you want when—'

'Oh, I'm not one of *them*,' the woman replied, glancing around in disgust. 'I'm doing a piece on Reginald Troughton. You said he was in Scotland?'

'I believe so,' Thomas glanced around for the manager, hoping that she could step in, do her bloody job and move this woman away. *He* didn't want to move her; someone could always misconstrue such things in this day and age.

'I spoke to him yesterday,' the woman replied. 'At home, in London. And he didn't seem to have any flu-like symptoms then.' She offered a business card, which Thomas took almost automatically. 'Care to make a comment?'

'Well, all I can go on is what my publisher told me,' Thomas really wanted to move on now as he faked a concerned expression for the woman. 'I believe the flu hit him overnight, or he would have made it. I'll check on him tomorrow. I'm sorry.'

'Well, if I can just ask—' *God, the woman simply wouldn't take a hint.*

The smile faded, and Thomas moved closer.

'Look, I've had an endless day, and I don't have time for interviews. If you want to talk to me, you can get me through my talent agent...'

He stopped as he looked at the woman properly for the first time.

'Have we met before?' he asked.

'Yes, we have,' the woman's face was emotionless now. 'I was one of the gang, not that you'd remember, or give a damn about. Have a nice day, *Mister* Williams.'

And as quickly as she'd arrived, the woman left, Thomas now standing alone and confused where he knew her from. The audience were still patiently lining up before the table, each with books in their hands, but before he could move towards them, Jane now marched towards him. Thomas looked towards the manager, nodding apologetically as he did so, and she smiled and nodded back at him in a *'no worries'* manner. The last thing she was going to do was stop two members from the Magpies from chatting to each other in her store. This was something that hadn't happened in years, and she could see that the audience, while waiting for the signature, were very aware of the *history* happening beside them and were *eating it up.*

'Thanks for outing me,' Jane smiled humourlessly.

'It was the least I could do,' Thomas said, shrugging. 'So what's it been, five years?'

'Seven.'

'Wow. How's—'

'He's fine,' Jane interrupted. 'We both are.'

One fan, a middle-aged lady with a book in her hand, who simply hadn't garnered the basic fact that *you left the talent alone,* walked up to them, breaking the moment.

'Hi, I'm sorry to interrupt, but I was hoping you could sign this?' she said to Jane. 'You're Jane Taylor, right?'

'Actually, it's Ashton now,' Jane replied, glancing at Thomas as she said so.

'Oh, like Luke Ashton?'

'Exactly like that.'

The lady paused at this sudden revelation. 'Oh. *Wow.*'

Thomas forced a smile as he leaned in.

'I'm sorry, we haven't seen each other for a while and only have a moment before I start my signing. Over there. Where you should be queuing,' he pointed at the line of now irritated women. 'Do you mind?'

As the lady finally got the hint and reluctantly left them, Thomas looked back at Jane.

'Can you wait around until after?' he asked softly. 'Catch up?'

Jane nodded, as Thomas grabbed and squeezed her hand before walking over to the signing desk to more applause.

Jane, meanwhile, pulled out her phone and, after reading a text on it, turned it off.

THE OFFICE IN THE TEMPLE INN APARTMENT HAD NEVER BEEN tidy, but now it looked like a bomb had hit it. Or, more accurately, that a fight had occurred there; a vicious beating of a sixty-five-year-old man.

A photo frame, one that held the same publicity photo of the Magpies that Waterstones had used was now discarded, broken on the floor, the glass smashed by the impact of a shoe's heel on it. A red smear of blood had been wiped across the broken glass, covering all the faces in the photo, smeared by the blood covered hand of Reginald Troughton, whose glassy, dead eyes stared vacantly ahead, as he lay face down on the carpet, his arm, stretched out rested beside the frame as if his last act had been to smear the photo with his own blood in some kind of message, or act of defiance.

Beside his body, the killer had also left the bloodied tyre iron on the floor, the end slick with the author's blood.

Reginald Troughton would never finish his tell-all adventure.

And the Magpies no longer existed to solve his *murder*.

1

FOR SORROW

DECLAN WAS STILL AT HIS DESK WHEN DETECTIVE Superintendent Bullman leaned out of her office.

'Where is everyone?' she asked, as if surprised at the empty room. Declan looked up at the clock on the wall; it read the time as just past nine-thirty in the evening.

'They've gone home for the night, Ma'am,' he explained, leaning back in his chair. 'Even the Desk Sergeant downstairs has gone for the night. Anjli's with her mum, I think Billy's on a date.'

'Oh,' Bullman raised an eyebrow at this. 'Anyone nice?'

'I find it's best not to ask,' Declan smiled.

'And why are you still here at—' Bullman looked up to the clock '—stupid o'clock at night?'

Declan indicated the monitor's screen, as if pointing at this would magically explain everything. 'I'm finishing up the notes on the Mason case,' he replied. 'Should be on your desk in thirty.'

'That could be finished tomorrow,' Bullman watched

Declan with a wry smile as she spoke. 'You didn't answer my question.'

Declan sighed, running a hand through his brown hair. It was peppering with a little white now, but that was to be expected with his line of work, although he was still proud that he'd shed a few pounds over the last month. 'I don't feel comfortable at home, Ma'am.'

'Why now?' Bullman leaned against the doorframe now. Declan shrugged.

'Small village mentality. Some still class me as the intruder, some still blame me for trying to arrest their favourite mechanic—'

'Karl Schnitter was a serial killer.'

'Yeah, but he was also a great mechanic,' Declan smiled. 'They just see me as trouble. And, since I moved in, I've had two armed units appear at my house, so there's a little bit of *no smoke without fire.*'

'Schnitter was a month ago,' Bullman muttered. 'We've got over it, they should too.'

'They're not the only ones,' Declan replied. 'Liz still won't allow me to meet or even speak to Jess. Which is completely understandable, considering what happened. So going home means I sit in the house alone. I might as well do that here and get work done.'

'You could sell the house?'

Declan grinned. 'I need to get some contractors in first,' he explained. 'I need a wall fixing. I might have taken out my dad's study with a sledgehammer a few weeks ago.'

He stopped.

'Anyway, why are *you* here this late, Ma'am?'

'Similar, actually,' Bullman shrugged. 'I bounced around for a year; Manchester, Birmingham and now here. Haven't even found a stable place to rent yet, in case they move me again.'

Declan nodded at this. Sophie Bullman had been a Detective Chief Inspector when they first met a couple of months earlier; she had been in Birmingham when DCI Monroe and Doctor Marcos had arrived looking for information on Angela Chapman, but after that had been on leave following the death of her colleague, DI White. While waiting for clearance, she had then assisted the Last Chance Saloon on two occasions; the first was in proving Declan wasn't a terrorist, and then she'd gone to Berlin with Monroe to check into Rolfe Müller's backstory. After that, it was revealed that thanks to some backroom shenanigans by Monroe, she'd been put forward and accepted as the newly created Detective Superintendent of the new, improved Last Chance Saloon.

Declan still wasn't sure if she was *happy* about this.

'Ma'am, did you need anything?' he asked. 'When you came out?'

'Actually, I do,' she replied. 'Just had a call. We've got a murder in the Inns, and we need to go have a look. I've already sent Marcos ahead.'

'Doctor Marcos still can't visit active crime scenes—' Declan started, but Bullman raised a hand to cut him off.

'It was a bloody stupid decision, she only has a month or so left on the suspension and we'd only have to find a way to break the rule, so I got Chief Superintendent Bradbury to remove it early.'

Declan smiled at this. He knew Monroe had also tried to reduce Doctor Marcos' 'sentence', but had been unsuccessful. That Bullman succeeded was sure to eat him up.

'What do we know about the victim?' he asked as he rose

from the chair, removing his suit jacket off the back of it and pulling it on. Bullman checked her notebook.

'Author,' she read. 'Married to a barrister so lives off Temple Garden Chambers. Reginald Troughton, sixty-five years of age--'

'Do you mean Magpies Troughton?' Declan asked in surprise.

'You know the books?' Bullman replied as she gathered her phone and a pen from her desk. 'They came out a bit after my time.'

'Hell yeah,' Declan met her at the door, adding a hasty 'Ma'am. My dad pretty much force fed them to me when I was about ten, eleven years old. Kept pointing out that these guys were only a couple of years older than me, and look what they were doing with their lives, solving crimes and all that. I pointed out that Hurley wasn't exactly a hotbed of crime—'

'Until Karl Schnitter arrived and started killing people.'

'Well, yes Ma'am, the obvious elephant in the room aside, I was a sleepy village kid, and these were city teens. I was a massive fan of all the books.'

They walked down the stairs, making their way to the entrance.

'If I'd known Troughton was living in Temple Inn, I'd have probably gained his autograph on a couple of them, passed them on to Jess. She loved the stories too when she was younger.'

'Sorry that you missed the boat then,' Bullman replied as they emerged onto the street. 'Still, you can take some crime scene photos and send them to her. Make your ex-wife hate you even more.'

Declan grimaced at the thought. 'Maybe not,' he mused. 'Do we know what the murder weapon was?'

'Some kind of tyre iron, I believe,' Bullman moved briskly across the car park. 'Anyway, the press have this too, so expect a bit of a circus. I know you're a shy, retiring flower, so this'll be an adventure for you.'

Declan smiled at that as he followed.

LUKE ASHTON SAT IN HIS KINGSTON THREE BEDROOM SEMI-detached house in the darkness and stared at the television silently, as if scared that the very act of speaking would alter everything.

In fact, it would have changed nothing, as Luke was alone in the living room, and nobody would have heard him. But the news on the television screen was momentous, and to speak over the newsreader felt almost like an insult to the memory of the man being spoken of.

'Reginald Troughton, the author of the bestselling Magpies series of books, was found dead in his London home earlier this evening,' the newsreader explained, and Luke felt a shiver go down his spine. Was it excitement? Shame, perhaps? He didn't know. What he did know was that it was change, and that change was good.

Absently he rubbed at the sleeve of his dress shirt; he was dressed in a white shirt and blue jeans over a pair of burgundy Solovair boots. He'd always loved his Dr Martens, but Jane had bought him these for his birthday, and he found them just as comfortable. Which was probably because they had *used* to be Dr Martens until the boots moved to China for production.

Looking at his sleeve, he saw that there was a wicked-looking smear of blood on it from where he'd been scratching, both arms speckled with the crimson liquid. Now turning his attention to his hands, he saw that both of them were bloodied and spattered with now-dried blood.

Sighing, he rose from the chair, his eyes still glued to the television as it showed old production stills from the days of the Magpies.

God, we all looked so young there, he thought to himself in almost disbelief as the carousel of images passed across the screen. And they *had* been young then. Young and innocent.

Not anymore.

Luke walked into the kitchen and, turning on the tap, washed his hands of the dried blood. This done, he pulled off his shirt, staring at the blood-covered arms. He knew he could probably get it off with some kind of stain remover, but then Jane might see it. *No, it was better to just throw the blasted thing away.*

He looked across the kitchen to his phone, charging beside the knife rack. There still had been no messages from Jane; he wondered if she'd even seen the news yet. Probably not. He considered texting her, letting her know, but he knew that she would have already gotten the text, would have known what was going on. Nodding to himself, Luke silently stared at the bloody shirt in his hand.

He should burn it.

Grabbing a box of kitchen matches, Luke walked out into the back garden and the fire pit.

THE PICCADILLY HYATT HOTEL HAD PROVIDED THOMAS WITH A double bed suite for the night of the talk; it was a requirement of his rider, and he always pushed for a suite rather than a train home, mainly as the talks were always filled with women, groupies even.

And Thomas loved groupies, especially the ones that had always dreamed of sleeping with him.

However, looking across the bed at the rumpled bedsheets beside him, he hadn't expected to be screwing Jane Taylor tonight.

The bathroom door opened, and Jane, still naked, still covered in a light sheen of sweat emerged, walking over to the bed and climbing back under the sheets, snuggling into Thomas's bare torso with what sounded like a contented sigh.

'We waited too long for this,' she mumbled into his chest.

'You're the one who got married,' Thomas replied. 'I mean, really? Luke?'

Jane pulled away now, looking up at Thomas. 'He's a good man, Tommy,' she said. 'He was there after…' she looked away again.

'Well, after.'

'I would have been there,' Thomas sulked.

'I couldn't get through to you,' Jane retorted. 'None of us could. Until you wanted the attention again, that is.'

'And by then it was too late,' Thomas shifted in the bed, reaching to the side table, pulling a cigarette from the pack, offering it to Jane. When she refused, he lit it himself.

'Why do you still do it?' she said, suddenly. 'Relive the books? I'd rather the bloody things were destroyed. Left in a corner to rot away.'

'They're all I have,' Thomas replied honestly.

'They drove Daniel insane,' Jane said.

'No, being Daniel drove Daniel insane,' Thomas took a drag of the cigarette and was about to reply again, when his phone beeped.

'I thought we said no phones?' Jane asked in surprise. Thomas picked it up, turning it on.

'No, *you* said no phones,' he replied. 'Mainly so Luke couldn't contact—'

He stopped, reading the text message.

'Christ,' he eventually said, scrabbling for the remote and turning the TV on.

'What's going on?' she asked. As *BBC News* appeared on the screen, a photo of Reginald Troughton filling it, Thomas threw Jane his phone.

'Read,' he said as Jane tapped on the screen to open the message, reading it slowly.

'Police have yet to comment on the attack, but it's believed that Mister Troughton was the victim of a home invasion that went horribly wrong,' the woman on the screen said.

Jane sat up now, her eyes widening as she looked up from the phone.

'He's dead?'

'Looks like it,' Thomas replied, leaning back. 'Shit.'

'You said he had the flu,' Jane said, eventually tossing back the phone and pulling on her clothes. 'You didn't say he was bloody dead.'

'Well, I didn't know, did I?' Thomas snapped back. 'And where the hell are you off to?'

'Where do you think?' Jane pulled on her jeans now. 'Home. The last thing we need now is the press finding me walking out of your bedroom the night Reginald died.'

She stopped.

'Is this what this was? An alibi?'

'You're the one to ask that,' Thomas stood now, naked in the room. 'I'm not the one who appeared out of nowhere for an old time's sake *shag*.'

He expected the slap, but didn't stop it. And, as Jane grabbed her jacket and shoes, already running for the door, he let her go.

What was done was done.

———

THE BAKER INSTITUTE WAS OFFICIALLY CALLED A *REHAB CENTRE*, but anyone who stayed there knew exactly what it was. And the orderlies who worked there knew what the inhabitants truly were, even if terms like *mental institution* were banned. Based just south of Hampstead, this was a place where the rich went mad quietly; some quieter than others.

Tonight, two of the orderlies walked nervously down a corridor towards one of the inmate rooms. In their years they'd seen everything, but there was something *off* with Daniel McCarthy, not least the fact that he'd volunteered willingly to stay at the institute, and that the institute itself was footing the bill for it.

'Do you think he'll be up?' the stockier of the two orderlies muttered. The taller one made a *tch*ing noise.

'What do you think?' he replied. 'I tell you, this one creeps me the hell out.'

'You ever read the books?' the stocky orderly asked. 'He's better in the books.'

'He's not as mental in the books.'

Knocking on the door, the two orderlies glanced at each other before opening it and entering.

Daniel McCarthy's room was a small, modest one. There

was an empty bookcase by the wall, a sideboard beside it. A single bed was against the opposite wall, with a plastic chair facing a small television on a writing desk. There wasn't much to give away who lived there, only the patient himself.

Who wasn't in the empty room.

'Ah, shit, he's gone again,' the taller orderly pulled out a radio, calling into it. 'Guys, get the dogs out. McCarthy's on the run again.'

OUT IN THE GARDENS OF THE BAKER INSTITUTE, THE LIGHTS LIT up the rain-covered grass as orderlies and evening staff exited the building, looking for the missing Daniel McCarthy. They didn't have to look for long though as, from the back wall, soaked to the skin and grinning, Daniel emerged from the bushes, waving happily to them as they approached. Small, Asian and bookish, he wore black trousers under the institute's regulation hoodie, both of which were utterly drenched in the downpour, plastering his dyed blond ponytail to his head.

'Mister McCarthy! What are you doing?' the stockier orderly called out. Daniel carried on grinning.

'It's a lovely night,' he explained. 'I took a walk.'

'It's raining!' A doctor, her greying hair now pulled back into a ponytail, and tucked behind her tortoiseshell glasses approached, appalled at the situation. Daniel sobered up now, the smile fading as he turned to look at her.

'That's what's lovely about it,' he breathed. 'God's crying.'

'We don't know how he got out,' the stockier orderly explained to the newcomer.

'That's because you never know how he got out,' the

doctor snapped back, looking over at Daniel. 'What's really going on here?'

'I saw it on the news,' Daniel replied calmly. 'Reggie Troughton's dead. I shouldn't really be telling you this, but you gave me apple pie for dinner tonight and I like apple pie.'

'Shouldn't be telling me what?' the doctor asked, confused. 'That he's dead?'

'They said it was a home invasion gone wrong, but it wasn't,' Daniel continued as if he hadn't heard the question. 'It was an execution.'

'How do you know that?' the taller orderly asked.

Daniel shrugged.

'Because I killed him,' he finished.

2

FOR JOY

Although the flat that Reginald Troughton had died in was in Temple Inn, it was officially classed as Middle Temple, as both Inner and Middle Temple had accommodation for barristers within the walls.

Declan had been stationed at the Temple Inn office for several months now, but during that time he'd never really walked around the Inns of Court, and he was a little ashamed at the ease with which Bullman navigated through the maze of corridors and marble archways en route to the apartments. That said, he clawed a little piece of self-esteem back by remembering that he was probably the only person on the team who knew how to traverse around the Inns by *rooftop*.

Well, *hopefully* he was, anyway.

'So you were a bit of a detective fanboy then?' Bullman asked as they approached Inner Temple Gardens. 'Or did you just fancy the girls in the books?'

'Bit of both, really,' Declan admitted. 'There was only a couple of years difference between us.'

He looked up at the apartments that faced him.

'Nice place to live if you can afford it,' he muttered.

'Being a barrister has its perks, it seems,' Bullman approached the main doors to the apartments, nodding to PC Morten De'Geer, currently standing guard, his immense Viking frame proving an effective, if noticeable barrier. Declan frowned as they approached.

'I thought you went home hours ago?' he asked. De'Geer shrugged.

'I was in Forensics with Jo—with DC Davey when the call came in,' he explained. 'Thought you'd need a *Scene of Crime* officer.'

'Rules state that should be a sergeant,' Declan replied.

'Come on, sir, when have we ever played by the rules?' De'Geer grinned.

'You were with Davey?' Bullman had the slightest hint of a smile. Realising what he'd said, De'Geer flushed.

'No, Ma'am, not like that,' he flustered. 'She's teaching me about blowflies.' At the blank expressions, he continued. 'Blowflies can be involved in breaking down decomposing bodies. And because of the specific life cycle of the blowflies, the time of death can be determined by comparing the two.'

'You hung around after work to talk about decomposing bodies and flies,' Declan sighed. 'If ever I wondered if the Last Chance Saloon was right for you, the last of my concerns were washed away right now.'

Passing De'Geer and moving upstairs, Declan and Bullman walked to the front door of Reginald Troughton's apartment. It was easy to work out which it was, purely because of the PPE-clad forensics officers already entering and exiting. Stopping at the doorway, Declan gratefully accepted a one-piece disposable suit; it was blue rather than the usual white, but it still performed the same task, covering his feet, body and head, ensuring he couldn't contaminate the scene. With a pair of blue latex gloves and a mask on, he was good to enter the apartment.

Doctor Rosanna Marcos, also in full PPE, was waiting for them when they entered. Her PPE suit however was light grey.

'How come you're different?' Declan asked as they approached. Doctor Marcos made what was likely to be some kind of shrug motion.

'Because I buy my own tailored ones,' she replied. 'The ones you're wearing always make me itch. And besides, I didn't want to look like a Smurf today.'

'What do we have?' Bullman asked, returning the conversation to the case at hand.

'Not sure yet,' Doctor Marcos turned to the Detective Superintendent. 'We only got here about ten minutes ago. I found Reginald Troughton on the floor, beaten to death with a tyre iron. No signs of forced entry, although there was a pane of glass broken in the kitchen.'

'Killer got in that way?'

'No, it looks like the glass was broken outwards. Apart from the body being thrown around a little, there wasn't that much of an even fight, from the looks of things. Definitely more of a one-sided beating.'

'He didn't defend himself... Could he have known his attacker?' Declan asked.

'Possibly, or he was taken by surprise, and they caught a lucky headshot,' Doctor Marcos nodded. 'You can't get through the main entrance unless you have a key or you were buzzed in, so there has to be a connection.'

'Unless they were buzzed in by someone else,' Bullman mused. 'We need to get De'Geer to check the other residents, see if they saw anything, or at least buzzed anyone into the building. Any CCTV?'

'Outside, and at the entrances to the Inns, but we can't find any in the building,' Doctor Marcos led Declan and Bullman into the study as she spoke. 'We're just going to have to rely on witnesses.'

Declan paused as he entered the study.

Reginald was still on the floor, a sheet placed over him while DC Davey examined his fingernails. The study itself looked as if a violent fight had occurred, with half of the contents of the desk strewn over the floor and around the body of Troughton, with a broken photo frame, Troughton's blood smudged across it, on the floor beside his hand. The glass of the frame was cracked in the middle, as if the heel of a shoe, or a boot had slammed into it, breaking the glass. Declan couldn't see whether the blood had been smudged onto the glass before or after the vandalism, but his attention was distracted by a tyre iron, discarded on the floor beside the body, yet to be bagged up by the team.

'Something the matter?' Bullman, watching him, asked. Declan knelt beside the tyre iron, close enough to examine it, but not crazy enough to touch the item.

'The weapon,' he murmured as he leaned in closer. 'It's not on brand, but at the same time it's more so than the books.'

'There's a brand to this?' Bullman was surprised. 'Do tell.'

'The first book was called *The Adventure of the Rusty Crowbar*,' Declan explained. 'The killer, Derek Sutton used it, you see. They caught him thanks to fingerprints on the weapon. But I remember seeing an interview, years later where Troughton said that the crowbar was an addition for the international audiences, and was changed before the first edition came out.'

'What do you mean, international audiences?' now Doctor Marcos was curious. Declan pointed to the discarded weapon.

'The original weapon in the books was a *tyre iron*,' he said. 'But they weren't sure whether it'd translate, and crowbar was more known around the world. It happens a lot, apparently. *Harry Potter and the Philosopher's Stone* was renamed *Harry Potter and the Sorcerer's Stone*, the Bond movie *Licence Revoked* was renamed *Licence to Kill*, that sort of thing.'

He looked up.

'What I'm trying to say is that if someone who had a passing knowledge of the books wanted to kill Troughton with a bit of irony, they'd use a crowbar, the weapon from the first book. If they had *more* than a passing knowledge, they'd use a tyre iron.'

'I knew your fanboyness would help us here,' Bullman replied. 'I bet you're a bloody joy at pub quizzes.' She turned to DC Davey. 'Got anything?'

'No blood or skin under the fingernails,' Davey placed the arm she was examining back onto the floor. 'No defensive wounds from the looks of things. He was battered, but as Doctor Marcos said, he didn't put up a fight.'

Declan observed around the study at the scattered items and broken ornaments.

'Are you sure?' Declan showed the carnage. 'Because this seems like a hell of a tussle.'

Davey shrugged. 'Just because he didn't put up a defence, doesn't mean he wasn't thrown around.' She quickly checked the other hand. 'I need to get Doctor Marcos to examine the body, but from a cursory glance here, I honestly don't think he threw a single punch,'

'We're still looking into how to get past the MacBook login,' Doctor Marcos moved the conversation away from the murder weapon. 'It's a Touch ID, but there's a password to unlock. I reckon Billy can work it out.'

'Good idea,' Bullman nodded. 'Get him using all that expensive equipment he requisitioned.'

Declan meanwhile had carefully picked up the photo frame, staring at the image within. It was one of the first promotional photos of the Magpies ever taken; he remembered seeing it as a kid in *Smash Hits* magazine. However, when he moved the frame, there was a slight thud within it, as if something was sliding around at the back. Doctor Marcos saw this and, nodding, took the frame from Declan, bagging it up.

'I'll check into that,' she said, passing it to Davey, who was already taking a box of samples towards the main door, and likely the laboratory at Temple Inn.

'Do you think he was trying to leave a message?' Declan asked as he watched the box leave the room. 'The blood smear?'

'Maybe he was trying to identify the killer,' Bullman suggested.

Declan clambered back to his feet, looking over to the wall of the study.

'There's something missing there,' he said, indicating a slightly lighter patch of wallpaper around the size of a large photo frame. 'It's bigger than the one on the floor, but it's definitely something that was there for a while. Note the discolouration.'

'*Note the discolouration*,' Bullman mocked with a wry smile. 'Thanks for the lesson on detecting, Sherlock.'

'Just keeping you on your feet, Ma'am.'

'Someone see if we can find a frame around here that matches this,' Bullman said aloud, as if expecting all the forensics officers to pause and do this. Seeing no response, she looked at Declan.

'Maybe we can give that one to De'Geer.'

As if hearing his name, PC De'Geer appeared at the doorway to the apartment, an arrival punctuated with Doctor Marcos screaming at him to *take one more step in without a PPE suit on and die.* Catching Declan's eye, he waved for Declan and Bullman to meet with him outside.

'Sorry to interrupt, Guv, Ma'am,' he said, looking back down the corridor as if expecting to have been followed, 'but there's a woman downstairs. A Detective Inspector. She wants to speak to whoever's in charge of the case.'

'That'll be Monroe tomorrow,' Bullman mused, already pulling off the PPE suit. 'But tonight she can talk to me. Did you get the name?'

'DI Theresa Martinez,' De'Geer replied as, joining Bullman, Declan peeled off his own PPE suit. Then, suitably disrobed and back in his normal clothes, he joined both De'Geer and Bullman as they walked down to the main entrance. There was something at the back of his mind that *tickled* on hearing the name, but it was gone as soon as it appeared.

Waiting outside was a frustrated and incredibly impatient woman. She was in her mid-forties and Mediterranean in looks; her bobbed black hair slightly frizzy over her sensible dark blue suit and black shirt. She looked like a detective who, even though she was attractive, was deliberately trying to *lessen* the impression, as if ensuring that the work spoke more than the looks.

'DI Martinez?' Bullman asked as she emerged.

The woman nodded, looking at Bullman and Declan.

'Theresa, Ma'am. Please.'

Bullman took the warrant card that Theresa Martinez had passed over, glancing down at it.

'Manchester police?' she asked in surprise. 'Can't see you getting down here that quickly.'

'Was in town on personal business, Ma'am,' Theresa replied stonily. 'Heard about the murder on the news.'

'And you're here because?'

'I'd like to help with the case,' Theresa replied, now sounding nervous as she spoke, stumbling slightly over her words. 'I knew Reginald, I mean the *victim* a long time ago. He helped me get into the force—'

'Christ, you're *Tessa Martinez!*' Declan blurted out.

There was a moment of silence as Bullman looked at him.

'Something you'd like to say, Detective Inspector Walsh?'

'Sorry,' Declan replied sheepishly. 'It's just that I realised that DI Martinez here was one of the Magpies.'

'That's true,' Theresa nodded. 'And that's why I'd like to help with the case. I'd like to find out who killed Reginald and put them away.'

'And that's admirable,' Bullman looked around the court-yard as she spoke. 'But at the same time, we don't know why he was killed, who killed him, or even what was going on in his life before that. And, as you can imagine, *Detective Inspector,* the fact that you're away from your post, and in the city that he's murdered in on the same day, on apparent personal business pretty much makes you one of the *suspects* in this murder.'

'I get that,' Theresa nodded. 'And I'm happy to sit down and answer any questions needed. But I'm asking for a little professional courtesy here, that someone can somehow keep me in the loop.'

'You want your little *Scooby Doo* gang to solve this crime?' Bullman almost laughed. 'Be serious. At best we'll link you into the round robin emails.'

Theresa went to bite back at this, but stopped herself before speaking.

'Thank you, Ma'am,' she eventually said stiffly, her body almost at attention.

All business, Declan thought to himself.

And then, pulling out a card, she turned to Declan.

'Here's my contact details,' she said, passing it across. 'I'll be staying in London for a while longer. We'll see each other again.'

This done, she turned and left the entranceway, visibly fighting to keep the anger held inside.

'Impressive,' Bullman mused as she watched her leave. 'I thought she'd kick off at the *Scooby Doo* line.'

'You were deliberately trying to provoke her?' Declan was surprised at this. He was even more surprised at the wide grin that Bullman gave him back in reply.

'I deliberately try to provoke everyone I meet,' she said pleasantly. 'It's the best way to throw them off balance, see what they truly think.'

'And that's why you called me a fanboy.'

'Hah, no,' Bullman pulled out her notebook, taking down the contact details on the card. 'You work for me. I say that for fun. If I wanted to provoke you, there are a lot worse things I can call you.'

She took a deep breath, taking in the evening air as she considered options.

'Right then,' she eventually decided. 'Call the band. We need to hit the ground running tomorrow.'

Declan looked back to the apartment block. The creator of the Magpies was dead, and one of the teenage detectives, now a DI in her own right, was muscling in on the case. The question though was whether it was truly to solve the crime, or whether it was to help guide it in the direction she wanted.

And how many other Magpies were about to crawl out of the woodwork, each with their own agendas?

One thing was definitely for certain. This was going to be a *circus* once the press really leaned into it.

And Declan *hated* bloody circuses.

3

FOR A GIRL

IT WAS RAINING THE FOLLOWING MORNING, WHICH FELT FITTING considering the circumstances. Declan had slept little; he'd returned home just before midnight and had wolfed down a cheese toastie before falling into bed. Rising the next morning, he'd quickly showered and dressed, noting as he was walking out of the door that he'd barely spent time in the house over the last month. Part of this was because of the whole Karl Schnitter incident, and the side glances he still received from the neighbours on the street, but a larger part was because he still didn't feel that this was his house.

Maybe it's time to listen to Bullman and buy something closer to London.

Declan had considered this a couple of times over the last couple of weeks, but there was a small part of him that felt that by doing this, he was giving up. He needed to decide whether moving on was a good idea, or a knee-jerk one. After all, this was a large house; he'd get nothing like this in London.

DCI Alexander Monroe was in his office when Declan

arrived; Bullman hadn't yet appeared, and both DC Billy Fitzwarren and DS Anjli Kapoor were likely car sharing again, although she had recently taken to bullying De'Geer into picking her up on his motorcycle. Declan expected her to buy one of her own within a couple of months, or realise before it was too late that *this* was her midlife crisis. Smiling to himself, he walked over to his desk, stopping as Monroe emerged from his office.

'You could have bloody well called me,' he moaned.

'I would have, guv, but you were home and Bullman was in the office,' Declan replied. 'And besides, we were there less than ten minutes, all said.'

'I know that, laddie,' Monroe smiled. 'I just wanted to see your tears when you realised that the writer you so loved as a bairn had been living not ten minutes from where you've been working.'

Declan grimaced. He'd forgotten that as a long-time friend of Declan's dad, Monroe had been privy to eleven-year-old Declan and his favourite books.

'I hear that one of the Magpies turned up too,' Monroe leaned against the door now, enjoying this. 'Was it the one you used to fancy?'

'I didn't 'fancy' any of them,' Declan replied haughtily, trying to focus on the computer rather than the chuckling DCI across the room.

'Oh, aye?' Monroe seemed surprised at this. 'Then those pictures you had of what's her name, Tessa? The ones you had over your wall, that *wasn't* a teenage crush?'

'I had photos of them all,' Declan blushed slightly, irritating himself. *He was a copper in his forties, Goddammit.*

'Aye, but you had more of young Tessa, now, didn't you?'

Monroe was warming to the hazing. 'Or should we call her Detective Inspector Theresa Martinez now?'

Declan grit his teeth. He'd hoped that this would have passed Monroe, but nothing ever passed the canny Scot.

'It was her, yes,' he replied. 'But she's not the teenage detective anymore, and I'm sure as hell not the innocent eleven-year-old.'

'Aye, you're right there,' Monroe replied, his tone softening. 'You've had your share of *shite*, Declan.'

As if realising he was being too kind to Declan though, he straightened.

'Still, must be a bastard knowing you'll never get your books signed.'

There was a noise at the doors, and Declan gratefully turned to see Anjli and Billy enter.

'Heard your childhood crush came to see you last night,' Anjli said with a grin. Declan leaned back in the chair, staring at the ceiling.

'How—'

'Doctor Marcos,' Billy replied as he walked over to his computer station, his three-piece Savile Row suit contrasting with the usual 'IT Guy' image that the cyber crime officers usually had. 'She sent it to all of us, I think.'

'Of course she did.' Declan looked over to Monroe pleadingly. 'Can we get on with the briefing now?'

'We need to wait for forensics,' Monroe replied. 'And the boss. Once they're here, we'll begin.'

Billy, starting up his bank of computer monitors, sang softly to himself.

'And they called it, puppy love....'

Declan threw a stapler at him.

'Right then,' Monroe said, standing at the front of the briefing room, Bullman standing slightly behind and to the left. 'Let's get this meeting going.'

Declan glanced around the room; Billy was as ever working the laptop, ensuring the images appeared on the plasma screen behind Monroe, Anjli sitting next to him and already writing in her notebook. At the back sat DC Davey and Doctor Marcos, chuckling to themselves about something, giving all the airs of naughty schoolchildren. The only person missing was PC De'Geer, who was currently on front desk duty.

Monroe turned to Bullman, indicating for her to take the stage. 'Ma'am?'

'Not my call,' Bullman replied, graciously waving Monroe forward. 'I'm the backup here, DCI Monroe. It's your case.'

Nodding, Monroe looked back to the detectives and police officers of the Last Chance Saloon. Behind him, on the plasma screen, an image of Reginald Troughton appeared.

'Reginald Troughton, sixty-five years of age. Widowed husband of barrister Michael Chadwick, who was part of the Inner Temple, not more than a hundred yards from here. Chadwick...'

'Died six months ago,' Anjli stepped in, reading from her notes. 'Hit and run on the Euston Road.'

'Convenient,' Billy replied. 'Did they catch the killer?'

'Yeah, the car, a Land Rover, was traced back to some drug dealer that Michael Chadwick had put away a year earlier. Two people were charged, but the case hasn't reached the court yet.'

'Thank you, DS Kapoor,' Monroe nodded. 'At nine-fifteen

pm last night, neighbours claim to have heard a ruckus coming from Troughton's apartment. When one eventually went to look, they found his body on the floor. They immediately called 999, which of course aimed this directly at us, being the closest coppers on the scene.'

A crime scene photo of the study now appeared on the plasma screen; Reginald's body was on the carpet, the arm outstretched towards a tyre iron, discarded to the side.

'When the first to respond arrived; that's PC De'Geer, DC Davey and Doctor Marcos, they found Troughton dead on the floor, apparently beaten to death with a tyre iron, one that had been left at the scene of the crime.'

He looked to Doctor Marcos who rose, walking to the front and turning to face the others in the room.

'No signs of forced entry, and no signs on the body of defensive wounds,' she started. 'Current hypothesis is that Troughton knew the killer, and that either they were let into the apartment, or had their own key. The wounds that Troughton had over his body are compatible with those given by a metal tyre iron, and blood found on it matches Troughton's.'

'So someone comes in, beats the crap out of Troughton, sending him flying all over the place and he doesn't defend himself?' Billy asked. 'Why wouldn't he put up a fight?'

'Depends who the attacker was,' Monroe suggested. 'He might have been begging for his life, or trying to talk them around.'

'Security footage?' Anjli asked. Billy shook his head.

'Not yet, but we're hoping to get it this morning,' he replied. 'That said, it's not well covered there, so someone who knows the area can probably work out how to bypass any cameras.'

'What do we know about Troughton?' Declan asked. 'Did he have anyone who hated him?'

'Checking into that,' Anjli replied, flipping the page on her notebook. 'One interesting fact though; before he died, Michael Chadwick was the on-retainer legal counsel for Johnny and Jackie Lucas.'

There was a moment of silence at this. Johnny and Jackie Lucas, known as 'The Twins' were well known to everyone in the room; not only had they crossed paths several times over the last few months, they'd actively assisted Monroe when he was being hunted by Rattlestone mercenaries. But that didn't make them allies. In fact, the worst kept secret in East London, in particular Globe Town and Mile End, was that Johnny and Jackie Lucas were actually *one man with two personalities*, and you never knew which 'twin' you'd be meeting.

'Are we so sure now that the hit and run was because of a case?' Billy commented.

'You might want to chat to them,' Monroe said to Anjli. 'See if they know anything.'

'You can ask them about Derek Sutton, too,' Doctor Marcos added. 'We found his fingerprint on the tyre iron.'

'Print or prints?'

'Print, singular,' Doctor Marcos replied. 'Usually I'd say they slipped up before putting on a glove, but this time, I'm not sure.'

'Why? Shouldn't we bring Sutton in then?' Billy asked. 'I mean, if his print's on the murder weapon...'

'We would, but he's got a solid alibi,' Monroe looked to Declan. 'If our resident expert here wants to weigh in?'

Declan nodded. 'Derek Sutton is in Belmarsh Prison, and has been for thirty-odd years,' he replied. 'He's been there since the Magpies proved he killed Narinder Singh and Jeetinder Gill, beating them both to death with a... well, if you read the book, it was a crowbar.'

'But there's more, isn't there?' Bullman asked, the first words she'd spoken since Monroe had started the briefing. Declan nodded.

'When the book came out, it was a massive success, but there was a rumour that right before the release there was a ton of rewrites, that the crowbar was added for the international audiences, and that it was originally a tyre iron.'

He straightened.

'Only the more devout fans know this, and the interview I read it in was a local paper, barely picked up on.'

'Christ,' Billy muttered. 'So the weapon used in the first book is used here, with the same fingerprints? Could it be the same weapon? Do we still have it somewhere? Maybe someone with police connections got it out?'

'Already looking into that, as there's a current police connection with DI Martinez,' Davey replied from the back of the room. 'Unlikely, though. Thirty years is a long time. Plenty of opportunities to lose things. And the one we found last night looks new.'

'If the tyre iron is a message, then it's going to be more Magpies related than Lucas Twins related,' Declan suggested. 'Do we need to get them in for questioning?'

'Declan has his autograph book ready,' Anjli grinned. Monroe however nodded.

'That's the next thing I was going to suggest,' he replied. 'All five of the Magpies need to be checked, especially with this new book being written.'

'I spoke with BadgerLock, the publishers right before the briefing,' Billy looked up from the laptop. 'Seems that the old publishing director, a woman named Julia Clarke, retired about five years ago, but when she did so, she paid a chunk of money into buying BadgerLock shares, ensuring she held enough in the company to control their direction. And with this, she convinced them to hire Reginald to write a 'lost' Magpies adventure to release this year, what with it being an anniversary. He took the money but delayed giving them the book.'

'There's nothing on the hard drive of his laptop?'

'We've not got into it yet,' Billy admitted sheepishly. 'For a retired writer, he's got some government level encryption going on there. What I can tell you however is that the publishers were expecting a book called *The Adventure of the Blacksmith's Apron*, but the only filename I can see is called *The Adventure of the Stolen Innocence*. Looks to me like Reginald Troughton might have gone a little off message.'

'Keep on with the MacBook,' Declan suggested. 'And while you're at it, look for any pictures of Troughton in his study. I found a spot on the wall where a photo used to be and I'd like to work out what's missing.'

'I can check what we have as well,' Davey commented from the back of the room. 'We took photos of all the other photos there.'

Billy nodded, writing some notes. At the back of the main office, De'Geer entered, walking over to the door to the briefing room, a piece of paper in his hand.

'Aren't you supposed to be on reception duty?' Monroe asked. De'Geer nodded.

'We've got a visitor,' he said, passing the piece of paper to Bullman who took it, reading the contents. 'It's the DI from last night.'

'I thought she was told to sling her hook?' Monroe was

both surprised and amused by this news. Bullman however passed him the piece of paper.

'Apparently she's gone above our heads,' she said. 'Took her case to Westminster. Got some Labour backbencher named Norman Shipman to push for her to be on the team.'

'He's more than a backbencher,' Declan paled at the sound of Shipman's name. 'He's government royalty, part of the Westminster Star Chamber with Charles Baker.'

'That explains why a nobody MP gets some serious sway in Whitehall then,' Bullman sighed. 'We'll have to bring her into the case. But to the law of the letter, no more. She's in the room, but not on the job.'

'There's something else, Ma'am,' De'Geer added. 'We had a call from Hampstead nick. They had a call from the Baker Institute, where Daniel McCarthy's been a resident for the last seven years. Seems that he disappeared from his room last night, and when they found him, he was in the gardens, soaking wet and claiming that he'd killed Reginald Troughton.'

'Well then, sounds like he should be our first point of call,' Monroe mused. 'Anjli? Take De'Geer and go see the Twins. Maybe we'll be lucky and get Johnny to talk to us.'

'I'd rather go alone,' Anjli glanced at Declan momentarily as she spoke, and Declan knew she was worried that talking to the Lucas twins in front of De'Geer could reveal that she was secretly passing them information, as payment for the help in her mother's breast cancer treatment a few months back. She'd come clean to Declan after the standoff at Beachampton a few weeks earlier, and had even offered to resign, but it had been decided between them it was a better idea to keep Johnny and Jackie Lucas on a short leash, and to provide them with fake tips to see where they emerged, maybe flush out some other corrupt coppers at the same time.

Monroe considered this, and then nodded. 'They know you, and I suppose having a hulking great Viking copper beside you isn't going to help things. Go alone, I'll take De'Geer with me to the Baker Institute, see what Mister McCarthy has to say. We'll then have a chat with Thomas Williams, the one who does the book tours. He's been told to stay at his London hotel, so we can catch him there.'

He looked at Declan.

'Have a chat with the right honourable Mister Shipman, see why he got involved, as I know you just *love* visiting Westminster.'

'And DI Martinez?'

'She can sit with Billy for the afternoon,' Monroe decided. 'Maybe she'll give the real reason she's here, while in a more casual setting. Next?'

Declan glanced over at Doctor Marcos. 'Last night, there was a photo on the floor. DC Davey took it to forensics.'

'The one that rattled when you shook it?' Doctor Marcos nodded. 'You were right. There was something in the back.' She nodded to Davey, who brought a clear bag to the front. In it was an unfolded note.

'This was folded up, and stuck in the back of the frame,' Doctor Marcos nodded to Billy. 'Can you put it up on the screen? The photo's in the main folder.'

Billy nodded, tapping on the laptop for a moment. On the plasma screen behind Doctor Marcos a photo of the paper appeared, the handwritten words visible.

Joyous winds blow hard
Mirthless through the dales
Hellacious tales of bards
Birthing hidden tales
Secretive and scarred
Devil's Holy Grails
Kissing 'til you're barred
Wishing you will fail

'Troughton's hiding teenage emo poetry?' Anjli muttered as she read the poem. 'I guess I'd want to hide this too.'

'It has to mean something,' Declan was leaning forward, examining the image as he spoke. 'A cypher?'

'I'll look into it,' Billy was already working on the laptop. 'He must have wanted someone to see it, maybe that's why he marked the frame.'

'Or he was marking his killer.'

'Maybe the poem is about the killer?' Anjli shook her head irritably. 'I hate cryptic shit like this.'

Declan rose from his chair, nodding to Bullman.

'And you, Ma'am?' he asked. Bullman smiled.

'My job isn't to run around like a headless chicken anymore,' she said, moving away from the door so that the officers inside the briefing room could leave. 'I'm the calvary. I'll be in my office if you need me.'

'I give you a week before you find an excuse to get into the field,' Monroe grinned. 'Ma'am.'

'I won't be taking that bet,' Bullman said as she walked back to her office. 'You know gambling on premises is frowned upon.'

Monroe choked back a laugh as he patted De'Geer on the

shoulder. 'Come on then, Thor,' he smiled. 'Let's go chat to a lunatic.'

Declan walked back to his desk, grabbing his notebook. Once more, he was returning to Westminster.

Where everyone there pretty much bloody hated him.

Things were going to be *fun*.

4

FOR A BOY

THE BAKER INSTITUTE WAS AN OLD, GEORGIAN BUILDING NORTH of Kentish Town and on the outskirts of the leafy suburbs of Hampstead, surrounded by well-manicured gardens that were held tight within high brick walls. A mixture of modern and old at the same location, it looked like someone had welded a small manor house to a *prison*.

Monroe stared up at the walls as he emerged from his car; they were built from red brick, and had broken glass mortared along the top. Anyone climbing over would have had to cover this with something thick and durable, or risk lacerations along their arms and legs.

That didn't mean it couldn't be done, though.

Taking a slow walk around the perimeter before entering the institute itself, with PC De'Geer walking alongside him, Monroe could spy at least three spots in the garden where the tree branches were close enough to allow someone to reach the top of the twelve-foot wall without clambering over glass shards, and close enough to enable a determined individual to attempt some kind of a suicidal leap over them to the pavement on the other side.

To try that was madness, of course.

But then again, Monroe only had to look around to remember where he was. Rational suggestions probably weren't that common around here.

Entering the main lobby of the Baker Institute, Monroe and De'Geer were greeted by a doctor, her greying hair pulled back into a bun as she cleaned her tortoiseshell glasses, peering through them at her visitors before placing them back on. She wasn't wearing a white coat; instead she was wearing a sweater and jeans, and Monroe realised that although the hair artificially aged her, the style of clothing made it hard to judge her correct age.

'You'll be here to see Daniel,' she said, holding out a hand. 'Doctor Hines. I'm, well, I'm the poor sod that has to deal with him.'

'He's that much of a nightmare?' De'Geer asked. 'We had the impression he's a voluntary admission.'

'Just because he feels he should be here, doesn't make it all singing and dancing once he enters the doors,' Doctor Hines replied with a weak smile. 'Come on, I'll take you to him.'

Daniel McCarthy's room was down a corridor to the side, and Monroe noted that as they walked to it, there was a distinct lack of security.

'There don't seem to be many bars around here,' he mused aloud. Doctor Hines looked at him, stopping in the middle of the corridor.

'What, you think 'Mental Institution' and it's all *One Flew Over The Cuckoo's Nest*?' she asked. 'ID cards and locked gates?'

'The thought had crossed my mind,' Monroe replied. 'How do you stop them escaping?'

'They don't want to escape,' Doctor Hines snapped. 'They want to be made better, or sometimes find a safe place to heal.'

'And is that what Daniel McCarthy was doing here?' Monroe kept his tone neutral and calm. 'Healing?'

'You can ask him that,' Doctor Hines arrived at a door on the right, knocking on it. 'Daniel? We have visitors who'd like to speak to you.'

Monroe nodded thanks to Doctor Hines, already walking back down the corridor, and opened the door to Daniel McCarthy's room.

Daniel was sitting on a plastic chair beside his bed, waiting for them as they entered, watching a small television placed precariously on a writing desk on the opposite side, as it silently played the news. Monroe had been told that he was Asian in heritage, but the bleached-blond hair and the black clothing made him look more like *Lucius Malfoy.*

'Daniel?' he asked. Daniel looked around and smiled, replying in a soft, sing-song voice.

'I'd hope so,' he whispered. 'Otherwise I have bigger problems than I thought.'

De'Geer stood beside the desk as Monroe sat on the end of the single bed. 'My name is—'

'You're Detective Chief Inspector Monroe of the City Police,' Daniel replied calmly. 'I've seen you on television. The Victoria Davies case, the gang war in Birmingham. You were drugged there. Did it leave any long-standing effects?'

'You're a fan?' Monroe was surprised. Daniel shrugged.

'I'm a detective,' he replied. 'I like to keep tabs on my peers.'

'Oh, so we're *peers*,' Monroe nodded. 'Good to know where I stand.'

'You're not standing, silly. You're sitting,' Daniel smiled.

Monroe went to reply but bit it back, forcing himself to smile in return.

'How right you are,' he said.

Daniel's face darkened. Gone now was the innocent, smiling man.

'Don't do that,' he snapped, the light, sing-song tone now gone.

'Do what?' De'Geer asked.

'Talk to me like I'm a child,' Daniel replied. 'Even when I was a child, I was more intelligent than either of you. Treat me like an adult.'

'How about we treat you as a *suspect*?' Monroe leaned forward now, tiring of this game. 'How about you explain to us why you told the orderlies last night that you killed Reginald Troughton?'

'Because I did,' Daniel replied matter-of-factly. 'But I wasn't the one that executed him.'

'Aren't killing and executing the same thing?' De'Geer walked across the room now, standing closer to Daniel, still sitting on his plastic chair.

Daniel, in reply, shook his head. Now understanding, Monroe nodded at this.

'You caused the death,' he said, 'but you didn't execute the action.'

'Yes,' Daniel looked back to the detective now. 'I caused his death, because I told him to write the book.'

There was a silent moment in the room as both Monroe and De'Geer processed this.

'Tell me about that,' Monroe eventually asked. Daniel shrugged.

'He was broke,' he explained. 'He wrote nothing after the Magpies books. No, that's not true. He wrote things, these bloody awful historical mysteries, but nobody wanted them. He was sullied, untouchable after the end of the Magpies.'

'Why?' De'Geer asked.

'Because of the truth,' Daniel shifted uneasily on his chair. 'Well, the truth until Bruno gets hold of it.'

'Who's Bruno?' Monroe pressed. 'Another Magpie?'

'No, there were only six Magpies,' Daniel was looking nervous now. 'Me, Tommy, Luke, Jane, Tess and Dexter. Oh, and Jane.'

'You mentioned Jane twice.'

'That's because you have to.'

Monroe glanced over to De'Geer, unsure whether he heard this correctly. But one look on the police constable's face showed him that no, he'd heard correctly.

'So this Bruno can tell me what sullied Reginald, but you can't.' It was a statement rather than a question. In return, Daniel nodded.

'Look, I know I'm tough to talk to. I've been here a long time, and it rubs off.'

'About that,' Monroe changed subject. 'Why are you in here? Records say that you self admitted seven years ago, and don't seem to want to return to the outside world.'

'Oh, I want to,' Daniel looked at the window, staring at the gardens. 'But I don't deserve to.'

'So what, you're punishing yourself by staying here?' Monroe was surprised. 'Why?'

Daniel opened his mouth to speak, but stopped.

'I can't say,' he replied.

'Okay,' Monroe was tiring of this. 'Let's say, for example, that you are the master detective you claim you are and let's say for example too that you're not the killer. Who is?'

'Could be anyone,' Daniel mused, his tone turning serious again as if this was a question worthy of his consideration. 'Tessa is too straight, but she loves those pills. Luke is a flunkie, but he's just been cuckolded by Thomas and Jane. And Dexter is dead.'

'Thomas and Jane are having an affair?' De'Geer asked.

'More a friends with benefits situation,' Daniel replied. 'There was always some sexual tension when we were a team. Then after... well, let's just say that after too many years of waiting for him to realise she was there, she ended up marrying Luke. Some habits are hard to break, though, as I hear they were together last night.'

'Who told you that?'

'I get told a lot of things,' Daniel smiled. 'Maybe the voices told me. Because I'm mad. That'd make things simple, wouldn't it?'

'Bet that causes strife at Christmas,' De'Geer said and, at Daniel's blank expression, added 'You know, because of Luke and Tommy being cousins.'

'Oh yes, I'd forgotten that,' Daniel forced a smile. 'Originally they were brothers, but Julia thought that was a little too much like Blyton.'

Monroe wrote the name down. 'Did you mean Julia Clarke?'

Daniel didn't reply, but there was a flicker of emotion across his face at the sound of the name. Monroe smiled.

Got you, you bugger.

'You know, the more I listen to you, the more I wonder if

you even knew each other before the first book was written,' he commented.

Daniel grinned.

'See?' he exclaimed. 'You are a detective after all.'

Monroe went to reply to this, unsure if it was meant as compliment or insult, but the door opened and an elderly man, in his sixties, thinning white and black hair blowdried into a back comb, as if to hide a balding pate, over wire-rim glasses, suited and with an expensive-looking briefcase in his hand entered without knocking.

'Sebastian Klinger. My client won't be answering any more questions,' he stated to Monroe. "If you want to talk more, you can do it during an arranged interview, on your premises, and with myself present.'

Monroe nodded, rising to his feet. 'Asked all we wanted to,' he said as he motioned to De'Geer to join him in leaving. However, as they walked past Klinger and crossed out into the corridor, Daniel called out after them.

'It wasn't Derek,' he said. 'No matter what the clues will state.'

'How would you know that?' Monroe turned back to Daniel, holding a hand up to silence his solicitor. 'I'm following up on a statement that your client made.'

Daniel shrugged. 'They said there was a tyre iron there,' he explained. 'Derek used one. Although it's probably not the same one.'

'And why would you think that?' De'Geer asked.

'Because they buried it,' Daniel replied, looking to the solicitor. 'Is it custard tarts tonight? I do so love those.'

And, realising that they wouldn't get any further, Monroe and De'Geer exited the room of Daniel McCarthy, and left the Baker Institute as quickly as they could.

Rory Simpson always liked the mornings.

The afternoons were always busy; Parliament usually started around lunchtime and Norman Shipman liked to work late into the night, and so his office staff were always finishing way beyond their regulated clocking off times. And more importantly, from the moment that Rory entered Portcullis House, his life wasn't his anymore.

He was owned, body soul and mind, by Norman Shipman.

That said, it wasn't all bad. Rory had been Norman's secretary now for over twenty-five years, ever since he joined the team in the mid-nineties as an eager, young advisor; in that time he'd found his star rising as Norman's star fell. The MP was old now, well into his seventies, and although he was still an elder statesman of the House, he wasn't going to be heading any ministerial departments in the near future. In fact, he'd been happy to stay a backbencher for the last twenty years; he always claimed that you could get more done when the press weren't watching your every move.

And move Norman did. He was busier than MPs twenty years his junior and, by simply being his go-to man, the party had seen and noted Rory Simpson over the last decade. There was even talk that they could parachute him into Norman's own constituency when the MP finally retired, likely before the next election, or even used in another battleground state. He was only in his fifties, looked younger than his age and was fairly fit for his sedentary lifestyle, although one spin session a week really wasn't enough these days with all the cameras in the House filming in high definition.

All he had to do was make sure that *Mark bloody Walters* didn't get there first.

Mark had been with Norman a far shorter time than Rory, but also didn't seem to be as ambitious. That was Mark's mistake, and *that* was what Rory would use to defeat him. And when he took Norman's place, Walters could be *his* bloody secretary.

But as busy as the days and the evenings were, the mornings were his own. He could take the time to stop and smell the flowers, to enjoy the scenery. And, for the last six months he'd taken to walking to work through St James's Park on his way to Whitehall, stopping at a small coffee shack in the park and buying his daily flat white, and sipping it as he stood on the Park Bridge, the small pedestrian walkway that crossed the lake that ran the length of the park. He knew that traditionally this was where the Cold War meetings between American, British and Russian spies had occurred, and the thought of standing here, where secrets had been passed, always sent a shiver of excitement down his body.

Of course, Rory Simpson had his own secrets.

'Your coffee, just as you like it,' a woman's voice broke into his thoughts, and Rory looked from the water towards the brunette who strolled across the bridge, two takeaway cups in her hand. She was around ten years younger than Rory, slim and attractive, her long dark hair left loose around her shoulders. Rory didn't know her name, and she didn't know his; they'd chatted every Wednesday morning when meeting here, and after a few weeks they'd passed the point when it was polite to actually ask for a name, even though they knew each other's coffee orders.

And besides, Rory liked the idea of anonymity. It made him feel like a spy.

'Thanks,' he said, taking the cup. 'I didn't know if I'd see you today.'

'Yeah, I had to move some meetings around to make it, but it was too nice a day to miss,' the woman smiled, sipping at her coffee as she looked up at the blue sky. Rory returned the smile, taking a large mouthful of his own drink. He'd been a fan of flat whites ever since he'd learned that Hugh Jackman, the Australian actor, had drunk them. They made it with espresso rather than coffee, and it gave Rory a little caffeine kick when he drank them, a kick needed when working for Shipman.

However this coffee felt a little off, a little oily.

He tried to keep the smile on his face though, as he gagged a little; the last thing he wanted to do was allow the woman to see him splutter coffee anywhere, because then any hope of seeing her in a more romantic setting would be completely destroyed.

Of course, any chance of seeing her in a more romantic setting would also have to involve Rory learning her name. All he had to do was to keep this mouthful down, even though he was coughing now, as if it'd gone down the wrong tube—

'You okay?' the woman asked, her face expressing concern as she watched Rory. 'You're flushing.'

'Yeah, it went down the wrong way,' Rory croaked as he placed the takeaway cup on the railing with one hand as he pulled his top button free, loosening his collar. 'I think I—'

He gasped for air as he felt his throat closing. He stared in horror at the cup.

'*Nuts*,' he croaked, reaching out for the cup, but accidentally knocking it into the water. 'Can't breathe—'

'Oh God!' the woman moved in now as Rory dropped to

one knee, clawing at his throat. 'Someone call an ambulance! He's allergic to nuts!'

Rory fell onto his back now, his eyes bulging, his face red and his breathing made in short, sharp gasps as he scrabbled with one hand for his messenger bag on the floor beside him.

'Epi... pen...' he whispered. There was a small crowd of people around them now, staring helplessly as the woman fumbled in the bag.

'Someone run to the coffee shack!' she shouted. 'They might have something to help!'

Two onlookers ran off as the woman looked back to Rory, horror in her eyes.

'There's no pen in there,' she said. 'We'll try something else.'

'Can't breathe...'

The woman kneeled closer, over Rory's face now, blocking it from the onlookers.

'I'll try CPR until the ambulance arrives,' she exclaimed. And, moving closer, she placed her hand on Rory's jaw.

And closed it, holding it tight.

As Rory's eyes widened, the woman moved in close, as if giving him the kiss of life, but her mouth barely brushed his in the lightest of kisses as, with her other hand she closed his nostrils, stopping all air entering his body.

'Ten years, I've waited to do this,' she whispered.

As Rory struggled to breathe, he realised that the woman must have spiked his coffee, and that he was living the spy life for real right now. But *why?* He wasn't...

important...

he...

was...

The woman, tears down her face, looked down at the

vacant expression of Rory Simpson, his lifeless, glassy eyes staring up at the sky as she pulled away from the body.

'No, God, no,' she cried.

A man placed a hand on her shoulder.

'There was nothing you could do,' he said. 'You did your best.'

Tears still streaming, the slim woman with the long brown hair nodded, taking her coffee cup, discarded on the floor when she knelt beside the body and casually placing it into Rory's hand with an ease that ensured that nobody noticed, ensuring his fingers touched the surface. Then, standing up, she backed into the crowd, disappearing amongst them as the paramedics arrived, quietly discarding her latex gloves into her handbag before moving off into the park, away from the murder scene.

5

FOR SILVER

Anjli had grown up in Mile End, and had pretty much spent her professional career there.

She'd also been transferred *from* there when she beat the living hell out of a domestic abuser and was tied to a local crime lord after he assisted with her mum's chemotherapy treatments.

Basically, Anjli Kapoor's relationship with Mile End was a little complicated.

Usually the Twins could be found in the Globe Town Boxing Club, but after Monroe had sought sanctuary there a month earlier, they'd spent more time away from it, as if realising that if the police knew where to find them, then anyone else could as well. That and the fact that operatives from a black op, government funded, military organisation named Rattlestone had their arses royally handed to them by some of the Twins goons in there, meant that keeping a low profile was probably a good idea.

She'd heard from one officer at Mile End that the Lucas Brothers were holding court in a vintage style pub at the top of Grove Road, close to the southern entrance of Victoria Park, so it was just before the lunch trade arrived that she entered the bar, spying Johnny Lucas at the back of it, lounging on one of the corner sofas, several of his men sitting around him as he animatedly spoke to them. He was tanned, his salt and pepper hair styled into a loose quiff, his deep blue shirt covered by a black suit jacket.

Anjli had hoped it would be Johnny, as he was the more rational of the two personalities that he had vying for control inside him; like a *Jekyll and Hyde* creation, the *Jackie* Lucas persona wasn't a twin at all, but a different, darker side of Johnny's psyche.

You never wanted to meet Jackie.

Johnny however was way more jovial than he usually was and, as he saw Anjli, he actively waved her over.

'DS Kapoor!' he exclaimed over his gin and tonic. 'What brings you here?'

'Couldn't find you at the Boxing Club,' Anjli admitted. Johnny smiled.

'Closed it up for a couple of weeks,' he explained. 'Had a little too much attention after your DCI used it as a bolt hole and hid from black op contractors.'

'Ones that your men beat the living tar out of?' Anjli returned the smile. 'I can see that not going down well.'

'I needed a holiday anyway,' Johnny lounged back on the sofa. 'And yes, I know I'm being a bit of a trope right now, what with being a gangster in a pub.'

He smiled, but it wasn't a warm one; more as if he was keeping an appearance while furious.

'For twenty years I did all kinds of business from that Boxing Club,' he said. 'And in the end it was helping a copper that killed it.'

Anjli shifted position, unsure what to say to this. Eventually Johnny snapped out of this melancholy and shook his head at her.

'I'm not in the mood for your reports,' he said. 'Come back some other time.'

'Actually, I'm here with questions,' Anjli replied.

'Of course you are,' Johnny sighed. 'Let me guess, Reggie Troughton?'

'How well did you know him?'

'I didn't really,' Johnny straightened in his seat. 'I only knew him from his partner, Michael.'

'Your go-to barrister?'

'For over thirty years,' Johnny frowned. 'And before you even go down that route, I didn't hit him with a Land Rover. If we have a problem with someone, I let Jackie say it to their face.'

Anjli didn't doubt this for a moment.

'Do you have any idea who would want Reginald Troughton dead?' she asked. Johnny smiled.

'I think his publisher might have wanted a word,' he replied. 'Last I heard he wasn't playing well with their plans for their long-lost book.'

'Did you ever meet any of the Magpies?'

'The kiddie coppers? Nah, taking on gangland crime didn't work well with their audience. 'Happier taking down *swarthy types* for more basic crimes.'

'Swarthy types?' Anjli raised an eyebrow at this.

'You should read the books,' Johnny Lucas took another mouthful of his drink. 'They're real eye openers. Books for their time.'

'Thank you, Mister Lucas,' Anjli placed her notebook away. 'And I'm sorry for any inconvenience we've caused you.'

'Of course you are,' Johnny chuckled.

'One last thing,' Anjli added. 'Did you ever deal with Derek Sutton?'

Johnny halted himself momentarily before he replied.

'I didn't know him well, but we had dealings with him back in the day,' he said. 'He mainly hung out with Danny Martin after running south from a murder charge in Scotland. Probably hangs out with him again in Belmarsh. Cut his teeth in Glasgow, though, worked for the Hutchinsons. Real vicious bastards. That's all I can tell you, I'm afraid.'

He smiled; a sly, suspicious grin making its way across his face.

'Of course, you have your own source to the Hutchinsons in your office,' he stated. 'Just have a chat with your Glaswegian DCI.'

And, as if deciding that the conversation was now over, Johnny turned away from Anjli, already discussing with his men what lunch they should have that day.

Silently, Anjli backed out of the pub and only when she found herself in the outside air did she let the breath that she'd been holding out.

The last thing she wanted was to find a link to Monroe, especially with Whitehall sticking their noses in.

She only hoped that someone else was doing better.

As a child, Declan had always wanted to visit the Houses of Parliament, but now he was bloody sick of them. After the Victoria Davies case he'd hoped to never return, but then after Kendis had died, he'd found himself once more in the building, this time making deals with Charles Baker to not only clear Declan's name but also to arrest Malcolm Gladwell.

And now he was here again.

It wasn't technically the Houses of Parliament; instead, Declan sat in the atrium of Portcullis House, across the street, leading to the Embankment and connected to the Houses by an underpass passageway. He'd called ahead to arrange the meeting and was surprised to see that it was accepted; he'd assumed that the person he'd asked to speak to wouldn't be happy about the meeting happening at all. In fact, as Declan saw Charles Baker, currently the favourite for the new leader of the Conservative Party enter from a double-door at the back of the atrium, he felt a little flush of pride at being able to cause such annoyance.

However, Charles Baker didn't look annoyed to see Declan. In fact, he seemed to positively light up as he saw him across the atrium, actually waving as he approached.

'Declan!' he exclaimed, sitting down across the table. He was wearing a modern navy blue suit with a blue striped tie, a change from his usual traditional pin-striped look, and his white hair was groomed perfectly, still lustrous and flowing despite his age. Even though he was a good fifteen years older than Declan, he actually managed, with his tanned skin and clothing, to look the same age as the now irritated Detective Inspector sitting opposite him.

'I thought you'd want to keep this under the table,' Declan replied, watching the atrium as he spoke, noting the faces now looking in his direction. 'You're quite a superstar these days.'

'Not at all,' Charles beamed. 'You're the one they're watching, Declan. The copper who not only saved Charles Baker's life and career but also took down a governmental conspiracy while being hunted as a terrorist.' He nodded to a server for a glass of water. 'They're all wondering what *exciting adventure* you're bringing to me this time.'

Declan leaned back in his chair, observing Charles.

'Do you remember the first time we spoke?' he asked. 'You met us in the quietest spot you could. You actively *avoided* us being seen together.'

'And look how far we've come since then,' Charles replied jovially. 'So come on, what is it this time?'

Declan shifted in his seat. He didn't like it when he wasn't in control of the narrative. 'I wanted to speak to Norman Shipman, but his office aren't taking calls, and they're saying that he's cancelled all his meetings today.'

'Yes, I heard,' Charles nodded at this. 'Poor bugger's had a rubbish morning so far. One of his aides died in St James's Park this morning. Silly bastard drank a hazelnut mocha before remembering they were allergic to nuts.'

He leaned closer, his eyes gleaming with interest.

'Is he under investigation?'

'No, but we want to know his connection to someone,' Declan replied. 'Detective Inspector Theresa Martinez.'

'Ahh.' Charles sat back now, nodding at this. 'You're here about Troughton.'

This surprised Declan. 'How would you know that?'

Charles shrugged. 'Troughton worked for the government when he wrote those books. Shipman was one of his controllers. Martinez was one of the Magpies. All links to the murder I saw on the news last night.'

'Shipman can't have been,' Declan retorted. 'Those books came out in the early nineties. John Major was in charge then. Tory government.'

'And Shipman was a Tory back then,' Charles smiled.

'What, you think I had the monopoly on changing sides before an election? Shipman was a Centrist Tory through both Heath and Thatcher's years; a little too left for them and dumped on the back-benches. And he hated Michael Foot and Neil Kinnock, so there was no chance of movement towards Labour in the eighties. He did a little better under Major, but it wasn't much. He would have jumped when John Smith took the reins of Labour, but then Smith died a couple of years later.'

Charles looked at his drink as he spoke; Declan knew that even as a Conservative Minister now, he'd started his career on the Labour side of the House, and had probably run because of politicians like John Smith.

With a deep breath, Charles forced a smile and continued.

'But when *Blair* became Opposition Leader, Shipman changed allegiances. He'd had some nasty calls in 1996, so it made sense to run. Besides, if Major lost, everyone knew Hague would replace him, and Shipman knew he wouldn't play well in that family.'

'So, going that he was a Tory then, what do you mean Shipman was one of Troughton's controllers?' Declan asked, returning the conversation back to its original course.

'Troughton worked in marketing, and that's where Shipman was,' Charles replied, his tone now a little too prepared, as if ensuring that he didn't go off message. 'Under-Under-Under Secretary to another Under Secretary. So far underground that you needed miners' hats to see.'

'Gotcha.'

Charles stopped talking, watching Declan intently for a moment.

'Why come to me for this?' he asked. 'You could have found this out from half a dozen other people.'

Declan shifted in his seat. 'I had another reason to speak to you.'

Charles Baker nodded at this, as if understanding the unspoken meaning.

'Ah, you mean our German friend.'

Declan nodded. A month earlier, Karl Schnitter, aka Wilhelm Müller, the Red Reaper had been taken by agents of Section D, a Whitehall black-bag operation controlled in part by Charles Baker. Declan had known that because of arrangements made with the CIA, Karl would have been sprung the moment he was arrested, and so had arranged with agent Tom Marlowe and Section D's head Emilia Wintergreen (DCI Monroe's ex-wife, and police partner to both him and Patrick Walsh back in the day) to have Karl taken by Section D instead, where he would spend his days in an MI6 black site, being grilled about his connections to the Russians before the fall of the Berlin Wall. He'd been the murderer of Declan's parents, both made to look like accidents, and to be brutally honest, Declan hoped that they had dumped him in a deep, dark hole and left him to rot.

'He's very talkative,' Charles replied, his tone still careful, choosing his words. 'He asks about you a lot. Claims he has information for you whenever you need it.'

'I don't need anything from him,' Declan snapped a little too forcefully. Several of the others in the atrium paused their conversations, looking at him. Declan reddened, sipping at his own water.

'Is he paying for what he did?' he asked. 'That's all I want to know.'

'I'll ensure you get copied into the next report,' Charles

said, checking his watch before rising. 'I'm afraid I have a committee to chair. I hope I could assist with the Troughton case? We only met the once. He was a bitter, back-viewing little runt of a man, but I'm sure he had his qualities.'

Declan nodded to Charles as he left the table, leaning back and glancing around the atrium. He needed more on Shipman, especially what his connection to Troughton had been back in the day. Of course, if he'd been around when Troughton was writing the Magpies books, it'd at least explain why Tessa Martinez had a relationship of any kind with him.

Getting up, he nodded to a couple of the suited MPs and advisors still watching him and left the atrium. However, as he exited Portcullis House, emerging out onto the Embankment and looking up at Big Ben to his right, he saw another suited man; mid-forties, his red hair balding and with thick, black-rimmed glasses on walk quickly towards him.

'DI Walsh?' he asked. Declan stopped.

'Who's asking?'

'I'm Mark Walters,' the man replied. 'I work for Norman Shipman. I heard that you've been trying to speak to him.'

'Nothing important,' Declan nodded now, observing the man as he continued. 'I heard you guys lost someone, so it can wait.'

'Thanks,' Mark replied. 'Rory was a real team player. Norman's right-hand man, even. We're all scrabbling around right now.' He pulled out a business card, passing it to Declan.

'You can probably guess that even without all this, talking to the best friend of the Tory King in waiting isn't going to be a popular option for a Labour Backbencher—'

'I'm not anyone's best friend,' Declan snapped, but then stopped.

Was this how his meeting with Charles had been perceived? A man who was all smiles, all camaraderie?

Of course people would think that.

Bloody Charles Baker had played him again.

'I just wanted to know why he personally got involved in reassigning DI Theresa Martinez to the Reginald Troughton case, nothing more,' Declan explained.

Mark nodded. 'Miss Martinez is an old friend of the family,' he said. 'When she asked for help, Norman gave it. That said, this was a single favour, not an ongoing one, if you know what I mean.'

'And Mister Shipman's connection to Reginald Troughton?'

Mark's face faltered for a second.

'Perhaps it's best if we talk about these questions another time,' he suggested, showing the card. 'In this instance, I'll be your focal point of contact.'

'And why would I be contacting Mister Shipman, or even you about the Magpies?' Declan asked. 'After all, I was only here because of Tessa Martinez.'

'Oh, I thought you realised,' Mark looked surprised at this. 'Norman Shipman asked to be kept informed about the Magpies, because he *created* them.'

6

FOR GOLD

Monroe disliked Thomas Williams from the moment they met.

Someone had once told him that your unconscious mind would decide within twenty or thirty seconds whether you liked or disliked someone upon meeting them; it was why salespeople worked so hard to give a great impression right from the start.

Monroe decided he didn't like Thomas Williams within ten.

They sat in the lobby of the Hyatt Hotel in Piccadilly; Monroe had suggested they returned to Thomas's room rather than make a scene in public; the sight of the muscled De'Geer in full police uniform was already gaining attention there, but Thomas had found a corner settee and plumped himself down on it, saying that *whatever he had to say could be done there.* Personally, Monroe wondered if there was something in his room that he didn't want them to see, but there was no way without a warrant to find out.

And warrants were way off at this point.

Thomas was in fitness gear and still slightly sweaty; he claimed he'd been in the hotel gym when they called him, and he hadn't bothered to shower yet.

'Can you tell me where you were last night?' Monroe asked. 'In particular, around nine pm?'

'Of course,' Thomas lounged, a lazy, seemingly arrogant smile on his face. 'I was on the fourth floor of Waterstones Piccadilly, launching the latest releases of Troughton's books to women and gay men in their forties, who most likely had the full set already.'

He leaned forward, grabbing the glass of diet soda he'd ordered from the bar before sitting back, sipping at it as he considered his next words.

'It started at seven, well they opened doors around ten past seven, anyway. I did a talk, answered some questions and then signed some books. The event ended around nine.'

'Aye, the event ended around nine, but you were gone before half-past eight, weren't you?' Monroe read from his notes. 'We've already checked with the manager. Seems she was a little pissed that you broke off the signing to leave early with a Jane Ashton.'

'I fulfilled my contract,' Thomas snapped back. 'I only ever sign the first forty personally. The rest were all signed earlier that day, so everyone got an autographed copy. If you want my opinion, that manager was only annoyed because she thought *she'd* be the one going to dinner with me.'

'Oh, so you went to dinner?' Monroe asked. 'With this Miss Ashton?'

'*Mrs* Ashton,' Thomas replied, the irritation audible in his voice. 'She's married to Luke. She used to be Jane Taylor.'

'The Magpie,' De'Geer confirmed. Thomas nodded.

'She turned up at the event. I hadn't expected her. It was a pleasant surprise, and we caught up elsewhere,' he explained. 'The problem was that the audience were a little forward in bothering Jane for autographs once they realised who she was. And although I'm happy to do that sort of thing, Jane's a little more, well, restrained.'

'So you decided that as they were all bothering her, you should go somewhere quieter.'

'Yes.'

'Even though it was you that outed her to the audience during that talk?'

Thomas nodded. 'I didn't mean to, well, I mean I saw her in the audience and I respected her privacy, but Bloody Troughton hadn't turned up. He was supposed to appear and do a little piece, and then we'd sign together.' He sighed.

'It's why I only do forty on a signing. He'd take so long, the night would be over before he hit thirty.'

'But Troughton didn't turn up,' Monroe was writing this down. 'And this was around what, seven thirty?'

'Seven forty-five,' Thomas confirmed. 'Anyway, I was a little screwed by this, as I knew that some of the audience were there for the 'surprise guest'.'

'What a shock, the audience being there for the *writer* of the book, rather than...' Monroe smiled '... you.'

'Wonders never cease,' Thomas was unfazed by the jibe. 'Still, needs must and all that. I had to find something big for them.'

'And there was Jane Taylor, fresh from the books, amid all the wolves,' Monroe nodded. 'I can see why you'd clutch at that straw. So let's move past the event. You left before eight thirty.'

'For a bite to eat.'

'If I can ask, where did you go?' De'Geer spoke now. 'We

can then confirm with them for CCTV footage to corroborate this, and that'll help both of you.'

'Both?' Thomas seemed surprised at this. 'Wait, we're *suspects?*'

'We're just getting the facts down,' Monroe placated with a smile. 'But currently, someone beat Mister Troughton to death with a tyre iron forty-five minutes after you and Jane Taylor—I mean Jane *Ashton* left an event. Piccadilly to Temple Inn is half an hour by foot, and only ten by cab. You could have left, grabbed a snack and then killed him together for all I know. But, if we can get some time-stamped CCTV of you, showing that you weren't killing the author of the books that you've sponged off all of your life, then that would be great.'

'We didn't go to a restaurant,' gone was the arrogant man now, as Thomas glanced nervously from De'Geer to Monroe, his voice now noticeably lower. 'We came straight here. It was quieter. Less chance of being hassled.'

'So you were at the hotel restaurant?'

'I'd rather not say,' Thomas replied.

'All you have to do is point out which—'

'*I said I'd rather not say!*' Thomas shouted, the raised voice attracting the attention of others in the lobby. Calming himself, he lowered his voice.

'Am I under arrest?'

'Not yet,' Monroe replied, his face expressionless.

'Then I won't talk anymore about last night.'

Monroe nodded, flipping the page on his notepad. 'Okay, that's fine. Maybe you can give me an example of your detective brain, instead. If it wasn't you, who do you think killed Reginald Troughton?'

Thomas thought for a moment.

'I genuinely don't know,' he replied. 'I mean, it's not like he had any major secrets or anything. They had left him alone for years.'

'Was he doing anything currently that could have changed that?'

'Well, he was writing a new book for BadgerLock,' Thomas offered. 'But they would have wanted him alive. And it was a made-up adventure, so there were no names being affected there.'

'What about the other Magpies?' Monroe continued the questions. 'Daniel McCarthy, perhaps? He's an interesting character. We spoke to him before we came here.'

'You spoke to Danny?' Monroe couldn't be sure, but he thought he heard a slight note of fear in Thomas' voice as he asked. 'How is he?'

'Oh, I'd guess he's very much the same as he was,' Monroe carried on writing. 'Although he didn't seem to be happy with all of you.'

Thomas snorted. 'He never was,' he muttered. 'What did the mad bastard have to say?'

'Well, he informed us you and Luke weren't actually cousins, and that you were most likely sleeping with Luke's wife, *Mrs* Ashton, last night,' Monroe gave a smile. 'I appreciate the gallantry on not giving her up when we asked about your dinner date, by the way.'

'As I said, mad bastard,' Thomas snapped back. 'His words aren't worth the paper they're written on.'

'What about the words of Bruno or Julia?' Monroe pressed. 'Bruno seems an interesting person. Can you tell me what happened between him and Reginald Troughton?'

Thomas had been about to reply to the previous statement, but as Monroe spoke the names he stopped, staring wide-eyed at the two police officers.

'Bruno Field was... um, he was a kind of mentor,' he eventually whispered. 'You know, when the fame from our books happened.'

'Was he the same to Troughton?'

Thomas continued to stare, making no answer. The name *Bruno* had awoken something inside him, but Monroe couldn't work out what it was yet. He considered asking more questions about the night, but he already knew that Thomas and Jane had entered his hotel suite less than fifteen minutes after they left Waterstones; he'd watched the footage with De'Geer before they even spoke to Thomas Williams.

'Before we leave you,' he said, placing the notebook down for a moment. 'When we spoke to Daniel, he named all the Magpies at one point, but said Jane's name twice.'

'I already said—'

'Aye, I know, laddie. Mad bastard and all that. But there was something in the way he said it. Something that made me think he was on the level here. So can you explain why he might have thought there were *two* Janes?'

Thomas looked torn.

'I have an NDA,' he whispered.

'Non-disclosure agreements are irrelevant in a murder enquiry.'

'Not when they're from the same people who do the Official Secrets Act.'

'And why would you have something like that?' Monroe leaned closer. 'Give me something, lad. Off the record.'

Thomas thought for a moment.

'Daniel was right when he said Jane twice,' he replied. 'During the run, we had three Dexters; the first had a tumour that killed him and the second was hit by a bus. Every time, the next day we had an exact duplicate waiting for us.'

'And Jane?' Monroe looked to De'Geer. 'Was she the same as Dexter?'

'Jane Terry didn't die,' Thomas whispered, barely a croak, as if ashamed of what he said. 'But yeah, they replaced her the very next day. Her *and* her mental brother.'

ANTHONY FARRINGDON WAS SITTING IN HIS USUAL ARMCHAIR, a dark green, leather one beside a bust of William Gladstone when Declan entered the members' room of the *National Liberal Club*, off Northumberland Ave. It was a high-ceilinged room, with red marble pillars running along each side, the spaces between filled with either the green wallpaper of the walls, or floor to ceiling green-draped bay windows that led Declan to Farringdon's low table.

Anthony Farringdon was an elderly man in a military blazer, his white hair neatly parted to the right. It wasn't the first time that Declan had spoken to him here; Farringdon was a one-time friend of Monroe and Declan's father. Declan had been sent to speak to him by Monroe during the Victoria Davies case, and he knew that Anjli and Bullman had spoken to him while Declan had been on the run a month or so back.

He was also the one-time controller of security for both Downing Street and the Houses of Parliament; an ex-soldier with an eidetic memory, who could deduce inhabitants of a parliamentary office simply by examining the office paper of the time.

'Declan,' he smiled, placing the newspaper to the side. 'Good to see you not in chains.'

'I don't think we use chains anymore,' Declan smiled, sitting down in the indicated chair. 'But yeah, it's good to be free. And I understand you assisted with some of that, with your help on the Star Chamber and Charles Baker.'

'One does what one can,' Farringdon waved for another drink. 'Stiffner?' he asked. Declan shook his head.

'On duty.'

'More fool you,' Farringdon replied. 'But you will have a drink. Malt Whisky used to be Patrick's choice.'

He nodded to the server again, who brought a second small whisky with Farringdon's refill.

Picking it up, he raised it, looking Declan dead in the eye.

'To your father, your mother, and that you avenged their deaths,' he said.

Declan leaned back in surprise for a moment, before taking his own glass and clinking it against Farringdon's.

'I didn't avenge them,' he said after taking a sip. 'Karl Schnitter got away.'

'Karl Schnitter hasn't been seen in a month, and even his daughter believes that he's dead,' Farringdon replied. 'I told you before, Declan. I might be retired, but I used to run Downing Street's security forces, and I still hear everything. What I hear right now is that Karl Schnitter will never be arrested, because he'll never be found.'

He raised his glass.

'So well done, Declan. From one military man to another, if you know what I mean.'

Declan kept silent, but still accepted the toast with another sip. Farringdon, happy with this, leaned back in the armchair.

'So what is it today?' he enquired. Declan pulled out his notebook.

'Norman Shipman,' he replied. 'I know you spoke to Anjli about him when they talked about the Star Chamber, but I was hoping you could tell me a little more.'

'About the Star Chamber, or about the Magpies?' Farringdon, usually so military, allowed himself a small smile at this. 'I read the news, boy. I saw that the author of them was dead. Makes sense that you'd come here and ask about Norman.'

'I spoke with one of his advisers,' Declan continued, 'who told me that Shipman apparently created the Magpies. And speaking with someone else, I learned he used to be Conservative and worked with Troughton, the victim who died.'

Farringdon steepled his fingers at this, nodding. 'He was an MP before even I turned up there,' he said. 'And yes, he was a Tory. Came in at the end of Heath's tenure, I believe. Youngest Tory in the room, back then. But Thatcher thought little of him, so for about ten years they dumped him in some small dark spot in Fisheries, until she was gone. Then Major used him, but he wasn't given a portfolio; he was just left on the back-benches.'

'How did John Major use him?'

Farringdon considered his reply. 'Marketing, mainly,' he answered. 'That and shaping the minds of children to come.'

Declan leaned back in the chair. 'Propaganda for kids?'

'Are you a fan of the books?' Farringdon seemed to change tack. Declan nodded.

'I was.'

'Then the propaganda worked,' Farringdon smiled. 'For behold, you are not criminal but work for the law.'

Declan took the tumbler of whisky and took another sip, his entire 'on duty' attitude thrown to the wall with this revelation.

'You're going to have to tell me more,' he said.

'So we're talking the start of the nineties,' Farringdon explained. 'Acid Raves were gone, but MDMA, or Ecstasy, was still being used by dance-crazed teenagers around the country. Ireland was bringing in the Childcare Act, while England was wearing plaid workmen's shirts and dancing to *Nirvana*. I mean, for Christ's sake, teenagers were being given a choice of downing alcopops on one hand, or Gordon the bloody Gopher and *Art Attack* on the other. The middle ground was non-existent.'

'So where do the Magpies come into this?' Declan asked.

'The Government needed to shape the minds of kiddies like you,' Farringdon replied. 'And, after seeing manufactured groups like *Take That* and *New Kids on the Block* do well, they decided to see if they could do something similar, but with books. Shipman was brought in to oversee the marketing side, and one of his copywriters, Reginald Troughton, was hired to author them. Good, solid, responsible books about responsible teenagers solving crimes and doing good. A contemporary *Famous Five*, or *Scooby Doo* without the rubbish ghosts.'

'Hold on, are you saying the Magpies actually auditioned to be in the books?' Declan was surprised at this. 'Rather than Troughton learning about them in the paper?'

Farringdon laughed. 'Not at all,' he exclaimed. 'The Magpies didn't even *exist* before the books.'

That's what Mark Walters had meant when he said that Shipman created the Magpies, Declan realised. But Farringdon carried on.

'It was the worst kept secret in Government,' he continued. 'Well, apart from Major and Edwina Currie. They thought they were being so clever, so secretive.'

'Who were?'

Anthony Farringdon started counting off names on his fingers.

'Norman Shipman, Reginald Troughton, Julia Clarke, Jim Sutcliffe and Bruno Field,' he finished. 'The kids might have had the adventures, but these were the *real* members of the Magpies.'

———

FOR SECRETS NEVER TOLD

BILLY HADN'T WANTED TO PLAY BABYSITTER TO DI MARTINEZ, but as the day went on, he found that he was actually enjoying her company. Considering her teenage credentials, she hadn't come across as arrogant or entitled in any way and, after a brief conversation in Bullman's office, she'd wandered over to Billy, introduced herself simply as 'Theresa' and pulled up a chair.

Billy had been working on the CCTV for Temple Inn, trying to find any clues as to who was visiting Reginald Troughton, but the security footage in the area wasn't that great; after Declan had been accused of terrorism and escaped from Temple Inn, the Inns of Court had decided to upgrade their cameras, but this was still in committee, and that simple fact had actively hindered this, as many of the cameras in the Inns were already being removed prior to replacement, including several on the courtyard outside Troughton's apartment.

Besides this, Billy knew that the security guards that watched the entrances were there more as a courtesy, something that was made painfully visible when DI Frost had entered the Temple Inn Control Unit and attacked Monroe without anyone realising several weeks ago.

Quite frankly, the CCTV situation around the apartments was a *mess*.

However, while waiting for the Temple Inn security to locate and send any additional footage, Billy had went through the recently applied for CCTV from the *Piccadilly Hyatt Hotel*, searching for Thomas Williams, trying to confirm whether he really had an alibi for the time of Troughton's murder. Monroe and De'Geer had already viewed it at the source, but Billy needed to have this logged and time stamped for future investigation.

Monroe had already told Billy what he'd seen on it, so it was no surprise to Billy to see Thomas enter the hotel with a blonde woman on his arm, laughing and snuggling in close as they walked through the lobby. Beside him, Theresa straightened.

'Know her?' Billy asked. Theresa nodded.

'That's Jane Ashton,' she replied. 'Used to be Jane Taylor. And used to be Tommy's major crush.'

'Ashton, as in Luke Ashton?' Billy whistled. 'I'm surprised that Reginald was the one murdered.'

Theresa didn't reply, watching the screen as Billy moved from camera to camera, following the couple as they entered the elevator, emerged on Thomas' floor and entered his room together.

'Eight-forty,' Billy marked the time down on a pad beside him. 'Still time to leave and reach Reginald.'

'I think Troughton is the last thing they're thinking about,' Theresa muttered, and Billy wondered if he detected a small amount of jealousy in her tone. He didn't answer this;

instead he fast forwarded through the CCTV footage of the corridor, pausing when movement from Thomas' door caught his eye.

'Ten thirty-seven,' he noted down as, on the screen, the door to the hotel room opened, revealing Jane Ashton, pulling on her shoes as, jacket in her hand she half ran towards the elevators.

'Looks to be in a hurry,' he said. Theresa nodded.

'Ten thirty the news was everywhere about the murder,' she replied. 'They probably received the text, realised the press would be all over this and decided that being caught together was a bad idea.'

Billy looked at Theresa Martinez, noting the comment.

Received the text.

'Did *you* receive the text?' he asked.

Theresa, watching the screen, nodded before realising what she had said, glancing back to Billy with a disarming smile.

'I mean, I received *a* text,' she explained. 'I said *the text* as I meant *the* text that gave the news.'

Billy looked back at the screen, nodding.

'How close were you to Troughton?' he asked.

Theresa, grateful for the subject change, shrugged.

'Not really,' she said. 'Luke, Thomas, Daniel, they were all closer. He was always friendlier with the boys.'

'Because he was gay?' Billy hadn't meant for it to sound like an accusation, but that he himself was gay had given the question a little more intensity than he had intended. Theresa, in response, jumped as if Billy had placed a taser under her chair.

'No, I didn't mean that at all,' she replied. 'I just meant he was closer to the boys. He'd always said that he'd wanted a son, but it wasn't to be. I just don't think he understood girls.'

'How did that make you and Jane feel?'

'Expendable,' Theresa answered honestly, with a wry smile on her face.

Billy didn't really know what to say about this, and so switched the screen to the crime scene photos of the study. At this, Theresa leaned closer.

'What are we looking for?' she asked. Billy showed the wall to the right.

'There's a picture missing there,' he said. 'I'm not sure how I intend to find it, but I know that there's a chance it—'

'I know the photo,' Theresa interrupted. 'That is, I think I do.' She leaned back in her chair, thinking.

'There was a piece done on Troughton in *The Independent* for the twentieth anniversary,' she continued. 'He's sitting in his study. It was a big, centre page pull out. Large photo.'

Billy started typing into his computer, pulling up a couple of lesser used, researcher-based search engines as he trawled the internet. After a couple of minutes, he leaned back in his chair.

'I think I have it,' he said, pulling up an image on the screen.

It was Reginald Troughton in his writing chair, facing a camera and smiling, holding a couple of first edition copies of the *Magpies* books in his hands. The corner of the room was behind him, and in the distance Billy could see a frame on the wall that matched the blank space now. It was blurred, the image resolution not great, but the fuzzy outlines of several figures could be made out in it, one smaller than the others.

'I can contact *The Independent*,' Billy was reaching for the phone. 'Even if this was a digital camera job, the raw photo image will still be in their archives. We might be able to zoom in.'

'You can, or you can instead email the *Uxbridge Informer*,' Theresa suggested. 'They don't exist anymore, so it might be tough; they were bought out by *Trinity Mirror,* who are now *Reach PLC.*'

'Why should I be contacting an out of print paper?' Billy asked.

'Because there was a *Blue Peter* competition back around '95,' Theresa replied. 'Winner got to meet Reginald and have an adventure with us in the *Blue Peter* garden, before appearing on the show.' She pointed at the blurred image. 'The winner was a girl from Ruislip, Eloise Lewis. That was the photo they used in the paper. It's Eloise with Reginald, Julia Clarke, Bruno Field and the MP, Norman Shipman. He claimed he was there as she was the daughter of one of his constituents.'

Billy looked over to Theresa. 'Shipman. Who gave you the all-access pass to be here.'

'He's a family friend, nothing more,' Theresa replied stiffly. 'There's no ulterior motive for me being here. I want the same as you. Justice.'

'That's good to hear, lassie,' Alexander Monroe said as he entered the office, overhearing her last words. 'Because in the spirit of finding justice, we have a couple of questions for you, too.'

Theresa rose, turning to face Monroe.

'As I said to DS Bullman, I'm an open book,' she said. 'So ask me what you want.'

'In a bit,' Monroe walked towards his office. 'I want DI

Walsh in on this. He's had an interesting chat with some Whitehall people about the *Magpies*.'

With that, he entered his office. Theresa, paling, looked to Billy.

'Where are the toilets?' she asked. Billy waved over to the back door and gratefully, Theresa left the main office, entering the women's toilets and locking herself into a cubicle.

Now alone, she pulled a small *altoids* breath mint box from her jacket pocket, opening it up. There weren't any breath mints in the box, but it was filled with small, round, white pills.

Her hand now shaking, Theresa carefully took a couple, closing the box and putting it away before her trembling could scatter the tablets to the floor, placing the removed tablets onto her tongue and swallowing without water with a practiced ease.

Then, after closing the box and shutting her eyes, she sat still on the seat of the toilet for a couple of moments, breathing slowly, calming herself while pressing at her right knee, massaging it gently.

Opening her eyes finally, she took a deep breath, rose and, flushing the unused toilet, left the cubicle. After checking her reflection, she returned to Billy, the mask of calm assurance back on her face.

'Anything new?' she said as she sat down, forcing a smile. Billy was once more working through CCTV images.

'Actually, yeah,' he replied, pointing. 'Temple Inn just sent us some more cameras. This is the main entrance to Fleet Street. It doesn't have a security guard and its usually closed after five, but the church had an event on, so they left it open.'

He paused the video. On it, a bald, Caucasian man in black was walking through the gate.

'I can't get a clear shot as the motion blur is bad here, but this man arrives at just before nine.' There was a flurry of movement on the screen as Billy fast forwarded. 'And here, fifteen minutes later, he leaves.' The image now showed the back of the bald man, with what looked to be a vertical scar on the back of the head.

'Can we get any better images?' Theresa asked. Billy shrugged.

'We know they left onto Fleet Street, so I can see if any of the shops picked them up,' he replied, changing the footage, showing a car park now. 'But that's not the only thing I saw. This man was seen arriving at eight forty-five by car.'

On the image, a black-haired man in a white shirt was seen walking across the car park. Theresa leaned closer, watching the image as Billy continued.

'He returns to the car twenty minutes later, as seen here,' he forwarded the footage twenty minutes before stopping; on the screen the man now walked over to his car, opening the back up, pulling a black messenger bag out of the boot. 'He then leaves again. The timestamp here shows nine-oh-seven.'

'Around the time when Reggie was murdered.'

'And here, ten minutes later, he comes back one last time,' Billy forwarded the footage until the man reappeared. But this time the figure was running, messenger bag on his shoulder, his hands dark with something on them, something that was spattered over the white sleeves of his shirt. On the screen, he almost slammed bodily into his car, looking around in some sort of bewildered daze before climbing into it and driving off at speed.

'Someone needed to get out in a hurry,' Billy said,

zooming onto the licence plate of the car. 'Was that blood on his hands? I'll check the plate and see who—'

'There's no need,' Theresa whispered. 'That's Luke Ashton. I'd bet my life on it.'

———

IT WAS ANOTHER HALF AN HOUR BEFORE DECLAN RETURNED TO the office. By then, Billy had confirmed that the car did indeed belong to Luke Ashton, and both Bullman and Monroe were standing around the computer screens as Billy tried to follow Luke's car through London.

'What did I miss?' he asked. Monroe looked over at him.

'Luke Ashton,' he said. 'Looks like he was in Temple Inn with what looked like blood on his hands shortly after Reginald Troughton's murder.'

'Can we get him in?' Declan looked to Bullman, but it was Theresa who replied.

'PC De'Geer has already gone with a car to pick him up,' she said. 'I offered to go with them, a friendly face and all that, but it was considered that it might be better for everyone if he didn't see someone he recognised, as they arrested him for murder.'

'We've also asked Morten to pick up his wife, too,' Monroe added. 'The two of them are the last *Magpies* we need to speak to.'

Theresa went to speak on that, but stopped herself. Declan, however, noted this.

'Something you wish to add, DI Martinez?' he asked. Theresa shook her head.

'No, nothing,' she replied.

Monroe turned to her.

'Are you positive about that?' he added. 'Maybe there's another member of the *Magpies* we need to speak to?'

Theresa Martinez stared at Monroe, her mouth opening and shutting quietly in small, almost imperceptible motions, as if trying to vocalise words. Finally, she did.

'No, sir.'

'That's a shame,' Monroe turned to Declan. 'If you'd told the truth, we wouldn't be resorting to this. DI Walsh, ready the interview room.'

'I don't know what—' Theresa replied, but Monroe spun to face her, stopping her words in her mouth.

'You lied to us, Detective Inspector Martinez. You said there were no other members of the *Magpies* to interview, but there are, isn't there? Jane Terry, for example.'

Theresa's face went even whiter. 'She wasn't a *Magpie*,' she whispered. 'She isn't in the books.'

'*Only because she was replaced!*' Monroe snapped. 'So how about you stop with the *secret history* bollocks and tell us the truth? Because I bet you, we already know most of it.'

'Like how you weren't crime solving friends, but auditioned for the roles,' Declan added. 'And that the *Magpies* were created in a government think tank and overseen by a Tory MP named Shipman.' He looked away in anger.

'I *worshipped* the *Magpies*,' he hissed. 'I *believed* you.'

Theresa leaned back in the chair, staring up at the ceiling.

'Do I need my federation rep or a solicitor in the interview with me?' she asked.

'That's up to you,' Monroe replied stonily. 'But we still class you as a suspect, no matter what Luke bloody Ashton was doing last night.'

DI Theresa Martinez stood up, straightening her suit.

'Then let's get this over with,' she said. 'You want the truth? I'll tell you everything.'

———————

JULIA CLARKE WAS RUNNING A BATH WHEN SHE HEARD THE phone ring.

She didn't like to answer the phone; it was usually cold callers or scammers from India trying to convince her that her Microsoft computer was hacked, even though she'd been an Apple user for the last five years. People who knew her would call her on her mobile, or send her emails or texts, knowing that she hated talking on the damn things.

It was usually *bad* when they called on the land line.

'*Julia, it's Thomas,*' the voice spoke through the speaker when the answerphone finally kicked in. Hearing this, Julia spoke a silent curse and left the living room, walking back up to the bathroom. Almost seventy years old, she'd been retired from publishing for five years now, bar a couple of consultancy jobs, and the last thing she wanted was to rekindle a relationship with *that* toxic prick. She'd arranged the new book with *Reginald*, not with bloody *Tommy of the Magpies*. Why was he calling *her* of all people?

Probably because you have the unfortunate joy of being his aunt, she thought to herself. *At least you can choose your friends. Family less so. And family can wait until after my bloody bath.*

The bath was almost filled now, but when she dipped her finger in, she winced; it was a little too hot for her liking. Before she could adjust the cold tap though, she heard a noise on the landing. A creak, as one of the hundred-year-old floorboards took the weight of something heavier than her Siamese cats.

'Who's out there?' she asked, nervously looking around for something to use as a weapon. The only thing she could see was a toilet cleaner, so she grabbed it, brandishing it like a club. In the doorway, a figure appeared, wearing shapeless black clothes and a full head latex mask of a bald man. Which, Julia supposed, meant that it could be anyone.

'Who are you?' she stood now, brandishing the toilet cleaner in front of her. 'I'm nothing to do with *BadgerLock Publishing* anymore. I can't help you—'

The intruder with the bald mask on said nothing, but lunged forward, knocking the toilet brush out of Julia's hand as they pushed her bodily backwards, tumbling over the edge of the bath and splashing into the hot water. As she screamed in both fear and pain, the figure grabbed at her throat with their black gloves, pushing hard, ramming her head under the hot water, scalding her skin as she fought to breathe, her arms flailing, her hand grabbing desperately at the latex head mask, tearing it off—

Julia's eyes widened in recognition of her killer, and the gasp that she made underwater released the last air she had inside her mouth. And, as the now unmasked killer continued to force her body under the water, Julia's eyes relaxed, no longer surprised as death took her, her now dead eyes stared blankly up at the killer.

Rising, panting with the effort, the killer grabbed the latex mask, pulling it back on and ensuring that the hoodie hid the neck. Then, having done this, they reached into their jacket and, from an inside pocket, pulled out a clear ziplock bag filled with white rose petals.

Emptying them into the bath, the killer stared down at

the face of Julia Clarke, half obstructed by petals and with a last, almost reverential nod left the bathroom and Julia's house, pausing only to listen to and then delete the most recent message.

After all, Julia Clarke wouldn't be listening to it any time soon.

8

FOR A WISH

THERESA MARTINEZ SAT IN THE TEMPLE INN INTERVIEW ROOM with the expression of a woman who'd already been condemned, as Monroe and Declan sat down opposite her.

'Smile lassie, it might never happen,' Monroe tried to joke, even though his expression was still one of thunder. 'This isn't a formal interview, as the others weren't. However, the others didn't strong-arm a prominent politician to give them a free pass to the front of the queue when it came to investigating, and we're yet to decide whether you're here to help us, or hinder us.'

'That's fair,' Theresa replied.

'So, why don't you tell us what you know?' Monroe continued. Theresa instead leaned back in her chair.

'Why don't you tell me what *you* know?' she countered. 'That way I know what not to double up on.'

Monroe looked to Declan, who shrugged. 'Makes sense.'

'Okay then, lassie, we'll go first,' the old Scot replied, pulling out his notebook and opening it. 'First off, let's talk about Daniel McCarthy.'

'He's a good man, but a broken one,' Theresa whispered, almost to herself.

'Aye, he's broken alright,' Monroe agreed. 'But at the same time, sometimes you wonder *why* he's like he is. Do *you* know why he voluntarily admitted himself to the Baker Institute?'

'No,' Theresa admitted. 'But I've heard rumours. He believed he deserved to be punished.'

'For what?'

'No idea,' Theresa shrugged. 'I was the copper in the gang. They didn't talk to me much over the last couple of decades.'

'Okay,' Monroe looked back to his notes. 'Tell me more about Jane Terry. And before you spout off about Whitehall NDA bollocks, know that we eat Whitehall lawyers for lunch.'

Theresa nodded. 'The NDAs mean little now Reggie's dead anyway,' she said. 'And Bruno pretty much tore them up after...'

She stopped.

'Jane Terry was the first Jane,' she admitted, returning to the question.

'So it's true? You auditioned for the roles?' Declan asked.

'Kinda,' Theresa tried to smile. 'Sorry to piss on your chips there. We spent a couple of months hanging out, getting used to each other. Luke and Tommy had to learn to be closer as they were brothers. Although, by the time the books came out, that'd changed to cousins. Danny looked after Dexter, well until the dog died, and then Jane looked after the replacement Dexter.'

'Which Jane?' Monroe asked.

'The second one,' Theresa confirmed. 'Jane Terry was allergic to dogs, which didn't help much.'

'So how long did the first Jane last?' Declan leaned closer. 'The photos always showed Jane Taylor.'

'Oh, Taylor was in position by the time the books came out, so she was used in the marketing, but the Jane that Reggie wrote about in book one was Jane Terry.'

'Why did she leave?' Monroe pushed.

'Didn't want to do it,' Theresa leaned back, remembering. 'She only came to the audition because her brother was up for the part that became Luke's. He didn't get it, but she did.'

'Bet that went down well.'

'Not really. He ended up coming with her everywhere, as if by being there he'd be written in like a sixth member of the team. She didn't get on with Tommy though, and Bruno didn't like her, kept shouting at her to get rid of Graham— that was her brother's name.'

She sighed.

'At the end of the first adventure, she said she wanted to leave, but at that point the books were already at the printers. Luckily Jane Taylor was on the backup list so Bruno swapped them. Terry was out, Taylor was in for the photos and when the second print came out they changed all the surnames, claiming that the first edition mentions of 'Jane Terry' was a mistake.'

'Lucky she had the same name.'

'She didn't. She was *Elizabeth Jane Taylor*. Named after the actress. They just told her to tell people she preferred her middle name. Nobody questioned it.'

'And what happened to Jane Terry and her brother?' Monroe asked.

'Graham was annoyed at what happened, but I think he understood. I think she became a teacher or something. I know Daniel kept in touch with her until...'

'Until?' Declan looked up from his notepad.

'Until she died, about eight years ago,' Theresa admitted. 'I don't know the full story; I know it was accidental. Maybe an overdose? Kind of like Heath Ledger. It's why I didn't reply when you asked if there were any more *Magpies* to interview. Technically, there aren't, as she's dead.'

'And Graham?'

'Christ knows,' Theresa looked directly at Declan. 'I never spoke to him after Jane left, and I got on better with the new Jane. Good riddance to the pair of them.'

She looked away.

'That's what I thought at the time, anyway.'

'And now?'

Theresa chuckled. 'Hindsight is always *twenty twenty vision*, DI Walsh.'

'So, tell us about Bruno Field,' Monroe said.

Theresa stayed silent for a long moment.

'He was one of the spin doctors in the room,' she eventually said. 'Worked with Shipman in Fisheries as Legal Counsel before Shipman came in out of the cold. Real bastard. He was part of the triumvirate. Reggie wrote the books, Julia published the books and Bruno did all the legal stuff and managed us. Like Simon Cowell, but years before he existed like that.'

'The publisher, that'd be Julia Clarke of *BadgerLock Publishing*, right?' Declan asked. 'They did the paperbacks when they first came out.'

'They've done all the books,' Theresa replied. 'Even the new ones. Well, I say new, but all that's different is some of the language and an introduction by Tommy.'

'But Reginald Troughton was writing a new one,' Monroe

butted in. 'And Daniel told us he believed he killed Troughton by suggesting that he did this.'

Theresa raised her eyebrows at this. 'Daniel did it?' she asked. 'I wouldn't have thought it'd be him. I was sure it was Tommy who begged Reggie for a new book.'

As if tiring of the questions, Theresa leaned forward.

'Look,' she said. 'I get you don't trust me, and that I appeared out of nowhere. But if it helps get me out of here, I'll be completely honest. I'm on leave from Manchester because I have PTSD. I've been having nightmares recently, of a case I was on ten years ago; the explosion at the Manchester Printworks.'

'You were there?' Declan asked.

'I was caught in the blast,' Theresa replied. 'I was in hospital for a couple of months while they put metal pins in my legs. I take painkillers for the pain in my right knee, still. And recently I've been having repeated dreams of this, so they signed me off.'

'You were lucky you're not dead.'

'I should have been,' Theresa replied. 'Weirdly, I had a call from Danny as we arrived. He never called me, so I took it, told him I was busy and would call back, and then followed my team in as the bomb went off. If I'd not taken the call, I'd have been at ground zero.'

'Sounds like Danny saved your life.'

'Danny has a knack for that,' Theresa smiled faintly. 'Anyway, I heard recently that Reggie was writing a new book, and I came to London to convince him not to. But I only arrived yesterday afternoon, and wasn't intending to see him until today.'

She took a deep breath.

'I'm Norman Shipman's God-daughter; that's how I got the part back in the day. I used this relationship to gain a letter from Whitehall, forcing you to bring me on. I'm not working for him, or Bruno, or anyone else. I've not seen any of the others, apart from Daniel a couple of years back, since we met up for some tenth anniversary TV special. I wasn't invited to Luke and Jane's wedding or the twentieth anniversary party, and Tommy pretty much wrote me out of all the intros he did for these books. Reggie was a drunk and Bruno was a sexual predator, but that was a long time ago.'

Quietly, she watched both Declan and Monroe for a reaction before continuing.

'I'm a Detective Inspector, and I'm a bloody good one. We all do stupid things as kids. The difference with me is that they published my stupid decisions to the world. I want to find out who killed Reggie, no matter where it leads. And I saw the tyre iron too, and heard that it has Derek Sutton's fingerprint on. Someone is playing silly buggers, and all it'll do is destroy our name. So charge me, kick me out or *put me to bloody work.*'

Monroe and Declan stared at Theresa before turning to each other. Eventually, Monroe looked back.

'One question,' he said, closing up his notebook. 'Did you actually solve any of the bloody cases?'

'Yes,' Theresa replied, straightening in the chair. 'Although we had help. A private detective named Jim Sutcliffe, who worked with Troughton at Whitehall. He showed us tricks of the trade and assisted us here and there. Reggie then edited him out of the story when writing the books.'

'Is that how you caught Derek Sutton?'

'Yes,' Theresa replied. 'Jeetinder Gill lived in Hillingdon, West London. There'd been some kind of conflict between him and Derek, and a few days later Gill, with another man, Singh were found beaten to death. Reggie got wind that it was Derek Sutton, and so Jim used his own connections to find the tyre iron, which 'we' then found and gave to the police. Reggie then made up some bollocks about a milkman to give us a reason to be there.'

'Did Reggie ever say who gave him the tip?'

'No, and we never asked.'

'Probably for the best,' Declan replied. 'So, Guv, what now?'

'Let's get a briefing going, see what's turned up and then chat with Luke Ashton when they bring him in,' Monroe rose from the chair. 'For the moment, DI Martinez, you can partner up with DI Walsh here. Any funny business though, and we'll bench you. Understand?'

'I'm okay with that if DI Walsh is,' Theresa looked to Declan. Monroe, though, smiled.

'Oh, he'll be fine with that, he used to have photos of you all over his wall.'

And, having placed Declan truly in the dock, Monroe left the interview room.

There was an awkward moment of silence before Declan spoke.

'He drinks,' he explained. 'It's a terrible thing. He doesn't know what he says.'

Theresa laughed. 'You can tell me all about the photos after the briefing.'

Declan inwardly groaned as he led Theresa Martinez out of the interview room.

'RIGHT THEN, TELL ME WHAT WE HAVE,' MONROE SAID TO THE briefing room, currently comprising Declan, Billy, Anjli, Theresa and Doctor Marcos. 'We know a tyre iron killed him, we know a fingerprint shows that Derek Sutton apparently did it. What else do we now know?'

'That the whole *Magpies* series of books were a manufactured fallacy?' Anjli replied sweetly, smiling at Theresa. Monroe frowned at her.

'True, but not helpful. Fill me in on Troughton, someone.'

'Worked for the government, under Norman Shipman,' Declan started. 'Helped create a crime solving team in the early nineties, under the remit of Shipman, Bruno Field, Julia Clarke and a private eye called Jim Sutcliffe. The kids were auditioned—'

'We weren't auditioned, as such,' Theresa interrupted. 'They did a subtle ask around to see who had children that fitted the bill. You couldn't audition for this without someone putting the dots together. They wanted a tomboy, someone good with mechanics. I was Norman Shipman's god-daughter, and I was adept by then at picking locks. They thought that would be a great thing to use.'

She chuckled.

'Although they got pissed off when I kept breaking into their cars. Even took Bruno's for a joyride when I was sixteen.'

'You could drive?'

'I was an expert in doing doughnuts in Landies when I was twelve,' Theresa said proudly. 'You know, when you spin the car around. All that *Fast and Furious* stuff before the films ever even came out. There was nobody better behind a wheel than me. Of course, we couldn't use any of that in the books as we weren't old enough to drive, and the whole point was not to do anything illegal, regardless of whether we did it in our spare time.'

'And the others?'

'Tommy was Julia's nephew, I'm not sure about the others.'

'We'll need all the family connections, when you have a chance,' Monroe looked back to Declan. 'Carry on.'

'The kids were gathered together and became marketed as the *Magpies*,' Declan continued. 'They would 'solve' crimes and Reginald would write them up. Although now we know that Jim Sutcliffe solved the crimes, and Reginald attributed the case solving to the *Magpies*.'

'Not all of them,' Theresa added. 'I already told you, Jim trained us as we went along. Although the first three were very much him, the rest were solved mainly due to us working it out. In *The Adventure of the Broken Clock*, Daniel solved the case before Jim did. We'd gotten quite good by then.'

'So why stop?' Billy asked. Theresa paused, looking at Monroe.

'The official reason was because we were all seventeen, eighteen by then,' she started. 'We were moving on, going to university, that sort of thing.'

She rubbed at her right knee, slowly letting out a held breath.

'The truth was that we broke up in 1996 after the publishing party for the last book, *The Adventure of the Vanishing Train*. Bruno had hired out a suite for the bash and had allowed us all to drink. Some of us were of age by then, and the rest of us were as near as dammit, so he pulled in a lot of champagne for everyone. We'd just done a deal for a TV series, America wanted us to do a UK-US crossover, we had another three books planned... And then we realised Luke was missing.'

'He'd left the party?' Anjli asked. Theresa shook her head.

'No,' she explained. 'He'd had a little too much to drink and Bruno, unknown to us, had taken him into the back bedroom. When we found them, Bruno was on top of a half naked Luke—who didn't even know where he was, he was so drunk.'

'Jesus,' Monroe exhaled. 'Did you have any inkling of this happening?'

'Yes and no,' Theresa admitted. 'We knew Bruno had a thing for Luke, and it had caused issues in the group. Tommy was supposed to be the leader, but Luke was more popular with the girls. It was a whole *Take That* situation, before they even existed.'

'*Take That?*' Billy asked, confused. 'I mean, I know the band, but I don't get the comparison?'

'The band showcased Gary Barlow, but Robbie Williams became more popular,' Anjli added. 'Not that I'm a fan or anything.'

'Luke wanted to quit, and we wanted Bruno fired, but everyone knew that this wasn't tenable. Word got out though, mainly because of the fight.'

'Fight?'

'Yeah,' Theresa continued. 'When Reginald found Luke with Bruno, he lost his shit. I mean, big time. Started kicking seven shades of hell out of Bruno—if Tommy and Julia hadn't interceded, he might even have killed him. The two wouldn't work or even speak to each other again. But rumours of the fight popped up around Westminster, and in the end the only option was to finish the series. And so we 'broke up'.'

'I bet that didn't land well on Shipman,' Monroe muttered.

'Could explain why he walked across the Commons floor a few months later,' Doctor Marcos suggested.

'No, that was because of the money,' Theresa added.

'How do you mean?'

'When the series collapsed, the Tories wanted the budget they'd given Shipman back. They were about to hit election year, and they'd given a fair few grand to the team for expenses. What they didn't realise was that the books were incredibly popular, bestselling even, and by the time they ended, there were about *four million* in book royalties inside the account. But when they eventually went in to get it, it wasn't there anymore,' Theresa replied. 'Blame fell on Shipman, as he was one signatory, but they couldn't prove it, and that's why he walked. A year later Labour got in, and the money was forgotten. Or, they found it and just didn't tell anyone.'

'Could Bruno have taken it?' Anjli asked. Theresa shrugged.

'Nobody knows, but after the news came out around Westminster, Bruno was blacklisted, couldn't get work anywhere.'

'Why?' asked Billy. 'I mean, this was a secret project, right? How did Westminster know?'

'They never gave the details,' Theresa answered. 'They just let it get out that he was caught grooming, and then trying to screw male interns. Which, as we weren't being paid by Westminster, I suppose that wasn't too far from the truth, while not telling the full story.'

She rubbed at the bridge of her nose.

'And when Shipman went, his entire team defected with him, as the Tories didn't want any of them around. Even the new boys in his team, like Simpson.'

'Was Reginald involved in this?' Anjli carried on. 'Could Luke have had some kind of issue with him that led to the murder?'

'No,' Theresa replied. 'And I can't see Luke killing Reginald. He...' she trailed off.

'I just can't.'

Declan noted the pause, writing it into his notepad. There was something more between Luke and Reginald. *If Tommy was connected to Julia Clarke, and Theresa connected to Shipman, could there be a familial connection there?*

'Okay, so what else?' Anjli looked to Monroe. 'Guv?'

'Thomas Williams and Jane Ashton seem to have alibis, purely through the fact that they were sleeping together in a hotel room at the time of the murder, and CCTV keeps them in the room,' he continued. 'Daniel McCarthy however was out of *his* room and found soaked in the garden after they released the news. Luke Ashton was seen on CCTV—' he looked to the plasma screen as Billy placed up the image of Luke beside his car, '—here, where it looks like he has blood on his hands.'

'That's not the only interesting suspect though,' Billy piped up, showing the image of the bald man leaving through the Fleet Street entrance. 'De'Geer interviewed the neighbours, and some of them saw this man leaving the apartments around the same time.'

'Any idea who it could be?' Declan looked at Theresa, who shook her head.

'It looks like Derek Sutton, but he's in prison,' she said.

Anjli whistled. 'You use Sutton's fingerprint on the same weapon he used, and at the same time you dress as him? That's dedication to the role.'

'So, we have two immediate suspects. This mysterious bald man and Luke Ashton. Anything else we're missing?'

'Jane Terry and her brother Graham,' Declan said. 'Jane apparently died eight years ago, but maybe there's something there.'

'Good thought. Let's look into that.'

'Johnny Lucas said that Michael Chadwick, their barrister, had been with them for over thirty years,' Anjli chimed in. 'When I checked the case, Derek Sutton fired him before he was arrested, and Chadwick refused to return for the murder trial, claiming a conflict of interest.'

'Hard to defend a suspect when your partner is writing a book about them *being* the killer,' Billy muttered. 'Maybe Chadwick was the source that told Reginald in the first place?'

'We'll never know, with them both dead,' Monroe mused. 'Billy, check into the scene reports. Anjli, go speak to Julia Clarke with De'Geer when he returns—'

'Shouldn't we go to see Sutton, Guv?' Anjli asked. 'I mean, I spoke to Johnny Lucas about that, and he might talk more to me—'

'I'm sure I'll be fine doing that alone,' Monroe replied. 'We're both Scottish, so worst-case scenario? We'll talk Celtic versus Rangers. You go see the publisher, and Declan and Miss Martinez? You find this Graham Terry. See if he knows anything.'

There was a buzz on his phone, and he paused, reading the message.

'For God's sake,' he hissed. 'Bloody Luke Ashton's in the wind.'

'And Jane?' Theresa asked. Monroe shrugged.

'All I have is that Luke wasn't there when they went to take him in. Bollocks.'

'One last thing,' Declan asked before people started leaving. 'Any news on what the poem meant?'

'Poem?' Theresa asked, confused. Billy nodded, pulling it back onto the screen.

> Joyous winds blow hard
> Mirthless through the dales
>   Hellacious tales of bards
> Birthing hidden tales
> Secretive and scarred
>   Devil's Holy Grails
>   Kissing 'til you're barred
> Wishing you will fail

'Troughton had it hidden in a photo frame of the lot of you,' Monroe explained. 'We don't know why.'

'I don't know why he was hiding it, but I know what it is,' Theresa rose, walking to the screen, staring at the poem. 'It's a message. We started doing them when we were together, a way to talk without the grown ups listening. You look for the words on each line.'

She rested her arm vertically against the screen, placing it around the middle of the verse, and blocking out the words underneath.

However, it was the words to the *left* of the arm that mattered.

Joyous winds blow hard
Mirthless through the dales
Hellacious tales of bards
Birthing hidden tales
Secretive and scarred
Devil's Holy Grails
Kissing 'til you're barred
Wishing you will fail

Monroe read the message. ' Looks like we have another clue to work out,' he said. 'Mainly who sent it, *why* they sent it, and *what the hell does it mean?*'

9

FOR A KISS

'I'M SORRY THAT I WASN'T THERE FOR YOU. I'M SORRY YOU'RE dead.'

Jane Ashton wiped a tear from her eye and looked away from the gravestone, staring out across the cemetery as she tried to plan her next words. Eventually, with no new thoughts coming to mind, she looked back to the gravestone in front of her; the monument for Jane Terry, dead for eight years. Beside the grave was a second, smaller stone, a simple cross with an inscription along the crosspiece. This stone was slightly newer and less weathered than the one beside it.

The grave of Graham Terry, dead for just under *seven* years.

Jane had never met Graham back then; she'd only crossed paths with the *other* Jane a couple of times since the *Magpies* ended. She'd always felt that she'd stolen the role of '*Magpie Jane*' from her, even though everyone had told her that the first Jane had asked for her release.

But Jane had found herself on a rooftop with her predecessor a decade ago. She hadn't meant to, but the twentieth anniversary party had been on the top floor of a hotel and, trying to find some area to escape to where nobody else was, she'd found herself on the other side of the building, on a rooftop and facing another attendee of the party, Jane Terry. She was there because of her dad, and she was about to throw herself off the edge.

They'd spent an hour talking, sitting on a precipice, finally learning the true stories of each other. Jane Terry learned that Jane Taylor hadn't known that there even *was* a first adventure before she turned up, that she'd arrived for a photo shoot and only learned that she was the second place Jane, when she read the galley proof of Book One. Meanwhile, Jane Taylor learned that Jane Terry had asked to leave, mainly because her brother was the one who truly cared about being in the *Magpies*, and seeing his face fall every day she was in the group was too much for her.

And therefore she quit, something she regretted every day following that action. Jane had felt there was something else, something *darker* the original Jane wasn't telling her, another reason for her leaving; but there was no way to press on the subject, and the conversation turned, never returning to a suitable moment to continue.

They'd talked more in that hour than they had in the previous two decades, and by the end both returned to the party, promising to keep in touch. They never did, mainly because of *Magpie* politics, including a potential reboot that Jane had wanted no part of, and two years later she'd learned of Jane Terry's death; some kind of drugs overdose, never explained or investigated.

And so, once a year since then, Jane came to this cemetery to talk to the woman she'd promised to all those years ago, yet years too late. She hadn't intended to come for another couple of months, but the recent events had drawn her here, to ask for forgiveness once more.

And she'd needed to be here right now.

There was what sounded like a rustling of leaves to the left; looking across the cemetery, Jane paused, her face paling, her expression one of horror. She looked around, her movements jerky, as if utter terror had taken hold of her.

There was the faint sound of laughter behind her; turning, she glanced across the cemetery and towards the main entrance where two elderly ladies walked towards her, gossiping and laughing as they did so. They hadn't seen Jane, but they were *safety*, and Jane started running towards them, stopping the two women as she approached.

'I'm sorry,' Jane exasperated as she almost ran to them. 'Can I stand with you a moment?'

'You look like you've seen a ghost!' The first one said, her expression one of concern. 'Are you alright?'

'I'm not sure,' Jane looked back to the graves; there was nobody there, and there was no longer movement of any kind. 'I was at the gravestones, and I saw a man.'

'I'm sure there's a lot of men around here,' the second elderly lady smiled. 'Place is filled with them.'

'I don't mean I saw a ghost, I mean I saw a living, breathing man,' Jane replied, her tone a little more forceful than it had been before. 'He was bald, white, and had a black hoodie on. He was by the trees over there.' She pointed at the area where she'd been standing.

'He was watching me.'

The joke seemingly over, the two elderly ladies peered off into the corner of the cemetery.

'Well, he seems to be gone now,' one of them said. 'But, better safe than sorry.' She looked back to the entrance to the cemetery, where one groundskeeper, a tall man in the green fleece jacket of the council, was pushing a wheelbarrow filled with tools along the path.

'Hey, Des,' she shouted out.

The man paused, looked to the three women and smiled.

'Ladies,' he grinned, nodding. 'I hope you're well.'

'Need a favour,' the second elderly lady motioned at Jane. 'Girl here's had a fright. Said there's some kind of stalker in the bushes over there.'

'Does she now?' Des left the wheelbarrow, but not before picking up a shovel. 'Show me where.'

Jane pointed back to the graves, and Des walked past them, examining the area carefully, before looking back to the three women.

'Nobody here,' he said, shrugging. 'If there was, he might have gotten out through the north entrance.'

'There you go,' one of the ladies smiled, 'All good.'

'What time is it?' Jane asked, her expression calming. 'I feel so stupid for wasting your time.'

'No need to worry,' Des replied as he walked back over to the ladies. 'I'd rather check and see nothing than not checking and... well, you know.' He looked at his watch. 'And it's just past two.'

'Thank you,' Jane shook hands with everyone and, with a last look back to the graves, she almost ran for the cemetery entrance.

'She probably saw a ghost,' one of the elderly women muttered. 'They're everywhere.'

'You and your bloody ghosts,' Des laughed as he returned to work, the scared blonde woman already fading from his mind.

'How many people knew about the code?' Declan asked as he climbed out of the Audi, looking around the estate. Theresa, emerging from the passenger side, thought for a moment.

'Me, Tommy, Luke, Jane and Daniel for a start, then maybe one or two others? I can't be sure, and it wasn't exactly that hard a code to break,' she chuckled.

'We didn't,' Declan replied. Theresa shrugged.

'You were doing what we hoped the adults would,' she said. 'Try to find the clues in the words and the letters, while missing the obvious clue in front of you.'

She leaned against the car now, taking in the surrounding estate. Billy had learned that the last known address for Jane Terry had been the Whitman Estate in Peckham, and even though she had died several years ago, an apartment there still had her there as *J TERRY*, a resident.

'What a miserable, God-awful place this is,' she muttered. 'And I work in Manchester.'

'There are parts of Manchester I really like,' Declan commented as they walked towards the main stairway. 'And *The Smiths* came from there.'

'You're a Smiths fan?' Theresa looked impressed.

'More a Johnny Marr fan,' Declan walked up the stairs to the second floor. 'Guy can seriously play.'

'There's hope for you yet,' Theresa smiled as they stopped at a door. 'So, what do you think we have here? Squatters?'

'That have paid council tax for eight years?' Declan shrugged. 'Probably just a case of notes not updating. Happens more often than you'd expect.' He rapped on the door, stepping back so as not to crowd the peephole.

After a moment, the door opened to show a short man in his early seventies. His hair was bottle black and slicked backwards across a thinning scalp, his skin mottled and parchment thin. He was stocky, like a rugby player rather than a man that liked a drink, and even though Declan had thirty years and a few inches of height on him, he didn't favour his chances.

The man was about to speak, but was interrupted by Theresa.

"Christ on a cross! *Jim?*"

The man now recognised as *Jim* looked at Theresa, staring at her for a moment, as if trying to reconnect the face to the voice; and then, with what felt like a sigh of relief, he smiled.

'Tessa Martinez!' he exclaimed. 'You got old.'

'You got older,' Theresa replied, looking at Declan. 'This is Jim Sutcliffe, the detective that we worked with. Jim, this is—'

'Yeah, I know Mister Walsh here,' Jim nodded to Declan. 'Anyone who read a newspaper a month back recognises that face. Detective Inspector.' He held out his hand, shaking Declan's. 'I'm guessing this is about Reginald?'

'Yes, but not in the way you might think,' Declan replied. 'We came here because of Jane Terry. This was her last known address, and her name is still on the records.'

'No, it's not,' Jim said, pulling the door back and waving them in. 'The records say J Terry, not Jane Terry. That's me. *James Terry.* Sutcliffe was the name I used as a private eye. You never wanted the bastards you were hunting learning your true identity, or they'd come after you.'

'So that means...' Declan started, but didn't need to finish the line, as Jim nodded.

'Yeah. Jane and Graham Terry were my kids,' he said. 'Come on, get inside. I've been expecting you.'

JIM SUTCLIFFE, OR JIM TERRY AS HE WAS OFFICIALLY KNOWN, was making coffee in the kitchen; small shiny coffee pods that went straight into the cup, the machine slurping and chugging away as he grabbed a half-eaten pack of chocolate *Hob Nobs* and threw them onto a plate, bringing them into the sitting room.

Theresa was flipping through a photo album, sitting on the sofa as Declan walked around the room, examining the photos on the sideboards, images of a younger Jim and his children; Jane was strawberry blonde and smiling, while Graham was ginger, his hair wild and untamed as he laughed on a beach. There didn't seem to be more than a year between them.

'Here you go,' Jim said, placing the biscuits on the table. 'Coffee will be here in a mo.' He noted the album in Theresa's hand. 'Ah, you found the scrapbook, then.'

Theresa showed the pages that she was currently looking at to Declan. They were newspaper clippings of the true life rescue of Count Emil of Bavaria, which had then been novelised as *The Adventure Of The Missing Prince*.

'Press had a field day with this one,' she said. 'Was utterly convinced that Emil had been inappropriate with me, and that he wanted me to be his bride.'

'Did he?' Declan sat down beside her, looking at the news clippings.

'God no, he was gay,' Theresa replied.

'Was?' Declan asked.

'Well, let's just say that he was more interested in Luke than me or Jane at the time, but then publicly claimed that he loved some duchess ten years later, so it was either a phase or he's doing that royal thing where you marry for heirs and damn your sexual orientation. You know, like Prince—'

Jim walked back into the room, a tray with coffee mugs in his hands, and Theresa, distracted by the entrance, faded off. Which was annoying, as Declan now wanted to know who she was talking about. Passing Declan and Theresa their mugs, Jim sat in an armchair facing them.

'So,' he said, looking at Declan. 'How much do you know?'

'About the books? Pretty much everything,' Declan replied. 'Although there are some holes in the narrative. One of which involves your children.'

'How so?' Jim sipped at his latte, but although his question was one of surprise, his expression gave the impression that this was something he'd been expecting.

'Whoever killed Reginald planned it,' Theresa answered. 'They used a tyre iron, knew the original story, and hated Reginald enough to kill him.'

'And you thought it was me?' Jim replied. Declan shook his head.

'We didn't know that you were here,' he said. 'We'd actually supposed that it could be Graham. Records for him were lost about seven, almost eight years ago, when he seems to have gone travelling. With the flat in the name of *J Terry*, we assumed he was staying here off the grid.'

'I'd be impressed,' Jim said. 'If he was, it would be only in spirit. He died about a year after Jane did.'

'He did?' Theresa looked thrown by this piece of news. 'Can I ask how?'

'Stabbing in Thailand, while addicted to heroin,' Jim replied sadly. 'I hadn't seen him for a couple of years by then. We never got on well after the whole *Magpie* thing. And there were other issues, father and son things. Anyway, in his twenties, he started hanging out with a dangerous crowd, started taking some serious drugs. I'd found him, dragged him out of some heroin den and placed him somewhere to get clean. I thought he had, but after Jane died he changed, and a few months later he disappeared. I learned later from Danny that he'd begun backpacking around the world, and had started on drugs again while in Thailand, a couple of weeks after the anniversary of her death. He'd been dead in some slum for a couple of weeks before they found him, multiple stab wounds in his chest. They found the killer a week later, some woman who lived in the same area. She was dead too, an overdose.'

There were no tears in Jim's eyes as he spoke; Declan felt it seemed more like shame than sadness. But there was something else that had been said there, something that struck home in the back of Declan's mind.

'Danny knew about this?' he asked. 'As in Daniel McCarthy?'

Even though Declan had asked, Jim looked to Theresa as he spoke.

'I thought you knew,' he said. 'Daniel and Graham were quite close after Jane's death. They helped each other through the dark times.'

Declan pulled out his phone, typing a message on it as he looked back to Jim. 'Daniel was quite distraught after her death?'

'Well, why wouldn't he be?' the question stunned Jim.

'Christ, what sort of monster would he be, if he wasn't broken up over the death of his fiancée?'

There was a moment of silence in the room. Jim, realising, broke it.

'You didn't know that they were engaged,' he said.

Theresa shook her head.

'We don't really talk anymore,' she replied.

'Yeah, I suppose you never really did,' Jim nodded. 'They got back together about a decade ago. Jane was at her lowest, and then at the twentieth anniversary party she met Daniel by chance again and started seeing him. Neither were in the headlines, because nobody cared about the *Magpies* anymore.'

Declan was writing in the notepad as he spoke.

'Sorry for your loss,' he said. 'Can I ask you one more thing? Where were you last night?'

'Pub Quiz at *The Willow*,' Jim picked up a piece of paper and wrote on it. 'I'm the quizmaster. Started at seven, finished just before closing. This is their number, you can check it there.'

Theresa took it with a smile. 'It's good to see you,' she whispered. 'I'm just sad it's under such circumstances.'

'All circumstances connected to the *Magpies* are sad,' Jim returned the faint smile. 'We just didn't recognise that at the time.'

STANDING IN THE ESTATE ONCE MORE, BREATHING IN THE AIR, Theresa turned to Declan.

'I can't imagine how that must have felt,' she said. 'To lose both children in just over a year.'

Declan's phone beeped, and he opened the message, reading it.

'We need to speak to Daniel again,' he said. 'This time about Jane Terry's death.'

'Surely you don't think that he had anything to do with that?' Theresa was horrified. Declan shrugged.

'All I know is that eight years ago, Jane Terry died. And a year after that her grieving fiancé checks himself into a mental institution.'

'Maybe he couldn't take the strain of it?'

'I thought that,' Declan put the phone away. 'So I texted Monroe, asking what Daniel had said when they talked. When asked why he was still at the *Baker Institute*, Daniel said that he wanted to leave, but he didn't *deserve* to. and when Monroe asked why he was punishing himself so, Daniel replied that he couldn't say. Also, there's no way that Daniel McCarthy can afford the rates of the institute, so how's he paying for his stay?'

He opened his car door, looking back up at the apartment.

'Eight years ago something bad happened, so bad that Daniel McCarthy believed eventually that he needed to punish himself, by locking himself away in an asylum. I think there's more to the death than we know right now, but what I can't work out is how it ties into Reginald Troughton's murder.'

10

FOR WEDDED BLISS

MONROE NEVER ENJOYED VISITING PRISONS. THERE WERE TOO many eyes watching him at any time, and he liked to keep his business to himself.

Especially when he was speaking to Derek Sutton.

He hadn't mentioned it to the others, but he'd had his crossings over the years with Sutton. Not as a police officer, but back when he was a teenager, living on the Glasgow streets. His parents had both worked long hours and as such, Monroe was a 'latch key kid', living day by day and with barely any parental control. In the grand scheme of things, it was amazing he'd done so well for himself.

It was also while he was a teenager that he'd started hanging out with the Hutchinsons. They were an affluent Glasgow family, with a large house, a tennis court and an indoor pool. Monroe's family lived in a small, two up-two down terraced house on Stoneyhurst Street in Possil, one of the scrappier areas of the city, and that was being *polite* to the area.

Monroe had a brother, Kenneth, or 'Kenny'; three years

older and more crooked than a three-pound note, Kenny was supposed to look after little 'Ali' Monroe, but most of the time he took his younger brother with him while he was working, often odd jobs, for the Hutchinsons. It was here that Monroe, barely thirteen and already aware that he had no future ahead of him, had been given a taste of a *far better* life.

He'd seen the world that Kenny worked in, but he hadn't really gotten involved; for all that Kenny was tangled in, there was still an element of brotherly protection for the runt of the litter that followed him around, and so little Ali Monroe was left to his own devices.

Unknown to Kenny though, many of those 'devices' were other minor jobs for the Hutchinsons; 'gopher' jobs, as in *go for this, go for that* jobs. And within a year Monroe was up to his neck in criminal activity. If they had caught him doing any of these things, he would never have been accepted into the police years later. But as the adage went, *you were only a criminal if you'd been convicted.*

He'd finally broken free when, at sixteen he came home from whatever dodgy activities he'd been up to that day, most likely being a lookout while someone else sold counterfeit wares on the street in Glasgow, to find that Kenny was *dead*, killed in a drive-by shooting at a Hutchinsons' bar in Blackhill. Whether or not Kenny had been the target was never known; all the police knew was that four people had been injured in the attack, but only Kenny had died.

It was then that Monroe met Derek Sutton.

Sutton was in his mid-twenties when the teenage Monroe was introduced to him. Built like a wrestler, with shaved black hair, Sutton was one of the go-to guys for the Hutchinsons whenever they needed some 'aggro' started. And, when he wasn't fighting for the Hutchinsons, he was fighting on the football pitch as one of the *Roman Catholic Casuals,* the hooligan supporters of *Celtic Football Club.* Sutton had known Kenny well, and considered himself a bit of a mentor over the years; so when Kenny was murdered in an attack that could honestly have been targeted at Sutton, he went looking for *revenge.*

And young Alexander 'Ali' Monroe went with him.

They never found the killers; if they had, then Monroe's life would have taken a far darker turn. Even now, standing outside the gates of Belmarsh Prison, Monroe couldn't honestly say whether or not he would have killed them. The rage was definitely there.

But the passion wasn't, and as Monroe and Sutton worked their way through the Glasgow underworld, Monroe found himself *sickened* by the glee and delight that Sutton had taken in the beatings and degradations he gave out.

Monroe was picked up one night by a police car; they'd been watching him for months, and decided that now was the time to speak to him before he went too far. The police had known Kenny, who turned out to be a confidential informant for them, and explained that during one of his last meetings with them, he'd expressed remorse at sending his wee brother down the same path as he'd travelled. They explained that Monroe was now at a crossroads; one way led to the world, the other *prison.*

The following day Monroe joined the police. Not because of some duty to the law, but because he'd realised that this was the only way he'd gain justice for Kenny, and properly find the killers.

Two years later Sutton shot the Wright Brothers in a Glasgow bar and left for London before the police could catch him. He needn't have worried though, as nobody ever informed on him to the police.

You didn't grass on Derek Sutton.

Years later, Monroe learned that the gang that killed Kenny were part of a rival, Southern firm that ran work-shopped arms from outside Leyton, in North East London. He'd called for a transfer down south, finding an opportunity to move to *detective* in the process. He'd worked well in Glasgow, and he'd been welcomed as a Detective Constable in North London, but he hadn't even unpacked before he'd met with Sutton, now working for the Lucas Twins, then in their early thirties and the scourge of East London. He'd told Sutton he'd learned the identities of the killers, but he was going to do it by the law.

That night, the nightclub the London firm worked from was burned to the ground, killing three. Of the dead, two had been involved in Kenny's murder.

Monroe never saw Sutton again.

He didn't know that at this point Sutton had been arrested for murder, and a gang of child detectives had solved the case. He only discovered this years later when, as a DS in Patrick Walsh's team, he'd learned from the eleven-year-old Declan about the *Magpie* case.

He was happy that Derek Sutton was behind bars. He felt it was a better place for him to be. And now, over thirty years since he'd last seen him, he was meeting Derek Sutton again.

Usually visitors would face the prisoner along a bank of cubicles, a Perspex barrier between them. The telephones of film and TV were barely used these days; small speakers would relay the conversation now, with tiny microphones on each side.

Today, however, Monroe had arrived outside of visiting

hours, and only one cubicle was occupied; Derek Sutton, now in his late sixties, his head bald and his body now more fat than muscle, still looked vicious as he watched Monroe approach.

'They said you're a DCI,' he spoke, his voice drawling, still with a Scottish twang. 'That you're here about the *Magpies*. Never gave me your name.'

'I told them not to,' Monroe replied as he sat facing Sutton. Although the man was recognisable, Monroe wondered, with his white hair and trimmed beard, whether he was as easy to remember.

Sutton frowned. 'That's a Glasgow twang to your accent there, pal,' he muttered, peering closer. And then, as if the years were suddenly pulled away, he leaned back, his eyes wide, and a smile on his face.

'Jesus and Mary, am I seeing *wee Ali Monroe* in front of me?' he asked.

'DCI Alexander Monroe, and I'm not so wee anymore.'

'Aye, I can see that,' Sutton grinned. 'I'd have thought they'd have kicked you out by now. Found out your dirty little secrets.'

'Having secrets isn't against the law,' Monroe said quietly.

'Aye, because if they were, you'd be in here with me,' Sutton replied. 'Did you know Danny Martin's in here? Yeah, he's nae fan o'yours.'

'I'm not here to talk about Danny—'

'Aye, I know. You're here about the murders of Narinder Singh and Jeetinder Gill, and the bloody *Magpies*.'

'Actually, no.' Monroe leaned in. 'I'm here because of the murder of Reginald Troughton.'

'Shame that,' Sutton smiled. 'Still, good things come to

those that wait. I hear he got a smacking too before he died. Good.'

'Did you hear how he died?'

'Aye. Tyre iron,' Sutton chuckled. 'Laughed my arse off when my brief told me. Just like the first time. Now, considering I'm locked up, I find that incredibly interesting.' He placed a hand on his chin, as if thinking hard.

'How could someone put my print on a murder weapon without my knowing? Probably the same way they did it last time.'

He lowered the hand.

'I never killed them. Said it at the time, and I'm still saying it now. I was framed.'

'You were seen at a *National Front* rally a week before their murders, amid a scuffle that they were also in,' Monroe replied calmly. 'A week later they're found dead with your prints on the weapon. Are you saying it's a complete coincidence that this happened to the two men who got a fair pop at you?'

There was a moment of silence as Sutton stared at Monroe.

'Ali, you knew me in Glasgow,' he said eventually. 'You saw my cuts and bruises from when I was at Celtic Park. Do you really think a slap from two *nancy boy pakis* would rile me up so much?'

Monroe stiffened at the racial slur. 'That you still call them that? Yeah, I reckon you would,' he said. 'You're a long way from Glasgow, here. Who knows what other habits you picked up.'

'So I'm not, what do you call it, *pee-cee*,' Sutton snapped. 'Don't change the fact they set me up.'

'And why would Reginald Troughton or the *Magpies* set

you up?' Monroe leaned back, folding his arms. 'What did you mean to them?'

'Troughton's boyfriend, the lawyer,' Sutton replied. 'He hated me. Said I was homophobic.'

'I can't guess how he got that idea.'

'Aye, anyway, I was doing gigs for Danny Martin, but I still wasn't in with the Twins, yeah? And I'd been picked up twice already. Danny had used Chadwick to get me out, and I know this caused friction in the firm. I told Danny I didn't want no *poofter* repping me, and if he tried anything I'd break his bloody fingers before moving to his throat. Chadwick probably heard, took it as a threat, told his boyfriend, and the wee bastards both planned for me to take the rap.'

'With a weapon that just so happened to have your prints on.'

'Look, Ali,' Sutton spoke, his voice softer now. 'I swear on your brother's grave; I might be a nasty bugger out there, but I never killed those men. Sure, I deserve to be in here, and the people I did kill are probably laughing. But someone else killed Singh and Gill, and every day I'm in here is a day they're still out there.'

He smiled, but it was an empty one.

'They said that my claims of scapegoating were laughable in the trial,' he said. 'That there was no way someone could fake my prints onto the tyre iron. So I wonder what they'll say when my brief points out that there's not a chance in hell I could have held this *new* tyre iron, either. I have a new one, you know. He's very good.'

He rose now, the meeting obviously at an end.

'Chadwick, Troughton, Clarke, all of them, they deserved what's coming for them,' he snarled. 'That smug prick of a kid, Tommy, too. Aye, I've seen his shite introductions, taking credit and all that. Ask yourself this, *Detective Chief Inspector*. If they framed me for book one, what about the people they caught in all the *other* stories?'

He smiled for a moment.

'Take care of yourself, Ali. It's still not too late to give up this folly and come back to the family. I'll see you soon.'

'I don't think so, Derek,' Monroe replied. In return, Sutton nodded.

'I've got high up Westminster types braying for my immediate release,' he said. 'Miscarriage of justice, mistrial, the terms are all favourable. There's talk that I won't even have to appeal. I'll simply be released quietly tomorrow. So aye, Ali. I'll see you *real* soon.'

And, with that last parting shot in the air, Derek Sutton nodded to Monroe and left the cubicle, walking back to the guard and exiting through the rear door.

Monroe didn't move for a moment; his mind was a whirl with thoughts. Sutton had named Michael Chadwick, Reginald Troughton and Julia Clarke at the end, saying that they all deserved what was coming to them.

Deserved. Past tense.

Pulling out his phone, he texted Anjli.

Get to Julia Clarke's now. No answer? Kick the door in.

Sending the message, Monroe looked at the guard on his side of the room.

'Does he get many visitors?' he asked. The guard shrugged.

'I wouldn't know,' he said. 'We alternate shifts.'

'Who would know?' Monroe rose from the chair. The guard thought about this.

'There's a visitors' log,' he said. 'That might help.' He leaned through the door. 'Jeff? Bring us the visitor log, yeah?'

There was a moment of expectant waiting until the door opened and another guard, an older, shorter one with shaved grey hair brought in what looked like sheets of A4 paper stapled together.

'Visitor logs for the last month,' he said, passing it to Monroe. 'Anything in particular you're looking for?'

'Just wondered if Sutton had any other visitors recently,' Monroe was already flipping the pages, working backwards through the log, pausing at a line. He showed it to the guard.

'This,' he said. 'Louise Hart. Last Wednesday, eleven in the morning. Would you still have the CCTV footage of her arrival?'

'I'd say so,' the guard scratched at his chin. 'Wanna have a look at it?'

'Very much so,' Monroe replied. There were too many complications involved here for such a simple murder, and Louise Hart, whoever she was, might untangle it all.

One thing was for certain, though. As a teenager, Monroe had known Derek Sutton. Even after these years, he could still read the man.

And Derek Sutton was telling the *truth*.

11

FOR THE MORROW

ANJLI HAD JUST LEFT THE POLICE CAR, PARKED UP IN A SUBURB just outside of Putney when the text from Monroe had arrived. Showing it to De'Geer, she looked up the path at the Victorian semi-detached house that faced them.

'Shit,' was all she said as she ran towards the door.

The house was quiet; the windows were closed, but the curtains were open, there were no lights on and Anjli could see no movement in the house as she hammered on the door.

'Mrs Clarke! Police! Open up!'

Nothing.

Anjli looked to De'Geer who gently moved her aside as he knelt to look through the letterbox.

'See anything?' she asked. Rising, De'Geer nodded.

'I can see the stairs,' he said, taking off his cap and passing it to her. 'There's water damage. Looks like it's streaming from upstairs. Probably a bath overflowing.' He took a step back and, with his arms folded, he slammed his shoulder into the door, shaking it. His size, his muscle build and his force meant that on the second attempt the wood around the lock splintered and the front door flew open. De'Geer went to run in, but Anjli grabbed him.

'Feet and hands,' she said, already pulling on disposable plastic booties with her latex gloves. As De'Geer pulled his own pair out, Anjli was on her way upstairs two steps at a time, feeling the squelch of the waterlogged carpet through the plastic as she did so.

The bathroom was at the end of the hall, and even from the first glance it was obvious which door it was, the trickle of water still emerging from it a giveaway. Entering the bathroom, she stopped for a moment as she took in the scene.

The floor was soaked and at least an inch deep with bath water. A toilet brush half floated in it, butting lazily against the sink. The floor also had several white rose petals floating on it, likely flowing out of the bath, now up to the lip with still-filling water, with several more petals spinning slowly in circles within it.

The taps were still flowing; Anjli turned them both off and stared into the bath. Under the water, still clothed, her eyes wide and dead, was a woman, late sixties in age. Anjli assumed that this was likely Julia Clarke.

De'Geer appeared in the doorway. 'Do we need an ambulance?'

'We need the coroner,' Anjli replied, looking around. 'This water's been flowing for ages. She's well past saving.'

De'Geer nodded and left the room. Anjli stared down at the body, wondering what the last image those eyes had seen was. Had she slipped and fell into the bath? Had she been held under? Doctor Marcos would know.

Walking down the stairs, Anjli entered the living room she'd seen from outside; the ceiling was bowing slightly, and there was a drip of water sliding down the light pendant.

Anjli knew the bathroom was pretty much above this room, and the last thing she wanted to do was see the bath crash through into it. Running a close second was seeing a police officer try to turn the light on. Looking around, she saw a small book nook beside the television, with a tiny desk and monitor on top of it. Walking over, she saw a Mac Mini computer connected to the monitor; quickly, she undid the cables and picked it up, walking it to the doorway and placing it on a still dry sofa. She knew that if she'd let this get wet, Billy would never let her live it down.

There was an answerphone on the desk, but the light wasn't flashing. Anjli dialled the last number recall service, noting down the time it was called, and the number that had done so. It might not lead to anything, but Anjli had learned never to leave a stone unturned.

On the shelf was a line of books, all by *BadgerLock Publishing.* In the middle were the *Magpies* novels in order. The first, *The Adventure of the Rusty Crowbar* was half out, as if recently removed and examined. The one next to it, *The Adventure of the Stolen Flowers,* was slightly visible because of this, as if the act of pulling the first book out had slightly dislodged the other. Something on the sliver of cover that was visible stopped Anjli, and so she pulled it out.

On the cover of the book was a bath, filled with water, and with white petals floating on it.

'Oh, damn,' she muttered as De'Geer entered the living room.

'Marcos and Davey are on their way,' he said, spying the book in Anjli's hand. 'Is that...'

'Yeah,' Anjli looked to De'Geer. 'I think it is. Someone's copied the murder from book two.'

DECLAN AND THERESA WERE THE SECOND PEOPLE CALLED AFTER Marcos and Davey, and it was around half an hour later when his Audi pulled up to the front of the house, parking next to a forensics van. Already the police forensics tent was up in the front garden; Doctor Marcos only had DC Davey on her team, but she had good relations with many of the Met units in Greater London, and there was a good chance she'd called in a couple of favours to gain some bodies on this. De'Geer, as first officer on the scene, was acting as Duty Officer, even though this would usually be a sergeant's role, and several officers were extending the crime scene perimeter. A police photographer was already leaving; Declan knew that the first person into a crime scene after the Divisional Surgeon, who mainly entered to confirm lack of life in the victim, was the police photographer, and would take as many shots of the scene *in situ* before people started moving things. Declan had heard of some kind of fancy 'in the round' device being used by photographers these days, something that could take a full three-sixty degree image, but most of the photographers he saw were old hands who preferred to use a solid digital SLS, and probably did a better job with it.

Doctor Marcos, in her custom made PPE suit, was waiting for him at the door to the house.

'Do you want to come in?' she asked. 'We've only just started, but there doesn't seem to be much here.'

'How do you mean?' Declan replied. Doctor Marcos shrugged.

'Neighbours claim they saw a bald man entering her property through the side gate. No alarm was raised as she'd been having garden work done, and people assumed he was a labourer. After about half an hour he left, and simply walked off.'

'So what else do we have?' Declan was writing in his notebook. Doctor Marcos looked up at the stairs as an officer walked past, before replying.

'Julia Clarke, sixty-nine years old, retired publishing director,' she said. 'Cause of death is drowning, but there are defensive marks on her fingers, so I think she was held under.'

'The bald man?'

'Makes sense,' Doctor Marcos scratched at her nose through the mask. 'He was seen around two this afternoon. And that's roughly the time of death, although I need to get her on a slab to have a proper going over.' She looked at Theresa. 'One interesting thing though,' she added. 'There were white rose petals in the bath.'

Theresa visibly flinched, and Declan knew why. The second novel had used this as a plot point, but the petals had been incredibly particular. 'Did you bag them?' he asked. Doctor Marcos nodded, waving to DC Davey, now walking down the stairs.

'Joanne bagged them,' she said. 'Any reason?'

'In the original case, we worked out that the murderer had used a particular rose petal,' Theresa replied. 'A faded white shrub rose, cultivated by David Austin and on show in Kew Gardens. The murderer, Gayle Holland visited there a day beforehand, and had been caught on a tourist's camera taking discarded petals.'

'If we've got a copycat killer, it makes sense they'd go the distance,' Davey mused. 'Fingerprint on a tyre iron, exact match on the rose—although thirty years is a long time for horticulture.' She nodded to herself. 'I'll contact an expert and get their opinion.'

Anjli, having been coordinating the officers on the street, now walked up the steps of the garden towards them.

'Hey, I've got something interesting,' she said, opening her notepad. 'Thomas Williams called Julia around the same time as she was murdered and left a message. There isn't one on the answerphone, so it's possible the murderer deleted the message.'

'Probably asking the publishers to pay for another night in the hotel,' Declan looked out to the street. 'Have we checked whether he left a message?'

Anjli nodded. 'Claims he was just checking in,' she replied. 'That said, it was incredibly convenient timing.'

'Two books, two deaths,' Theresa muttered. 'Who's next?'

Declan was going to reply when he saw a man standing at the police cordon; in a suit and tie, he was looking completely out of place as he waited to catch Declan's eye. Declan recognised him instantly; it was Mark Walters. Seeing Declan glance at him, he pushed his black-rimmed glasses back up his nose and waved at him to come over.

'Excuse me a moment,' Declan left the doorstep and walked over to the cordon, indicating to an officer to let Mark through. 'Just passing by, Mister Walters?'

'Of course not,' Mark replied, looking nervously around. 'I heard there was an incident at Julia's house, and knew you'd be here. Can we speak?'

Declan walked Mark Walters over to the side of the cordon, away from the onlookers. 'If this isn't a social call, what is it?' he asked. 'If you're telling me Norman Shipman wants you in the loop, we can always send you emails. You don't have to turn up to crime scenes.'

'I came because I needed a favour,' Mark said. 'I was hoping your Divisional Surgeon could look at a body for us.'

Declan stopped, staring at the bespectacled man. 'Any particular one?'

'Rory Simpson,' Mark replied carefully.

'The man who died on the bridge,' Declan commented. 'Why would you want him examined? I'll be honest, if it's for insurance reasons—'

'We think he was murdered,' Mark cut in. 'I wanted to find out a little more about the incident, so I went and talked to the coffee shack that he bought his drinks from. I wanted to know why they gave him the wrong drink, but they explained they hadn't, that they'd made him the same drink he had every day. However, on this day, the order had been picked up by another person, a woman, as part of a two drink order of a flat white and a hazelnut latte.'

'You think he took her drink by mistake?' Declan thought about this. 'Could still be an accident.'

'That's what I thought,' Mark nodded. 'So I asked around, tried to speak to some witnesses. They said that he dropped his cup into the lake before he fell. They also said this woman was talking to Rory when he had his attack, and that he scrabbled for his bag, crying out that he needed his epi pen. She looked, but couldn't find it, and so tried to give him CPR until the ambulance arrived.'

A dark shadow fell across Mark's face.

'I went back to the office; they'd sent his things there as Rory didn't really have a family to send them to. I looked in his messenger bag. Detective Inspector Walsh, the epi pen was right there. I'm sorry, but there was no way this woman didn't see it.'

'I think we need to speak to this woman,' Declan replied

cautiously. 'Although—'

'That's not all,' Mark interrupted. 'When the ambulance came, witnesses said that she got up and left before anyone could talk to her about this. But before she did so, one woman I spoke to said she was absolutely sure the woman took the drink that she was holding before the incident, and placed it in Rory's hand.'

'To make it look like he'd drunk the latte,' Declan was seeing a pattern. 'But if he hadn't, and he was simply drinking a flat white, then what gave him the anaphylactic shock?'

'Exactly,' Mark nodded. 'I could really do with your best forensics person performing a postmortem on Rory's body. I've already spoken to Norman, and he understands, and stands beside the idea. We need to know what Rory had in his stomach when he died, because if it *isn't* an accidentally drunk hazelnut latte—'

'It's murder,' Declan looked back to the house, where Doctor Marcos was talking to Theresa. 'Let me see what I can do.'

Mark shook Declan's hand and turned to leave, but Declan placed a hand on his arm to stop him.

'One thing though,' he added. 'What would anyone gain by killing Rory?'

Mark paused, thinking this over.

'Nothing at all,' he replied eventually. 'It's why nobody's even considered looking into it deeper than an unfortunate accident.'

'Was Rory involved with The *Magpies* at all?'

'He was there in the final year or two, but in a junior grade, never making decisions back then,' Mark replied honestly. 'Maybe the reprints, or the introductions to the recent editions that Thomas Williams wrote. I heard Reginald was writing a new book, so maybe that too?'

Mark looked to the doorstep, watching Theresa carefully.

'Or, it was to stop Theresa Martinez from gaining access to the investigation. Maybe they didn't know she'd already managed it?'

Thanking Mark once more, Declan moved away from the cordon, walking back to the house. Monroe had sent a text as they were arriving stating that Louise Hart, a female, brunette journalist, had been to see Derek Sutton a week earlier, but surely they couldn't be the same person. And why kill Rory Simpson the day after Reginald Troughton?

Declan believed there were more threads to this case, more plot lines that led away from a simple revenge killing. Shipman was involved too, Declan was sure of it. Mark Walters appeared earnest, but there was something *off* about him.

Theresa Martinez, talking to Doctor Marcos, looked over to Declan, concern on her face. And for a moment, Declan wondered whether that was genuine concern to his wellbeing, or concern that she was about to be *found out.*

One thing was certain. There were a lot of bodies piling up, and with Jane and Luke in the wind, Daniel locked up and Thomas hiding in a hotel room, there was currently only one *Magpie* around to investigate them right now.

But whether that *Magpie* was also *creating* them was something he'd need to monitor. He may have had a crush on Tessa Martinez when he was a teenager, but now things were incredibly, scarily different.

He was so focused on Theresa, that he didn't notice the hooded man who, amongst the crowd of observers, was also watching her, before turning and walking away from the police cordon and down the street.

Now out of the sight of the police, Luke Ashton pulled the hood off his head, picking up his speed as he headed towards the train station.

Reggie, Rory and Julia were now dead.

Things were coming to an end.

12

FOR THE MIRTH

DECLAN HAD RETURNED TO TEMPLE INN AFTER THE FORENSICS had closed up Julia Clarke's house. He knew they would be there for hours, and the night was drawing in. De'Geer was assisting Davey in his own time, still fascinated with the workings of the forensics department, and so Declan had taken his leave, Theresa driving back to Temple Inn with him.

Bullman was in her office when they arrived, and Monroe was with Billy, working through CCTV images of Belmarsh Prison. Declan brought them both up to speed with what he'd learned, and then returned to his desk, staring at the monitor. It was almost eight; he could be home in less than an hour.

Although it still didn't feel like home.

Sighing, Declan stretched in the chair, glancing at the Funko Bobby on his desk. He knew it was a dumb idea, but he really wanted to speak to Jess right now, to make sure that she was all right. However, he also knew that there was a very strong chance that Liz wouldn't even take the call, and at best would only pass on a message. She'd changed Jess' phone number so Declan couldn't even call or text, and he'd agreed to keep his distance. There was nothing he could do.

'You look like the weight of the world's on your shoulders,' Theresa Martinez stated as she sat down in a chair to the left. 'You okay?'

'Family issues,' he replied. 'Ex-wife annoyed I almost killed our kid. So now her number's been changed, and I'm barred from calling her on the land line.'

'Yeah, I heard about the drama in Hurley,' Theresa nodded, and Declan wasn't surprised. That Jessica Walsh had been captured and almost killed by Ilse Müller in Hurley a few weeks earlier was common knowledge, as well as the fact that Jess had not only escaped her bonds, but almost restrained the insane German woman before Anjli and Billy arrived to save her.

Declan was proud of Jess. He knew she'd make an incredible police officer. But she was fifteen, coming on sixteen and was in her last year of GCSEs; he had no right to even involve her in the case, regardless of what she wanted. He had made a serious error, and now he deserved the punishment that he was getting.

'She won't take your calls?' Theresa asked. Declan shrugged.

'I don't know,' he replied. 'Liz, that's her mum, she gate-keepers the calls now.'

'From everyone?' Theresa smiled. 'I mean, if I called, perhaps?'

Declan looked from the monitor. 'Why you?'

'You mentioned in the car that she read the *Magpie* stories too,' Theresa suggested. 'Maybe I can help.'

Declan thought about this. 'What's in it for you?'

'Does there have to be anything?' Theresa laughed. 'Jesus, Walsh. What women do you hang out with?'

She stopped, her eyes widening as she realised what she'd said.

'Oh, sorry.'

Declan actually laughed at that. The last woman he'd 'hung out with' had been publicly labelled a terrorist; this was why Theresa froze.

'No, you're right,' he replied. 'I have a lousy taste in women.'

'Tell you what,' Theresa suggested. 'It's gone eight, so if I do this, you buy me dinner somewhere. Nothing too fancy. Even a pizza is good.'

Declan must have flinched slightly at this, as Theresa immediately continued. 'Look, it's obvious that you don't want to go back to Hurley, and Monroe mentioned that you've been working late to stay here recently. After what happened there, I totally get it. I wouldn't either. But at the same time, I'm a Mancunian in London, I don't know anyone and if you say no, I'm just going back to my hotel room to watch *Repair Shop*. So you'd be doing me a favour. And, we can talk about the case.'

Declan nodded at this. There was a part of him that wanted to keep talking to Theresa, to ask about her days as a *Magpie*, but it scared him that the further he fell down the rabbit hole, the more lies he'd learn. Pulling out his phone, he scrolled to LIZ on the *contacts* list.

'Here,' he said, passing it over. Taking it, Theresa pressed *dial* and held it to her ear.

'Hi, is that Liz Walsh?' she asked, eventually. 'It's Detective Inspector Theresa Martinez here.' She paused as Liz spoke, inaudible to Declan. 'No, it's fine, he's fine, actually I'd asked him if I could speak to your daughter, Jess? I understand she liked the *Magpies* books when she was a kid and, well, I was one of them, so I thought it would be nice to say hello.'

There was another pause, a long one. Declan didn't know whether this was because Liz had gone to get Jess, or because Liz was giving Theresa an earful. After a moment, and judging from the expression on Theresa's face, Declan knew it was the latter.

'Look, Liz, can I be blunt?' Theresa's face had hardened slightly and Declan knew that the conversation wasn't going well. 'You can't know how your daughter is feeling, because you've never been in that situation. I have. I spent my teenage years being captured by criminals I was hunting. I risked my life more than once, and I did it because I believed it was the right thing to do. I was younger than your daughter when I had my first gun rammed in my face, and all it did was make me more determined to become a copper. And, from what I hear of Jess, she'll be an incredible copper, a definite credit to the force and the family.'

There was another pause, but strangely this time Theresa smiled.

'I agree,' she said. 'My parents hated that I was a *Magpie*. But eventually they understood that if they told me no, I'd do it anyway. And it was better to have responsible people who knew what they were doing helping me, rather than have me going off on my own and *Scooby Doo*ing it. And soon, I guarantee, you'll have to consider this with Jess.'

Theresa listened down the line, said 'Absolutely. Just let Declan know,' and then disconnected the call, passing the phone back to him.

'I think that went quite well,' she said. 'You can't really take the high ground about teenagers in danger when the person you're talking to pretty much made a career of it. She's still angry, but I think she might cool down a little.'

'And Jess?' Declan leaned closer.

'Liz is going to speak to her, arrange a meeting with me. I'll answer some questions, tell a story or two. And, of course, say how great her dad is, and how he bought me a lovely dinner to make me feel welcome.'

Declan laughed. 'You've definitely earned that,' he said, rising from the chair. 'Come on, let's get out of here—'

'Guv, you need to see this,' Billy interrupted, looking back at Declan. As they looked to him, Theresa and Declan saw Monroe turn from the monitor, also nodding.

'This is a twist we weren't expecting,' he said.

Declan and Theresa walked over to Billy's bank of monitors. On each one was a different CCTV image, frozen in place. On the left was a prison waiting room; in the middle was a CCTV taken in St James's Park, and on the right was an image from a camera in a library, or bookstore. Billy pointed at the three images, showing a dark-haired woman in each one.

'Belmarsh Prison, St James's Park, and Waterstones, the night that Thomas Williams did his signing,' Billy said. 'This woman was at all three. Now the CCTV isn't great, but the details we have indicate that this is the same woman, especially as in the first two, she has the same hairstyle and jacket.'

'So this is the woman that may have poisoned Shipman's assistant,' Declan mused.

'Belmarsh had her details,' Monroe continued. 'Louise Hart, freelance journalist. The manager of Waterstones said that she was also an attendee of the signing, and was seen confronting Thomas before the end. But in that photo she's pulled her hair back, looks a little harsher, older, even.'

Billy tapped on the screen, and the driving licence of Louise Hart appeared on the screen. It was a few years old, but the hair and the facial structure were similar.

'So a journalist visits Derek Sutton, confronts Thomas Williams, and is possibly linked to Rory Simpson's death,' Declan looked to Theresa, to see her staring in horror at the screen.

'Put up the photo,' she said. 'The one of the *Blue Peter* girl.'

'What is it?' Monroe asked as Billy brought up the older photo. 'She looks like the picture, but the BBC said that her name was Eloise Lewis, not Hart—'

'She took her mother's maiden name when she was in University,' Theresa whispered. 'She was Lewis and then became Hart. And I'd heard she felt *Eloise* was a little too posh, so shortened it. Eloise Lewis became Louise Hart.'

'How do you know this?' Declan asked. Theresa turned to him.

'I followed her for a bit back then,' she admitted. 'After she broke up with Tommy.'

'Louise Hart dated Tommy Williams?' Monroe exclaimed. 'How did we not find this in the records?'

'Because Eloise Lewis did,' Theresa replied. 'It was a couple of years after the photo. She was fifteen, he was seventeen.'

'I thought Tommy fancied Jane?' Billy looked up. 'Or was that another lie?'

'Put an image of Jane up from the books,' Theresa requested. 'One of the later ones. Next to the *Blue Peter* picture.'

An image of Jane, taken from the cover of the fifth book, appeared. She was wearing baggy stone-washed jeans and an oversized plaid shirt.

'Compare the two,' Theresa said. 'They weren't related, but they could have been sisters. Tommy couldn't have Jane, mainly due to all the legal contracts we'd signed when starting; there was a *'don't date your co-stars'* sort of clause in it, but Eloise was fair game. A brunette Jane 2.0.'

She looked around the group.

'I don't know how they met back up, but one minute Tommy was a team player, and then the next he'd gone all *John and Yoko*, saying that if Eloise wasn't added to the *Magpies,* then he'd leave,' she continued.

'I'm guessing she wasn't?' Billy asked. Theresa shook her head.

'Bruno explained bluntly that they would rather lose Tommy than gain another,' she said. 'The books were declining. And there had been accusations.'

'Accusations?'

'Girls, claiming that Tommy had been sexually abusing them,' Theresa's voice was barely more than a whisper. 'Not penetration to my knowledge, and there were no rape allegations or anything, but stories were being told of Tommy pressuring female fans to show him... well, to strip. This was before the internet, so I don't think there were dick pics or anything, but he was a little forceful, according to the girls.'

'Christ,' Monroe looked to Declan. 'Wee Tommy's a piece of work.'

'Wee Tommy sounds like a piece of shit,' Declan snapped. 'Jess is the same age. I'd have killed him if he'd tried anything.'

'That was the problem,' Theresa continued. 'There wasn't

any proof, and Tommy apologised for any confusions or inopportune behaviour, but claimed he was being victimised. The powers that be ensured it was hushed up, and they chaperoned Tommy from then on. But it killed his relationship with Eloise. There was even talk that during this time he'd forced himself on her, but it was never proven.'

'And nobody did a damned thing,' Declan muttered. Theresa shook her head.

'No, we did,' she replied. 'Luke kicked the living shit out of him one day. It was from out of nowhere too; it was almost as if Luke had taken this attack on Eloise personally.'

'And then a year or so later the *Magpies* disbanded,' Declan finished. 'Tommy Williams got away with it.'

'So far,' Theresa pointed at the screen. 'Looks like Louise Hart is on a mission again.'

'And you didn't think this was important?' Monroe was glaring at Theresa now.

'It wasn't relevant to the case at hand, so no,' she replied. 'I wasn't dragging in a competition winner who had a shit time with Tommy two decades ago until I knew it was important. You want me to call up my ex-boyfriends too?'

'We need to know what she said to Thomas at the signing,' Monroe muttered, moving on from the conversation. 'We also need to bring this woman in. And, Billy, we need better images than these, because currently we can't confirm she was in St James's Park, and that's the key moment here so far.'

Billy went to reply to this, but there was a ping and an email appeared on his screen.

'Guys,' he said as he read it. 'Police have been examining Luke Ashton's house, and have found charred remains of a white shirt in a fire pit in the garden.'

'He was wearing a white shirt in the CCTV,' Declan replied. 'It looked like something was on it.'

'Yeah, blood,' Billy continued. 'It was on some of the unburned parts of the shirt. Forensics have confirmed that it's a match for Reginald Troughton.'

LUKE ASHTON ALMOST RAN ACROSS THE ROAD TOWARDS THE Kingston apartment block facing him, but he knew he had to take it slow, to ensure he wasn't noticed. It was gone nine in the evening now; he'd spent the afternoon in Richmond Park after leaving Julia's street, but he couldn't relax in the open. He knew that at any moment someone could recognise him.

And it wasn't time to be recognised yet.

Keeping his hood up, he looked to the floor as he passed late night pedestrians on the street, focusing on the door to the apartment block, now half open and inviting. Sliding through, he took a breath as he started up the half-lit stairs, feeling a little of the weight of the world lift from his shoulders; in here, he was no longer on view, or under scrutiny.

Walking up two flights, he stopped at a black painted door, a number 7 in brass upon it. Knocking, he looked around urgently, ensuring there were no cameras or witnesses to his arrival.

The door opened, and Daniel McCarthy stared out of the doorway at him.

'What the hell are *you* doing here?' Luke asked angrily, pushing past Daniel, entering the apartment, closing the door behind him before he pulled off the hood.

'Making sure you're sticking to the plan,' Daniel replied calmly. 'The hard part is over.'

'Oh, you're an expert on the hard part?' Luke exclaimed. 'Tell me, you killed anyone recently?'

'You know I have, so shut the hell up and sit down,' Daniel snapped. 'This shouldn't be a shock to you. You've had this sorted for months.'

'I didn't think Jane and Tommy would be *shagging!*' Luke shouted. '*How could they?*'

'How could *she*, you mean?'

'Dammit, Danny. All you have is a mental home room. I have a life!' Luke pleaded. 'Police are going through my house with a fine-toothed comb, Julia and Reggie are dead while Tommy still lives, and—'

He stopped.

'Where are we, anyway?' he asked. 'I got the text with the address, assumed it was *his* place, but it looks a little too feminine. Who's flat is this?'

'Louise Hart's,' Daniel replied, standing at the window of the apartment, glancing out at the estate below. 'Police are on their way.'

'What did you *do*?' Luke whispered, looking to the bedroom. 'Is she—'

'She's in there,' Daniel replied, still watching out of the window. 'She took an overdose before I arrived. Looks like she's been dead a few hours now, surrounded by photos of her and Tommy.'

'You bastard,' Luke snapped. 'She wasn't supposed to be *dead.*'

'I didn't expect her to *kill herself!*' Daniel snapped back. 'I expected her to be angry at being shunned, and ready for phase two. But the door was open when I arrived.'

'They'll blame me for her death!'

Daniel shook his head, still looking away. 'No, she's made

it clear that this was her doing. Trust me on that one. Anyway, I'm sticking to the plan.'

He turned from the window.

'If they haven't done the DNA tests soon, you'll need to subtly suggest it to Tessa. Make them think it's their idea. You'll be okay.'

Luke looked around the apartment helplessly. 'When I texted, I was asking for help.'

'We *are* helping,' Daniel replied, walking to the door. 'And I'm making the best of an unpleasant situation. Just remember to aim at the correct target when they interrogate you.'

Luke nodded, moving over to the window, looking out.

'This is almost over,' Daniel continued soothingly. 'Soon we'll finish this, and we'll all start our new lives. And nobody will pin any of this on you.'

'On *us*, you mean.'

With a curt nod, Daniel left the apartment, leaving Luke Ashton alone in the apartment with a dead woman in the next room as, in the stairwell, the sounds of approaching officers could be heard.

13

FOR A FUNERAL

'HERE YOU GO, A GUINNESS, A CIDER AND A WINE FOR ME.' Anjli sat at the table with a grin. 'Did I miss anything while I was gone?'

Declan looked up from the menu. 'Just food options,' he said. 'We have about ten minutes to order before the kitchen closes.'

Declan had kept his side of the deal, and had brought Theresa to *The Old Bank of England*, a pub based on the other side of Fleet Street from the entrance to Temple Inn, and therefore only a couple of minutes away from the offices if they were needed. An imposing Grade II-listed building, the pub was once the Law Courts branch of the *Bank of England* from 1888 to 1975, but after falling into disrepair, it was restored by *Fuller's* brewery two decades later in neoclassical style, complete with marble, specially commissioned murals, chandeliers and sculptured high ceilings. Now a *McMullen's* brewery, the pub was a welcome distraction for the officers, especially as the pub was only half-full when they arrived. Declan had been about to sit Theresa down at a small table by the wall, when Anjli had patted him on the shoulder, having entered the pub moments behind them.

'Aye aye,' she smiled. 'Room for one more?' she winked at Declan. 'Unless you need me to leave, you know, if you're putting on the charm?'

Declan inwardly groaned as he forced a smile. 'Billy turning up as well?' he asked. 'Monroe too?'

'What, and turn your intimate date into a works outing?' Anjli thought for a moment. 'Could work.' She dodged a clip around the ear, laughing. 'I haven't eaten all day, but if you want...'

'You're buying the first round,' Declan had said, now picking a larger table to sit down at. And dutifully, Anjli had done just that, bringing them back as Declan was trying to decide on whether he wanted a healthy salad, or a pie and chips.

Theresa had made her mind up about three seconds after looking at the menu, and was now watching Declan with a small amount of amusement.

'Is he always like this?' she asked with a light smile. Anjli sat down, doling out glasses as she did so.

'Depends,' she replied. 'Has he started with his rant about bloody pies yet?'

'It's not a rant, it's a valid argument,' Declan muttered. 'The dictionary describes a pie as a *baked dish of fruit, or meat and vegetables, typically with a top and base of pastry.* The important part is top and base.' He tapped at an image of a pie on the menu. 'That's not a pie, that's a casserole with a puff pastry lid on.'

'Pies are split into three types,' Theresa answered. 'First there's the filled pie, which has an open top. Then there's the top crust pie, which you're annoyed at here, and then there's the two-crust pie, which I think is what you want.'

'I didn't realise the Manchester police had to be pie experts,' Anjli grinned.

'I know a little about them because of the name,' Theresa tapped the menu. '*Pie*. Taken from the Latin word *pica*, meaning magpie. The birds didn't get the *mag* part of their name until the seventeenth century.'

'Sod it, I'm having the gammon and egg,' Declan surrendered the menu to Anjli, who stared at him in horror.

'Way to piss off the vegan guest,' she said, indicating Theresa. Declan paled.

'I didn't—' he started, but stopped when both Theresa and Anjli laughed.

'I'm having sausage and mash,' Theresa said when she could breathe again.

'He's so easy to play,' Anjli was still chuckling.

'I find it adorable,' Theresa mocked. 'The guys I work with are all so desperate to prove themselves better than me. This is a welcome change.'

Declan rose from the table. 'I'll get the food in,' he said, glowering at Anjli. 'You want something? I'm buying so get in quick.'

Anjli pointed at the lasagna, and Declan stomped off irritably to the bar.

'He's genuinely a good copper,' Anjli said, watching him leave. 'There aren't many like him. He's the one who joined to make a difference, you know?'

'Yeah,' Theresa said, watching Declan at the bar. Anjli, noting this, leaned closer.

'And he's had his heart torn out and fed to him recently,' she added. 'So, if you screw him over in any way, *Detective*

Inspector Martinez, know that I will personally make it my mission to destroy you.'

Theresa watched Anjli silently for a moment, before nodding.

'Understood,' she breathed. 'Does he know how you—'

'Oh, God no,' Anjli held her hands up. 'Not even close. He's my friend. I'd say the same if you were smacking onto Billy, although you'd need to be male to be a threat.'

'I think *the lady doth protest too much*,' Theresa smiled softly, reaching for her drink.

Anjli, not replying, reached for her own.

'I read about his ex,' Theresa said after sipping at her cider. 'She died, right?'

'There's been a lot of death around Declan of late,' Anjli replied. 'Not by his choosing, neither.'

'I'll play nice.' Theresa nodded.

'You can play how you like,' Anjli forced a smile. 'Just remember that you have an unfair advantage. You were the object of his affections as a teenager.'

She paused, thinking.

'I mean, the things he must have *done* while staring at the poster of—'

She stopped, grinning at Declan as he returned to the table.

'You're smiling. That's not good,' he said as he sat facing Anjli, before turning to Theresa. 'Whatever she said, ignore her. She's a pathological liar.'

'Shame,' Theresa replied, rising from her own chair. 'She said pleasant things about you.'

With that bombshell, she grabbed her handbag and walked off towards the ladies' toilets.

'Ah, the old double bluff,' Declan muttered.

Anjli leaned back in her chair.

'Got a problem,' she said. 'While we're alone.'

'Go on.'

'When I spoke to Johnny Lucas, he made a comment, a suggestion that Monroe may have known Derek Sutton in Glasgow, and that Monroe may have had connections to the Hutchinsons, a criminal family up there.'

Declan took a mouthful of Guinness before replying. 'Could be screwing around with you, seeing if you report back to Monroe.'

'I looked into it a little,' Anjli replied. 'Not much, as I didn't want it getting back to him. But Monroe had a brother, Kenny, who worked for the Hutchinsons. Killed while working for them, part of some rival gang war thing. But here's the problem.'

She leaned closer.

'There was a fire, killing two of the gang members who were believed to have performed the hit on Kenny Monroe. The arson was never closed, but it was an open secret in the force that it had been the Hutchinsons, and performed by Derek Sutton, after he moved down to London.'

'Sutton avenged Monroe's brother,' Declan shook his head. 'Christ. And Monroe pretty much demanded he visit Sutton alone.'

'It also happened a week or two after Monroe arrived in London,' Anjli continued. 'And we know that Sutton and Monroe both had Lucas connections back then. The question now is—'

'Whether Monroe helped Sutton start the fire, or even told him where the killers were,' Declan finished the sentence.

'I think we need to be watchful here,' Anjli returned to

her original position. 'The Guv's on pretty thin ice as it is. The last thing we need is some gangland connection he's accused of that's set before the *last* gangland connection he's accused of.'

Declan picked up his pint again, taking a sip as he tried not to catch Anjli's eye. In the office was a USB stick that Billy had been quietly checking for viruses; it hadn't been opened yet, and had been given to Declan a few weeks earlier by Tom Marlowe, a spy who was Monroe's adopted nephew, and passed on to him by his boss, Emilia Wintergreen, who was Monroe's ex-wife. Declan shut his eyes, remembering what Marlowe had said to him, in the house in Hurley, before leaving.

'Your dad didn't just have folders on the Red Reaper on the drive you gave us; there were some other things, about... other people. Things you should look at and know.'

The implication had been that the drive had information on Monroe within, information that Declan hadn't wanted to see, and had therefore taken his time on. If Patrick Walsh had this information and had done nothing with it, then Declan didn't see why he should. But this Scottish revelation was another reason why Declan *should* see what secrets Monroe had in his past, if only to be aware of them when they slammed into his investigations like a freight truck.

'How was Johnny?' he asked, changing the subject.

'As loveable as ever,' Anjli replied, a wry smile on her face. 'They've all decamped to some pub in Mile End. The Boxing Club is currently closed; too hot for them right now.'

Declan grinned. 'That's what you get for helping the police,' he said.

The conversation was halted however as Theresa returned, sitting back down with a grin on her face.

'There's a board on the wall,' she said with delight. 'Apparently this pub is set between *Sweeney Todd's Barbers*, and *Mrs Lovett's Pie Shop*.'

'Half of Fleet Street claim that,' Declan replied. Theresa shrugged.

'Doesn't matter,' she said. 'Just be grateful that you didn't have the pie here.' She winked. 'You'll never know what they put into it.'

Declan laughed, but paused as he stared up at one of the television screens in the bar. As most London bars did, they had BBC news on all the time but with the sound on mute, closed captions giving poor translations of the live spoken words, while the news chyron below scrolled the important up to date moments. Declan hadn't meant to stop, but the image on the screen had caught his eye. An elderly, suited man with wire-framed, slightly tinted glasses and a peppered back comb that made him look like a blow dried badger was speaking to the cameras, while the captions underneath repeated what he said after a five or six second delay. Underneath him was the headline

DEREK SUTTON APPEALS CONVICTION CITING NEW EVIDENCE

Theresa followed his gaze upward.

'Oh, Christ,' she murmured.

'Can we get the barman to turn the volume up?' Anjli asked, but Declan was already typing into his phone.

'It's mostly passed now, and by the time they do that we'll be onto the sport,' he replied. 'They'll have it on the website.' And, finding the video, Declan turned his phone around so that all three detectives could see it.

The man with the badger haircut was holding what seemed to be a press conference; from the lighting outside, it'd been recorded earlier that day, so possibly before Julia Clarke had been found.

'*My client, Derek Bruce Sutton, has contested his incarceration for over thirty years,*' the man with the badger haircut explained. '*He has always been innocent of the crimes thrown at him, in particular the murders of Narinder Singh and Jeetinder Gill.*' He was reading from a piece of paper, looking up to emphasise points as he spoke. '*He was convicted on the testimony of children, and by a piece of evidence, his fingerprints on a tyre iron that the prosecution claimed could not, in any way have been faked; my client had to have held the weapon, and had to have used it to murder these two men. However, last night, Reginald Troughton was also beaten to death with a tyre iron, and we have learned that this weapon, this modern version of the weapon used all those years ago, also bore his fingerprints. As my client has been incarcerated in Belmarsh Prison for three decades, we find this something of a paradox, as we were told, emphatically, that this couldn't happen.*'

He looked up to the cameras now.

'*Reginald Troughton had a personal grudge against my client dating back decades, and my client had recently fired his boyfriend, the banister Michael Chadwick. That an author of children's books had such sway over the legal system is beyond ludicrous, and has made a joke of the entire legal institution. We are appealing this long-standing injustice immediately, and my client—*'

Declan turned the video off.

'Seriously,' he said to Theresa. 'Did he do it?'

'Yes,' Theresa replied, but then followed it with 'as far as we were told.'

'Were told?' Anjli exclaimed.

'It was the first book, so Jim Sutcliffe led us,' Theresa admitted. 'He was the one who learned of Derek, and he arranged it so that 'we' could find the murder weapon.'

'How exactly did he find it?' Declan asked. 'Because that's the question that might free Derek Sutton.'

Theresa didn't reply for a few seconds.

'I honestly don't remember,' she replied. 'But it was all sanctioned and signed off, so we assumed that they'd ensured everything was correct. Bruno wouldn't have done anything if it wasn't, he knew the law like the back of his hand.'

Declan leaned in the chair, looking at Anjli.

'We thought this was some kind of ironic revenge,' he mused. 'What if it's more than that? What if they killed Reginald just to bring doubt to Derek Sutton's case?'

'There are easier ways to do that,' Anjli replied. 'Although if this was a *kill two birds with one stone* situation, or rather a *kill two Magpies with one stone...*'

Declan went to reply to this, but paused as his phone went.

'Looks like Monroe saw the news too,' he said before answering it. It wasn't Monroe, though, and he listened for a moment, nodding to himself before replying 'thanks' and disconnecting the call.

'We're gonna have a busy day tomorrow,' he said to Anjli.

'What's happened?' she replied.

'They've found Luke Ashton,' Declan was already texting Monroe as he spoke. 'That was a friend in the West London Met. They brought Luke into Hammersmith Hospital half an hour ago after being tasered.'

'The police tasered him?' Theresa looked confused at this. 'Did he resist arrest?'

'Apparently he was arrested in Louise Hart's apartment,' Declan replied as his food was brought over, Theresa's bowl of sausage and mash placed down beside it, a second server bringing Anjli's lasagne. 'A neighbour called the police, and when they arrived he was ranting, violent, so they took him down with a police issue X26 Taser.'

'Was Hart with him?'

'They found her in the bedroom, dead,' Declan replied. 'Apparently she'd taken an overdose earlier in the day and had laid on her bed surrounded by images of Tommy.'

'Jesus. Maybe we should get these to go?' Theresa asked as she looked down at it. Declan shook his head.

'Luke's being observed by nurses now,' he replied. 'They'll need to check him before processing, so we have ten minutes or so to eat.'

Anjli stared at her lasagne. 'I'm not sure I'm hungry anymore.'

She looked up at Theresa with a wicked smile.

'I'm guessing this wasn't how you expected your first date to go,' she grinned. But Theresa wasn't smiling, staring down at the mash, her right hand lightly scratching at her upper left arm.

'Ignore her,' Declan glared at Anjli. 'And I'm sure there's a valid reason why Luke was at Louise's place.'

'Yeah,' Theresa rose from the table, grabbing her bag. 'I'm just popping outside to get some air, back in a moment.'

'Sorry if I offended you—' Anjli started, but Theresa smiled and leaned closer to Declan.

'Next time, we don't need a chaperone,' she whispered. 'Just so you know.'

Declan paused, staring after Theresa as she left the pub.

Anjli, chuckling, prodded him on the arm to bring him back to the present.

'You noticed she takes that bag with her when she goes everywhere?' she whispered. 'You think she's popping a pill?'

'Your childhood friend was accused of murder,' Declan replied. 'Wouldn't you? Besides, I think they're painkillers.'

'Still not good. And she might be a suspect,' Anjli muttered sullenly. 'So don't go too *Basic Instinct* on us, okay? She could be far more dangerous than a poster on a wall.'

Declan couldn't help it.

He smiled.

'God, I hope so,' he said, before tucking into his food.

14

FOR A BIRTH

THOMAS WILLIAMS WAS ANGRY. HE WAS ALSO DRUNK. HE SAT on his bed and glared balefully at the TV screen, attached to the wall in front of him, as if believing the television itself caused his anger.

It had been quietly suggested by the DCI who spoke to him earlier that he shouldn't leave any time soon; and to be honest, with people dying all around, the safest place he could be in was a room of a busy hotel with CCTV on every floor. He'd even bought a Wi-Fi camera, now in the corner of his room, aimed at the door in case anyone tried to make their way in, although he had no idea whether he'd even turned it on correctly.

On the TV the *Ten o'clock News* was showing Sebastian Klinger, the solicitor for Derek Sutton. Thomas knew him in passing, as he was also the go-to solicitor for the *Magpies,* ever since Chadwick had died, which seemed a little strange when considered properly; *the murderer and the solvers both represented by the same firm.* Thomas almost laughed. The idea was so ludicrous. But then much of what had happened over the last twenty-four hours was equally insane.

Reginald was dead.

Julia was dead.

Rory was dead.

Luke was on the run.

Tessa was actively investigating them.

On the screen, Klinger talked about Sutton, and there was something in his voice, his tone that seemed *familiar*. Had he been involved in any other court cases with them? He was certainly old enough.

And Sutton was going free.

Thomas sighed, turning off the TV. He wanted to go to Daniel, to see if he knew anything; he had always been the cleverest in the team, even if he was the craziest. But there was a nagging concern at the back of his mind, a worry that if he did, then Daniel would tell him something, *reveal* something that he didn't want to know.

No, he thought to himself. *I don't have any secrets.*

But he knew that was a lie. Thomas still remembered what had happened the previous night with Jane.

Jane.

He'd always loved her, ever since she joined the *Magpies*. But they weren't allowed to have relationships, and although they both fancied each other, the bloody contracts and NDAs that the government had landed on them meant they couldn't do a damn thing. Although the *story* had them as boyfriend and girlfriend, they'd not been allowed to do anything outside the given parameters, and those parameters had been *minimal*. They'd intended to meet up when the books were finished, but then he'd started seeing the *Blue Peter* girl, what was her name—

Thomas drunkenly rose from the bed, the room spinning, but his mind finally having a moment of clarity.

Shit. The woman from last night.

It was Eloise—no; she was *Louise* now; it had to be. Her hair was pulled back, angling her face and she'd lost weight, a *lot* of weight, but the eyes, the *eyes* gave it away. She was skinnier than Jane now, but they still looked alike. He was annoyed at himself for not guessing; what was it she'd said?

'Have we met before?'

'Yes, we have. I was one of the gang, not that you'd remember, or give a damn about.'

One of the gang. That bloody *Blue Peter* event, and that bloody *reboot* idea ten years ago.

Thomas stumbled over to his jacket, pulling out a collection of ticket stubs and receipts from the inside pocket. She'd given him her business card, he was sure of it. He'd stuck it in his pocket without even looking.

Idiot. She wanted to talk. Why else would she turn up?

He stopped. To be fair, they hadn't ended well. The rumours of him with other girls, the asking for Polaroids of their naked bodies, it'd all been a bit of fun, nothing serious. He'd wanted to see how far they'd go, how much they wanted to impress him. So he'd kissed a couple of them, maybe gone a little further. It was only because they wanted him to. And he was a teenage boy, being offered the keys to the candy shop. What would *anyone* do in that situation?

But Eloise never understood, even when Thomas explained that he had urges. Nobody understood terms like *sex addict* back then. He hadn't meant to force himself on her; she'd given the wrong signals, made him think she wanted it. And then Luke, finding out, blindsiding him, taking him down in an unfair fight...

Luke deserved everything he got from Bruno. Thomas almost felt bad about setting that up, telling Bruno that Luke had been confiding about his confused, mixed feelings for the man, even sending him love letters, spurring him on, winding him up like a top.

The business card was now in Thomas' hand. It was simple, just her name, a telephone number and an email. The last time he'd even seen her was just under a decade ago, when they'd had the idea for the sequels. They'd been okay back then. She'd even forgiven him.

Thomas reached for his phone but then stopped.

Why would she want to talk to him? Why was she speaking to Reginald?

The knock at the door halted him from dialling. Walking quietly towards it, he stopped as he looked through the peephole. Confused as to who he saw through it, he opened the door.

'Who are you?' he asked, swaying a little as he held onto the door. 'I was told nobody would call on me. It's after ten pm.' He squinted at the man in front of him. 'Are you from the hotel? Have we met?'

'I'm Mark Walters,' the red-headed man said as he passed Thomas, entering the suite, taking off and cleaning his glasses as he did so. 'I work with Norman Shipman.'

'Ah,' Thomas spoke as if this simple statement explained everything. 'I didn't tell them anything,' he replied.

'Of course you did,' Mark said as he placed his glasses back on, looking around the room as he did so. 'I would have as well. Not bad.'

'Paid for by the police,' Thomas stumbled to the sofa that was against one wall, sitting on it as he observed Mark. 'They told me I had to stay, the publishers didn't want to pa, but the bill was paid so I'm assuming they did, anyway.'

He forced a cunning smile.

'If they think *I'm* paying it, they're going to have a bloody shock.'

'Are you drunk?' Mark asked. Thomas shrugged.

'I'm not paying for the room, so why should I pay for the minibar?' he asked wolfishly.

'You won't be paying for it,' Mark replied, walking to the window and staring out of it, down at Piccadilly Circus. '*I'm* paying for it. That is, I'm covering it on behalf of Mister Shipman.'

He looked back.

'It's the least we can do.'

'Are you also the one paying for *Daniel's* room?' Thomas' tone changed to one of suspicion.

Mark nodded, walking to the chair beside the desk, sitting down on it.

'Luke Ashton has been arrested,' he replied. 'They found him in the apartment of Louise Hart.' He looked at the desk; on it were the phone and business card. Mark picked the card up, examining it.

'A woman who you seemed to be about to call,' he tossed the card back to the table. 'A woman who saw you last night, saw Derek Sutton a week ago and who is believed to have killed a colleague of mine this morning.'

He rubbed at the bridge of his nose.

'So much in one day,' he whispered. 'Sometimes I feel like my head will explode.'

'I didn't realise who she was,' Thomas slurred. 'She didn't give her name.'

'You hung out with her ten years ago,' Mark replied. 'Are

you telling me she changed so much, or are you that much of a *narcissist* that you simply don't notice other people?'

'People change,' Thomas mumbled. 'I can't be expected to recognise everyone I've met.'

'No, I don't suppose you can,' Mark nodded, leaning closer. 'You never were good at seeing the things right in front of you.'

'I *do* know you,' Thomas replied. 'Where do I know you from?'

'We've mainly dealt with each other by phone,' Mark muttered, rotating his neck, trying to get the kinks out of it. 'I think this might be one of the first times we've ever properly met face to face. Oh, Jane Ashton is on her way back here.'

'Jane? That's insane?' Thomas blurted. 'There are press outside!'

'I think that's the point, don't you?' Mark rose now, walking around the room. 'You, however seem quite calm, to be honest. I thought that hearing about the murder of your aunt would have concerned you.'

'She was an aunt in the loosest of senses,' Thomas snapped. 'She spent years trying to stop me cashing in on the books. All the money she made was fine, but me? One of the bloody *Magpies* gaining something from the books that I made famous? Bitch.'

'I'm guessing you can guarantee where you were when she died?' Mark smiled now, dropping a half torn piece of paper into the wastepaper bin, but the smile was cold, like a child playing with an insect before squashing it. Thomas squirmed a little now, realising that this wasn't the innocent visit he'd assumed that it was.

'What do you want, Mister Walters,' he said, not as a question but a more monotone statement. With the glasses now off, Mark Walters looked familiar, more than just *a meeting with Shipman here and there* familiar.

'You were a prick to her,' Mark said. 'She told me. How you made her feel so special and then threw her away.'

Thomas looked back to the desk and the business card.

'For Christ's sake, is this about Eloise, or Louise, or whatever the hell she calls herself?' he exclaimed. 'I've not seen her for years! Of course I wasn't going to bloody well recognise her!'

'*I'm not talking about Louise Hart!*' Mark snapped, and Thomas saw for the first time the murderous intent in his eyes. 'I'm talking about Jane! *Jane Terry!*'

Thomas rose unsteadily now, standing opposite Mark, his eyes narrowing as he tried to recollect where he knew the intruder from.

'I think it's time for you to piss off, mate,' he slurred. 'Before I call security and have you removed.'

'Security will be here soon enough,' Mark smiled. 'They'll be alerted to you when Jane arrives.'

'Alerted about what?' Thomas was shaking now, forcing a brave face, but behind the expression he was confused, his mind fogging up, a leaden feeling in his limbs. Reginald, Rory and Julia were dead; *was this the man that killed them?*

'I... I don't feel right,' he muttered. 'I need to throw up.'

'That'll be all the drinks you've finished,' Mark smiled. 'Thomas Williams. Ace detective. So good that he didn't even notice that the minibar bottles had all been opened.'

'What?' Thomas was swaying more now, his eyes unfocusing.

'I told you, I paid for the bar,' Mark replied. 'So I ensured what you drank. And each bottle had a tiny amount of Rohypnol in it.'

He moved closer.

'You remember Rohypnol, don't you?' he asked coldly. 'It was your drug of choice when you were a teenager.'

Thomas was trembling now, terrified and confused as Mark pointed at the bathroom and the under sink counter.

'The hotel didn't clean your room today, did they?' he asked. 'You were scared they'd realise you slept with someone in here. Nobody's been in here, not even the police.'

'So?' Thomas was looking at the under sink counter, as if drawn there by Mark's finger. Mark dropped it as he shrugged.

'I know someone who *was* in here.'

Thomas couldn't take any more of this; he staggered into the bathroom, opening the under sink counter.

Inside it was a latex mask of a bald man, a full head piece, a slit down the back, and a pair of black gloves, blood on them. On the top were two white rose petals, as if garnished.

'Jane was in here,' he whispered. 'After we...'

'Poor Tommy Williams,' Mark mocked, walking to the coffee table, picking up a square glass ashtray, weighing it in his hand as he spoke. 'So happy to get one over on Luke, he didn't even wonder why Jane was so eager to get into his room.'

He walked to the door of the bathroom, staring at Thomas.

'She did a good job, too,' he said. 'She's even got some of your hairs in it.'

Thomas thought hard, fighting through the fuzz; he remembered a moment, during when they... well, *during*. She'd grabbed his hair, pulling hard. He'd thought that she was playing rough, that she *wanted* it rough—

'Yes, that's right,' Mark nodded. '*Now* you're starting to see.'

'Why are you doing this to me?' Thomas slurred now, more a whine than a comment. 'What have I ever done to you?'

'You destroyed my life,' Mark replied.

Thomas frowned, his expression one of bemused stupidity.

'I don't even know you!' he mumbled back. 'Who are you? Really?'

Mark *told* him.

And then he moved in quickly, striking Thomas hard on the head with the edge of the ashtray, sending him to the floor.

———

JANE MADE A SHOW OF RUNNING INTO THE *HYATT* LOBBY, collapsing against the reception counter as if the world was chasing her. Which in a way, it was as behind her were half a dozen paparazzi, all smelling a story here.

'Quick!' she shouted at the first receptionist. 'Call Tommy Williams! I think he's in danger!'

The receptionist, a middle-aged woman with her hair in a bun and already aware of the celebrity on the upper floor, tapped in the number, waiting for the phone to answer. Jane, meanwhile, was pacing, rubbing her face with her hands.

'Haven't you had enough?' she snapped at the photographers. 'Haven't you had your pound of flesh?'

'Did you know Luke was going to kill Reginald Troughton?' one of the press asked. 'Did you plan it with him?'

'Luke didn't kill anyone, especially Reggie,' Jane argued back. 'Thomas was the one who hated him. Told me last night, said he made him look like a fool.'

'How long were you with him last night?'

'That's between me and Tommy,' Jane insisted. 'But it was all innocent. We went to his room, he went out to find us takeaway, got back about half hour later and then we ate alone. I left a couple of hours later.'

'Did you sleep with him?'

'No comment!' Jane looked back at the receptionist, placing the phone down. 'Well?'

'No answer,' the receptionist was now tapping on the screen. 'I'll check security, see if we can—'

She paused. On the screen was the corridor that led to Thomas Williams' room. There was no movement on the screen, but Thomas's door was slightly ajar.

Reaching to a walkie talkie, the receptionist spoke into it.

'Clive, do me a favour, go check out Thomas Williams?' she said, looking back to the paparazzi. 'And can I get a couple of guys down here to clean up the lobby?'

She motioned for Jane to come behind the counter, and follow her into the back office 'They'll keep asking questions if you're out there,' she said. 'Best to stay out of the way.'

Jane nodded slowly. 'Just make sure Thomas is okay.'

'One of our best is going there right now,' the receptionist replied soothingly. 'I'm sure it'll all be okay.'

———

AT THE DOOR TO THOMAS WILLIAMS' SUITE, CLIVE MANTLE, assistant head of security for the *Piccadilly Hyatt,* knocked loudly on the door. It slowly opened as he did so, and he saw it hadn't automatically closed because the inside lock, the metal bar that worked as a stronger version of a door chain had been placed across the frame, ensuring that the door would stay open. Added to that, the DO NOT DISTURB sign that had been on the handle all day was now gone.

As if he wanted someone to enter, Clive thought as he opened the door, entering the suite.

It was quiet; *too* quiet. Walking through the living area, he saw a small pile of mini bar spirit bottles on a chair, all empty.

Maybe the stupid bastard's passed out, he thought as he entered the bedroom. But no, Thomas Williams wasn't in bed.

'Mister Williams?' he asked. 'Are you in here?'

No answer.

Clive was about to leave when he spied something in the bathroom. Walking in, he stopped, staring down in shock.

'Clive to security, I've found Thomas Williams,' he said. 'We're gonna need an ambulance here.'

'What's he done?' The voice came back on the radio. Clive swallowed.

'I think he's fallen in the bathroom and smashed his head open,' he said as he stared down at the body. 'I'm not touching anything.'

'Is he breathing?'

Clive leaned over the body, currently face down and placed two fingers on Thomas' neck.

'I think there's a pulse, but I ain't going any closer.'

He paused, noticing something large and rubbery on the floor. Pulling out a pen, he used the tip to gingerly turn it over, stepping back in horror as a man's face stared at him.

However, after a moment, rational thought came back, and he even laughed at his skittishness.

It was a mask. Nothing more than that.

'Yeah, security?' Clive spoke again into the radio. 'We definitely need the police. Like, right now.'

15

FOR HEAVEN

'I THINK I'M CURSED,' DECLAN MOANED AS HE LEANED AGAINST the side of the elevator. 'I'm cursed never to go home or sleep.'

'Well, you're working with a *Magpie*,' Anjli mocked. 'You know, *one for sorrow, two for joy?*'

Declan smiled, but it was a tired one.

'We could have done this tomorrow,' he muttered.

'Tomorrow will be the interview of Luke Ashton,' Monroe tapped at the floor button to open it. As the doors opened onto the hotel floor, he walked out into the corridor, with Anjli and Declan following.

They'd heard about Thomas Williams while preparing to interview Luke; Declan, Anjli and Theresa had returned to the Temple Inn Command Unit after a quick evening meal, half of which had been placed in 'to go' containers to save time. De'Geer, downstairs with forensics while Doctor Marcos examined the body of Rory Simpson took the call, alerting upstairs that not only had Thomas Williams apparently collapsed drunkenly in the hotel bathroom and smacking his head open, he'd also been found in possession of a latex, *bald man* mask.

'Look,' Monroe pointed at the CCTV camera. 'There's no bloody way he got out of here without us seeing!'

Declan glanced up the corridor and saw that Monroe was correct. That said, anyone trying to move now would have a shock, as the corridor was filled with police and forensics officers, the latter in their blue PPE suits. Grabbing their own, Declan and the others quickly dressed in the disposable one piece before entering the hotel suite.

'You didn't need to do that,' Doctor Marcos, in another of her custom grey PPE suits, said as she emerged from the bathroom, indicating their own masks and suits. 'There's not much here.'

'Davey not with you?' Monroe peered into the bathroom. On the floor was a bloodstain, the colour matching the smear on the side of the marble counter. Just outside the bathroom was a scrunched up towel, but there was no Thomas Williams; the paramedics had already taken him away. Doctor Marcos followed his gaze.

'You seen in there?' she asked, and Declan knew that behind the mask, she was smiling. 'Bloody hotel bathroom, isn't it. I've been in phone booths larger.'

'So, what do we have?' Monroe tried to regain a little control of the situation. Doctor Marcos pointed at the towel.

'Current hypothesis is that Williams drank the contents of the minibar, staggered into the bathroom, his bare foot went on the wet towel, which slid back because of the tiles underneath and, with his momentum sending him forward, he slammed his head into the countertop at a pretty bloody fast speed.'

She pointed at the puddle of blood on the floor.

'He's out cold, severe head trauma, and losing blood. Security comes in, finds him sparked out, and that on the floor beside him.' At this, she showed the latex full head mask on the floor, a pair of black leather gloves poking out of it. In a clear bag beside them were two rose petals.

'Obviously we haven't looked at it properly, but it seems to be the same style of mask that we've seen on CCTV,' she said. 'And there's blood on the gloves which I reckon will match Reginald Troughton, and petals which look similar to the ones found with Julia Clarke.'

'So this was an accident?' Declan asked. Doctor Marcos frowned behind her mask.

'I'm not sure,' she said. 'The smear on the counter is close, but doesn't quite match the injury. But that could be because of the way he fell. We'll know better after we check him over.'

'Is he likely to recover?' Monroe followed up. Doctor Marcos shrugged.

'Personally, from the amount of alcohol he seems to have ingested, I'm stunned he's still alive.'

'Any visitors?' Declan was examining the mini bar bottles now. He wasn't speaking to Doctor Marcos, more asking the room, but it was Doctor Marcos who answered.

'CCTV shows a man enter and leave about an hour ago. We're still waiting for reception to tell us who it is, but we're in the night shift right now, and they're a little slower.'

'What I can't work out is if he *was* the one wearing the mask, how he got to Reginald's,' Anjli said, looking around the room. 'I mean, Jane being here aside, the CCTV didn't show anyone leaving until she went around half ten.'

'Ah, I can answer that,' Doctor Marcos walked the three detectives back out of the room, pulling off the PPE mask and hood once back in the corridor.

'Look down the corridor,' she said. 'It's an optical illusion on the camera, as the walls merge into one.'

Declan looked up the corridor and saw that about two rooms further on was a turnoff to the right, one that couldn't be seen on the tight angle of the CCTV camera.

'Another set of rooms?' he asked, walking towards them. A man in the uniform of *Hyatt Hotel* security, standing in the corridor with one of the officers, looked over to him.

'No rooms down there,' he said. 'It's mainly a quick route to the back stairwell, in case of fire.'

'CCTV?' Declan asked. The security officer shook his head.

'Never really needed it there,' he replied apologetically.

'The suite that Thomas was in used to be two rooms,' Doctor Monroe continued. 'Clive there was telling me all about it.'

'Oh aye?' Monroe looked back to the security officer, now looking a little pale at this sudden attention. 'Maybe Clive can tell us too.'

'I just told your Divisional Surgeon that we never used to have suites on this floor,' the security officer, now identified as Clive explained. 'But when we got more suite enquiries than room enquiries, the higher ups renovated. As such, rooms on this floor and the one above were merged.' He walked down the corridor, motioning for the others to follow. As they turned into the side corridor, Declan saw it was only about thirty feet long, leading to a window, a door to the back staircase beside it. On the opposite side of the corridor, a door was positioned midway along it.

'That used to be the door to the other room,' Clive explained. 'Once the suite was finished though, there was only one door needed, so rather than brick it up, they simply locked it.'

'Why lock it rather than removing it?' Anjli asked.

'You never know when you need a side door,' Clive replied. 'Cleaning staff are encouraged to use these corridors, so that they don't bump into the guests.'

'Is it still locked?' Declan asked. 'Who has the key?'

'Only people assigned to the floor, and security,' Clive replied. 'Any usual issues would involve entrance through the main door.'

'So you could hypothetically leave through this door without being picked up by the camera, go down the back staircase and leave the hotel?'

'That's right.'

'And how many cameras would you pass?'

Clive's silence was damning.

'Jesus,' Monroe swore. 'He could have been in his room and out within a matter of minutes.'

'No, because the door's locked—' Clive grabbed the door handle and twisted, and was surprised to see that the door swung gently open.

'When was the last time this was definitely locked?' Anjli asked. Clive thought for a moment.

'Cleaning yesterday,' he replied. 'We couldn't get in today as Mister Williams was in the room all day, well apart from when he went to the hotel gym or met with the police downstairs, and he had the *do not disturb* sign up those times, so nobody would have tried.'

'So if he checked in yesterday afternoon, he could have had this open from then until now,' Declan suggested. Clive nodded.

'Pretty much,' he replied.

'Has Mister Williams been here before?' Anjli asked. Clive smiled, grateful for a question he could attest.

'Yes, twice before,' he said.

'And has he ever stayed in this suite before?' Anjli continued.

'Both times,' Clive continued. 'He makes it a part of his contract rider that this suite is always booked for him. And if they can't, they need to rearrange the date of the event he's attending to ensure it is.'

'And that doesn't seem odd to you?' Monroe raised an eyebrow.

Clive shook his head.

'I've worked in London hotels for twenty years,' he explained. 'This isn't even in the top ten.'

WITH CLIVE NOW SHOWING A POSSIBLE ESCAPE ROUTE FOR Thomas Williams to use on the night of Reginald Troughton's murder, Monroe, Declan and Anjli stripped off their PPE suits and made their way back down to reception. The lobby was quiet; it was almost midnight now, and the bulk of guests had checked in. The lobby was mainly filled with police officers, primarily there to stop photographers from entering.

'I understand you have someone in the back?' Monroe asked the receptionist, who nodded, leaning back and rapping on the door with her knuckles. A female police officer poked her head out, nodding as she saw Monroe.

'Guv,' she said, closing the door behind her as she walked over. 'Jane Ashton was very distraught, and the paramedics have given her a mild sedative. She's on the sofa but pretty unresponsive, if you know what I mean.'

'Balls,' Monroe was annoyed at this. 'I wanted to have a little chat with her about her choice in bed partners.'

'If it helps,' a female receptionist spoke up, 'I was the one she spoke to, when she arrived.'

'Oh, aye? And what did she say?' Monroe looked over.

'She was very distressed,' the receptionist answered. 'She was arguing with the paparazzi. They were questioning her, I think it flustered her.'

'Did she answer them?' Monroe asked. 'If she did, it'll likely be all over the news by morning.'

'She did,' the receptionist admitted. 'She spoke about last night, said that it was all innocent. She went to Mister Williams' room, he went out to get a takeaway and then they ate alone. She left a couple of hours later—'

'He went to get a *takeaway*?' Monroe spluttered in surprise. 'Are you sure of that?'

'I am,' the receptionist faced Monroe now, straightening as she patted at her bun, as if affronted she would invent such a story. 'She repeated it to me when we were in the back room.'

'We'll need to get that from her when she wakes up,' Monroe said to Declan. 'We also need to know who the visitor was that came to see Thomas an hour before Jane arrived—'

'That'd be me,' a voice spoke from the other side of the lobby, and Declan turned to see Mark Walters walk over to them. 'Mark Walters, I work for Norman Shipman,' he said to Monroe and Anjli. 'I've spoken to DI Walsh here a couple of times already.'

'And you always seem to be where the action is,' Declan replied cynically. Mark shrugged.

'It's London,' he answered casually. 'Throw a stone any direction and you'll hit something going on.'

'And why are you here, Mister Walters?' Monroe asked suspiciously. Mark shrugged.

'Because you wouldn't pay Thomas Williams' bill,' he replied, before turning to Declan. 'When your DCI here told Thomas to stay in town, it gave him a bit of a problem. *BadgerLock Publishing* only gave him a night, and the hotel is fully booked for rooms. The only way to stay, was to keep the suite. And Thomas is, well, let's just say he's maxed out on all his cards. So, he called in a favour from Mister Shipman.'

'Pay the bill?' Declan whistled. 'Glad to see where my taxpayer money's going.'

'Actually, it's not,' Mark shook his head. 'I've covered the bill personally. However, it was at the express demand that Thomas only use essentials. Not drink the whole sodding minibar. I was here to confirm that he hadn't, but the front desk told me they hadn't been able to enter the room to check. I went to the room, entered and found Thomas in a state, sprawled out on the settee, bottles all around him and spouting gibberish.'

'So he was still conscious then?' Anjli asked. Mark nodded.

'He was teetering, but yeah, just about,' he replied. 'Kept muttering that *she deserved it;* I guessed that the she that he was talking about was Julia, as I'd recently seen DI Walsh at her house, and it's all over the news.'

He paused.

'Although I've also heard that Louise Hart was found dead today, and knowing their history, he might have been talking about her, I suppose.'

'So you did the right thing and called the police,' Monroe smiled humourlessly.

'Of course not,' Mark snapped. 'I didn't know he had a bloody mask in the bathroom, and I didn't know he had a secret entrance like James Bond. I assumed he was having a relapse or something, so I phoned Jane.'

'Jane Ashton, who's ignored our calls all day?'

'Well yeah,' Mark looked around. 'She doesn't know your numbers, and I'm on speed dial.'

'And why is your number on speed dial?' Declan looked up from his notebook.

'All the *Magpies* have my number on speed dial,' Mark pulled his phone out, scrolling through a long list of numbers and names. 'My phone is effectively *Norman Shipman's* phone.'

'So how did you leave Mister Williams?' Monroe continued.

Mark took his glasses off, cleaning them with a lens cloth as he spoke.

'Angry and bitter,' he said with a hint of remorse. 'I told him we weren't paying for sundries, so he'd better find a way to pay the stupidly large drinks bill he'd racked up. He threw a tiny vodka bottle at me and I left.'

'And then an hour later Jane turned up,' Anjli said.

'I assume so,' Mark replied. 'I only got here a few minutes before you did. A friend on the concierge desk gave me the nod.'

'Don't leave the hotel,' Monroe ordered Mark. 'We might need to speak to you again.'

Mark Walters nodded and wandered back to the other side of the still quiet lobby.

'There's something off about that man,' Declan muttered. 'He's always around when there's shit going on.'

'Yeah, but Westminster pays a bundle for people like that,' Anjli replied as her phone beeped. In fact, all three phones beeped as Declan, Monroe and Anjli all pulled out their devices and stared at the same text, sent to all of them from Doctor Marcos.

Receipt in bin from McD last night timed at 9.22pm

'That'll be the takeaway that Jane mentioned, then,' Monroe placed his phone back in his jacket with irritation. 'And it looks like we have a bow to tie on our case.'

Declan nodded. With Thomas Williams now able to come and go at leisure without being seen, there was every chance that he *was* the man in the latex headpiece that had been seen at both Temple Inn and outside Julia Clarke's house.

'Something's not right here,' he muttered. 'This feels a little too Rolfe Müller.'

Rolfe Müller had been the son of Karl Meier, and had believed all his life that he was the biological son of *Wilhelm* Müller, better known as *Karl Schnitter*. He'd died in a crypt in Hurley, his death made to look like suicide, and with erroneous evidence on his person that labelled him as the *Red Reaper* serial killer. Declan and his team hadn't believed this though, and had continued the case, finding the true killer in the end.

Thomas Williams found by accident with the mask, petals and gloves beside him was *way* too convenient.

'Get some sleep,' Monroe replied. 'By the time you get home it'll be gone one in the morning, and I need you back bright and eager tomorrow morning. We've got more work ahead of us.'

He glanced across the lobby at Mark Walters, laughing with one receptionist.

'A *lot* more work,' he finished.

16

FOR HELL

BILLY AND THERESA HADN'T GONE WITH THE OTHERS TO THE hotel, and so it was a quiet office as Billy worked at his bank of monitors, idly snacking with a fork on Anjli's to-go lasagne.

'She'll be angry when she finds out you stole her dinner,' Theresa commented, sitting at Declan's desk as she went through images of Belmarsh Prison on the screen. Billy shrugged in response.

'I've bought her enough dinners since we started here, it's about time she gave me something,' he replied with a smile.

'The least you could do is microwave it.'

'What, and spoil the taste?' Billy looked horrified. 'That said, the best thing cold is pizza, stuck in the fridge overnight. Yum.'

As Theresa grimaced at the thought and returned to her work, Billy returned to his own monitors, watching the screens as he moved through banks of coding. He'd been trying to open Reginald Troughton's MacBook for over a day now, but the encryptions were Government-level in security, which made sense if he was still working for them. There were literally half a dozen fail-safes to get through, and he was on the final one now. He just hoped that what he found the other side was worth it.

At the same time, on another screen he was going through the details of Gayle Holland, the arrested perpetrator of the murders in *The Adventures of the Stolen Flowers*, the second *Magpies* novel. She'd been discovered and convicted after the Magpies proved that she alone had taken the petals that she placed on the victims after drowning them. Like Sutton, she too had claimed that she was innocent and had been framed, although she admitted to the other offences that she'd been accused of, including embezzlement and theft. It was almost as if they'd caught her dead to rights on some lower level crimes, but had thrown in a couple of murders just to spice it up.

Billy had started a deep dive through Gayle Holland's life; he'd wondered if, like Sutton's confrontational relationship with Michael Chadwick, Gayle had any connections with people involved in the creation and running of the *Magpies* as well, and was surprised to find that actually, she had. A year before the arrest, Gayle Holland had been in a scuffle with Julia Clarke in a nightclub in London; apparently Julia, while drunk, had barged past her at the top of the stairs, causing her to fall badly down them, and Gayle was in the midst of taking Julia to court over injuries suffered during the incident.

Reading the police report it looked like Julia had been incredibly intoxicated when knocking into Gayle, and had claimed it was accidental, but records from the prosecution showed that Gayle had actually met Julia two months before, during a gala at Kew Gardens where Gayle had claimed that

Julia had tried to sleep with her boyfriend at the time, causing a scene when Gayle confronted her.

That Julia had been in a confrontation with Gayle and then, two months later had possibly tried to throw her down some stairs had not been missed by the press, and the only way that Julia could get out of this was if Gayle's own character could somehow be pulled into question.

Luckily for Julia, Gayle turned out to be a murdering embezzler; one who Julia's personal team of child detectives could prove guilty.

Billy leaned back in his chair.

'Jesus,' he whispered.

'You okay?' Theresa asked. Billy, not wanting her to know what he'd learned just yet, nodded.

'Lasagna's repeating on me,' he replied.

'Told you that you should have reheated it,' Theresa was already back working as she spoke.

Billy scrolled further back through the timeline of Gayle Holland, pausing around a year earlier. Gayle had always, like Derek Sutton, protested her innocence, and for over twenty-five years had continually spoken out against the Magpies. However, around a year ago, Gayle's legal firm had released statements saying that Gayle had found proof, conclusive evidence that she had been targeted by Julia Clarke, had been scapegoated as the murderer, and had been damned by public perception after the book came out. But now, she was going to show the world, prove her innocence and then bankrupt *BadgerLock Publishing.*

Yet eight months ago, Gayle Holland had changed her mind, and had taken her own life one night while alone in her cell.

Billy frowned at this. *If you seriously believed you had a cast iron way out, why would you end it?* Taking the date of the suicide, he made a digital request to HM Prison Drake Hall, the Woman's Prison in which she'd been incarcerated, asking for dates and names of visitors. He'd expected this to come back in the next couple of days, so rather than wait, he used some back-end data encryptions to see whether he could gain it through quicker, less official routes. After all, the information *would* be coming. He just had to wait.

After ten minutes of hacking through Government systems, Billy found himself in a spreadsheet that gave him all he needed. And, as he moved back through the digital record, seeing if anything out of the ordinary showed up, he paused on the week of her death.

She'd had a meeting with a solicitor, *unnamed* at 10am on the 7th August. It wasn't her own solicitor, as there was a note stating this was an unusual situation. There was something about the timing, however that niggled at Billy; looking back through Gayle's solicitor's statements, he saw there was one sent out later the same day, a final one saying that she was reconsidering the appeal, and that more news would be forthcoming.

The following day, the 8th August, she was dead.

Who was the unnamed solicitor?

Taking the data he already had, Billy started a search for 'drake hall', hoping that something might trigger a new line of enquiry. But what he found surprised him. A diary entry, taken from a digital calendar.

```
8th Aug 10-11 Drake Hall
```

Michael Chadwick's diary. Who, it seems, had been in the same prison at the same time.

Billy whistled gently to himself. If this was true, then Michael Chadwick could have been the man that convinced Gayle Holland to stay silent, which could have led to her death.

Michael Chadwick, who would die himself in a hit and run, two months later.

Michael Chadwick, who was married to Reginald Troughton.

This was too coincidental. However, Billy had to sit on this until the official request was fulfilled.

That was going to be difficult.

'DO YOU KNOW WHAT SODDING TIME IT IS?' DCI HANNAH Miller rubbed the sleep out of her eyes as she stared down the camera of her phone at Bullman. 'You'd better be dying, Sophie.'

'I think the term you mean to say is 'Ma'am', Hannah,' Bullman replied with the slightest hint of a smile. She'd worked with Hannah and her team while up in Manchester a couple of years earlier, and according to the files, it was the same Command Unit that had housed Theresa Martinez recently.

Miller sighed, mocking a salute. 'What do you want, Soph?' she half whined. 'I was just getting to sleep.'

'Do me this favour and I'll owe you,' Bullman replied. Hannah thought for a moment and then nodded, rubbing her face again to wake herself up.

Having a Detective Superintendent owing you was worth a night of broken sleep.

'Go on.'

'DI Theresa Martinez,' Bullman continued. 'She was in

your department, right?'

'No, but she was at the Unit,' Miller replied. 'I hear she's your problem now, right?'

'What can you tell me about her?'

'Good detective. Well, she was, til about a couple of months back,' Miller replied, the background behind her shifting as she moved from the bedroom into her study. 'We had a shitty bust and there was some bloodshed on both sides. Martinez was caught in the middle of it. Not good.'

'She was injured?'

'More mentally, but yeah,' Miller was typing on a laptop, the light of the screen giving her face an ethereal glow as she continued speaking. 'She was wound up tight before this, because of an explosion she was involved in a decade back, but something that night snapped her. Started beating on one of the suspects, had to be pulled off. They prescribed her some mild antidepressants I think, but we learned at the time that she was *majorly* self-medicating for knee pain.'

'Christ,' Bullman noted this down. 'Anything else?'

'Yeah,' Miller nodded. 'You know that thing, where you lie so much about something you actually believe it yourself? She did that, convincing herself of things that simply weren't there. She was given leave, but she kept coming back to work. She was *suspended* and kept coming back to work. It was as if she simply didn't get that we wanted her gone.'

'How did it end?' Bullman looked through the glass of her office into the main bullpen, where Theresa could be seen at Declan's desk. There was a long pause, as if Miller didn't know quite how to reply.

'How is she with you?' she asked. 'I mean, what allowed her to join the team?'

'She has a note from Parliament, effectively telling us

she's now a DI in our team, and on this case,' Bullman replied. 'Why?'

'Because that's the only way that she *could* be on your team,' Miller sighed. 'Soph, they *fired her* from the police two weeks ago.'

Bullman looked back to the bullpen, looking for Theresa—

But she had gone.

'Shit.' Bullman ended the call and stared at the ceiling. Norman Shipman had ensured that Theresa Martinez still had a position and a rank in the police. He'd effectively re-hired her into her team by Governmental decree.

But why? Was it to *solve* the case, or *something worse?*

THERESA MARTINEZ DIDN'T RETURN TO HER HOTEL; IT WAS almost one in the morning by now, and central London had quietened, especially the area around Fleet Street, where the only traffic seemed to be Uber drivers, cabs and buses.

It felt peaceful.

But Theresa wasn't at peace. She was shaking, her hands trembling as, while she walked towards St Brides Church, she shakily opened up her *Altoids* box, grabbing two tablets and popping them, swallowing quickly, breathing deeply as she continued walking, as if the simple act of putting one foot in front of the other would help her calm down, find a way to get through this.

Her career was over.

Either way, this wasn't ending well. She'd either solve the crime and, once finished, the letter from Whitehall would be invalidated, or the team would learn the truth of her and kick her out there and then. Theresa was stunned she'd actually made it this far. She only needed to keep straight a few more days.

Yes, a few more days, and then she could take a break, maybe wean herself off the pills.

Why are you conning yourself, the voice in her head mocked. *You love the pills.*

'Shut up,' she hissed at the voice, pausing in the middle of the pavement as she did so. She knew that a figure was walking up behind her; grabbing the small can of pepper spray in her handbag, she spun to confront her potential attacker—

'Talking to yourself in the middle of the street?' Daniel spoke calmly. 'And I thought I was the crazy one.'

He was in a long black overcoat; the collar pulled up, and his blond hair bundled up under a Baker Boy cap, but it was unmistakably him. Dropping the can, Theresa ran at him, pulling him into a deep embrace.

'God, Daniel, you scared the shit out of me,' she mumbled into the coat. Daniel for his part hugged her back, just as tightly.

'Missed you, buddy,' he said when they finally parted.

Theresa looked around. 'How are you even here?' she asked. Daniel, in reply, took her by the hand, leading her down a side lane, away from the lights and shops of Fleet Street.

'They don't watch me after I take my tablets,' he explained. 'Then it's sleepy time and I get to disappear all night if I want.'

'Danny, Tommy's been hurt,' Theresa stopped now, turning Daniel to face her. 'They took him to hospital this evening.'

She leaned in.

'This has to stop.'

'And it will, don't worry,' Daniel placed a calming hand on Theresa's shoulder. 'It will end soon and everything will be fine again.'

Theresa stared at Daniel. 'How?' she asked. 'How can *anything* be fine again?

'Can't tell you,' Daniel sung, skipping around Theresa. 'You'll tell your new copper boyfriend. I wonder, does he know you were the one that stole the evidence and sent it to Gayle Holland, giving her hope? I ought to thank you for that. If you hadn't killed her with kindness, we'd never have started.'

And, as Theresa stared in horror at Daniel McCarthy, he waved for a taxi, its orange light glowing in the night.

He turned, grinning at Theresa as the taxi pulled up.

'Don't bother telling anyone about this,' he said. 'They won't believe you. After all, I'm in a secure room, watched over by experts. How could I be here?'

He opened the cab door and then paused, looking back at her, leaning close once more, almost swinging off the door frame.

'Thomas Williams and Louise Hart killed them all, and justice will prevail,' he said. 'Go home, Tessa. You're just in the way here.'

As the taxi left, en route for Hampstead, Theresa Martinez shakily reached for her *Altoids* box, opening it up and spilling the contents onto the pavement.

And then Theresa Martinez fell to her knees and started to cry.

17

FOR THE DEVIL

MONROE HAD BEEN CORRECT; BY THE TIME DECLAN HAD returned to Temple Inn, gathered his things, climbed into his car and driven back to Hurley, it was gone one in the morning before he fell, still fully clothed, back into his bed. Temple Inn had been more of a ghost town than the hotel when he had arrived, with Theresa having left the office without telling anyone, and Billy having left around the same time.

The following morning's alarm had blared at Declan for a good twenty seconds before he finally mustered the strength to turn it off. He'd deliberately left his phone to charge across the room, so that he had to actually get out of bed and cross it to get to the damn thing; and, once up, he could avoid returning to the bed, instead stripping off his previous day's clothes and standing under a cold shower for a minute to wake himself up. He'd seen videos on YouTube on how cold showers increased metabolism and circulation, but all he cared about was the sudden jolt of morning adrenaline that kept him awake *just long enough* to reach his first coffee of the day.

After showering, dressing and driving back to Temple Inn, Declan arrived in the office shortly after eight thirty. Unsurprisingly, he was the last to arrive, with Billy and Anjli already working together on CCTV footage, Monroe and Bullman in their respective offices, and Theresa Martinez sitting at Declan's desk, staring blankly at her notepad. She looked more tired than Declan was, and he wondered for a moment how many hours she'd slept after returning to her hotel.

'Ah, good, the part-timer's finally arrived,' Monroe mocked from his office door. Declan decided not to reply that literally every other member of the team lived a couple of miles from the unit, but remembered that he'd chosen to stay in the Hurley house, and that this was yet another reason why selling up and moving closer to London was a probable solution.

Bullman joined Monroe as she emerged from her own office.

'Briefing room,' she said simply, walking into the glass walled briefing room with Monroe trailing behind. Declan rose from his chair and followed them in.

It was a couple of minutes before everyone entered; Doctor Marcos and DC Davey looked like they hadn't slept all night, which, with the amount of evidence examining and autopsies they had on their plate right now, was probably true. PC De'Geer sat at the back with them, as beside Declan sat Anjli and Theresa, Billy at his usual spot beside the laptop that controlled the plasma screen.

'Well, wasn't yesterday a busy bloody day?' Bullman mused. 'Well done, all of you, as it was an absolute shitter.'

She looked to Monroe.

'Your case,' she said, giving him the floor.

'So, we're all over the place right now,' Monroe started. 'We thought this was a simple murder, but now we don't know what the hell it is. So, let's go through the facts.'

On the screen, the crime photo of Reginald Troughton's study appeared.

'Two nights ago, Reginald Troughton was murdered in his apartment in Temple Inn. Beside the body was a tyre iron, newly bought, with fingerprints of Derek Sutton on it.' He held up a hand to pause Anjli. 'We'll get to that little gem in a moment,' he said, continuing. 'CCTV and witnesses saw two people entering his apartment, at least one of whom had keys and passes that gained them access not only to the building but also his premises.'

Two CCTV images appeared on the screen. One was the bald-headed man, leaving, the other was Luke Ashton, his arms covered in what looked like blood as he stood by his car.

'Now Luke Ashton here had blood on his hands, and from DNA residue on charred clothing that he attempted to burn, we know this is Reginald Troughton's blood. However, gloves found at the hotel room of Thomas Williams also had blood from Reginald Troughton on them.'

'Maybe they did it together?' De'Geer commented. Monroe looked at Theresa.

'Is that possible?'

Theresa shrugged. 'They hated each other, but who knows.' She seemed reticent to answer, and Declan observed her carefully.

Something was wrong there.

'So here's our first enigma,' Monroe continued. 'Two people, both possibly with Reginald when he died. Now, we also have another fun little tidbit. When searching Luke's house, we did a DNA test on a few of his personal items, to make sure we knew which items were his, and which were his wife's. On putting the test through the system, DC Davey found out something we didn't know.'

'Luke Ashton's DNA is a partial match for Reginald Troughton,' Davey spoke from the back of the briefing room. 'They're blood relatives, most likely father and son from the closeness of the samples.'

'Luke can't be Reggie's son!' Theresa exclaimed. 'He's gay!'

'What, so gay people can't have children?' Billy asked, and Declan detected a hint of confrontation in his tone. Theresa must have also noticed this, because she shook her head.

'Of course I don't mean that,' she blurted. 'I mean, he always said he wanted kids, but couldn't because of his sexuality.'

'Reginald was sixty-five when he died. Luke is forty-four,' Declan noted. 'Reginald could have had a son when he was at university; we don't know what his sexuality was back then.'

'Find out,' Monroe ordered. 'And find out if Luke and Reginald knew about this connection. Ask your buddy who works for Shipman if this was why Luke was brought into the *Magpies*.'

'If Luke was Reginald's son, he might have tried to save him,' Billy mused. 'That could explain the blood.'

'And the fact he didn't call for help?' Anjli shook her head. 'Something's off here.'

'So, while we're on the scene, let's talk about the murder weapon,' Monroe looked to Doctor Marcos who rose, walking to the front and turning to face the team.

'The tyre iron used in the murder was a Draper 07054 19mm or 3/4 inch wheel nut wrench,' she explained as behind her an image of the weapon appeared on the screen. 'It's a heavy duty forged wrench with a long leverage handle, with a socket on one end, and a flat-end hubcap remover on the other. It's sold loose, available anywhere.'

She indicated the image.

'As you can see, there's no grip, so the killer held onto the flattened end, using the heavier socket end as a club. Because of this, we have a good fingerprint on the metal.'

'How?' Declan asked. 'We know the killer wore gloves.'

'True, but we also know the fingerprint couldn't be that of Sutton, because he's in bloody *prison*,' Doctor Marcos replied. 'We thought they'd taken it from something else, some other item, and we looked into it.'

The screen changed and now they saw two thumbprints, side by side, identical apart from a gash down the middle of the one on the right.

'On the left is the print used to convict Derek Sutton thirty years ago,' Doctor Marcos explained. 'On the right is the one found on the tyre iron. Identical apart from this gash.'

She looked back at the team.

'The problem here though is that Derek Sutton gained this scar on his thumb during a scuffle four weeks ago. It's still healing, so likely affected the print because it hasn't had enough time to fade.'

'So someone gained the print from Sutton in the last couple of weeks.' Billy leaned back. 'Louise Hart?'

'That's one option,' Monroe replied. 'There's a multitude of ways he could have done this. What we need to know is why.'

'Because he was framed,' Anjli said. 'Or, because he believes that.'

'I think he's telling the truth on that,' Monroe looked to

Theresa. 'Which brings us to the second problem. If Sutton didn't do it, who did?'

Theresa shook her head, still reluctant to speak up.

'I don't know, Guv,' she replied.

'Aye, well, let's move on,' Monroe continued as a photo of Rory Simpson appeared on the screen. 'Because here's the next bag of fun.' He looked at Declan. 'You want to take this one?'

Declan rose. 'Rory Simpson, aide to Norman Shipman, died yesterday morning in St James's Park after accidentally drinking a coffee with nuts in. However, Mark Walters, another aide to Shipman, did his own investigating and found that Simpson had been bought his drink by a brunette woman, someone that not only misplaced his epi pen, but left the scene before the ambulances came. De'Geer?'

PC De'Geer rose, addressing from the back of the room. 'I visited the coffee stall this morning with an image of Louise Hart, taken from her National Union of Journalists pass,' he said as the image of Louise Hart appeared on the screen. 'They couldn't be sure, but they thought it was the same woman, as they had the same eyes.'

'So now we have Rory Simpson, murdered the morning after Reginald Troughton, and seemingly for no reason,' Declan explained. 'We need to know what he did to deserve that.'

He looked at Theresa. 'Simpson was Shipman's secretary. Knew you all from back in the day. Did he give you the pass?'

'No, I went to Shipman to gain access, but when I arrived, Simpson barred me from talking to him. However, Mark Walters appeared, told Simpson to bugger off out of things that didn't concern him and gave me a pass from Shipman.'

Theresa shrugged. 'I thought nothing of it, assumed that it was backroom political oneupmanship.'

The screen now showed an image of Louise Hart meeting Derek Sutton, CCTV taken from a week earlier on one side of the screen, and a more blurred CCTV image of her confronting Thomas in Waterstones, two nights before. They were both lousy resolution, but with the hindsight of knowing who the dark-haired woman was, Declan could tell they were both incredibly similar, and had to be Louise.

'Louise has been busy,' Monroe stated. 'Two nights ago she spoke to Thomas Williams, and as it wasn't recorded, we'll never know for sure what they said, although an hour later Reginald Troughton was dead. A week earlier, she met with Sutton, and again we have no information on the conversation. Yesterday morning we think from witnesses that she was with Rory Simpson when he died, and they arrested Luke Ashton in her apartment, with her dead of an overdose in the next room.' He looked at Billy. 'Anything else?'

Billy tapped on his keyboard, and the *Blue Peter* photo returned to the screen.

'Eloise Lewis,' he started. 'Won a competition to meet the *Magpies* through the BBC show *Blue Peter* in 1995. Started a secret, on-off relationship with Tommy, aka Thomas Williams, possibly because she bore a resemblance to Jane Taylor, who he had a serious thing for, which lasted until three months before her sixteenth birthday, when he, aged seventeen tried to have sexual relations with her. The resulting argument ended with Luke Ashton knocking Thomas out, and Eloise being banned by Bruno Field from ever meeting the *Magpies* again.'

'Good old Bruno,' Theresa muttered. 'Misogynistic piece of shit that he was.'

'Her parents split up after this, and she ended up going to Hull University, in the process changing her name from Eloise to Louise, and taking her mother's maiden name, Hart. She trained as a journalist and mainly worked for local newspapers and radio stations.' He looked at Declan.

'She wrote the piece you remembered reading,' he said. 'The one about crowbars and tyre irons.'

He stopped, reading a note to the side of the laptop.

'This isn't confirmed,' he said, 'but I heard from one of her work colleagues that she was ill; another mentioned that they'd heard that she had been fighting the onset of Huntingdons for a few years.'

There was a moment of silence as everyone took this piece of news in. Huntington's disease, sometimes known as *Huntington's chorea*, was a severe genetic neurological disorder with no cure; anyone who was diagnosed had fifteen, maybe twenty years at best. If Louise Hart had been fighting it for years, that timeline could be *halved*.

'We checked Thomas Williams' phone last night,' Billy continued. 'It was in the hotel room, and there was a deleted message, sent to her phone around ten thirty on the night of Reginald's murder.'

A phone message popped up on the screen.

Tell anyone and I kill your family. Finish him tomorrow or I do the same.

'What does it mean?' Anjli asked.

'The following morning she killed Rory Simpson, allegedly, so maybe he was confirming that she'd do it?'

'What, and then come home and kill herself?' Anjli shook her head. 'Too convenient.'

'Maybe she didn't want the guilt?' De'Geer suggested. 'Maybe she thought by doing that, she was saving her family?'

'Table that thought,' Monroe nodded to Billy. An image of Julia Clarke appeared on the screen.

'Julia Clarke,' Monroe continued. 'Murdered by drowning yesterday afternoon, with a specific set of petals left in the bath. Witnesses stated they saw a bald man enter and leave the premises, which again could be a mask, not unlike the one found with Thomas Williams. The petals found with the mask in Thomas Williams' room also matched, and under her nails were traces of latex, so I think she tried to pull the mask off. Whether she was successful, we'll never know.'

'Any idea where the petals came from?' asked Theresa. 'Was it Kew Gardens?'

'No,' DC Davey replied. 'There's an alkaline discrepancy, but I spoke to the head gardener at Kew. She said that there was only one other location that had the exact same strain of *faded white shrub roses*. The gardens of the *Baker Institute*, in Hampstead.'

'Where Daniel McCarthy is,' Monroe sighed, looking down at his notes. 'What have I missed?'

'Jane Terry,' Anjli added. 'Turns out she was the fiancée of Daniel McCarthy, and when she died eight years ago he blamed himself, and a year later placed himself into the *Baker Institute* voluntarily.'

'She was also the daughter of Jim Sutcliffe, the private eye that Bruno and Shipman used,' added Declan. 'His real surname was Terry, and both Jane and Graham, who died almost a year after his sister, were his children.'

Monroe nodded. 'Anything else?'

'I have something new,' Billy raised a hand.

'Bloody hell, Billy, how long have you been here?' Monroe snapped. 'No need for hands.'

'Gayle Holland,' Billy stated. 'Second murderer in the books, always claimed she was innocent, then eight months ago she stated that she had evidence that could free her. I asked for details from the prison she was at, and they came through this morning.'

'Did you wait for them?' Monroe raised an eyebrow. 'Or did you go hunting?'

'They're on my PC now, and that's all that matters,' Billy replied, stone faced. 'Anyway, she had a meeting with an unnamed solicitor, the same time and date as Michael Chadwick visited the prison.'

His tone changed as he finished.

'The same day, she removed the appeal and then killed herself, taking a drug overdose.'

'Jesus. Poor bloody woman. We need to know what they said, and why Michael was there,' Monroe mused. 'Unfortunately, we'd need a ouija board for that.'

'Why Gayle?' Anjli asked. 'I mean, we know Sutton had issues with Chadwick, and that he was likely suggested as a good fit-up to Reginald. But what had Gayle done to ensure she was dumped in prison?'

'She was suing Julia for injuries caused in a nightclub accident,' Billy explained. 'Julia was contesting at the time, claiming a simple accident, but there was proof they'd met before, and Julia had propositioned Gayle's then boyfriend. The papers had got hold of it, and—'

'And they needed to ensure her word was worth shite,' Monroe snarled. 'If Julia wasn't dead already, I'd be dragging her into the cells right now.' He calmed himself. 'What else?'

'About Thomas Williams,' Doctor Marcos nodded to Davey, who brought a clear bag to the front, with what looked like a camera inside. 'Thomas Williams bought this yesterday, had it couriered over to the hotel. It looks like some kind of Wi-Fi webcam, but we don't know if he'd connected it up. We can't get into it, and we don't know if it was even recording yesterday, but we were hoping DC Fitzwarren could have a look.'

'Status on Williams?'

'Conscious but confused,' Davey spoke up now. 'Doesn't remember a thing after five pm yesterday.'

'Convenient. We'll bring him in for questioning too,' Monroe nodded.

'Did you find out anything about Walters?' Declan added, looking at the others. 'He seems to be everywhere. He was at Julia's house after the murder, and in the hotel last night, apparently paying for Thomas's room. I know he claimed that was his job, but there's something not right.'

'Not much, but there's a little out there,' Billy tapped on the keyboard and a passport image came up. 'Mark Walters is actually the *Viscount Marcus Sebastian Walters*; his parents died ten years ago and left him just under six million and a couple of properties. He'd basically been living the rich prick allowance lifestyle, but when mummy and daddy died in a helicopter crash, he went off the rails, travelling around the world, hopping from jet-set party to jet-set party. Disappeared in Asia for a few months and then came home, seemingly with a change of heart. Started working for Norman Shipman in his office about seven years ago, and has been moving up ever since. Probably aiming for a House of Lords position.'

'Where in Asia was he, and when?' Declan asked.

Billy typed on the laptop again.

'Thailand for about six months,' he replied. 'Right before he returned. Why?'

Declan stared at the passport image of the red-haired man who'd been his principal liaison to Norman Shipman. And, as he did, a memory of a conversation he'd had with Jim Sutcliffe about the death of Graham Terry the previous day came to mind.

'He died about a year after Jane did.'

'He'd begun backpacking around the world, but had started on drugs again while in Thailand.'

'He'd been dead in some slum for a couple of weeks before he was found, multiple stab wounds in his chest. They found the killer a week or so later, some woman who lived in the same area. She was dead too, an overdose.'

Graham Terry and Mark Walters had been in Thailand at the same time. It could have been a coincidence, but this felt right, like he was onto something.

'You mentioned he owned two properties,' Declan looked to Billy. 'Is one of them the *Baker Institute*, perhaps?'

Billy searched through some records, looking back at Declan in surprise.

'He doesn't own it, but he holds shares in the company that runs it,' he replied. 'How did you—'

But Declan wasn't listening. Already in his head, he was making connections.

Daniel McCarthy was engaged to Jane Terry, and had been close with Graham.

Jane had died somehow. Daniel blamed himself for it.

Graham travelled to Thailand, and was there at the same time as Mark Walters.

Mark Walters was the mysterious benefactor paying for Daniel's Baker Institute room.

The same institute where the rose petals had come from.

Everything was connected.

But what did it all *mean?*

18

AND FOR YOURSELF

LUKE ASHTON SAT ON HIS CHAIR AND LEANED ON THE DESK, HIS hands on his face when Monroe and Theresa entered. Looking up, he glowered.

'Chosen your side, then,' he hissed. Theresa, ignoring this, sat down across the table from him.

'So, you've been a bloody pain to get hold of,' she said, looking to Monroe who, sitting beside her, turned the recorder on.

'Interview with Luke Ashton, eleven thirty-three am, DCI Monroe and DI Martinez attending,' he said before looking back to Luke. 'Sorry to hear about your father's death, son.'

Luke stared at Monroe, silently. However, as there was no surprise to the statement, Monroe took this as confirmation as to knowledge of the situation.

'Do you want to tell us why you were there that night?' he asked gently.

'Do I get a solicitor?' Luke muttered. Monroe leaned back. 'Do you need one?'

Luke thought about this for a moment.

'I visited him a lot, at the end,' he said. 'Reg. Dad. Whatever you want to call him.'

'Why didn't you tell us he was your father?' Theresa asked.

'We were finished when I found out,' Luke replied. 'I can't remember *how* I found out, but Reg didn't want people to know. I don't think he wanted Michael, his partner, to know, either. That hurt a little, but I got it.'

He smiled.

'I mean, we've all got our secrets, right?'

'Did you know about the book?' Monroe asked. Luke nodded.

'I was helping him with it,' he said. 'It's the reason I was there that night.'

'No other reasons?' Monroe leaned forward. 'After all, your wife was at Thomas Williams' talk.'

'Not been a fan of those, or him for a few years now,' Luke folded his arms.

'Did you know Jane was there?'

'Of course,' Luke replied, but his tone betrayed his expression, and Theresa now leaned closer.

'So you knew they were together when Reginald was killed?'

Luke didn't answer.

'For the recording, Luke Ashton isn't responding,' Theresa said.

'What do you do for a living, Mister Ashton?' Monroe asked. Luke smiled.

'I work for the MOD,' he replied. 'the Ministry of Defence.'

'I know what the MOD is,' Monroe smiled back. 'And what do you do there?'

'I can't say.'

'You can't or you won't?'

Luke shrugged. 'I work in computer decryption. and that's as much as you'll get until you reach my grade.'

'So it's an *I could tell you, but then I'd have to kill you* type of thing?' Theresa nodded. 'Good to know.'

'Tell us what happened the night Reginald died,' Monroe changed direction. Grateful for this, Luke nodded.

'I was with Reg,' he explained. 'I went to my car to pick something up, and when I got back... he was there, on the floor. Dead.'

'Did you see anyone else?'

'No,' Luke shook his head. 'I went to give CPR, but it was too late. I saw I had blood on me, and I just panicked.'

'And that's why you left, without phoning the police?'

'I thought I could find the killer, drive around, maybe see him.'

'But you said you didn't see anyone,' Monroe questioned. 'So how could you know who you were looking for?'

There was a moment of silence in the room, before Luke eventually shrugged.

'I wasn't thinking straight,' he continued. 'Reg didn't want to go to the launch, he hated Tommy. We all did. The prick wouldn't let the books die, you know? So I was helping Reg with his new book. That's why I was there that night. It was pretty much a Tommy Williams exposé.'

He relaxed into the chair, more comfortable now he was talking.

'Tommy didn't realise, none of them did, but the book wasn't an adventure. It was the truth. How we were hand picked, how we were threatened with prison for our families if we told anyone the truth.'

Monroe looked at Theresa. 'Is that true?'

Theresa nodded. 'Pretty much.'

'The book was going to explain everything,' Luke continued. 'How the crimes were staged, and how people that the cabal didn't like would take the rap—'

'Cabal?'

'Yeah. Bruno, Julia, Shipman, even Reg and Michael. They picked the criminals and set them up. After the first two books, we were unquestionable. I could look at anyone, blame them for something, and everyone would believe me.'

His expression darkened.

'Well, unless I was accusing someone of *molestation*, or another of *rape*.'

'I'm guessing you're talking about Bruno Field in the first instance. I'm assuming the second was Thomas? With Eloise Lewis, now Louise Hart?' Monroe enquired.

'Yes.'

'Louise Hart, whose apartment you were arrested in?'

A pause.

'Yes.'

'Who was dead in the next room?'

'Yes.'

'Did you know she was dead when you went there?'

'No.' Luke leaned back, pinching at the bridge of his nose, as if staving off a headache. 'I was worried about her. I'd heard that she was at Tommy's thing, I guessed it didn't end well. I called on her first thing in the morning, but she wasn't there. So, I tried later, and she still didn't answer. I got in through the main door, went to her flat and the door was ajar. I entered and found her on the bed.'

'Did you call the police?' Monroe asked. Luke shook his head.

'Didn't need to,' he replied. 'One of the people living in the apartments recognised me from earlier. *They* called the police.'

'What was your relationship with Miss Hart?' Monroe continued.

'I didn't have one,' Luke stopped pinching at the bridge of his nose. 'We knew each other in passing, and I'd heard about the... Well, about the illness. We'd chatted a few times in the last couple of weeks, nothing more.'

'Did Jane know?'

Luke nodded. 'I don't keep things from my wife.'

'Is that the same the other way around?' Monroe glanced at Theresa as he spoke; she was being unnaturally quiet here. Luke glared at him.

'You mean did I know they were screwing?' he snapped. 'No.'

'Why did you run?' Theresa changed the subject now. 'After burning your blood-stained shirt? Why not simply turn yourself in, save us the hassle of hunting you down?'

'I was scared,' Luke admitted. 'I knew that because I'd gotten blood on me, after trying to save Reg, that I'd be prime suspect. I thought I could get some help, maybe solve the case.'

He smiled; a wry, humourless one.

'I believed my own press, I suppose.'

'Is that why you went to Louise?' Theresa asked again.

'Yeah,' Luke replied softly. 'I knew Tommy wouldn't help me, and I thought Louise could at least give me advice. Both of us were adept at *rock and a hard place*.'

'What did you speak to Louise about?'

'Nothing much,' Luke shifted in his chair. 'Good old days stuff. Although the last time we spoke, a week or so back, she said that Tommy was contacting her again, trying to pressure her into doing stuff.'

'What sort of stuff?' Monroe was writing in his notepad now.

'I don't know,' Luke admitted. 'And when I next saw her, she'd killed herself.'

'You sure it was suicide?' Theresa frowned. Luke nodded.

'Yeah,' he replied. 'She left the door open because she had cats. She wanted to be found quickly.'

'Why did you resist arrest?' Monroe changed subject.

'I didn't,' Luke said simply. 'I was telling them to go check on her, they were telling me to get on the floor. I was annoyed. They tasered me.'

There was a moment of silence.

'She died the same way as Jane Terry,' he eventually spoke. 'Tommy took another.'

'What do you mean?' Theresa asked. 'Tommy took what?'

'Come on, Tessa,' Luke snapped. 'Tommy's toxic. Everyone around him gets hurt or dies. All he gives a shit about is himself. Even the bloody reboot.'

'What reboot?' Theresa insisted. Luke paused in replying, watching her.

'God, you don't even know,' he said. 'You really were so far out of the loop.'

'Tell us now,' Monroe suggested. 'Put us *in* the loop.'

'It was a decade back,' Luke started. 'The twentieth party. You weren't there.'

'I wasn't invited,' Theresa's response was stiff, hurt even. Luke nodded.

'Nobody wanted you there,' he replied. 'And don't do the hurt thing with me. You never cared about us. Christ, you couldn't get out of there fast enough, and you made it perfectly clear there was no love lost on any side.'

'That's not true,' Theresa retorted, but didn't elaborate further. Luke shrugged.

'Either way, the anniversary was a minor affair. We'd all gone because they paid us to. The Tories were back in power since the Blair ousting, and someone in Cameron's cabinet had remembered the *Magpies* were a thing. Tommy was there, doing his usual pitch, saying that there was room for a new series, and someone somewhere started to consider it.'

'I bet Shipman wasn't happy with this,' Monroe mused, 'especially as he was on the Labour benches then.'

'He wasn't, but he still sent his aide, Simpson, to the party in his absence,' Luke replied. 'Snivelling little shit, the man was. Instantly hit it off with Tommy. Cut from the same cloth.'

'Rory Simpson.'

'Yeah,' Luke continued.

'You'd met before?'

'He was around at the end of the books, I think,' Luke thought back. 'But back then I think he made the tea.'

'But he was at the party, twenty years later?'

'Yeah. Anyway, they talked about reforming the *Magpies*. You were out,' he said to Theresa, 'you were deep in the force by then. And you weren't particularly liked by any of us.'

'Feeling's mutual,' Theresa's expression was one of stone.

'I said I wouldn't do anything with that prick, and Jane wasn't happy about returning,' Luke carried on. 'So now they only had Tommy, and maybe Danny. But they had options.'

'Let me guess,' Theresa folded her arms. 'Jane and Graham Terry.'

Luke nodded. 'Jane was a teacher, primary schools.

Graham was some kind of club promoter. They were pressured into getting involved, replacing Jane and me.'

'And who replaced me?' Theresa asked, her eyes widening as she realised. 'No.'

'Louise,' Luke answered. 'They explained that Jane was the original Jane, and that the printing error had been in itself an error, wiping her from history. And, having the *Blue Peter* winner turn up and help gave a nod, a connection to the old team.'

He chuckled.

'And the fact that Danny now had a thing for Jane Terry ensured that while she was in, he was in.'

'So, why didn't this happen?' Monroe asked. Luke shrugged.

'I dunno,' he said. 'I wasn't there.'

He leaned in.

'I heard some rumours though,' he said. 'They were taking a leaf out of the first book, creating the story and fitting up someone for it.'

'Me?' Theresa looked surprised to hear this.

'No,' Luke shook his head. 'They were going after Bruno.'

'Bruno's been gone for decades.'

Luke leaned back in his chair. 'They thought they knew where he was. Working in marketing somewhere in Sheffield. He was apparently happy there. That pissed them off.'

'I thought that he'd run away with the missing millions?' Theresa asked. Luke shrugged.

'Maybe he spent it all. Either way, they were going to fit him up.'

'Fit him up for what?' Monroe asked.

Luke looked at Theresa.

'Look, this was all gossip mongering, so probably

bollocks, but I heard they were discussing having you murdered,' he said, softly. 'And that Bruno would be arrested as the one that did it.'

There was an uneasy pause in the room as both Monroe and Theresa took this in.

'The explosion in Manchester,' Theresa replied. 'That was ten years ago.'

'Yeah,' Luke nodded. 'It was. And I don't know much about what happened, but I know Danny learned of this, and called you up, delaying you just long enough to get there a little too late. You were injured, rather than killed. After that, it was a little too real. Jane Terry threatened to go to the press, claiming she'd been taping meetings. She was going to expose everything. Nothing happened though, and the whole reboot plan fell apart. Louise found out she had Huntingdons disease around then and Graham, seeing his second chance slip away, fell back into drugs and started backpacking through Asia, while Danny asked Jane to marry him.'

Luke shook his head.

'But Tommy, bloody *Tommy* couldn't let it lie,' he snarled. 'Word is that he convinced Louise to help him pressure Jane into staying quiet. That if she spoke to the press, she'd be convicted too, as would Danny, because of his connection to the earlier books miscarriages of justice. I heard that Reg, Julia, Rory, even Reg's bloody husband all took shots at her. They started spreading lies about her professionalism; she lost her job, it was bad.'

'And then she killed herself.' Monroe looked up from his notepad. 'And you did nothing?'

'I didn't know this was happening,' Luke explained defensively. 'I learned this over the last few months, through Reg.

It's why he wanted to write the book, to put the true story out there.'

There was a commotion outside the interview room, and the door opened as Sebastian Klinger entered.

'That's enough of that,' he said. 'My client hasn't had time to properly speak to me, so I'd like this to be ended and a quiet place provided for us to talk. Alone.'

Monroe rose, seemingly unsurprised by the arrival. 'Of course,' he said, waving for Theresa to come with him, turning off the recorder and waving at the CCTV camera to turn off. 'Have as much time as you want,' he continued. 'We have two other suspects to interview.'

'Jane Ashton is under my counsel too,' Klinger retorted. 'I'd suggest—'

'And Tommy Williams?' Theresa interrupted. 'Is he under your wing?'

Sebastian Klinger smiled.

'No, Miss Martinez,' he replied. 'He's not under my wing, as you say. So go wild with him.'

Leaving the interview room, Monroe looked at Theresa.

'Something you want to tell me?' he asked. Theresa looked around to ensure that they were alone.

'Norman Shipman provides Klinger,' she said. 'He's there to sort us out if we have any issues, but he's mainly there to make sure we don't say something stupid and reveal everything. Up to six months ago, it was Michael Chadwick. After the hit and run, Shipman brought in Klinger.'

'Surely this isn't a surprise?' Monroe asked. 'I'm sure this happens a lot.'

'Of course, but the thing is, I've been sure I *know* him,' Theresa looked back to the interview room, as if worried they were being watched. 'Klinger literally appeared out of nowhere about eight years ago. Before that he was apparently on private retainer for a wealthy family, but there're no records, no photos of him.'

Monroe now looked back at the interview room.

'Go on.'

Theresa clenched her jaw. 'I could be completely wrong,' she said. 'The hair's different, and the glasses are new. He's lost a lot of weight, and it's been a few decades, but the moment he said 'under my wing' I got chills.'

'Why?'

'Because I think Sebastian Klinger is *Bruno Field*.'

DECLAN WAS BESIDE BILLY, STARING AT REGINALD Troughton's MacBook as Monroe and Theresa entered the main office.

'Billy, I need you to find everything you can on Sebastian Klinger,' Monroe said as he walked across to them. 'I want to know where he gained his degree, when he was called to the bar, everything—' he stopped. 'What have you found?'

Declan looked back from the laptop.

'Billy broke the code,' he said. 'We've opened Reginald's computer. There's two files on it; one is *The Adventure of the Stolen Innocence,* and the other one is, well, a little strange.'

'Strange?' Monroe walked over.

'Look for yourself,' Billy replied, leaning back. The screen was a block of words, continually repeated across the pages.

One for sorrow Two for joy Three for a girl Four for a boy Five for silver Six for gold Seven for a secret never been told Eight for a wish Nine for a kiss Ten for a life of wedded bliss Eleven for the morrow Twelve for the mirth Thirteen for a funeral Fourteen for a

birth Fifteen for heaven Sixteen for hell Seventeen for the devil and for yourself One for
sorrow Two for joy Three for a girl Four for a boy Five for silver Six for gold Seven for a
secret never been told Eight for a wish Nine for a kiss Ten for a life of wedded bliss
Eleven for the morrow Twelve for the mirth Thirteen for a funeral Fourteen for a birth
Fifteen for heaven Sixteen for hell Seventeen for the devil and for yourself

'The entire document is this,' Billy said. 'About seventy thousand words.'

Declan looked at Monroe.

'This was hidden in a subdirectory,' he said. 'I'm not sure what it is.'

'Research?' Monroe suggested. 'Maybe he needed to note the poem down?'

'Ten thousand times?' Billy shook his head. 'I think this is something more. It was hidden too well.'

He swallowed nervously.

'I think *this*, rather than the book he was writing, is the reason that *Reginald Troughton was killed.*'

19

FOR FATAL WITNESSES

AFTER THE INCIDENT WITH THE PAPARAZZI THE PREVIOUS evening, Mark Walters had arranged for Jane Ashton to be given a room in the *Piccadilly Hyatt* for the night; after all, the photographers were still outside, and the police were working through her house, finishing up their search and, even if they had left by now, and she'd been allowed to return home, there were even more photographers waiting for her there.

Anjli actually respected the idea; keeping Jane out of the public eye was the best thing for her right now, especially in the highly emotional state that she'd been in the previous night. That said, Anjli also wondered whether this had been altruism on Mark's part, or an order from Norman Shipman, ensuring that at least *one Magpie* was under his control.

Jane was waiting for her when she arrived around midday; Anjli had asked Billy to call ahead and warn her of the arrival, as the last thing she wanted was to turn up and find Jane in her underwear.

Although Declan would probably like that, fanboy that he was.

Looking around, she wondered where Declan was; she'd expected him to jump at the chance of interviewing one of his childhood heroes. Maybe the truth about them was souring his palate.

There was however someone else that she recognised in the lobby, rising from the chair and putting aside a copy of *The Guardian* as she walked over.

'Ma'am,' Anjli said, 'I didn't think you were getting involved?'

'That bloody office is claustrophobic,' Bullman replied. 'And with all hands needed right now, I thought a day trip was required. If you're okay with that?'

She sighed.

'Although Monroe will have a field day, knowing he was right.'

'Nobody I'd rather have,' Anjli grinned. And this was true. They'd worked together a lot while Declan had been accused of terrorism a few weeks earlier, and Anjli found she enjoyed working in tandem with Bullman's more relaxed, almost sarcastic level of interrogation.

'You're just saying that, so I put you up for DI,' Bullman smiled as they walked to the elevators. Anjli gave a mock surprise expression.

'Is that a thing?' she asked, astounded. 'Can it be a thing?'

Bullman kept quiet as the doors closed.

THEY HAD GIVEN JANE ASHTON A SUITE, WHICH WAS QUITE generous of Norman Shipman, or rather Mark Walters, as he was likely paying this bill as well. Maybe even the hotel, realising the amount of press outside could give them either a good or bad day, sacrificed a room. There was also the fact that this had been decided around midnight, so the chances were the suite was empty, and there was no major money lost either way.

Jane was in a towelling robe when they arrived; her hair was wet, hanging lankly down her back as she dried it, sitting at the desk and using the hotel hairdryer.

'Sorry,' she shouted over the noise. 'I thought you'd be a little while longer, and I spent too long in the shower. They've said I can stay another night, and I'm making the most of it.'

'Not a problem,' Bullman replied. 'If you want, we can do this downstairs in the lobby?'

'No, I'm good,' Jane smiled, grabbing a brush. 'They've really been great to me here. Even found a change of clothes in my size. Two secs.'

Jane Ashton walked into the bathroom, the door left open.

'So what did you want to talk about?' Jane asked from inside it. Bullman and Anjli looked at each other silently. It was almost as if Jane was treating this like a newspaper or magazine interview.

'You *are aware* we're conducting a murder enquiry?' Bullman replied stiffly.

There was a moment of silence, and Jane emerged back into view, now with a sweater and jeans on.

'Sorry,' she said, almost apologetically. 'It's my defence mechanism. I'm so used to doing interviews back in the day, you know.'

There was a beep on Anjli's phone; opening it, she read

the message. It was from Monroe. Placing the phone back in her pocket, she looked back to Jane, who now sat on the end of the bed, facing the two detectives.

'Last night,' she started. 'I don't know what it was, I think there was something niggling at me all day, you know? Anyway, I'd had a few weird encounters during the afternoon, and I was walking the streets, trying to make sense of it. I went to visit Danny, and we had a walk in his garden.'

'What time was this?'

'Before his dinner, so maybe four? I was in the area.'

'Why were you in Hampstead?'

'I was visiting Highgate Cemetery,' Jane replied without pausing. 'Jane Terry's grave. I do it once a year. After Reginald... I felt I had to go tell her what was happening.'

'You went to talk to a grave,' Anjli confirmed. Jane glared at her.

'You might think it strange, but to some of us it gives peace,' she said, reaching to her side table and picking up her handbag. 'Mind if I smoke?'

Bullman indicated it was fine with her, passing across a glass ashtray as Jane lit up a cigarette, taking a deep drag.

'Okay,' she continued. 'And then you came here?'

'No, then I walked home.' Jane shook her head. 'I mean, I walked to a bus stop and made my way home. I didn't walk from north London. But when I got there, I saw police and press everywhere. I didn't want to be interviewed or papped, so I left.'

'Papped?'

'Hassled by the paparazzi.'

'Understandable,' Bullman was writing in her notebook. 'Where did you go after that?'

'I thought they'd go away, so I went to Leicester Square and watched a film. The new Tom Cruise one.'

'Any good?' Bullman asked.

'He runs a lot.'

'And then?'

'I started having a bad feeling,' Jane leaned back on the bed, her arms propping her up as she answered. 'I don't know why, maybe it was the film, but I realised Tommy had been a little distant the night before, like something big was weighing on his mind. I'd tried to ignore it; after all, we'd done some *off* things ourselves that night, but then I got the message that Julia had died. And I heard Luke was arrested and Louise Hart was dead.'

'How did you hear this?'

'Mark Walters,' Jane pointed at the phone on the hotel suite desk. 'He was letting me know about Luke. The rest came out later.'

'And then you came here,' Anjli noted. Jane nodded.

'I was in Leicester Square, and I thought maybe I should see Tommy,' she explained. 'But then I had a text from him.' She waved to Anjli to pass the phone over. Anjli did, and after opening it, Jane showed a text message, sent the previous night from Thomas Williams' phone.

I'm sorry. I can't go on.

'What would you think if you read that?' Jane asked. Anjli nodded.

'Fair point.'

'Let's talk about a couple of things following this,' Bullman moved on. 'You were recorded by the press while in the lobby. You spoke out.'

'I was stressed and annoyed.' Jane shrugged. 'They pissed me off.'

'I get that,' Bullman nodded. 'You said to one that Thomas had gone to get fast food.'

'*McDonalds*, yes.' Jane nodded.

'And he was gone half an hour?'

'Around that, yes.'

'Long enough to travel to Reginald Troughton, kill him and return.'

Jane stubbed the finished cigarette out in the ashtray on the bed, passing it to Anjli. 'No, I don't think he would do something like that,' she said. 'Reg was his cash cow. Could you put that on the table again? Thanks.'

'Did you know about the side door?' Anjli asked as she did this.

Jane shook her head. 'I only used the main door.'

'Which you used at ten thirty-seven to leave.'

'Well, yeah,' Jane replied. 'I knew the press would be hunting *Magpies* the moment Reginald was announced on the news. The last thing I wanted was to be seen with Tommy.'

'Because you're married.'

Jane stared at Anjli now. 'Are you married, detective...'

'*Detective Sergeant* Kapoor,' Anjli shook her head. 'And no.'

'Then don't presume to know what it's like, yeah?'

Jane sighed.

'Sorry, didn't mean to snap. Luke and me, we're... well, it's complicated. He works for the MOD, and it's all secret, and we can't just tell each other everything when we get home from work. We're in a rut. And Tommy...' she smiled, a faint one, as she finished. 'He was a stress reliever. Nothing more.'

'Did you return home afterwards?' Bullman continued. Jane nodded.

'Yeah, got back around eleven-thirty,' she replied. 'Luke was already asleep, so I just checked the news for any updates and then went to bed.'

'And the following morning?'

'I woke about eight, and Luke was already gone,' Jane admitted. 'I'd taken a tablet, so I was out like a light. Probably bumbled around the house for an hour or so, and then went to the gym.'

'You weren't working?'

'I knew the press would be waiting, so I sent the school principal a text,' Jane held the phone up again, as if to offer it for examination. 'She understood, and to be honest she didn't want press around the kids.'

Anjli waved the phone away.

'It's okay, we'd need to check the cell towers, anyway,' she gave a smile. 'So, after the gym?'

'I had some lunch with a friend, I can give you her details, and then I went to Highgate.'

'Can anyone confirm you were there?'

'Actually, yes,' Jane nodded, leaning closer. 'Something weird happened there, but I think it was an overactive imagination.'

'How so?'

'Well,' Jane started. 'I was at Jane Terry's grave and I was sure I saw someone in the trees, watching me.'

'What did he look like?'

'Funnily, like Derek Sutton,' Jane said. 'But *not*. He was in a hoodie, but it was for a moment, and then he was gone. Probably me thinking about the news report and seeing things, but it was enough to make me run for help.'

She spoke softer.

'We had fans, back in the day. The *wrong* kind of fans, if you know what I mean.'

'Did someone give help?'

'Yes, a couple of ladies who were visiting, and a groundskeeper,' Jane nodded. 'I think his name was Desmond, or Des.'

'Did he find anyone?'

'Christ, no,' Jane almost laughed. 'It was my overactive imagination. I left there and went straight to find Danny, and he calmed me down.'

Anjli looked to Bullman, as if checking whether there was anything else to be asked.

'That's everything we need, I think,' she said, rising. 'Oh, one last thing, if you don't mind. Can I get a selfie?'

Jane was a little surprised at this. 'I'm sorry?'

'Declan, one of our DIs? Big fan of you. I thought it'd be amusing to get one, just to annoy him.'

'Sure, yeah,' Jane shrugged, moving next to Bullman, who passed her phone to Anjli.

'Thanks,' she said as Anjli took the photo. 'Oh, and can I get one of you alone? That way at least we can give Declan something.'

Again, Jane patiently smiled as Anjli took another photo and then, with this done, walked both detectives to the door, promising to let them know if she remembered anything else.

Anjli didn't speak until they reached the elevator.

'Okay, what was the photos thing?' she asked.

'We don't have a good, recent shot of Jane, and unless she's brought in, we won't get one,' Bullman replied. 'And did you see her with the wet hair? It made it darker. That's triggering my Spidey Sense.' She stared off down the corridor.

'And something else is nagging at me, I'm sure I'm missing something—'

She smiled.

'I know what it was,' she said. 'The cemetery. She said that she imagined that someone was watching her, bald in a hoodie.'

'And?'

'And we haven't released that information to the public,' Bullman entered the elevator as it arrived. 'So Jane Ashton's been *talking* to someone.'

———

It was raining when De'Geer arrived at the *Baker Institute,* which made it difficult for him to find someone willing to traipse out into the garden with him to examine a rose bush. In fact, he was about to consider pulling rank and threatening to arrest someone unless they put a coat on and follow him, when Daniel McCarthy emerged from his room, smiling.

'I hear you have a thing for roses,' he said. 'I'll take you if you want.'

De'Geer expressed his gratitude and followed Daniel out into the rain, but there was a small part of him that felt uneasy, probably because *Daniel* made him feel uneasy. There was something about him, as if he knew all the answers before you even thought up the questions. But then again, he was apparently a detective genius, so maybe he did.

'I hear they arrested Tommy for the murders,' Daniel spoke as they walked across the open garden, towards the wall and the bushes that ran along the sides. 'I wasn't surprised.'

'You weren't?' De'Geer was having to hurry to keep up. 'Why?'

'Because he was always a two-faced wanker,' Daniel replied calmly. 'He only ever called when he needed something.'

'When did he last call you?' De'Geer asked.

'About a week back,' Daniel turned left, towards the corner of the garden. 'It was a nice day. And they were serving salmon for dinner. We walked around the garden, just like we're doing now. He went to the toilet behind that tree over there.'

'You don't have toilets here?' De'Geer meant it as a joke, but he'd forgotten that Daniel McCarthy didn't seem to *do* jokes.

'We have lots of toilets,' Daniel corrected. 'I can show them all to you. But Tommy was only caught short for a wee. He ran to the back rather than spend five minutes going through the institute.'

He smiled; a knowing, secretive smile.

'But he didn't wee,' he breathed. 'He pretended, but he made a mistake.'

'What?'

'He forgot that I'm clever,' Daniel replied, walking to a bush at the edge of the left-hand side of the wall, beside a large, overhanging oak tree. 'He treated me like he'd treat one of *you*.'

He stopped at a bush, and De'Geer could see several white roses blooming from it.

'This is the same strand of rose as the ones found in the second book,' Daniel explained as he stroked the petals of one. 'It was a gift from a friend when I—well, when I came here.'

He smiled.

'He was allowed to plant it here, so I'd aways have something from the *good old days* to remind me.'

'Were they?' De'Geer asked. 'Good old days?'

'Oh, yes,' Daniel's voice had taken the light sing song tone again as he spoke. 'My life fell apart when I was a grownup. Being with Jane was the only good thing.'

'Jane Terry.'

Daniel nodded, staring at the roses. 'Tommy didn't need a wee,' he said. 'He needed time by the roses. When I came by later to tend them, I saw that a dozen petals had been removed.'

'And Thomas Williams did that?'

Daniel shrugged, still looking at the roses. 'I can't prove it,' he said. 'But they were definitely taken that day, and Thomas didn't wee behind the tree.'

'How do you know for sure he didn't?' De'Geer asked.

'Because I went behind and checked after he was gone,' Daniel explained with a smile. De'Geer didn't dare ask how Daniel checked such a thing, and images of Daniel on his hands and knees sniffing the base of the tree came to mind.

'Thank you for this,' he said, looking at the roses. 'May I take a petal too? For comparison?'

'Of course,' Daniel said, picking a fallen petal from the ground and passing it to De'Geer. 'Here, take this one. No need to damage the roses.'

De'Geer placed the single petal into a ziplock bag and, thanking Daniel, turned to leave. But, as he walked away, a sudden urge paused him, looking back to where Daniel had been standing.

Where Daniel was *still* standing.

Staring at De'Geer.

Smiling.

20

FOR PRIME SUSPECTS

WHEN THOMAS WILLIAMS WAS RELEASED FROM HOSPITAL later that afternoon, he wasn't brought directly to Temple Inn; with Luke still there, and the press outside hoping for a scoop, it was decided to take him to a closer Command Unit, in this case an interview room in New Scotland Yard itself. Declan wasn't a fan of this building; he preferred to work on the edges of the law rather than under the direct scrutiny of it, but there was nothing he could do, and so Declan and Anjli, recently arrived back from the *Piccadilly Hyatt* with Bullman (to Monroe's great delight) reluctantly travelled along the embankment to sit down with the prime suspect in not only Reginald Troughton's murder, but now also the murders of Julia Clarke and Rory Simpson; although that last one seemed by *proxy*.

'What do you reckon the chances are of him playing the memory loss game?' Anjli asked as they made their way through security, showing their IDs and passing through the metal detectors. 'I mean, you're the expert on him.'

'I was the expert on him when he was a kid,' Declan replied. 'I haven't got a bloody clue about the grownup.'

Thomas Williams was waiting for them in an interview room; his face was bruised, and he had a wicked-looking bandage on his head. He'd lost a lot of blood through a vicious gash on his temple, made when he slipped and fell, but the doctors at the hospital had explained that he didn't seem to have a concussion, although he would have a killer headache for a few days.

As Declan and Anjli sat down opposite him, he glowered angrily at them.

'This is a joke,' he muttered. 'I'm not even safe in my hotel.'

'I don't see a solicitor,' Anjli said conversationally. 'Did you request one?'

'Do I need one?' Thomas replied cautiously. Declan looked up from the papers that he was arranging.

'Depends on whether or not you intend to answer our questions,' he said.

'I'm innocent,' Thomas replied. 'I don't have anything to hide.'

'Great, then let's begin,' Declan smiled, pressing the record button. There was a slow beep as the recording prepared and, once it stopped, Declan looked to it as he spoke.

'First interview with Thomas Williams, DI Walsh and DS Kapoor attending, two-fifteen pm,' he said. 'Mister Williams has waived his rights to a solicitor.'

'For the moment,' Thomas muttered.

'For the moment,' Declan agreed. Then, turning to Anjli, he nodded.

'Mister Williams,' she started, leaning closer. 'Where were you on the night of the murder of Reginald Troughton?'

'You know this,' Thomas snapped. 'I've already told your DCI. The Scot with the attitude.'

'That was a conversation, not an interview,' Anjli replied. 'We need a reply for the record.'

Thomas shrugged. 'I was at a talk in *Waterstones*. I was launching a new series of books.'

'And then?'

'I met with Jane Ashton,' Thomas said, but his voice was softer, more cautious.

'Was this expected?' Declan asked. Thomas shook his head.

'I haven't seen her for years,' he replied. 'Was completely out of the blue.' He winced a little. 'Sorry, my head still hurts.'

'No worries,' Declan looked at his notes. 'For the record, Mister Williams is suffering from a painful head wound. And you went back to your hotel for dinner, right?'

'Yes,' Thomas nodded. 'I didn't want to find the fans following us. I'm fine with it, but she isn't.'

'CCTV shows you going to your room,' Anjli interrupted. 'Not to the restaurant. I'm guessing you were considering room service?'

Thomas paused for a moment. Then, as if deciding something, his body language changed, and he slumped back.

'We weren't in the room for food,' he said.

'You were there for something else?' Declan asked.

'Come on, don't be a dick,' Thomas snapped. 'We were screwing, okay? Having an affair. Doing the nasty. Whatever the hell you want to call it. I didn't say this last time because I was trying to keep Jane out of it.'

Declan nodded.

'I understand,' he said. 'So, for the record, you didn't order room service.'

'No.'

'And you didn't go out for takeout?'

'You saw we didn't,' Thomas muttered. 'I know you've been checking the CCTV.'

'True, but we both know that there's another door out, one that isn't covered,' Declan watched Thomas for a reaction; all he got was surprise.

'That's locked,' Thomas said. 'Always is.'

'Wasn't yesterday,' Anjli interjected.

'I didn't know,' Thomas looked to her.

'You just told us you knew it was locked,' Anjli replied calmly.

'Come on,' Declan almost laughed. 'You've booked that room deliberately for the last three times. You're telling me you never knew?'

'I didn't book them!' Thomas half rose as he replied. 'The publisher ordered it! They go on what—' he stopped.

'Something the matter?' Declan asked.

'There are many people involved in the public events,' Thomas stated warily.

'I see,' Declan nodded. 'And you don't want to put anyone who doesn't need to be, into the spotlight. So let's make it easier for you.'

He leaned closer.

'How much say does Norman Shipman have in your events?'

Thomas opened and shut his mouth, and Declan knew he was on the right track. In fact, he wondered if he could play a hunch right now.

'Or is it Mark Walters that liaises with the publisher?'

'I don't know who in the office organises it,' Thomas replied carefully. 'I've spoken to both Rory and Mark over the years.'

Declan looked to Anjli as she wrote this down.

'So, let's go back to dinner,' he said. 'You're stating that you had no food while together?'

Thomas shook his head. 'We didn't have time, if you know what I mean.'

Declan nodded at this, and Anjli took the hint, pushing across the table a half-torn receipt, held within a clear plastic folder.

'For the recording, I am showing Mister Williams a receipt, found in his room's wastebasket,' she said. 'It's a *McDonalds* receipt, picked up from the Piccadilly *McDonalds* on the night in question at nine twenty-two pm.'

Thomas stared at the receipt in confusion. 'I don't know how that got there.'

'Jane Ashton told journalists last night that you had left for fast food, and were gone for half an hour.'

'I didn't—' Thomas looked around the room, as if expecting someone to leap out going *gotcha*. 'I swear, we just had sex.'

Declan nodded again, and Anjli brought out a larger, clear bag. This one had a mask within.

'For the recording, I'm showing Mister Williams a full head latex mask, in the style of a 'bald man',' she said. 'Inside the mask are strands of hair, matching Thomas Williams.'

She pulled out two more clear bags, pushing them across the table.

'It was found with these gloves, with Thomas Williams' DNA inside and Reginald Troughton's blood on the outside, and these rose petals, which match the same ones found at Julia Clarke's murder scene.'

'No...' Still in his chair, Thomas did his best to back away from them. 'Where did you find them?'

'Under your bathroom sink,' Declan replied. 'Did you walk to Temple Inn or grab a taxi when you left the hotel?'

'I didn't leave, I swear,' Thomas looked at Declan pleadingly. 'Ask Jane. She'll tell you.'

'I don't think Jane's the best alibi for you right now,' Declan nodded to Anjli, and she passed across a piece of A4 printout.

'I'm showing Mister Williams a printout of a text message,' she explained. 'A message sent from his phone, but then deleted.'

'I don't understand,' Thomas read the text. 'What does it mean? Who did I send it to?'

'*Tell anyone and I kill your family. Finish him tomorrow or I do the same,*' Thomas read. 'I think it's quite self explanatory, don't you? It was sent to Louise Hart at ten-thirty three on the night of Reginald Troughton's murder.'

'Louise?' Thomas was clutching at his temple with one hand now. 'I don't even know her phone number.'

'Her card was on the table beside your phone,' Declan replied. 'Given to you the night before, when you spoke to her at the signing. Witnesses say the confrontation seemed argumentative.'

'The night... The signing...' Thomas' eyes widened. 'Jesus, that was Louise? It's been so long...'

'So long for a woman whose name and number is in your contacts list?' Anjli shook her head. 'A woman who, the morning after this text was sent, went to St James's Park and murdered Rory Simpson?'

'No, this can't be!' Thomas leaned back in his chair. 'Speak to her! She'll tell you—'

'Louise Hart committed suicide yesterday afternoon,' Declan interrupted, his tone harsh and cold.

There was a moment of silence in the room. Thomas stared blankly at the two detectives.

'How did you fall over, Mister Williams?' Anjli asked. 'Last night?'

'I don't remember.'

'Do you remember drinking the entire contents of the minibar?'

'I... I don't remember.'

'What's the last thing that you *do* remember?' Declan asked. Thomas closed his eyes, scrunching them tightly as he tried to gain any sort of memory from the previous twenty-four hours.

'I remember ordering lunch,' he replied, but now his voice was higher, almost a whine.

'You don't remember the afternoon?'

Thomas shook his head, and tears were welling up in his eyes.

'No, it's blurry.'

'Let me tell you what I think,' Anjli leaned back as she watched Thomas. 'I think you arranged for Louise Hart to meet with you at the signing. I think you told her to kill Rory, and then used Jane Ashton as a convenient alibi while killing Reginald, using the unlocked door to the suite that you've repeatedly used.'

'No...'

'I then think that after Rory was murdered, you went to Julia Clarke and drowned her before returning here and drinking yourself into a stupor.'

She cocked her head slightly as she watched him.

'Was it a celebration? The drinks?'

'I... *I can't remember!*' Thomas shouted.

Declan decided it was time to change the subject again.

'When did you last see Louise?' he asked.

'Ten years ago,' Thomas wasn't as arrogant or as entitled as he'd been at the start of the interview. Declan almost felt sorry for him.

'Was this the reboot?' he continued, nodding. 'Yeah, we know about it all. Luke explained it to us.'

'Luke wasn't in the room. He knows shit,' Thomas muttered.

'So enlighten us,' Anjli commented. 'Tell us how Rory Simpson convinced you to do it all over again.'

Thomas stared at Anjli for a long moment before continuing.

'Rory came in at the end of the books,' he explained. 'Shipman was getting cold feet by then. He wasn't happy with the way the party was going. Then we had the fallout, Bruno stealing the millions—'

'You know that for definite?' Declan asked. Thomas shrugged.

'I don't know what his issue was. All I knew was that after twenty years, Reg, Jim, Rory, Julia, they were all coming back on board. But they wanted to remove the troublemakers, so they dumped Tessa and Luke to the side.'

'I get why Tessa was dumped, we already know she wasn't well liked, but why Luke? He was the most popular character,' Declan asked.

Thomas went to reply, but bit it back at the last moment.

'Because I wanted to be the lead for a change.'

'So you have your new team of you, Louise, Jane and

Graham Terry and Daniel,' Anjli read from her notes. 'No dog?'

'No bloody dog,' Thomas muttered. 'Although they gave us a bloody stupid talking computer that had its name.'

'Didn't last long though,' Declan mused, watching Thomas. 'Didn't even get a book out.'

'Jane kept to tradition,' Thomas muttered sourly. 'Quit the band before we started the first book. There was an incident involving an ex-*Magpie*—'

'The explosion in Manchester,' Declan added. Thomas nodded.

'Jane thought we caused it,' he replied. 'Silly bitch didn't realise the books were fiction.'

'Were they?' Declan asked. 'I mean, Derek Sutton, Gayle Holland...'

'Above my pay grade,' Thomas smiled, but it was a feral, cunning one. 'Can't blame the kids.'

'But you weren't kids this time.'

'No,' Thomas sadly shook his head. 'No, we weren't.'

'What happened after it fell apart?'

Thomas thought for a moment. 'Graham fell off the wagon, Eloise, or Louise then disappeared, Jane... Jane died.'

There was a moment of silence.

'You can see how bad this looks, right?' Declan asked. Silently, Thomas nodded.

'I didn't do anything,' he mumbled. 'I didn't kill anyone.'

'Not doing anything and not killing someone are two different things,' Declan leaned back. 'Even if you're innocent of the latter, your figurative fingerprints are all over a ton of different events, from setting Bruno and Luke up to the issues with Eloise Lewis—'

'We patched things up!' Thomas whined.

'Then why were you arguing two nights ago?'

Thomas started to cry; soft, silent tears streamed down his face.

'Because I didn't recognise her,' he whispered. 'She was my Jane, and I didn't recognise her.'

DECLAN STOOD OUTSIDE THE ENTRANCE OF NEW SCOTLAND Yard, breathing in the afternoon air as Anjli emerged out of the building to join him.

'What do you think?' she asked.

'Nailed dead to rights,' Declan replied. 'There's no way that a court would consider him innocent. He's got no real alibi for the times of the murders, the texts alone show coercion of Louise and testimony from Jane has him leaving the hotel.'

'But?' Anjli watched Declan carefully.

'As mad as it sounds, I think he's telling the truth,' Declan replied sullenly. 'He's a terrible human and a piece of garbage and all that, but I genuinely think he's being set up.'

Anjli nodded.

'Me too,' she said. 'But if it's not him, then who?'

'That's the problem,' Declan sighed audibly. 'Louise Hart can't be interviewed, so she's out. Luke could have killed Reg, but then there's the bald man. Possibly Daniel, maybe even Louise?'

'Jane?'

'If she's throwing him to the wolves, she has to be at the hotel, or else he'd have given her up,' Declan shook his head. 'But she and Luke may have planned this. There's more going on here than we realise. We need to work out who has cast iron alibis for the murders and work back from there. We also need to find Bruno Field, and work out if he's the next potential victim.'

'Bruno? Why would you think that?' Anjli reached into her pocket, pulling out her phone as she spoke.

Declan shrugged. 'He's the only one left in that photo, and there's a lot more animosity for him out there than the others.' He started for the road, and the journey back to Temple Inn.

'Someone has a lot of money in their pocket. Enough to convince people to kill.'

He paused, however, noting that Anjli hadn't followed him, still reading her phone.

'Problem?' he asked. Anjli turned the phone to show the screen to him; it was the BBC NEWS app.

'I had a name alert,' she said as he read the lead story.

DEREK SUTTON TO BE RELEASED FROM PRISON

'Well, that's about to make things a lot more interesting,' Declan said as they started back towards Temple Inn.

21

FOR RACEHORSES

the offices, Monroe and Theresa beside him.

'You know, you could just share the Netflix account, and save you all having to watch the same screen,' he joked. Monroe moved aside, and Declan could see two images; one was the man with the badger haircut, the solicitor Klinger; the other was Bruno Field.

'Glad you're here, laddie,' Monroe waved him over. 'And you, lassie.' He pointed at the screen. 'We're playing *Guess Who.*'

Declan stared at the two images, looking at Billy. 'Same?'

'Possibly,' Billy was playing with Photoshop, stretching and morphing a third image, which was both images on top of each other. 'There's weight loss, and the hair's different, but the eyes and the nose are matching. It could be.'

Anjli leaned in. 'We heard Bruno was working in Sheffield,' she said. 'Any way to check?'

'Already ahead of you,' Billy tapped on his keyboard and

another of the monitors lit up. 'Apparently he quit the marketing firm ten years ago.'

'Two years before Mister Klinger here appeared,' Monroe mused. 'New identity, legend, driving licence, everything.'

'That costs,' Theresa replied. 'You can't get something this good for less than maybe fifty grand.'

'Unless the government do it,' Anjli nodded. 'Maybe we should have a chat with the Guv's ex-wife—' she stopped herself. 'Sorry.'

'No offence taken,' Monroe smiled. 'If I thought she could help, I'd be the first on the call.'

'I suppose he could have saved up,' Billy suggested.

'Or maybe he stole the missing millions, and now he's spending it,' Declan suggested to the group. 'Nobody's claimed it.'

'Maybe we should call him out of his meeting with Luke and then arrest him for questioning?' Billy suggested. Monroe looked to Bullman's office.

'I'll pass it by the higher up,' he replied, leaving the group and walking over to the office. Declan went to walk over to his desk, but stopped as another image on the bank of monitors caught his eye.

'Why is there a selfie of Bullman and Jane Ashton?' he asked. Anjli grinned.

'Jealous?'

'Little bit.'

Billy brought the second image up on the primary screen, but here it was against a transparent background, with no Bullman. This one was an image of Jane Ashton with nothing behind her.

'Bullman asked me to have a play with this,' Billy explained as he pulled up adjustment layers. On the screen, the image of Jane changed, as her wet, dark blonde hair suddenly changed to brunette.

'God, that's the spit of Louise Hart,' Theresa muttered. Anjli nodded.

'That's what Bullman thought it would be,' she said. 'Close enough for doubt, anyway. We should send this to De'Geer, get him to take it to that coffee guy in St James's Park.'

Anjli walked off to her desk as Declan and Theresa still stared at the screens.

'Your ex-wife called,' Theresa said, out of the blue. Declan looked at her as she continued. 'She's given me a time tomorrow to meet your daughter, so if there's anything you want me to say to her, write it down before then.'

'Sure, thanks,' Declan replied. 'I mean it. Thanks.'

Theresa smiled warmly and walked off to the desks, leaving Declan and Billy alone at the monitors.

'Bruno has to be the lawyer,' Billy muttered as he looked back at Declan. 'And that's not even the craziest thing we've heard here.'

Declan laughed. 'What do we know about this missing money?' he asked.

'You think it could be connected?' Billy started tapping on the keyboard. 'I'll be honest, I don't think I'll find much. And we didn't find any piles of cash under the beds of Reginald or Julia.'

'Where *would* you find piles of cash?' Declan was thinking aloud now. 'Like four million pounds' worth?'

'Are you asking me rhetorically, or because you know I come from money?' Billy asked suspiciously.

'Can't it be both?' Declan smiled. Billy thought for a moment.

'That'd be straight into a bank if it was me,' Billy said. 'Probably Swiss, maybe Cayman Islands. All you need is a twelve digit account number and a password.'

'How would you ensure nobody else got into it, though?' Declan was looking at another of the screens, where the strange, repeated poem that Reginald had been writing was revealed.

'I'd make sure I'd hidden the bloody things well,' Billy replied. 'Maybe commit it to memory, like a phone number.'

'Yeah, but if you forget even one number, you lose it forever,' Declan remembered something his daughter had told him, something about cryptocurrencies, back during the Bernard Lau case, before he'd joined Monroe's band of merry misfits. 'What about *seed phrases?*'

'Aren't used in banking,' Billy shook his head. 'Banks are numbers. Seed phrases are only really used in crypto, and are usually a list of words...' he stopped, pulling up the image of the note found in Reginald's house.

Joyous winds blow hard
Mirthless through the dales
Hellacious tales of bards
Birthing hidden tales
Secretive and scarred
Devils Holy Grails
Kissing 'til you're barred
Wishing you will fail

'Seed phrases,' he muttered, pointing at the document on the second monitor.

One for sorrow Two for joy Three for a girl Four for a boy Five for silver Six for gold

Seven for a secret never been told Eight for a wish Nine for a kiss Ten for a life of wedded

bliss Eleven for the morrow Twelve for the mirth Thirteen for a funeral Fourteen for a

birth Fifteen for heaven Sixteen for hell Seventeen for the devil and for yourself

'It's the racehorse joke,' he whispered. 'Has to be.'

'Enlighten me about the racehorses,' Declan smiled. He could see that Billy was onto something; he just didn't know what it was. In answer, Billy quickly wrote on a post-it note, passing it to Declan.

11 was a racehorse 22 was 12 1111 race 22112

'That's gibberish,' Declan replied.

'Read it aloud,' Billy said, writing on another note.

'Eleven was a racehorse,' Declan started. 'Twenty-two was twelve—'

'Stop,' Billy passed Declan the second note. 'Now read it *phonetically.*'

'One-one was a racehorse, two-two was one too, one-one won one race, two-two won one too.' Declan smiled. 'Clever. And how does this relate?'

'Instead of the numbers being words, the words are numbers,' Billy pointed at the screen. 'One for sorrow, two for joy. So joy is...'

'Two,' Declan looked at the line of words. 'Which makes Mirth twelve.'

Billy was already writing the numbers down. After a moment, he showed Declan.

2 12 16 14 7 17 9 8

'Eight numbers,' Billy shook his head. 'Not enough.'

'Yes there are,' Declan took the notepad and pen and rewrote the numbers below.

2 1 2 1 6 1 4 7 1 7 9 8

'Twelve numbers,' he said. 'To what, we don't know.'

'Bloody writers,' Billy smiled. 'Always making things complicated.'

'At least it's not a bloody *anagram safe*,' Declan replied, remembering the *MacNeale & Urban* letter combination safe that Malcolm Gladwell had owned.

'I can compare these to Swiss bank numbers,' Billy was already typing the numbers into his computer. 'The problem is that people use Swiss banks for a reason, to ensure people like us *can't* find things.'

'So go in as an account holder,' Declan suggested. 'Find the bank and type in the account number. Use Reginald's name as the user ID.'

'We'd still need a six letter pass code,' Billy replied.

Declan counted on his fingers.

'Try *Magpie*,' he smiled. 'The universe has crapped on us enough times. Maybe this time it'll throw us a bone.'

'Even if we get in, it probably won't give us the account details of who's been using it,' Billy was typing as he spoke, scanned websites already flashing past as he worked.

'But it might give transactions, right?' Declan was already working the possible options through this in his head. 'If we find a chunk of money is removed at the same time as, say, a house is bought, or some *fake ID*, then we have a solid connection to move on.'

Billy stopped.

'It can't be Troughton,' he said. 'He took the last book gig because he was broke. Why would he do that if he had all this money waiting for him?'

Declan patted Billy on the shoulder. 'Let's see if this is an account, first,' he said. 'We'll burn the other bridges when we get to them. And while you're at it, think of anything else that needs twelve one-digit numbers.'

'What are you going to do?' Billy asked as Declan grabbed his jacket. Declan looked at Theresa, nodding for her to join him.

'I'm going to visit a politician,' he said.

NORMAN SHIPMAN STORMED THROUGH THE CORRIDORS OF Westminster in a foul mood; he'd been about to attend a bill reading that was important to his constituents, and he knew painfully that at his age, there weren't many of those left.

He'd received the message ten minutes earlier from Charles sodding Baker. Seemed like Sir Hiss had got his knickers in a twist over some *Star Chamber* business, and as the *de facto* head of it right now, it would be up to Norman to fix whatever issues Baker had. As much as being in control empowered Norman, he was looking forward to the day that he could give it up.

'Are you sure you don't need me to go for you?' Mark Walters half ran beside him; almost half Norman's age and still hurrying to keep up.

'*Star Chamber* business doesn't concern you,' he replied, waving Mark off. 'We'll catch up back at the office after I've sorted this, and after I've been to the bill reading.'

They were in the Central Lobby now; a beautiful and ornate, eight-sided meeting area for members of both houses, although many preferred not to meet here, if only because both the public and the press could get in, and secret deals weren't exactly secret when a BBC News crew were filming you. With Mark veering off down one of the side corridors, Norman carried on down the main corridor towards the Great Hall, and the small tearoom that was beside the entranceway. It wasn't a usual spot for meetings, but it was the nearest thing to 'outside the halls of power' that you could get without actively standing on the lawn itself.

Charles was sitting at a table in the corner as Norman entered, the full-length window behind him, giving Norman a view of the fountain of New Palace Yard, installed in 1977 to commemorate the Silver Jubilee of Elizabeth II. Based on the lost and re-discovered medieval fountain of Henry VI, the fountain stood in an octagonal pool, a large welded steel sculpture decorated with depictions of birds and beasts from six continents, topped by a gilded crown. Norman thought it was horrible; he also found it amusing that they had unveiled it the same year that he had arrived in Parliament, following a closely fought by-election in April.

It's also not worked for five years, he thought to himself. *Bugger got to retire before me.*

'Norman,' Charles smiled, pointing to a scone and a cup of tea on the table facing him. 'I got you a cream tea. I hope I got it right.'

'What the bloody hell are you playing at?' Norman asked, sitting down. 'We're a clandestine organisation. And you're the most visible bloody Tory out there.'

'I'm performing a favour for a friend,' Charles replied, rising from his chair and nodding to the side doors, where Declan and Theresa stood. 'They needed ten minutes with you.'

Rather than being annoyed at this, Norman Shipman's eyes widened in delight.

'Tessa!' he explained, pulling Theresa into a bearhug. 'Why didn't you tell me you were in town?'

'I did,' Theresa replied, pulling away and bringing Declan forward. 'This is—'

'I know who DI Walsh is,' Norman nodded. 'Perhaps we should sit?'

As Charles, nodding to Declan, left the cafe, Norman, Declan and Theresa sat at the table.

'Sorry for your loss,' Declan started. 'We heard about Rory.'

'Yes, utter shock,' Norman replied. 'But I don't understand why you're involved in it?'

Declan looked to Theresa for a moment before turning back.

'Because you asked us to,' he said. 'Or, rather, Mark Walters asked us to on your behalf.'

Norman frowned at this. 'He did? He didn't tell me.'

'There seems to be a lot that Mark hasn't been telling you,' Theresa continued. 'If it's okay, we'd like to ask you some quick questions. Just give us some simple, mainly yes or no answers.'

'Do I need a solicitor?' Norman looked to Declan, who shook his head.

'No, but I think someone will be later,' he smiled. 'You were involved in creating the *Magpies*, yes?'

Norman looked at Theresa. 'Well, if my God-daughter's here, I'm guessing you already know that's a yes.'

Declan nodded. 'Thank you. Now, did you keep involved with the *Magpies* after you moved across to Labour?'

'Of course not,' Norman replied. 'It was a Tory thing.'

'What about the anniversaries?'

'I attended a couple,' Norman admitted. 'That was it.'

'The twentieth anniversary bash?'

'No.'

'Did you send Rory Simpson to it in your stead?'

'No.'

Norman frowned.

'That was a leading question,' he said, looking at Theresa. 'Was he there?'

'Yeah,' she replied. 'And it's worse than that. Norman, were you involved in a rebranding, a reboot of the *Magpies*, using Rory Simpson as your proxy?'

'Of course not!' Norman's voice rose. 'That would be unethical!'

He looked at Declan.

'What is this?'

'Sir, we believe that Rory Simpson used his position in your team to push to create a new version of the *Magpies*, featuring Thomas Williams, Louise Hart, Daniel McCarthy and Jane and Graham Terry.'

'He said nothing to me about it,' Norman muttered. 'When was this?'

'Ten years ago.'

'Christ, we'd just been in the middle of a Labour Leader election back then,' Norman replied. 'There was no way I could have been involved. I was being pulled in a dozen different directions. I'm guessing that Rory could have been working on his own initiative.'

'Do you currently provide legal assistance to the *Magpies*, in the form of lawyer Sebastian Klinger?' Declan continued.

'Never heard of the man,' Norman replied. 'Look, if it makes things quicker, I haven't had anything to do with the

Magpies, bar Tessa here for a good twenty years or more. I left the whole experiment the day I walked across the Commons.'

Declan opened his notepad.

'I had a feeling you'd say that, sir,' he said. 'I tried to contact you, on the day that Rory was murdered, but was told you weren't talking to the police.'

'Rory was murdered?' Norman was astonished. Declan looked up.

'You didn't know this?'

'How would I know this?' Norman looked at Theresa now. 'What's going on?'

'Let me give you a timeline,' Declan said, 'and this should explain everything. On the morning that Rory Simpson was murdered, I came to speak to you at Portcullis House. Understandably, you were busy. Instead, I spoke to Mark Walters.'

'That's right,' Norman replied. 'In that he'd be the one who took on that role, not that I was aware of you.'

'Mister Walters told me he would be our liaison to you. I next saw him later the same day, when he met me at Julia Clarke's house.'

'Yes, I heard about Julia. Shame.'

'He said at that time that there was a belief that Rory Simpson had been poisoned, and wanted our forensics to confirm. He said, and I quote, *I've already spoken to Norman and he understands, and stands beside the idea.* I'm guessing he hadn't, and you didn't.'

Norman was glowering now. 'I didn't know any of this.'

'Maybe he was trying to keep some of the stress from you,' Theresa answered.

'Did you ask Mark Walters to cover the expenses of Daniel McCarthy's stay at the *Baker Institute?*'

'God no!'

'Did your office arrange and cover the expenses of Thomas Williams' hotel suites whenever he was in London?'

'It's a Labour office!' Norman retorted. 'Why would we fund a *Tory experiment!* Bloody *BadgerLock* would cover that!'

'And you wouldn't liaise with them at—'

'You seem to not be listening to me, DI Walsh,' Norman interrupted angrily, his face flushing. 'I've already told you I have had nothing to do with the *Magpies* for two decades.'

'Then this is a memo that wasn't passed to either Rory Simpson or Mark Walters,' Declan replied. 'As both have been keeping you out of the loop while using your name to forward as-yet unknown intentions.'

'I'm going to bloody kill them,' Norman hissed. 'Well, Mark, anyway.'

'Actually, I'd like you to hold on that,' Declan smiled. 'You see, I've had an issue with Mister Walters for a while now. There's something a little off, and I want to see how much rope he'll take from you before he hangs himself.'

'When you do that, call me,' Norman muttered, angrily spreading clotted cream on his scone and furiously biting into it. 'I'll help string the bugger up myself.'

Declan looked to Theresa, who gave an approving nod. He knew that somewhere, a cog had clicked into place in this, and the end was moving into sight. Mark Walters had been playing the police from the start. He'd ensured that Theresa was involved in the case rather than risking her speak to her God-father. He'd aimed the police at Rory Simpson's death, and therefore Louise Hart. And, more importantly, he'd embedded himself into the lives of the modern day *Magpies*, hook, line and sinker.

The only thing that Declan couldn't work out was *why?*

22

FOR MASKS AND LEGENDS

MONROE WAITED UNTIL KLINGER LEFT THE INTERVIEW ROOM before cornering him.

'Can I have a wee word?' he asked, a disarming smile on his face. 'In my office, perhaps?'

Reluctantly, and claiming that he had to be at Belmarsh soon for Derek Sutton's release, Sebastian Klinger followed Monroe down the stairs and into the main office, taking the offered seat facing Monroe as, after shutting the door, the grizzled DCI sat down to face the solicitor.

'I've got a problem, and I'm hoping you can assist me,' he said.

'I'm probably out of your pay grade,' Klinger smiled. 'I charge a lot.'

'Ach, it's not for me,' Monroe shook his head. 'The problem is *Magpies* related. And you represent them all, right?'

'Only Jane and Luke Ashton, and Daniel McCarthy.'

'Aye, you mentioned you don't cover Tommy Williams,'

Monroe nodded. 'But you don't represent Theresa Martinez either?'

'Not to my knowledge,' Klinger shrugged. 'But then I represent many people, always changing.'

'She seems to think you do.'

'She seems to be mistaken.'

'Must be odd for you,' Monroe leaned back in his chair, 'you know, representing the *Magpies* and the man they put away.' He pulled out a bottle of whisky and two glasses. 'Drink?'

'No, thank you.'

Monroe nodded, putting the bottle away. 'Aye, that's probably not a good idea during work hours, anyway.'

He rose and walked to his bookcase, picking a bottle of water from the side. Walking back, he poured two waters, passing one to Klinger.

'In case you're parched after your long talks with Tommy,' he offered. 'And so you can be on form with Derek.'

Patiently, Klinger took the glass and placed it back on the desk as Monroe sat back down.

'Derek Sutton understands the complexities of the situation,' Klinger straightened in his chair. 'And like several of the *Magpies*, he too has had his last three decades defined by a decision in a Westminster backroom. We'll be commenting on that tomorrow, when we have a press conference about his release today.'

'Aye, I see that,' Monroe smiled, but there was no humour in it. 'The bastards in that backroom, playing God with people's lives. It makes me sick. It must make you sick too, aye?'

Klinger didn't reply. In fact, he was looking incredibly uncomfortable.

'What did you want to talk about?' he asked.

'I've been doing a lot of audial research,' Monroe said, leaning forward and knitting his hands together in front of him. 'I had a pal, in Glasgow. He was a true Scot, you know? The whole *jings, hoots mon* kinda accent was going strong for him. And then, when he came down to London, he had the right royal piss taken out of him. Wanted to be an officer in the *Royal Marines*. Was almost laughed out of the room. Nobody would follow a man with such a caricature of an accent.'

'Shame.'

'Aye, but the thing is, my pal? He went to elocution sessions. He learned, over time, to lose the broad Scot's accent, and make it more *'generic south England'*. After a couple of years down here, you wouldn't have guessed where he came from. He had the most middle-class accent you could get.'

'Impressive,' Klinger was obviously boring of this conversation. Monroe leaned in closer.

'But sometimes, late in our cups, when we'd had a few and were putting the world to rights? My *old* pally, the *Scot,* would come back. In turns of phrase, or colloquialisms. You see, Mister Klinger, no matter how hard we change things, your accent can be as damning as a fingerprint sometimes. Especially to those who know you well.'

He looked to the window.

'Like wee Theresa Martinez out there. Well, not there right now, she's out on a job. But before she went, she came to me with a concern, something rattling around in her brain. She thought you were *Bruno Field.* Can you believe that!'

He laughed, with Klinger nervously following along.

'Of course, I knew she had to be wrong,' Monroe continued. 'But she had such conviction that I had to check. And so, while you've been talking to your client, I've been listening to old news clips of Bruno Field. And you know what?'

'What?' Klinger asked, his eyes flickering around the office.

'You're Bruno Field,' Monroe replied calmly, leaning back.

'Preposterous,' Klinger exclaimed.

Monroe shrugged.

'Sure, it's a reach, but here's the thing,' he said. 'I believe Miss Martinez, I've heard what she heard in your tone and I'm convinced that you're Bruno Field, but what confuses me is why the other *Magpies* don't see it.'

'Because you're wrong,' Klinger rose angrily now. 'And if that's it, I'll—'

'*Sit down.*' Monroe's tone was sharp and commanding, and Klinger did exactly that, as it was Monroe's turn to rise now, walking around the desk and leaning against it, facing Klinger from above. Nervously, Klinger grabbed the glass of water, downing it.

'In 1995, we pulled Bruno Field over for drink driving,' Monroe explained. 'It never went to court as someone in Westminster magically quashed it. It disappeared like magic. But do you know what didn't disappear?'

'No,' Klinger was mesmerised now.

'His *fingerprints*,' Monroe smiled. 'When he was processed.'

Pulling his pocket square handkerchief out of his jacket pocket, he used it to pick up the glass that Klinger had recently picked up, walking back around to his side of the desk, placing it down.

'We have a forensics lab downstairs,' he said. 'Best crew in the force. What do you think they'll find when they look at *this?*'

Klinger was silent now, as if weighing up his options. Monroe made the decision for him.

'Look, if we wanted to arrest you, and question you next to Luke and the others, we would,' he said. 'But we don't. This is a bloody minefield, and if you want to keep your past hidden, then that's fine by me. But you can answer some questions for me first.'

Sebastian Klinger, whose actual name was Bruno Field, silently nodded.

'Luke Ashton,' Monroe asked. 'How come he's letting you rep him?'

'Because he was told to,' Bruno replied.

'Who by?'

'Mark Walters,' Bruno looked out of the window now. 'He hired me to represent Luke and Jane Ashton, Daniel McCarthy and Derek Sutton. In fact, I sent a message to all of my clients to let them know of Reginald's death.'

'But not Theresa Martinez or Thomas Williams?'

'No, although to be honest Theresa may have assumed I was her brief, simply because Michael had been, and in a way I replaced him.'

'And why would Mark Walters want you repping the *Magpies*, considering you killed the franchise?'

'I did nothing of the sort,' Bruno snapped. 'Tommy Williams conned me into thinking that Luke was attracted to me. He forged letters, got people to play along. It was all because I wouldn't back him when he was caught trying to rape that *Blue Peter* bitch.'

'*Blue Peter bitch*,' Monroe nodded. 'That's a lovely way with words you have.'

'She was, and I'm glad she's now dead,' Bruno replied, calming. 'She got her teeth into Tommy and destroyed everything. I got her out of the room, so to speak, but then Tommy was angry, saying I was sabotaging his love life. They were falling apart by then, anyway. He had this pervy fascination for Jane, and then Luke beat the living shit out of him when he molested Eloise in a green room after *Live and Kicking*.' Bruno almost spat. 'I mean, for God's sake, *anyone* could have walked in!'

'Looks like you were more angry about the location than the action.'

'I never said I was a saint,' Bruno leaned back in the chair. 'But that little prick destroyed my life after that. My reputation was in tatters. I couldn't get legal work, Westminster had blackballed me.'

'Yet look at you now,' Monroe indicated the suit that Bruno wore. 'That looks incredibly Savile Row. We have a chap here who dresses just like you. *Bespoke*.'

He paused.

'So if you didn't kill the franchise, who did?' he asked.

Bruno rubbed at his temples. 'Eloise Lewis did,' he replied. 'She threatened to go to the press after Tommy… well, after Tommy. We also knew there were a dozen others, all girls who'd been paid to keep quiet, but who, if one person came forward, might add their names to the list. It'd be a PR nightmare. *MeToo* but thirty years too early.'

'So what did you do?' Monroe asked. 'I'm guessing something, because she never went public.'

'She wanted to be a *Magpie*, so we made her one,' Bruno shrugged. 'We were finishing what was to be the last book, so we sat her down and gave her the same NDAs and contracts as we gave the others. She'd be brought in during the next book, we'd phase Tessa out and she'd end up replacing her. Eloise was over the moon with this. She had her people look at it, and then she signed.'

Monroe smiled. 'And then you killed the franchise.'

'And then we killed the franchise,' Bruno agreed. 'It was Rory's idea. He'd come across from Shipman's office, and he saw this as something that could derail his career before he even started. We never said she'd be in the books in the contracts she signed, just that she'd be a *Magpie*. And, when she was locked in, we cancelled the books. She couldn't tell anyone anything, because we had those bloody NDAs nailed down.'

He looked at the floor.

'Of course, by then we'd had the after party, and I'd— well, I'd misread signs by Luke, mainly thanks to Tommy, and so when it ended, it looked like it was because of me.'

Monroe was about to reply when the door opened, and Bullman was standing there.

'A word, please,' she said. Monroe looked at Bruno.

'Stay,' he hissed. 'You move out of this office, and I'll bloody arrest you myself.'

'Look, I'm sure this is an overreaction—'

'That's probably what Julia Clarke said,' Monroe walked to the door. 'Just before she was drowned.'

Emerging out into the main office, Monroe looked at Bullman.

'Problem?' he asked. Bullman nodded to Billy, working at his monitors, Anjli and Doctor Marcos behind him, watching him work.

'You need to see this,' she said, leading Monroe across. Billy, seeing Monroe smiled.

'Declan and I worked it out,' he said happily. 'The words were numbers and the numbers were an account.'

'What words, and what bloody numbers?' Monroe was exasperated now. Billy threw up the poem onto one of the screens.

'The first words were used in the Magpie poem that Troughton had on his laptop,' he explained. 'One for sorrow, two for joy, etc. We matched the words here to the numbers they represented in the poem and found twelve digits, all of which match a *Credit Suisse* account in Geneva.'

'Swiss banks are notoriously hard to crack,' Doctor Marcos mused. 'Even *Interpol* has—'

'I'm already in.' Billy's grin was even wider now. 'I used Reginald's name, and the password *Magpie,* but with an *at sign* as the a, and a *one* as the i. It was a gamble, but it paid off.'

'So what did you find?' Monroe asked as, on one of the screens, lines of numbers appeared.

'Well, the point of Swiss bank accounts is that they work well with anonymity,' Billy explained as his fingers danced across the keyboard. 'However, there are things you can work out even without names.'

He pointed at one line of what looked to be code.

'The account was opened up in early 1996, as you can see here,' he said. 'Four million pounds was placed into it.'

'By whom?' Anjli asked and then shook her head. 'Swiss bank. We won't know.'

'No, but we know a few things,' Billy tapped again on his keyboard and a series of statements appeared. 'There were some stipulations placed on the account from the very start. Withdrawals and deposits could only be made for twenty-four hours, and that was every five years.' He showed one of the statements. 'See? Basically, the only activity we see here is on the thirty-first of March, in the years 2001, 2006, 2011 and 2016.'

'What are the numbers?' Monroe peered at the screen at the amounts. 'They're going down.'

'That's the interesting part,' Billy turned to face the team behind him as he continued. 'Five years after they put in the money, five accounts made transactions on the thirty-first of March. Five equal amounts of a hundred and ninety-three thousand pounds each were withdrawn. In total, that was nine hundred and sixty-four thousand, six hundred pounds.'

'Interest?' Bullman asked. Billy nodded.

'In the years between '96 and '01, the Swiss bank interest rate fluctuated, but hung around the five percent mark. And because of this—'

'They made almost a million in profit,' Doctor Marcos nodded. 'Two hundred grand, every five years. So why do the amounts drop?'

Billy looked back to the screen where the numbers for the withdrawals were shown. 'Because the interest rate dropped,' he explained. 'In 2006 they only made five hundred and sixty-five grand, so about a hundred and ten grand each, In 2011 they made four hundred and ninety-eight grand interest, so only about ninety-nine grand each.'

He tapped the last line.

'But here's the kicker,' he said. 'Over the last few years, Swiss banks have actually moved into *negative* interest; you're literally paying them now to hold your money. And because of that, the last payment, back in 2016, was only a hundred and seventeen grand, which was about twenty-three and a half grand each.'

'Why the end of March, though?' Bullman asked. 'End of account year, perhaps?'

'It's the book launch anniversary of the first *Magpie* novel,' Doctor Marcos replied. 'And today's the thirtieth of March. Tomorrow is the thirtieth anniversary of the book—'

'And the next payout,' Billy added.

'They'll get a shock when they try to open it,' Monroe smiled. 'Especially if it's now lowering the money. No payout this time.'

'No, this time is the bumper payout,' Billy tapped on the screen, returning to the first document. 'When it was opened in 1996, it was agreed back then that after twenty-five years, the remaining money would be split between all surviving accounts and then closed.'

He looked back at Monroe.

'Unless I can stop it, from midnight tonight, whoever has the account details gains the money,' he said. 'And if any of the five people involved die before this, that leaves more for the survivors.'

'Can we prove who the five names are?' Anjli asked. 'Not that we have to, but I'm assuming this is Shipman, Troughton, Chadwick, Clarke and Field?'

'Why Bruno Field?'

'Because this was before his fall from grace, and ten years ago he changed his identity,' Anjli tapped the screen. 'Ninety-nine grand can buy a good legend off the black market.'

'And you know this how?' Bullman enquired sweetly. Anjli shrugged.

'Being in the Mile End Crime Unit for a few years teaches you a lot of things, Guv.'

'In 2006, Reginald Troughton and Michael Chadwick bought a house, cash for two hundred grand,' Billy was reading some notes to the side. 'I saw that when checking through their records earlier, as it had to be declared. They sold it at a loss though a few years later after the banks crashed. And Julia Clarke bought large amounts of shares in *BadgerLock Publishing* every five years, eventually holding a controlling percentage.'

'Shipman?' Anjli asked.

'Nothing on him,' Billy shook his head. 'He has to declare everything anyway, so if it *was* Norman Shipman, he'd have to be a lot cleverer.'

'Look into Rory Simpson,' Monroe suggested. 'He was around in 1996, and I'm seeing his fingers on this.'

'So it's money,' Bullman said, looking back to Monroe's office where, still sitting alone and reading his phone was Bruno Field. 'Five accounts. And if they *are* Troughton, Chadwick, Clarke, Simpson... That leaves one. *Bruno Field.*'

'Who looks to gain all the money at midnight tonight, winner take all, unless Billy can work some magic,' Monroe nodded. 'The question is though, is he the one *doing* this, or is he going to be the *next victim* on the list?'

IT HAD BEEN ALMOST THIRTY YEARS SINCE DEREK SUTTON HAD stood as a free man, but here he was, standing outside Belmarsh Prison in the early evening, drinking in the cool night air.

They'd told the press that he'd be released in the morning, but for some reason had chosen to move it forward; most likely didn't want a press circus outside the prison.

Sutton didn't care.

Sutton was free.

God bless you, Klinger, he thought to himself. *You did what you promised.*

There was a car approaching; it looked like a limo. Derek hadn't heard from Sebastian Klinger since they brought him out of his cell, but he knew that there had been plans for this situation.

The car, a black limo pulled up in front of him, and the driver, a woman, her blonde hair bundled under her cap, smiled at him.

'Mister Sutton?' she asked. 'Compliments of Sebastian Klinger. He couldn't make it, but wanted you to know that there will be a press conference tomorrow at ten am, where you'll be starting proceedings for compensation against her Majesty's Government.'

'Good, aye,' Sutton smiled. 'Have we met before?'

'Not to my knowledge,' the driver smiled back. 'I'm to take you to a nearby five-star hotel and spa, where you'll spend your first night of freedom. Mister Klinger said that it could cater for any urges you have, *free of charge.*'

'Does it have the football?' Sutton asked as he climbed into the limo. 'That's all I care about.'

'I'm sure it does, sir,' Jane Ashton replied as she climbed back into the driver's seat, closing the door and pulling back out into the road. 'Make use of *all* the complimentary drinks.'

23

FOR BRIEFINGS

DECLAN AND THERESA ARRIVED AT THE TEMPLE INN COMMAND Unit about ten minutes after Billy's revelation; and because they were almost back, Monroe had told Billy to *hold* on letting the two detectives know, partly to streamline the upcoming briefing, but also because he wasn't yet a hundred percent sure about Theresa Martinez. Still, when they arrived, Billy happily went through it with both of them to bring them up to speed.

Coincidentally, PC De'Geer, still in full motorcycle gear, had also arrived at that point, so Monroe took the opportunity to pull everyone into the briefing room, after curtly informing Bruno to stay a little bit longer in his office.

'Okay. Updates. Go,' he said. 'I'm guessing you're all aware of the Swiss bank account? Good.'

De'Geer rose first. 'I took the photoshopped image of Jane Ashton to the coffee shack; they said that was more recognisable than the one of Louise Hart we'd shown them.'

'Jane Ashton texted her school at the same time though,'

Anjli replied. 'And Billy said the phone pinged from a tower near her home.'

'The *phone* texted,' DC Davey commented. 'Maybe it was Luke?'

'Either way, let's pick her up from the *Hyatt*,' Monroe nodded. 'Any news on Norman Shipman?'

'Didn't have a clue about any of this,' Declan said, looking up from his notebook. 'Everything seems to be done either by Rory Simpson or Mark Walters, both of whom seem to be playing their own game.'

He paused before ending. 'Well, at least Mark is still present tense.'

'Julia Clarke?'

'Still checking the witnesses,' DC Davey nodded. 'Hoping that whoever wore the mask took it off near someone who could have seen it.'

'Reginald Troughton?' Monroe raised a hand. 'We know about the account, so what else do we have?'

'I've been reading the book,' Billy raised a hand momentarily before dropping it again. 'It's not favourable about anyone in it.'

'Go on.'

'I think Reginald's trying to burn everything down,' Billy explained. 'And in the middle, he's placing Thomas Williams front and centre.'

'But why the encryptions?' Bullman asked. 'Surely Reginald would have wanted people to see this? Why write it otherwise?'

'That we don't know yet,' Billy stated. 'However, I checked with a source—'

'He asked Trix,' Anjli muttered loud enough to be heard.

'I checked with an *unknown source,* who confirmed that

these were Ministry of Defence grade encryptions, and there was no reason for them to be on his computer.'

'Luke Ashton,' Bullman mused.

'Has to be,' Declan replied. 'This is completely within his remit. Again though, why?'

'That's why it's called *detective work*, laddie,' Monroe nodded as he looked to the room. 'Get detecting.'

He straightened.

'Some of you know that Sebastian Klinger is in my office. What isn't known by all of you is that he's actually Bruno Field.'

He waited for the raised voices and questions to die down before continuing.

'I know, we have a lot of questions, but these can wait for the moment. We know that the Swiss bank account set up to hide four million pounds of government money twenty-five years ago closes at midnight tomorrow, so for twenty-four hours from midnight, that money can be removed by someone with the right credentials and passwords. Originally there were five, but we've worked out that Julia Clarke, Reginald Troughton, Michael Chadwick and Rory Simpson were four of the account holders. Which means that Bruno Field is the only one left.'

'Could Bruno be the killer?' Theresa asked. Monroe shrugged.

'He was taking questions in a press conference when Julia Clarke was killed, so if he was, he's using proxies,' he said. 'Again though, Bruno, or Sebastian as he's now called, has been working for Mark Walters, and has been the go-to guy for most of the *Magpies* since Chadwick died.'

'Most?' Declan replied. Bullman, by the door nodded.

'Apparently he doesn't represent Theresa Martinez or Thomas Williams,' she replied.

'Looks like they dropped me off the list when Chadwick died,' Theresa muttered.

'And he's the one who sent his clients the text message about Reginald,' Monroe finished. Declan went to speak on this, but noticed a strange expression, a confusion on the face of Billy on hearing this news, so held his tongue.

'So what's the next step?' he asked instead. 'Thomas Williams is banged to rights as the killer, and all the evidence points at him. But none of us in this room believe that. He's been set up, and by someone good. No one person could have killed these people. Chadwick was a hit and run by a drug dealer, Simpson was possibly by Jane Ashton, who was across the city from Julia when she died, Reginald died before Luke Ashton could get to him while the killer left into Fleet Street and Julia was killed in the middle of the afternoon, supposedly by the same man.'

Monroe nodded.

'This is a real pain in the arse,' he muttered. 'Of the account holders, only Bruno Field still lives, and there's every chance that by the end of today he might not, if we can't sort something out.'

'We need to lock him somewhere safe,' Anjli muttered. 'Like we did with you when you were being hunted,'

'I stayed with a gangster in a boxing club,' Monroe retorted. 'We need to find something a little cleverer here.'

I think everyone needs to be brought in,' Declan added. 'Daniel McCarthy, Jane Ashton, bring them in to sit with Luke. Mark Walters, too. Although I have no idea what his beef with the creators of the *Magpies* is, considering he's a bloody *Viscount*. Maybe he—'

Declan stopped.

'Anything more?' Bullman asked, half amused.

Declan shook his head.

'I need to check something first,' he replied. 'Sorry.'

'Doctor Marcos?' Monroe asked. Doctor Marcos rose, walking to the front.

'We did a blood toxicology on Thomas Williams, and he's telling the truth,' she said. 'He doesn't remember a thing last night because he has a shit ton of Rohypnol in his system, probably through the minibar bottles, which also had trace amounts in.'

'What, so every drink was opened and spiked?' Billy looked impressed. 'That's dedication.'

'It was also almost fatal,' Doctor Marcos continued. 'I don't think they expected him to drink them all. If he'd had a couple, we might not even have noticed until it was too late.'

She nodded to Billy, who brought up an image of the bathroom.

'Now, the belief is that he fell, cracking his head against the sink, but as you can see here, the bowl is more rounded, while the injury was more of a pointed dent,' she explained. 'In addition, the smear is a little more man-made than accidental damage.'

'So what did hit him?' Declan asked.

'I might have something on that,' Anjli said. 'They put Jane Ashton in the same kind of suite as Thomas, and on the table was a square glass ashtray. I didn't see it in Thomas' room.'

'Maybe he was in a non-smoking room?'

'No, his was a smoking room,' Declan nodded. 'You could smell it.'

'That would fit the wound,' Doctor Marcos nodded.

'However, as there wasn't one found, whoever did it took it home with them.'

'Okay, so we're playing hunt the ashtray,' Monroe interjected. 'What else?'

'The rose petals in the Hampstead institute are a match for the ones in Julia's bathwater,' she said. 'Currently, we only have Daniel McCarthy's word for Thomas Williams taking them. We've already examined Troughton and Simpson, but DC Davey had a look back at Michael Chadwick's death.' She nodded again to Billy, who pulled up a folder, opening a CCTV video on the screen. It was the Euston Road, six months earlier. In the distance, you could just make out a man crossing the road, towards the station.

'This is the best angle we have, unfortunately,' Doctor Marcos apologised. 'But it gets better.'

On the screen a black Land Rover slammed into the man walking across the street; there was no sound, but Declan could almost envision the screams and the screech of tyres as the Land Rover spun in the road, heading northwards up Eversholt Street.

'Whoever did it knows how to drive,' De'Geer muttered. 'That's some solid drifting.'

'Drifting?' Anjli looked over to De'Geer.

'It's like you're oversteering,' De'Geer explained. 'You intentionally lose traction, so that when you kick the clutch, you're moving one way while you're pointing the other.'

'Skidding,' Doctor Monroe replied.

'More a *controlled* skidding, but only for a turn,' De'Geer nodded. 'However, Land Rovers aren't supposed to be able to *do* that. Either they have a BMW in the engine instead, or the driver's been overdosing on *Fast and the Furious* movies.'

'The problem is, the two we have for this crime only

just about know how to drive a stick shift, let alone do that sort of thing,' Davey continued. 'Makes me wonder if someone else killed him and used the dealers as a handy excuse.'

'Which is the *Magpie* M.O.,' Anjli said, looking at Theresa. 'Present company excluded.'

'No, it's true,' Theresa was watching the screen intently. 'Or it was your crime Twins, or even Derek Sutton, ordering it from prison.'

'Must be great being so hated,' Declan replied sardonically. 'Let's check into all of those.' There was something niggling at the back of his mind, though. Something *skewed*, again, about the hit and run.

'Anything on that camera in his suite?' Anjli asked Billy, who shook his head.

'Dozy bugger set it up but forgot to press record,' he said. 'It's utterly empty.'

'Right then,' Monroe clapped his hands together. 'Billy? Keep on with the accounts. DI Walsh? Bring that bugger Mark Walters in for a chat. Doctor Marcos? Go with De'Geer and pick up Daniel McCarthy, will you? Have a look about while you're there, see if we missed anything.'

'You invariably did,' Marcos nodded. Monroe smiled.

'I'll grab the lassie from the *Hyatt* and bring her here,' he finished. Anjli raised a hand.

'Gods, child, not you too,' Monroe moaned.

'You didn't give me anything,' Anjli smiled. 'I'm guessing I'm on babysitting duty for Field?'

'Aye, you and DI Martinez,' Monroe nodded. 'Get him somewhere safe and off the grid. Keep him there until we've sorted things out, and for the love of God don't let him log onto any Swiss bank pages.'

Everyone rose, but Declan paused at his chair, waiting for Billy to pass, matching step with him.

'What was it?' he whispered. 'You flinched. When they talked about messages.'

Billy kept quiet until they reached the bank of monitors. Then, ensuring they were alone, he spoke.

'Back when DI Martinez first arrived, she was stuck with me for a while,' he said. 'At some point we talked about when she found out about Reginald.'

'And?'

Billy picked up his notepad. 'I wrote what she said later,' he explained, flipping through it. 'It's pretty much word for word, but she was talking about the other *Magpies*, and she said *ten thirty, the news was everywhere about the murder. They probably received the text, realised the press would be all over this and decided that being caught together was a bad idea.*'

'Okay, and this piqued your interest why?'

'*Received the text,*' Billy replied. 'Not *a* text, but *the* text. I asked if *she* received the text, and she changed what she said, saying that she received *a* text, as in *the* text that gave her the news.'

'Maybe she meant that,' Declan suggested, hoping deep down that Theresa was indeed innocent of this, and hadn't received anything from Bruno Field.

'Let's hope so,' Billy nodded. 'Because if I try to get hold of her text history, as a serving officer there'll be a lot of paperwork and it could affect her career.'

'Hold on it for the moment,' Declan nodded. There was still a niggling feeling in his gut, something that he couldn't quite put his finger on. 'That said, can you check her police record *without* raising attention?'

'What exactly do you want to look at?'

'When she's taken time off over the last year,' Declan replied, watching across the office at Theresa, currently preparing to leave with Anjli. 'In particular, around the time that Michael Chadwick was killed.'

'Shouldn't be too hard, as it's just the online diary,' Billy sat at his desk. 'Also, I might have something we can do with the accounts.'

'Can you move the money?'

'I can't really do anything,' Billy admitted. 'But I might be able to play with it.'

Declan stared in confusion. 'You know you're making no sense, right?'

'My family used to work with the Swiss a lot,' Billy explained. 'One of their biggest client base? Russian Oligarchs. So, I had a thought, and realised that you have to think like a Russian sometimes,' he said. 'Anything else?'

'Actually, yes,' Declan replied, sitting down beside Billy. 'Two things. First, send me a crime photo of Thomas Williams' hotel room. Doesn't matter which one, as long as it shows the camera in it. Actually, stick it on a USB drive. The three before it, too.'

'Can do.'

'Also, the study of Reginald Troughton, when we examined it, there were tons of photos on shelves, on walls, everywhere. All we concentrated on was the photo on the floor, and the one missing.'

'Both valid reasons, though.'

'True,' Declan nodded. 'At the time, we didn't know what people looked like, then. Now we do. I was hoping we might still have images of the photos? I know the crime scene photographer would have taken shots of them all.'

Billy nodded, looking over to DC Davey, walking past.

'Joanne, can you help us?' he asked.

Davey nodded and walked over. 'What's the issue?'

Declan explained what he was looking for, and Davey nodded.

'I know where they are,' she said, moving over the keyboard. 'They're on the forensics server. Scoot aside, pretty boy.'

After a minute of file browsing across the Command Unit's personal cloud, Davey eventually leaned back, nodding to Declan.

'There's your folder of photos of photos,' she said. 'What were you looking for?'

'Nothing involving Reginald with awards, or famous people,' Declan considered. 'I'm just thinking, that with the marketing shots of both the *Magpies* and the *Blue Peter* winner being on his wall, he might have had a photo up of the revival.'

Davey thought for a moment.

'Group shot,' she said. 'I think there was something like that.'

She moved back onto the keyboard, once again pushing aside a frustrated Billy as she searched quickly through the thumbnails, eventually pulling up an image.

It was monochrome, and taken in an office. Definitely marketing related, as it was posed. Thomas Williams was standing next to a computer, the letters D.E.X.T.E.R on it; he was bearded and ten years younger, but it was definitely him, with Daniel beside him, his peroxide dyed hair shorter here, more *Draco Malfoy* than *Lucius*. Beside him was a woman that Declan didn't recognise; he assumed that this was Jane Terry, and the man to her right, his short, obviously red hair even in the monochrome image standing out as he smiled. And, to the right, as if placed in by accident, was Louise Hart, not as skinny as she was in her most recent photos, but almost positively the same woman.

'The reboot,' Declan said, scrutinising the image. 'Can you print me a copy?'

'Already ahead of you,' Billy reached to the printer beside him, which was currently spewing out an image on a sheet of A4 paper. Taking it, Declan picked up a black sharpie from Billy's desk and, holding the page close, started drawing on it. After a moment, he showed it to Billy and Davey, who looked at him in confusion. He smiled, looking back to the now vandalised image.

'Gotcha,' he said to it. 'Someone grab Anjli before she leaves.'

Davey waved to Anjli, gaining her attention.

'What exactly have you worked out?' Davey asked as Anjli, motioning for Theresa to wait, walked over to the group around the monitors.

Declan shrugged, looking back at the piece of paper. The other niggle he'd had was also clear now, no matter *how bad* it was.

'Actually,' he replied, 'I think I might have worked out everything,' he said.

'And I know how to prove it.'

24

FOR REBOOTS

Declan didn't bother calling ahead to announce he was heading to Portcullis House. In fact, he didn't even know whether Mark Walters would be there; however, he had a pretty good idea that on this day in particular, and having heard that Norman had spoken to Declan the same day, he'd be keeping his head down while trying to garner more information.

Norman had wanted to castrate Mark, after learning he'd been kept out of the loop and used like a patsy, and Declan, knowing the power Norman currently had as head of the *Star Chamber,* didn't really want to see this. He had however asked for a couple of days to work on the case, to ensure Mark didn't know he was being investigated in any way. And so Norman Shipman had agreed to pretend that everything was fine, drop a hint he'd had a surprise chat with Declan, but throw questions asked by Mark about the details of the meeting onto Rory Simpson, and how Norman was *stunned* that Rory could have done so much behind his back.

Which, in effect, was actually all true; Norman *was*

furious that he'd been played for over a decade, but with *both* advisors.

Norman had also agreed to keep Mark in the primary office, but at the same time couldn't confirm he'd be able to keep him there for long. Declan had hoped to drop back to Temple Inn, update and then return, but so much had happened since, he was worried that he'd missed the chance.

He hadn't.

Mark Walters sat in the now dark and up-lit atrium, having an evening cup of coffee while he took a break, oblivious to the world of problems that he was about to face. Being late in the evening, most companies would have emptied with their workforce going home hours earlier, but with Parliament often working into the early hours of the morning, so did their staff.

Declan was grateful for this.

'Hello, Mark,' he said as he sat down opposite the advisor. Norman had allowed him access through security, and there hadn't been the slightest of clues to his arrival. Nevertheless, Mark looked up with a smile, as if he'd been waiting patiently all evening.

'Declan,' he said, placing down the iPad he'd been reading. 'How's the day been treating you?'

Declan noted the familiarity; it was different to every other time, as if Mark had been preparing for this moment.

'All good, actually,' he replied. 'What are you reading?'

'Boring reports,' Mark leaned back, stretching. 'Long day. Especially after the late finish yesterday.'

'Yes, yesterday,' Declan nodded. 'Interesting times.'

'I hear Thomas is still in custody?' Mark asked. 'So sad to see a man fall from grace like that.'

'And the paranoia,' Declan added. 'That was a real shock.'

For the first time, Mark faltered.

'Paranoia?'

'Oh, sure,' Declan smiled, reaching for the iPad. 'Is this government or personal?'

'Personal—'

'Awesome,' Declan pulled out a USB drive. 'Oh, do you have some sort of dongle for this?' he asked. 'I was told that the new ones allow external drives.'

Mark reached into his briefcase, pulling one out. 'Here.'

'Excellent,' Declan smiled as he plugged the USB drive into the dongle, and then the dongle into the iPad. 'Honestly, we were stunned.'

On the screen of the iPad, a folder appeared; the external drive that Declan had just added. Angling it so that the screen pointed at Mark, Declan opened the folder; a crime scene image of Thomas Williams' room appeared on it.

'You were only in the room for a moment, weren't you?' he asked. Silently, staring at the image, Mark nodded. Declan scanned through the first three images quickly.

'We knew he was a little paranoid as he kept saying he was being set up, and as you can see here, he managed to drink the minibar.'

He looked at Mark.

'You'll have to pay for that, won't you? Sorry about that.'

Mark nodded, his eyes glued to the screen, unsure what this was exactly. Declan flipped to the fourth image.

'This was the one that got me,' he said, zooming in on the image with his fingers. 'See that? It's a Wi-Fi camera. Seems that Thomas bought it yesterday afternoon without anyone knowing and set it up about three or four hours before he passed out.'

He looked directly at Mark.

'As you can see, it gives a superb, panoramic view of the entire room,' he said. 'Can you guess what's on it?'

To his credit, Mark Walters didn't change appearance.

'I don't know,' he said calmly. 'Me having a row with Thomas over a bar bill?'

'Possibly,' Declan nodded. 'Or, maybe we'll see Graham Terry hitting Thomas on the skull with a glass ashtray.'

'Graham Terry is dead,' Mark replied, his voice wavering slightly.

'Is he?' Declan smiled. 'Scroll to the next image.'

Mark did so, and the picture of the reboot *Magpies* appeared on the screen.

'Look closer,' Declan said softly. 'Maybe take off your glasses? They're plain glass, anyway.' He'd noted this as he watched Mark; the lenses would usually distort the outline of the face when watched from an angle. These didn't.

'What exactly are you implying, Detective Inspector Walsh?' Mark replied.

'Oh, so I'm no longer Declan? I'm hurt,' Declan made a sad face to show this. 'Can I give you a theory? Stop me if you've heard it.'

He leaned forward now, lowering his voice.

'Graham Terry leaves the UK after the collapse of the reboot. He's using again, and he's pretty blissed out all across Thailand. Lots of local goods to sample, you know. He's having a blast. And then he learns his sister is dead.'

'I feel for him.'

'So do I,' Declan said, using his finger to scroll to the next image on the screen. It was a picture of Mark Walters, taken in Thailand at one of the parties he was at. It was a tabloid shot, but was clearly Mark.

'Then, he meets Mark Walters. What a joy! Another

redhead Brit, travelling the world. And, more importantly, they look the same. Well, if you squint.'

He leaned back now, still with his finger over the screen.

'What I can't work out is how you befriended him,' he said. 'Also, I can't work out how you got him to turn from this —' he showed the picture, before scrolling one more time.

Now, the crime scene photo of the death of Graham Terry was on the screen of the iPad. It wasn't a great shot, and the detail wasn't brilliant; but the body on the bed was still mostly visible. It was a red-headed man, his hair straggly and unkempt, matching his wispy beard. He was painfully thin, due to what was known as *heroin chic* and had been stabbed repeatedly in the chest and torso. The blood was everywhere, including the face.

'—into *this*,' Declan finished.

Mark stared at the image for a few moments before pushing the iPad away.

'Okay, it's true,' he said, 'I knew Graham when he was in Thailand. We were both partying with the same crowd, and they found it amusing, that we were both these pale Brits who could have been cousins. And, as I was the one with the money, we made an arrangement. I'd fund Graham's... Well, his *interests* while he became my courier, taking the money and swapping it for merchandise.'

'And by merchandise you mean...'

'Heroin,' Mark admitted. 'Graham was a big fan.'

DOCTOR MARCOS HAD DRIVEN DE'GEER TO THE *BAKER Institute*, insisting that even though the two of them could easily double up on a pillion, trying to add Daniel McCarthy to a police motorcycle as well was just asking for trouble. In fact, they were still discussing this as they walked to the entrance, pausing as Doctor Hines, pushing her glasses up her nose emerged from the building to meet with them.

'Problem?' De'Geer asked, seeing her expression. Nervously, Doctor Hine nodded.

'I wasn't sure how you'd heard,' she said. Doctor Marcos stepped forward at this.

'Heard what?' she asked. Doctor Hine's expression turned to one of actual surprise.

'Oh, I thought you were here because of Danny,' she said. 'We only phoned the police ten minutes back.'

'What happened with Daniel McCarthy?' De'Geer replied. Doctor Hine wrung her hands as she answered.

'He's run away,' she explained. 'He's packed his bag and escaped.'

———

MONROE WALKED INTO THE *PICCADILLY HYATT* LOBBY, marvelling at the marble facades that lined the entranceway. He'd always been a *Bed and Breakfast* traveller, and the thought of even spending the amount of money needed for a regular room here made his skin itch, let alone a suite. He'd seen the bar bill for Thomas Williams' room last night, and it was in the *hundreds*.

The receptionist looked up, smiling as he approached. 'Welcome to the *Piccadilly Hyatt Hotel*,' she said. 'How can I help you?'

Monroe flashed his warrant card, smiling to show that it wasn't a concerning visit. 'Picking up a guest,' he replied. 'You had a Jane Ashton in suite—'

'Oh, she checked out,' the receptionist was already reading the screen. 'Just after lunch.'

'She did, did she?' Monroe stepped back, looking around the lobby. 'Any idea where she went?'

'No, sorry,' the receptionist replied apologetically. 'She wasn't paying, so all she did was pass us the key card and leave.'

'Did she call for a cab? Anything like that?' Monroe asked, and as the receptionist sadly shook her head, he turned and left the hotel.

Jane Ashton was in the wind again.

'WERE *YOU* AS MUCH A FAN OF HEROIN?' DECLAN ASKED. MARK shrugged at this, looking around the Portcullis House atrium.

'Not really,' he replied carefully. 'I'd had an unpleasant experience. I was giving up.'

'Unpleasant experience?'

'Death in the family,' Mark said before adding 'my parents.'

'Ah, yes, the helicopter crash,' Declan nodded. 'And then, after Thailand you had what, your *come to Jesus* moment and returned home?'

'Something like that,' Mark nodded. Declan looked at his watch, as if working something out.

'The one thing I can't explain is how you took the identity,' Declan continued. 'I mean, signatures can be forged, but you weren't *that* identical. And trust me, I've dealt with identical twins and the problems they entail before.'

'Anything can be fixed if you have the money,' Mark said,

and then stopped himself, as if realising that he'd said too much.

Declan smiled; the smile that a shark might make as it found its prey.

'Tell you what,' he said. 'Let's carry this on at the station, *Graham*. You can catch up with Luke, Jane, Danny, and we can have a good old chinwag about the millions of pounds in a Swiss account that are going to simply disappear tomorrow.'

Mark shifted in his seat, but it wasn't the movement of a scared, nervous or guilty man. Instead, it was the mannerism of a man who was in control.

'I don't think so,' he said. 'I'm not *feeling* that.'

'I don't believe it was a request,' Declan replied calmly. 'You've played your cards, I've played mine, and you've been out-matched.'

'Have I, though?' Mark leaned closer, raising his eyebrows as he asked. '*Have* I? I think you'll find there's one more hand to be played.'

As if on cue, his phone beeped. Answering it, he listened.

'Exactly what I wanted to hear,' he said, disconnecting, looking back to Declan.

'Now, how about you call your station, and get them to release Luke?' Mark asked. 'Tell them you've got some additional proof, something amazing that places Thomas square at the murders. And then, once he's out, you and me? We'll go for a stroll to a location of *my* choosing.'

'And why would I do that?' Declan replied.

Mark Walters, now revealed as Graham Terry *told* him.

ANJLI AND THERESA HAD KEPT EVERYTHING UNDER THE RADAR when taking Bruno Field out of Temple Inn; they'd deliberately taken Billy's Mini rather than a police car and had made sure the location Anjli now drove them to wasn't on any police list of safe houses.

Bruno was an unhappy passenger; he sat in the back, alternating between arguing that this wasn't necessary, and that he should be allowed to go about his business, as they had no right to restrain him, while then switching at a moment's notice to a terrified man, convinced that everyone and their *dog* was about to leap out of the shadows and *brutally murder him,* with a little more brutality and murder for good measure.

Anjli was almost ready to do it herself.

'Where are we?' Theresa asked as Anjli pulled the car up in the middle of an East End estate, in a small alley beside a red brick building.

'The Globe Town Boxing Club,' Anjli replied, exiting the car. 'It's owned by Johnny and Jackie Lucas, but I know they're not around at the moment. It's shut up, and nobody would think of finding a police witness there.'

'I've heard of the Twins,' Theresa looked concerned. 'You sure they'll be happy with this? Shouldn't we ask them?'

'I'm all about asking forgiveness than permission right now,' Anjli smiled, showing the door to the boxing club. 'Declan said you were good with locks?'

'You don't even have a key?' Theresa sighed as she knelt beside the door, examining it. 'I might have a skeleton that matches this.'

After a couple of failed attempts at unlocking the door by Theresa, Anjli pulled the mat up, revealing a brass key taped to the bottom.

'Well, what do you know,' she said triumphantly. 'Got a key right here.'

'They seriously leave it under the mat?' Theresa took the key, opening the door.

'When you're Johnny and Jackie Lucas, only an idiot breaks into your house,' Anjli replied, pushing the protesting Bruno through the door.

'That's what we're doing,' Theresa said, walking in behind Anjli.

The boxing club had recently been renovated, and now state-of-the-art equipment lined the walls, with shiny, new-leather smelling heavy bags surrounding the boxing ring itself.

'It's not much, but it'll do for the moment,' Anjli said. 'Although don't think about getting snuggly with Declan in the back office when he arrives—'

She turned to see Theresa standing in the doorway, closing it, a phone to her ear.

'It's me,' she said into it. 'We're at the Globe Town Boxing Club.'

Finishing the call, she placed the phone in her jacket pocket and, with the hand still in it, she walked towards them.

'You might want to sit down,' she said. 'We're expecting visitors.'

'Now listen here—' Anjli went to reply, but stopped as Theresa pulled her hand back out of her jacket pocket.

She now held a Glock 17 pistol in it, pointing directly at Anjli.

'I wasn't asking,' Theresa said, almost apologetically.

'Sorry. Looks like I wasn't one of the good guys after all.'

25

FOR REVELATIONS

'THE LEAST YOU CAN DO IS EXPLAIN HOW YOU MANAGED IT,' Declan muttered as he followed Mark Walters, AKA Graham Terry down the Embankment, walking towards Blackfriars from Westminster. 'And maybe call a cab?'

'Cabs can be tracked,' Graham replied, watching down the road. 'Your car won't be.'

'Great,' Declan sighed. After Graham had been revealed, and then had explained that Theresa was a reluctant mole, placed in the organisation specifically for this moment, he'd told Declan in no uncertain terms that unless he left the Portcullis House atrium right now, DS Kapoor's life would be cut tragically short. Understandably, Declan had agreed to follow him, and had been doing so for the last fifteen minutes. In fact, they were walking south of Temple Inn right now, where Luke Ashton, freshly released thanks to a phone call from Declan, would wait for them with Declan's Audi, taken from the car park outside the Command Unit.

'I still think you could at least answer some questions

while we wait,' Declan repeated. 'I'm guessing that Theresa tipped you off about Shipman?'

Graham nodded. 'She told me you'd grassed me up to him,' he said. 'That's why I was in the atrium, rather than the office. Didn't want you confronting me around witnesses who actually knew me.'

'Or your darling boss taking a punt at your head,' Declan replied. 'Did you take the glass ashtray as a souvenir? Would he have thrown *that* at you?'

'I kept the ashtray,' Graham stated, exasperated. 'I left the bloodstains on it too. It'll keep me warm at night, thinking about it. So, when did you *really* know?'

'I had my suspicions,' Declan shrugged. 'You knowing what was found in Thomas' room before being told was a giveaway.'

'Yes, I realised I screwed up there,' Graham nodded. 'So, what would you like to know?'

'What actually happened in Thailand, for a start,' Declan gave a winning smile at his captor. 'Genuinely curious how you managed the whole *Talented Mister Ripley* thing.'

'I intended to kill myself,' Graham said, leaning against the railings. 'I'd just heard that Jane had died of an overdose; news travelled slowly to where I was. I didn't want to carry on. Life was just so unfair...' He stopped, watching Declan rub his thumb and index finger together, as if listening to the sound. 'What are you doing?'

'Smallest violin,' Declan replied. 'Go on, you were saying. Boo hoo, sister dead, heroin good?'

'Yeah, it was,' Graham's face was shadowed now as he stared away from the piss-taking detective. 'You know, you really should take this seriously.'

'No offence mate, but this isn't my first rodeo,' Declan

shrugged. 'In fact, nine out of ten of the cases we've solved usually end up with someone holding a weapon or threatening someone's life.'

He smiled.

'You're not even in my top three *threatened by someone who isn't who they said they were* moments.'

Graham watched the Thames across the road for a moment.

'I didn't want this,' he said. 'I just wanted to be a *Magpie*.'

'So did I,' Declan replied. 'But the difference between us is I never killed anyone.'

'How do you know I have?' Graham enquired. 'What, because there are dead people, I have to be the killer?'

Declan shrugged again. 'Touché,' he said. 'Please, go on.'

'So, there I was in an opium den on the Thailand and Laos border, and who should I meet? But the Viscount Marcus Walters himself. Seems the party boy was on a solid bender, just like me. And, as we were the only Westerners around, we formed a bond.'

'Gingers of the world, unite,' mocked Declan. Graham ignored him.

'We ended up in Bang Kapi, sharing some kind of, well, squat, I suppose. And somehow, over the weeks we'd spent together, I'd fallen into a servant type role.'

'Bet that made you happy.'

'I've spent my life working for people. Why not work for someone who's giving me heroin?' Graham sighed. 'He really was a nice bloke, but then I learned of his... *urges*.'

He spat on the floor.

'He was in Thailand because at thirty years old, and with his new inheritance, he was richer than Croesus in a land where human life, especially *children's* life, was cheap.'

'Still thought he was a nice bloke?'

'I learned that he'd been with a kid. A child, no older than ten. Something had happened, and the child had died. I had to tell the mother that there'd been an accident. She cried on me, before grabbing a carving knife and attempted to kill me,' Graham replied, his voice soft, lost in sad memories. 'That was the point I decided to get myself clean. Took a couple of weeks, but I'd done it before and as I got better, he got worse. By the time I was clear-headed, he was bedridden, his only interest the next needle. But if he couldn't walk to his bank, he couldn't get money out. And no money—'

'No drugs,' Declan nodded. 'So, let me guess. He made some kind of arrangement, that you'd take his place at the bank, go in his stead?'

'At first I was just a messenger,' Graham explained. 'I didn't know how much money he had, and I was never told. But then the manager I was dealing with moved branches, and the new manager kept calling me 'Mister Walters.' Finally, I could see my account, and—'

'It wasn't your account,' Declan interrupted. Graham glared at him.

'I could see *the* account,' he altered. 'I saw the millions that he had. Millions he was squandering, wasting on dirty drugs and deviant behaviour.'

'So what happened then?'

'I made a game of it with Mark; made him tell me a secret, or a fact about himself in return for the merch. He was pathetic by then, eager to do this for a hit, and I let him fall. After a couple of months he was almost unrecognisable, he'd lost so much weight. You never want to eat, you see. Just inject.'

He sniffed, looking around the street.

'Meanwhile, I'd actively put on weight, cutting my hair and growing my beard to look as close as I could to his passport photo. When I felt I was ready, I went to the British embassy, explaining that I'd lost my passport and my wallet, and that I needed to gain new ID. And of course the bank manager, who'd believed from the start that I was Mister Walters, was more than happy to vouch for me, helping me get them. The only issue I had was with my fingerprints on the passport, but ten grand passed to the right customs official sorted that out. And then, six long months after I'd met the real Mark Walters, I *was* Mark Walters. And he was now Graham Terry.'

'And then you stabbed him to death.'

'God no,' Graham almost laughed. 'I didn't kill him. I found the mother, the one whose child he had killed, and I told her who he was and what he did. Gave her a thousand pounds and a kukri knife, and let her go to town while I was gathering my visas at the embassy. He was dead after the first stab, but she just kept going, screaming as she did so.'

He shivered.

'I then explained to her that I had the whole thing on camera, and if she told anyone, I'd kill her. I needn't have worried because a week later she overdosed. Weirdly, it was the day I returned to England.'

'And you weren't scared of being recognised?'

Graham laughed. 'Mark didn't have friends, and his family were all dead. I arrived in London and immediately went to his family solicitors. They'd never met him in person as he'd gone travelling the moment he gained the money, and my passport was documentation enough. I'd learned about my extensive portfolio through my Q&As with Mark before giving him his heroin, and realised that I'd been given a second chance.'

There was a beep of a car horn; a familiar beep, and Declan's Audi pulled up, Luke Ashton driving.

'Get in,' Graham prodded Declan along. 'Story time's over.'

IN TEMPLE INN, MONROE WALKED INTO THE MAIN OFFICE, noting that Doctor Marcos, PC De'Geer and Billy were all around Billy's monitor, watching the screen.

'Something good on?' he asked. Doctor Marcos looked over at him.

'Guessing your *Magpie* was missing too?'

Monroe nodded.

'As of this moment, Daniel McCarthy and Jane Ashton are both in the wind,' he said. 'Any news from Anjli?'

'Nothing yet,' De'Geer replied. 'And Processing called to say they'd let Luke Ashton go after DI Walsh called, telling them he had some information that led to his innocence.'

'Did they clear it with the boss?' Monroe asked.

'They did,' Bullman replied, walking out of her office. 'Currently, the only *Magpie* in custody is Thomas Williams.'

'Just the way we want it,' Monroe smiled. 'Any news on Sutton?'

'Picked up by a limo outside of Belmarsh earlier this evening,' De'Geer checked his notes. 'No idea where it went, and the guards didn't take the licence number.'

'I'm sure he'll turn up soon.' Monroe looked at the screen. 'What are you doing?'

'Playing with time zones,' Billy explained. 'I'm bouncing my IP code and spoofing a Moscow data stream.'

Monroe nodded as if understanding this. 'Computer stuff,' he replied. 'I knew we kept you from leaving for a reason.'

He looked at Bullman now.

'Give the word,' he said softly.

Bullman looked at the clock on the wall, noting the time.

'The word is given,' she said.

IT WAS ALMOST TEN IN THE EVENING BY THE TIME DECLAN arrived at the Globe Town Boxing Club, Graham Terry pulling him out of the car as Luke emerged from the driver's side.

'Seems like your request to find a nice, quiet place was listened to,' Graham smiled. 'Let's go inside.'

Entering the boxing club, Declan immediately saw that Anjli and Bruno were standing in the boxing ring, with Theresa waiting on the floor beside them, gun in her hand.

'This the main event?' Declan asked, unconcerned. 'My money's on the copper.'

He looked at Theresa now.

'I've changed my mind,' he said. 'I don't want you talking to my daughter. I think you could be a bad influence.'

He couldn't work out if it was mocking or actually genuine, but Theresa Martinez's face actually fell at this.

'I would have steered her in the correct direction,' she said. 'I never lied about how I felt for you.'

'No, just everything else,' Declan replied as he looked up at Anjli, currently leaning on the ropes. 'You okay?'

'Just dandy,' she said. 'We're in here because we need to be watched.'

'I'd do the same,' Declan smiled, looking back at Graham. 'I'm guessing you have a game plan,' he said. 'I mean, this has all been very well planned. Meticulous, even.'

'Of course we have a plan,' Luke snapped from across the club. 'One that makes us a lot of money.'

'Your dad would be proud of you,' Anjli muttered.

'Reg wasn't my dad,' Luke snapped back at her. 'No matter what he believed. He kept me hidden! What kind of dad does that? He deserved everything that he got.'

'Not really a *father's day card* person then?' Anjli mocked as ignoring her jibes, Luke pulled his messenger bag from his shoulder, one he'd picked up from the passenger seat when he left the car. Opening it, he pulled out a laptop and what seemed to be some kind of Wi-Fi booster. Setting them up on a table by the wall, he logged in.

'You know you can just tether it to your phone these days,' Declan suggested. 'Saves a whole ton of time.'

'Sure, and allow people to see exactly where I am?' Luke scoffed. 'I'd rather bounce it around some satellites.'

'Fair point,' Declan admitted before he turned and smiled at Graham. 'Care to tell me the plan? I'm guessing we're waiting here until midnight, and then Bruno there will open up his account details for you?'

'That's not going to happen,' Bruno spat at Graham. 'I trusted you!'

'It's okay, we don't need you for that,' Graham replied. 'I mean, we did, but then we didn't expect Declan and his team to work out Reginald's details.'

He smiled.

'Now you're here to help with the story.'

'Is it a scary story?' Anjli asked, still lounging against the ropes. 'I don't like scary stories.'

'Live with disappointment,' Graham snapped at her. Anjli rocked against the ropes, smiling. There was a noise at the door, and it opened to reveal Jane Ashton, in a driver's uniform, and Daniel McCarthy, still in his *Baker Institute* hoodie.

'And the band's all here,' Declan looked to Anjli. 'That'll annoy the others, when they go to pick them up, and find everyone gone.'

'Do you have him?' Graham asked Jane, who nodded.

'In the back of the limo, unconscious,' she replied.

Graham clapped his hands together. 'Excellent.'

He looked back at Declan.

'The problem is, Detective Inspector Walsh, that the plan is a little too complicated for the average layperson to understand.'

'What, stealing money from a Swiss bank account?' Anjli laughed from the boxing ring. 'That's not really that complicated.'

'*Shut up,*' Theresa muttered, glancing up at Anjli who stepped away from the ropes and, with a nod, waved her into the ring.

'Come and make me, you *junkie bitch,*' she smiled. 'Ding ding, round one.'

'People, please!' Graham shook his head. 'No need for bloodshed yet. We have time to kill, and I'm happy to tell some fireside stories.'

He turned to Declan.

'You said that you wanted to be a *Magpie.*'

Declan nodded. 'As a child,' he replied. 'But now I think they kinda *suck.*'

Daniel laughed at this from across the boxing club, currently examining the fitness equipment. Graham cocked his head, conceding the point.

'So, how about you act as a *Magpie*?' he suggested. 'Why don't you tell us what the solution is? Solve *The Adventure of the Soon-To-Be-Dead Detectives?*'

Declan scratched at his chin, looking around the boxing club; at Anjli, nodding at him, at Bruno, confused as to what was happening, at Luke and Jane, now standing beside the laptop, at Daniel, watching him from the back, his eyes glittering in the shadows, at Theresa, staring sadly at him, as if realising what she'd lost by double crossing him, and then finally at Graham, eagerly awaiting his answer.

'I thought you'd never ask,' he replied.

26

FOR A MAGPIE

'It's going to take a while, but let's be honest, we've got time,' Declan said, looking up at the clock, reading five minutes past ten. 'And there are a lot of moving parts, so give me some leeway as I work through it.'

'This is stupid,' Luke muttered.

'This is exciting,' Daniel retorted. 'First live theatre I've seen in years.'

Declan nodded to Daniel as he paced around the ring now, thinking.

'Okay,' he started. 'So, we know the *Magpies* were fake, that they collapsed and that you were all left in the dirt.'

He stopped.

'We also know that there was an aborted second version, one pioneered by Rory Simpson without Norman Shipman's knowledge.'

'Boring,' Daniel called out. 'We want *Poirot*, not *Clouseau*.'

'We also know that Graham Terry, after the collapse of the reboot and the death of his sister Jane, went to Asia where he met the Viscount Marcus, or 'Mark' Walters, and over the next six months took his identity, leaving him dead in his bed, and ensuring that the police believed it was the body of Graham Terry.'

He looked back at the *real* Graham.

'No longer revenge on a paedophile, and instead a drugs deal gone wrong.'

'I literally told you this an hour ago,' Graham sighed. 'I expected better.'

'So here's where the *we knows* and *I thinks* merge,' Declan smiled. 'I *know* that when you returned to the UK, you learned you had at least a controlling share in the *Baker Institute*. I also know that Danny McCarthy was having a bad time, and had spent the last year blaming himself for his fiancée's death.'

'Because I did kill her,' Daniel replied, his voice now sad and quiet.

'I think you found a way to get into Norman's good graces here,' Declan continued. 'I think you met with Danny, told him who you were, and gave him a way to pay his own personal penance, staying in the institute. At the same time, Rory Simpson would have been tearing his hair out, as his big reboot plan failed, and now he was worried that Danny would tell everyone. But here comes the *Viscount Walters* with a way to save the day, and all he wants in return is a job in Shipman's office. How am I doing now?'

'Better,' Graham nodded.

'Now I'll be honest, I genuinely think you weren't thinking of all this back then,' Declan mused as he continued pacing around the ring. 'It almost feels like you were trying to make your own amends. Rory knew you from the reboot, but now you've got those glasses on and an expensive suit.'

'If it works for Clark Kent,' Graham raised his hands in mock surrender.

'I think for a couple of years you just sit back, learn the ropes. Maybe you're trying to find another way to bring the *Magpies* back. Maybe not. And then we reach five years ago.'

Declan stopped, looking at Graham.

'I don't know if he bought something stupid, or he was flashing it around, but Rory Simpson suddenly comes into some money, on the twenty-fifth anniversary of the books. And this makes you a little suspicious. You dig around.'

'He asked 'Mark' for stock advice,' Graham replied, nodding. 'Explained that he'd had a bonds windfall, and that it was with another windfall he'd received five years earlier. Didn't know if he should buy gold or not.'

'And so you started playing *Magpie*,' Declan carried on walking.

'I didn't *play* at anything!' Graham snapped back. 'I *was* a *Magpie!*'

'Yeah, but *were* you?' Declan enquired. 'Really?'

There was a moment of silence. Taking that as an answer, Declan continued.

'Whether you played or believed, you dug into it. Probably around this time you learned about the missing millions, probably governmental scuttlebutt. And, as a millionaire yourself, and with probably your own Swiss account, you probably had an inkling that something was up. I mean, Troughton and Chadwick were buying houses, Julia was gaining controlling stock in her publishing company; they weren't exactly hiding this. But I genuinely think you didn't know of it for sure until you found Bruno there.'

He pointed up at the badger-haired lawyer in the ring.

'I'm thinking it was in the last year, probably some kind of accidental meeting, or maybe you found him, and located the new identity he'd created for himself with his share of the interest. Either way, you learned of the deal.'

Bruno nodded. 'He came to me in my offices,' he said. 'Told me who he was, told me who *I* was, then explained that he wanted revenge on the others.'

He looked to the boxing ring's canvas.

'I told him how the deal worked, and how in under a year there'd be five payouts. He suggested that perhaps the other four could be paid to different people, and I was happy with that.'

'Because Troughton, Chadwick, Simpson and Clarke had destroyed your name,' Declan nodded. 'I get that.'

He looked at Luke and Jane.

'Of course, at this point we know Danny was on board, but now we turn to the remaining three members of this new cabal.' He looked up to Anjli. 'Want to tag in?'

'Gladly,' Anjli grinned, looking around the ring as she spoke. 'I think he came to each of you, explaining that the plan was to gain revenge on those that had wronged you, leave it all at Tommy's feet and walk away with a million each.'

She looked at Theresa.

'That's enough to walk away from a distinguished career, right?'

'*You know nothing about my career!*' Theresa shouted angrily. 'Danny told me, explained to me how they'd tried to kill me ten years ago! I've had two disciplinaries for excessive pain medications because of that! I have night terrors because of that! They would have destroyed my career—'

'What career?' Anjli interrupted. 'They *fired you* a couple of weeks back.'

It was almost as if everything was frozen for a moment. Theresa stood stock still, her mouth open as if to reply, but with nothing emerging.

'Yeah, we know,' Anjli continued. 'The only reason you got on the case was because 'Mark' there gave you a hall pass.'

She walked to the ropes, staring down at Theresa.

'What was your plan?' she asked. 'Take the money and run?'

'It's not what you think,' Theresa muttered. 'If it worked, they'd have to reinstate me.'

'Ah, so you were going to be the *saviour of the case*,' Declan nodded. 'Solve it, be the true *Magpie* and gain all the accolades.'

'*It wasn't like that!*' Theresa was shaking now, reaching for her *Altoids* box, taking a handful of tablets and swallowing them. 'Eight months ago, I found evidence that showed Gayle Holland was innocent. I took it to my superiors, but they did *nothing!* That woman had been stuck in prison for years! And they were *leaving* her there!'

'And so you gave the evidence to Gayle.'

'Yes,' Theresa nodded. 'I thought that maybe her lawyers could use it, help her. But then after she started appeal proceedings, Michael Chadwick visited her and threatened her family, threatened her friends...'

She looked at the floor.

'Gayle killed herself because I gave her hope,' she mumbled. 'The next day Michael contacted my superiors. He told them what I'd done. All of it. I was suspended, told that I'd likely be fired after the tribunal.'

She looked back up, tears in her eyes.

'That's why Chadwick had to die,' she said. 'He was toxic. He killed everyone he met, eventually.'

Declan stared at Theresa coldly.

'So one last case to be solved for you,' he said, turning back to Graham. 'Let me guess. The deaths of me, Anjli and Bruno, by whoever you have in your car outside.'

His face brightened.

'Christ, is it Derek? You brought Sutton back for an encore?'

'Enough!' Graham snapped, but Declan shook his head.

'You told me to solve this, and solve it I will,' he said. 'Anjli?'

'Sorry, got distracted,' Anjli smiled, walking back to the centre of the ring. 'So one by one he pulls you all in. Jane, out of guilt for the other Jane's death. Luke, for a chance to hurt Tommy and kill Bruno. Theresa for...'

She grinned.

'I dunno, bag of pills maybe?'

Theresa glared up at Anjli, but said nothing as she continued on.

'So now, they're all in, but you still need to have someone on the inside. You're still the new boy, even though you've been there for years. Chadwick has to be removed. Which is a good thing, as it'll place Reginald on his own, and also free up one of the account spaces.'

'You set up a meeting with him, but either don't show, or cancel,' Declan took over. 'Chadwick is angry, not thinking clearly, and steps into the road in front of a Land Rover, who mows him down and drives off.'

He looked at Theresa.

'A Land Rover driven by you.'

'And how did you work that out?' Theresa asked, regaining her composure now. Declan shrugged.

'Actually, *you* told me,' he replied. 'When you said *you used to do doughnuts in Landies.* As in Land Rovers. We also looked into your attendance around then and saw you were on a day's holiday. Can you guess where we found your phone that day, when we asked for the tower data?'

'Euston Station,' Anjli added. 'For a good few hours. And then an hour later? Back to Manchester on the first train out.'

'You knew,' Theresa said, softly. 'You knew, and you still got in the car with me.' She looked at Graham.

'We're being set up.'

'Don't be stupid,' Graham replied irritably. 'Nobody knows where you are, and you both turned off your phones to ensure that.'

'Then we move on to you,' Declan looked at Daniel now, moving the conversation on. 'Telling people Tommy planted roses in your gardens, when only the governors can decide foliage.' He turned to Graham.

'Governors like 'Mark Walters' there.'

Declan was pacing around the ring once more, the eyes of everyone on him as he spoke.

'Now, everything's planned and ready. Luke, just before Chadwick's death, 'discovered' that Reginald is his father and contacts him, maybe after the funeral. Reginald never wanted to tell him, but now he has a new outlet for his grief.'

'He never grieved over Michael,' Luke laughed. 'They hated each other at the end. They were divorcing. Reginald told me he was my dad two years ago. Some fling he had in University gone wrong. He'd always known, and he never told me, even when I was spending days at a time with him.'

The smile faded.

'He offered me Michael's spot, you know. Told me about the accounts, how it worked. And *I* was the one that told Graham, when he came to me.'

'That's how you knew about the ticking clock,' Declan smiled. 'I hadn't worked that part out. So, now Chadwick's dead, and Danny convinces him to write a tell-all book. I'm guessing this was so that Tommy's character is destroyed? After all, you needed a reason for him to go nuts and kill all the people who'd been putting food on his table for all of those years.'

Luke nodded. 'Danny and I both pushed him into it,' he said. 'Got him an advance, told him they couldn't do anything if he changed the plot, all of that.'

'Meanwhile, 'Mark' here sorts out the hotel suite, making sure it's the same one, Reginald is convinced to stay home and then Jane is whored out to ensure he's got an alibi for the night, one that crumbles under pressure.'

He stopped, nodding.

'Loved the brief touch of having Louise Hart there.'

'She helped kill Jane,' Graham replied. 'Of course we were going to do the same to her as Tommy.'

'But it didn't go to plan, did it?' Anjli said from the ropes. 'You wanted both of them being arrested as co-conspirators, but Thomas didn't recognise her. Distraught, she went home and killed herself.'

'She was supposed to be alive, so she could be arrested, but dead also works,' Graham shrugged.

'Nice touch getting Jane to put on a wig and visit Sutton,' Declan added. 'That's where you got the fingerprints, right? I'm assuming that Bruno, as Klinger ensured it happened?'

Bruno, sitting on the canvas of the ring, nodded.

'I'm guessing Luke opened the door to Reginald's apartment,' Declan carried on. 'He would have been given a key by daddy. Thomas and Jane were away, Theresa was getting ready to make her arrival... I'm thinking Danny was the bald man at this point. He came in, killed Reginald and then left the weapon, complete with fingerprint, on the floor.'

He shook his head.

'One thing I don't get is why walk back to the car before returning?' he asked Luke. 'Was it to give some plausible deniability to you being there?'

'Partly,' Luke nodded. 'But also because I had to get my toolbag. When we got Reginald to write one last book, we hadn't realised that he was a Luddite. Still wrote on a type-writer. So, when Michael died, we wiped his MacBook and gave it to Reginald to use. He only had one file on it; the book. But then he started getting paranoid, and the next thing I knew, he'd stolen some of my encryptions, and had locked up his files nice and safe.'

He looked over to Theresa.

'We only learned later from Tessa that he did this because he also had his account seed phrase now on there.' Luke sniffed.

'Honestly? I thought your cyber guy would be cleverer, work it out faster.'

Declan stared at Luke. 'And you had no qualms about killing your father?'

'I already said that man wasn't my dad,' Luke snapped. 'He used me, discarded me and only told me because he was unhappy with Michael and wanted someone new to adore him. Bastard should have bought a puppy instead.'

Anjli, deciding not to reply to this outburst turned to Daniel.

'Why break the window?' she asked. 'It broke outwards, so we know it wasn't to add to the scene.'

Daniel shrugged. 'I wasn't aware of how heavy it was,' he replied. 'The tyre iron. I wanted to test a swing, and it kinda got away from me.'

'So Danny kills Troughton and runs back to the institute,' Declan counted off on his fingers. 'Luke tries to unlock the laptop to ensure we can all read the new book, finds that he can't, I'm guessing he then checks through Troughton's pockets in case there's a password hidden, finding nothing but in the process getting blood on his arms, and then cleans up as well as he can, taking the photo so Theresa could lead us to Louise. Did you also put the photo on the floor?'

Luke shook his head. 'Danny did that for fun,' he replied. 'Although if he hadn't, you wouldn't have found the account details.'

Declan looked over to Jane now.

'So Troughton's dead, and Theresa is installing herself in our department,' he said. 'You go home after staying with Tommy, and the following morning you call in sick. But you don't, do you? Luke does it for you, as you're wearing the same wig you had in Belmarsh, and you're adding concentrated nut oil into Rory Simpson's flat white order.'

'My phone shows I was at home,' Jane replied smugly.

'True, but it also shows you repeatedly visiting St James's Park, every Wednesday morning for the last few weeks,' Declan waggled his finger. 'Playing hooky from school? What must they think?'

'Oh, they thought she was having therapy sessions before work,' Anjli replied helpfully. 'We asked them.'

'So you may have left your phone at home this time,' Declan stated, 'but it's the other times you've been damned by. Also, we showed a photo of you with dark hair to the vendor, and he recognised you.'

'That's the problem with long-term plans,' Anjli carried on. 'Time isn't your friend. And as you saw, because of her advanced stage Huntingdons, Louise Hart had lost a lot of weight recently. You weren't quite the twin you used to be.'

'Which leads us to Julia Clarke,' Declan was on a roll now, enjoying this as he looked back at Graham. 'Danny's in the institute, Theresa's with us, you're in parliament with Shipman and Jane's conveniently had a scary moment in a graveyard miles away, which involves her gaining a witness that not only remembered her but also the exact time she was there.'

He walked over to Luke, facing him.

'You, however, have no alibi for this one,' he said. 'Also, Daniel could have passed you the petals when he saw you the previous night. You put on the bald mask, or at least *a* bald mask, enter the house and kill Julia, deleting a voicemail by Thomas at the same time. I thought I saw you in the crowd, but I was distracted by 'Mark', who'd suddenly appeared.'

He looked back at Graham.

'Chadwick, killed by Theresa Martinez. Troughton by Daniel McCarthy. Simpson by Jane Ashton, and Clarke by Luke Ashton. Each of the four, killed by each of your conspirators. Which leaves you and Bruno Field.'

'Very good,' Graham clapped his hands. 'And now what happens?'

Declan thought for a moment.

'You want the money, but you also need a clean win,' he said. 'You don't want people coming after you, the last thing you want to do is look over your shoulder all of your life. So, you needed a scapegoat. And who better than the original one, Derek Sutton.'

At this, Bruno looked down at Graham from the boxing ring.

'You said we were getting him out to ensure justice prevailed!' he whined. 'Not to be arrested as a murderer again!'

'Ah, but this time he won't be arrested,' Declan walked over to Theresa now, standing only a couple of feet from her as he spoke. 'The story will be that Thomas Williams was working with Bruno Field who, under the identity of Sebastian Klinger, had released Derek Sutton from prison. What Bruno hadn't bargained on was that Derek had worked out who Bruno was, and, now free had gone after him. There's a fight, in which DI Walsh and DS Kapoor are tragically killed in the line of duty. How am I doing so far?'

Theresa said nothing. Declan walked back to Graham now.

'Luckily, brave DI Theresa Martinez, assisted by Mark Walters, who had been lied to and led astray by Bruno and his partner in crime, Rory Simpson arrive just in time, thanks to information gained by the *Magpies* and kill Derek Sutton in self-defence, but not before poor Bruno is murdered.'

He pointed at the gun, still in Theresa's hand.

'I'm guessing with that gun.'

'No, actually, *this* one,' Graham pulled a .45 revolver out of his pocket, aiming it square at Declan. 'Well done. You would have been a worthy addition to the *Magpies*. Unfortunately, after we kill you, they'll be taking the millions and disbanding forever.'

He cocked the gun, about to pull the trigger.

'Yeah, about that,' Declan said, his face belaying no

expression of fear, his voice cool and calm. 'The money that you're all expecting to take in a couple of hours?'

He shrugged, with the slightest hint of a smile on his lips.

'I don't mean to piss on your chips or anything, but it's *already gone.*'

27

FOR THE END

'*You lie!*' Graham screamed out. '*You're playing with us!*' His finger was twitching, his eyes wide and angry. Declan, meanwhile, was completely at ease.

'No, really,' he shook his head. 'All gone. Kaput. Get your cyber guy there to look.'

Luke was already ahead of him, leaning over the table and typing quickly on the laptop, reading from a piece of paper to the side; most likely the account number, name and password that the Temple Inn team had found, now passed onto him by Theresa Martinez.

He sat back, his eyes filling with tears.

'It's gone!' he exclaimed. 'All of it! I looked ten minutes ago, and it was there!'

He rose from the table, storming across the boxing club and grabbing a non-retaliating Declan by his lapels.

'What did you do!' he hissed.

'Get your boss to lower the gun and I'll tell you,' Declan explained. Luke looked across the floor at Graham, who lowered his revolver, uncocking it as he did so.

'Look, it doesn't matter—' Graham started, but Luke interrupted him.

'*Of course it doesn't matter to you, Graham!*' he snapped. 'You've still got *his* money! And the houses and all that! You gonna share *those* with us?'

Graham and Luke were now facing each other, both tense, as if waiting for the other to make the first move.

'I'm guessing you *don't* want me to tell you?' Declan interjected between them. 'It's really good.'

'How?' Graham glared at Declan now. 'You couldn't beat the clock.'

'Yes, but you can *move* the clock,' Anjli replied from the boxing ring, where she now leaned forwards across the top rope once more. 'Billy, he's *our* cyber guy, he worked out how to make the account work to *Moscow* time.'

She pointed at the clock on the wall, now showing eight minutes past ten.

'It meant that we could remove the money before you, eight minutes ago. Two hours ahead of us right now due to British Summer Time, and twelve am Moscow time.'

Declan faced Graham, while pointing at Luke with his thumb.

'Honestly? I thought your cyber guy would be cleverer, work it out faster,' he said, repeating Luke's earlier comment.

'You've been delaying us,' Graham spun on the spot, looking around the boxing club. 'All this talking, all this walking round the ring, you just needed to talk out the clock.'

'Pretty much,' Declan nodded. 'Thanks for being such a helpful criminal.'

'You're gonna die,' Graham brought up the revolver again.

'Wait,' Theresa spoke now. 'Something's not right. If they knew I was part of this, why come here at all?'

She turned back to Anjli, raising her own gun.

'You wouldn't have walked in here willingly, knowing there was no police backup.'

'She might do if she had *other* backup,' a voice spoke from the shadows, and as Theresa looked to the door that led into the back room, she saw a man, blue shirt under a black suit, with amazingly groomed hair emerge, with Derek Sutton walking out behind him.

'We left the key for DS Kapoor,' Johnny Lucas said. 'She needed a favour. And we've been listening to everything you said. Even pulled our boy out of your limo. Thanks for springing him, though.'

'Who the hell are you?' Luke walked up to Johnny, but Theresa pulled him back.

'That's Johnny Lucas,' she whispered. 'You don't—'

'Listen to your friend,' Johnny smiled, but to all there it looked more like he was baring his teeth. 'You don't. *Full stop.*'

He looked back at Theresa.

'You killed my solicitor, you bitch,' he hissed. 'We're gonna have *words*.'

'No, you won't,' Monroe said as he walked into the room behind Johnny, with De'Geer, Billy, DC Davey and Doctor Marcos behind him. 'I gave you Derek on the basis that they live.'

He looked at the door to the boxing club, where Daniel McCarthy had slowly sidled his way. He said nothing as the blond-haired Asian quietly opened the door to a barrage of flashing blue lights and the grinning form of Detective Superintendent Sophie Bullman.

'Hey Danny,' she said. 'Should have stayed in Hampstead.'

'Oh, I wasn't trying to escape,' Daniel smiled warmly. 'I

was doing this—' he quickly smacked the bank of light switches on the wall, and for a moment the entire boxing club was plunged into darkness. Declan felt someone barge past him, likely Graham Terry, and started after him, reaching the back door as the lights returned on. Graham was already at the fire door, slamming the bar down as he ran out into the Globe Town street. There were no blue lights; the chances were that nobody had considered checking the back of the building yet, but Declan wasn't letting him escape this time. Ducking to the side, he flinched as Graham waved his revolver, firing backwards blindly.

Screw this, Declan thought to himself. *You destroyed my childhood. I'm not letting you get away now.*

———

THE MOMENT THAT THE LIGHTS HAD TURNED OFF, ANJLI HAD dived across the ring towards Theresa Martinez, sliding through the gap under the bottom rope, and slamming boldly into the other woman, sending her Glock 17 tumbling across the matted floor. As the lights came back on, Theresa fell back into a defensive fighting position, something akin to Kung Fu, perhaps, but Anjli wasn't intending to fight.

She was intending to brutalise.

'I warned you what I'd do if you hurt Declan,' she said, punching hard at Theresa's gut, but finding it blocked, as Theresa grabbed the arm, spinning her to the floor, Anjli tumbling onto the mat amongst the surrounding chaos. Luke and Jane were trying to run, but had been cornered by Doctor Marcos and DC Davey, Derek Sutton was being physically restrained from attacking Bruno Field by Monroe and

Billy, while Bullman and De'Geer seemed to play tag with Daniel as he ran around the boxing club in delight.

'Yeah, yeah, you'll hurt me,' Theresa said, waiting for Anjli to get up. 'Heard it all before—'

Slamming her boot heel hard down onto Theresa's damaged right knee, Anjli watched her opponent crumple to the floor in a wave of intense pain.

'I said I'd *destroy* you, bitch,' she said as she pulled Theresa's chin, forcing her to look up with her left hand as, with her right she slammed a wicked punch to the face, sending Theresa sprawling to the floor, her nose now busted and spewing blood.

'You know, with a punch like that, you should start training here,' Johnny said, currently lounging against the table with Luke's laptop on.

Anjli smiled.

'Where do you think I learned?' she asked.

RUNNING TO THE END OF THE ALLEY BEHIND THE BOXING CLUB, Graham stopped as he saw the blue lights of police cars blocking his way. Sighing, he tossed away his gun and looked back to Declan, now walking determinedly towards him.

'Well played,' he said. 'I thought you were a little too casual, but I just assumed you were arrogant.'

He held his hands out to be handcuffed.

'You won't be able to prove that I'm not Mark Walters though,' he smiled. 'Graham Terry is dead.'

'I think a DNA test with Jim Sutcliffe will probably prove that a lie,' Declan replied, pulling out his cuffs, and turning Graham around.

'Unlikely,' Graham replied. 'Didn't you ever wonder why my sister was blonde and I was ginger? Why I didn't get on with him later in life? I was the cuckoo in the nest.'

He laughed.

'A cuckoo in the *Magpies!*'

'Then you'll be tried under *this* identity,' Declan said.

'And Mark's vast amount of money will provide me with a team of lawyers that'll get me out in minutes,' Graham laughed. 'All those in there? I was fooled into doing it by Rory, and he's dead. Or Norman made me do it, and he's too senile to realise.'

Declan turned Graham around to face him.

'You know? You might beat this,' he said. 'At worst, make a comfortable life in there. But I don't think it'll get that far.'

'Why?' Graham looked nervously around now, as if expecting Declan to kill him right there. Declan did nothing of the sort though; instead he grinned widely.

'For the next few months, your pissed off ex-boss is still head of the Westminster *Star Chamber*,' he said. 'I had a run in with them and it was a nightmare. And I was *innocent*.'

He leaned in.

'Imagine how much worse it'll be when you're *guilty*,' he whispered. 'Personally, I'd be looking to make a deal as quickly as I can.'

And with that subtle warning made, Declan walked the Viscount Marcus Walters, otherwise known as Graham Terry out to the front of the boxing club, and the awaiting police.

As the police cars filled with arrested suspects, Johnny Lucas walked over to Anjli, currently holding an ice bag to her knuckles.

'Can I have a word?' he breathed. 'Alone?'

'I'm still on duty,' Anjli replied, not moving. 'Give me your demands some other time.'

'No demands,' Johnny smiled. 'Just a gift.'

He looked over to where Derek Sutton was giving a statement.

'Derek just informed me and my brother that you're the one that pushed for his release to help with the arrests. You got one of my old guys out, and even if he's a right royal pain in the arse, I know you could have just as easily left him there.'

'I didn't push for his release,' Anjli shook her head. 'It was—'

'Of course not,' Johnny tapped his nose. 'Whatever it was, your debt to me is cleared.'

Anjli stared in shock at Johnny, as he nodded one last time before turning and strolling off.

'See you around, DS Kapoor. I'll be sending you a cleaning bill for my boxing club.'

Anjli looked around the street, her mind a whirl. The release of Derek Sutton really had been nothing to do with them—

She glanced across the road at Monroe, laughing with Doctor Marcos. He looked back at Anjli and a small half-smile crossed his lips, before he carried on with whatever anecdote he was telling, and judging from the expression of Doctor Marcos, telling *badly*.

Had Monroe told Derek Sutton to say that? Anjli knew they had known each other, back in the day. *Had Monroe deliberately engineered this purely to get her out of Johnny Lucas' debt?*

She couldn't help it; Anjli Kapoor laughed.

DECLAN WAS WAITING BY THE POLICE CAR WHEN THERESA, HER nose plugged up with tissue paper, was brought over by De'Geer.

'Can I have a moment?' he asked. De'Geer nodded, nodding to Theresa.

'Ma'am,' he said, walking off.

'He's a good copper,' she said. 'Calls me Ma'am, when I'm a suspect. And, technically no longer on the force.'

'You *are* a good copper,' Declan replied. 'I've read your jacket. I saw what you've done over the years.'

'All for nothing,' Theresa sighed. 'Hey, apologise to your daughter for me. I don't mind letting you down, but it sucks to do that to her.'

'I will,' Declan nodded.

'So, was this the last goodbye?' Theresa had a wolfish smile. 'I mean, we can still have that proper dinner, but you might need to wait a few years.'

'I have something for you,' Declan pulled out his phone. 'I have some friends in... well, in places where information is easier to obtain.'

'Spooks.'

'Of a sort,' Declan smiled. 'I asked one of them to have a look into the Manchester Printworks explosion.'

'Why?' Theresa asked. 'We both know who sorted that.'

'That's the thing,' Declan replied. 'You don't. A week before the attack, MI5 had picked up chatter on some extremist sites, hinting at something like that happening. When the bomb went off, they compared it to some other devices and linked it to the *Flames of Abraham*, an extremist organisation that MI5 were following. It was never announced though, as the *Flames* never took credit for it. But last year, one ex-member, one that was now an asset to MI5, admitted it was a bomb that went off prematurely, and was disowned.'

'That can't...' Theresa shook her head. 'Danny...'

'Danny called you then purely by accident,' Declan explained. 'Maybe they were intending to do something, but the bomb blast was a pure coincidence, and one they've used on you for ten years.'

He backed away now as another officer walked over, opening the rear door for Theresa to get into the car.

'It's time to stop listening to people and start listening to yourself,' he said as the door was closed. 'You were a good copper, but the accident, the constant pain, the tablets, and then Gayle? They took you down a destructive path.' He nodded to himself.

'But at the trial, if you need a character witness? Call me.'

Theresa, tears streaming down her face, wouldn't even look at him, and as the squad car drove off, Declan found himself a little hollow inside.

'Girlfriend left you?' Anjli said, punching him on the arm with her good hand. 'Best for all of you. I mean, you'd only let her down or get her kidnapped, or killed, or...'

'You're stupidly chipper,' Declan smiled. 'Why are you so bloody happy for a change?'

'I've had my debt cleared,' Anjli pointed to Monroe. 'I think he had a word with Derek Sutton on my behalf.'

Declan shook his head.

'It won't be Monroe,' he muttered. 'He doesn't like you. None of us like you.'

He looked at Billy, walking towards them.

'Here comes Billy. He doesn't like you either.' He raised his voice.

'Hey, Billy, you like Anjli?'

Billy stared in confusion at Declan and Anjli as they started laughing, unable to stop.

'I work with bloody children,' he muttered. 'Seriously. The *Magpies* were more grown up than the pair of you.'

EPILOGUE

EVERYTHING THAT MARK WALTERS, OR GRAHAM TERRY HAD promised came true.

DNA proved he wasn't the son of Jim Sutcliffe, AKA Jim Terry, but at the same time couldn't accurately prove he was the son of the *previous* Viscount Walters, and some second cousin three-times-removed had placed an injunction on him, freezing his bank accounts until it could be proven.

Which, as he *wasn't*, meant that Mark Walters wasn't going to be able to pay for the fancy law firm he'd wanted. Even Bruno Field, released with no charges and still allowed to practice law under his legal name of Sebastian Klinger, refused to represent him.

Thomas Williams had been released without charge, and had immediately started claiming damages against the *Piccadilly Hyatt Hotel*, claiming they'd somehow been in league with his previous team, and that he expected innumerable damages to be paid.

It was, unfortunately, around this time that *BadgerLock Publishing*, the paid for and legal owners of Reginald

Troughton's final work, released *The Adventure of the Stolen Innocence*, in which Thomas Williams did not fare well. And within a week of the hardback release, the book was in the *Times Bestselling List*, and over fifty women, all in their late thirties and forties, horrified at what they'd read in the book offered their *own* stories from three decades worth of Thomas Williams, the now accused *sexual predator.*

Jane Terry was finally named as the original Jane of the *Magpies*, in a ceremony that involved Norman Shipman and Jim Sutcliffe, the only untarnished members of the original team. Sutcliffe, having never known that his son was still *alive,* was overwhelmed by the additional information that Graham wasn't even his son, the seemingly A-list detective never realising the clues in his own home life.

With Julia Clarke no longer there to demand otherwise, *BadgerLock* pulled all copies of the newly released versions of the *Magpies* books from their lists. The truth was out there now, and they felt that with Julia now dead, the original books should stay as memories, whether for good or for bad.

Derek Sutton returned to Glasgow, claiming his new legal team were going for the Government's jugular, and that he'd be expecting a pretty large windfall. He intended to buy shares in *Celtic FC,* and watch the matches in the owner's box. Monroe, not believing a word and expecting to hear news of Sutton caught fighting in the stands within three home games had agreed to ensure that he caught the night train up to Scotland, and had arrived into work the following morning like a bear with a sore head, complaining about *dodgy peanuts* making him sick, rather than the god knows how much alcohol he'd drunk in the King's Cross pub they'd said good-bye in.

The money taken earlier from the Swiss bank account

was never found, with Billy Fitzwarren claiming to any politicians who asked that the amount in the account was actually less than thirty thousand pounds, money instantly handed over to the government. However, seventeen worthy charities all had *bumper donations* given to them that day.

And Declan stayed at the house in Hurley, rather than move to London. He needed a break, and although the drive could be a pain, the scenery there was excellent. The locals were even being nice to him, even if a few more were now pissed at him for destroying their childhood book loves.

But that was fine, because he'd done the same to himself.

'THE PROBLEM IS, IT'S JUST SO BLOODY QUIET,' he moaned, sitting at his desk and staring at the Funko Bobby that stared back at him. 'So I end up staying here, which means I end up working late, and then I don't unwind.'

Anjli nodded. 'Yeah, but it's an incredible house in a beautiful village,' she said. 'I mean, there's what, four bedrooms? In London it'd be called a mansion.'

'Still lonely,' Declan replied. 'Especially with Jess being barred from me.'

'I thought Liz was getting over that?' Anjli asked. Declan nodded.

'Yeah, my new friend the childhood detective turned actual police detective was helping with that,' he said. 'And then the childhood detective turned actual police detective turned out to be a killer, and that kind of fell apart.'

He sighed.

'I haven't called them yet.'

'Well stop being a wussbag and do it,' Anjli snapped.

'Hey, if you're truly finding it hard there, why not find a housemate?'

'Trust issues,' Declan grinned. 'That and the fact that I'd need to finish fixing up the study.'

There was a quiet moment; Anjli looked like she wanted to say something, but wasn't sure how to say it.

'For Christ's sake, just say whatever's on your mind,' Declan muttered. 'We'll be here all bloody day otherwise.'

'Do you remember when we went to the house?' Anjli asked. 'When they broke in and stole your iMac?'

Declan thought back.

'Because if you ever need a housemate, let me know. I feel like I've fallen into Midsomer Murders here.'

'You asked if I needed a housemate,' he replied. Anjli nodded.

'Offer's still open,' she said. 'I have a rolling contract at the moment and my place is expensive and tiny. Have a think about it.'

She rose from her desk.

'And call your bloody ex-wife.'

Declan watched Anjli walk off, his mind already considering it. He got on well with Anjli, her friends group seemed to only involve people who worked at Temple Inn, she was a damn sight more fastidious than he was, and she was more likely to annoy the locals than Declan, which meant that they might leave him alone for a moment.

He saw Billy leaning back on his chair, watching him.

'She hates the people she shares with now,' Billy said. 'I mean, she hates you too, but you're a superior, so she has to be nice.'

'You think it's a good idea?'

'Yeah, guv, I do,' Billy replied. 'You're a damn good detective, nobody's doubting that, but since Kendis died you've retreated into this shell, emotionally. I thought Theresa Martinez might have broken through but...'

Declan nodded. 'I'll consider it. Anything else?'

'Actually, yes,' Billy held out his hand. In it was the encrypted USB drive Declan had given to him weeks earlier, that had been given to him by Tom Marlowe. 'I think I've cracked this, and I didn't know what you wanted to do with it.'

Declan looked at the drive, and then turned, staring out across the office towards the glass windows of Alex Monroe, currently holding his head in his hands as he valiantly tried to drink a glass of *Alka Seltzer*. Tom had said there was information on Monroe that should probably be seen, information gathered by Declan's father. But at the same time, Declan had learned a little too much about Monroe this case; the day after it ended, Monroe had pulled the team in and told them about his childhood in Glasgow. He trusted them to understand his life choices, and in return Declan needed to trust Monroe.

'Reformat it,' he said, turning back to Billy. 'I don't want to know what's on there. And if there are any problems down the line, Monroe can tell us himself.'

Billy smiled with relief and pulled a small, cordless drill out of the desk drawer, drilling into the USB with a piercing crunching noise.

'There,' he said, holding the damaged USB drive. 'Formatted. Nobody will ever see what was on it.'

'For the love of sweet baby Jesus!' Monroe screamed from the door, clutching at his pounding head, *'What the bloody hell are you clatty bawfaces doing out there! Cut it out!'*

Billy and Declan couldn't help it; they started laughing, which seemed to anger the hungover Monroe even more.

'I swear, I'll have them all demoted to *Community Support Officers*,' Monroe snarled to a patient and sympathetic Doctor Marcos who, with a grin and a wink back to Declan and Billy, sat him back at his desk, passing the unfinished glass of *Alka Seltzer* back into his hands.

Turning his chair back to his desk, Declan picked up the phone. Moving through the contacts, he stopped at a number, dialling it. After a few rings, it was picked up.

'Liz, it's me,' he said, 'No, I'm alright. I just wanted to talk to you about Jess, and how I can convince you to let me see her again.'

There was a pause in conversation, and Billy, who hadn't meant to eavesdrop on any of it, and had only been privy to it by closeness of location, glanced over at Declan, worried that he was getting some kind of ear bashing.

As it was, Declan was leaning back in the chair, half laughing as he listened to the phone.

'*I know!*' he exclaimed. 'Imagine how bad it'd have been if she met her!'

Billy smiled, looking around the office. De'Geer was walking back from the canteen room with DC Davey, both deep in conversation about *maggots*, Anjli was talking to Bullman outside her office, re-enacting the punch she'd made in Globe Town, Declan was laughing with his ex-wife again and Monroe was being force-fed the *Alka Seltzer* against his will by Doctor Marcos.

The team had never been closer.

It was a *family.*

Billy looked down at the USB drive, the cordless drill bit still pierced through the middle. He was glad that Declan had decided to destroy the data. Billy just wished that he had the strength of will to do it to the *real* USB.

Because after decoding the encryptions, Billy had read the drive's *contents*, and had seen the documents that had been encrypted; pictures, notes and clippings saved by Patrick Walsh over the years.

All about Detective Chief Inspector *Alexander Monroe.*

Billy had read them all. And he now understood why Patrick Walsh had made this dossier, encrypting it to USB, and more importantly why Tom Marlowe had passed it on, however misguided, to Declan.

One day the news *would* come out.

And when it did, Declan would need the USB drive; the *real* one, if only to give him the unbiased information held within, to help him deal with it.

Billy opened the drawer, placing the drill and the broken, fake USB stick into it, closing it with a slight shiver.

Until then, though, it could wait.

DI Walsh and the team of the *Last Chance Saloon* will return in their next thriller

A RITUAL FOR THE DYING

Order Now at Amazon:

http://mybook.to/aritualforthedying

And read on for a sneak preview...

PROLOGUE

Simon wasn't sure if this had been one of his better ideas, and he was very vocal in explaining it to Alfie. However, the words were simply swept away, flying off like notes on the wind as Alfie chose, as per usual, to ignore them.

They were currently standing at the Southern entrance to Greenwich Park in South East London; giant, wrought-iron gates held between six tall, pale brick pillars, each adorned with an enormous lamp and with the gates themselves spiked, the black painted vertical tines of the wrought-iron resembling spears, as if warning all who enter to play by the rules... or be punished.

Simon had seen photos of Blackheath Gate, as it had been called from around ten years earlier; they used to be far more ornate, with large, flowing gold motifs along the top but sometime in the last decade it had been decided by the council to remove these and renovate them into the stark, cold gates that the park now had in order to widen the roadway entrances, allowing larger vehicles to enter.

Alfie didn't care about the gates; for him, they were too

modern, too normal. Alfie was there for the mysteries and the histories. Simon envied Alfie for that. He'd been like this ever since school, and university hadn't exactly pulled him away from his passion, allowing him to join organisations like the university paranormal society, which had led him down the path towards other, non-university based esoteric organisations.

Simon hadn't gone to university. Simon had left school after his GSCEs and had joined the post office. But he'd still kept in touch with his best mate, even in their late twenties.

Alfie was now examining the railings, checking his watch. It was close to eight pm now, and the sign on the gate stated that in April, the park closed then. Simon knew that for the plan to work, they needed to get into the park and hide in the undergrowth before the rangers and park police did their last sweep of the area, which didn't exactly give them much time.

'Dude, we need to leave,' he hissed. Alfie turned, smiling. He was dressed in a black bomber jacket over a similarly black hoodie, black jeans and black boots completing his all-black ensemble. He had a charcoal grey backpack over his shoulder; this carried the tools of his trade, and the items that they'd be needing tonight, as well as a cheese ploughman's sandwich, some *Quavers* crisps and two bottles of Wild Cherry *Lucozade*.

'I think we should do the intro here,' he said. 'It'll only take a moment.'

Simon looked around. They were a little exposed but at the same time there were about a dozen other people nearby, all talking into cameras, either on their phone or on gorilla-grip hand-held mounts, likely recording for their *YouTube* channels.

Which was exactly why Simon and Alfie were also there.

'Sure,' Simon said, dropping his own backpack to the pavement and pulling out a Canon EOS SLR camera with a slim, fur covered directional mic sticking out the top and facing forward. Simon loved this camera; it was his pride and joy, and he knew that part of the reason that Alfie had let him join the channel was partly because he was an expert cameraman and amateur editor in his spare time but more importantly he was the owner of this beauty, which had cost him over a grand when he bought it new. Sighting through the digital screen on the back, he nodded to Alfie, now finding a suitable spot on the pavement to stand.

'Ready whenever you are,' he said.

Alfie nodded, counted to five and then made a circular motion with his arms; he did this so that they could tell on a continual clip when a new take had started. It made it easier to skim through the footage when working on *Final Cut Pro*.

'Hi there, and welcome to another episode of *Ghost Bros*,' he grinned. 'Tonight, in a last-minute change of plan, Simon and I are examining the mystical and horrifying tales of Greenwich Park, here behind me.'

Simon forced himself not to laugh at the name of the channel; he'd done so the last time, and they had a nightmare removing it from the edit. It had been Alfie's idea, to follow on from some of those American paranormal shows like *Ghost Adventures, Ghost Hunters* or *Haunted Towns,* as they had been more grounded than the UK options such as *Most Haunted,* which mainly revolved around scared people wandering around dark rooms with a Spiritualist medium, which meant that a lot of the 'evidence' found was often through the mouth of a man or woman who honestly could have read the wiki page of the location before they arrived. Although they'd used a medium themselves a few months ago, Alfie had wanted a fresh start recently, mimicking the US shows that were more grounded in technology; EVP, or *electronic voice phenomena* sessions, where questions were asked into a digital recorder and then listened back to see if spirts had manifested answers, specialised devices that recorded EMF, otherwise known as *electromagnetic fields*, which gave scientific proof that something was or wasn't around them and other items, such as handheld and static digital video cameras, including thermographic and night-vision options, although a lot of this was for show.

Simon and Alfie had all of these, although one of the static night vision cameras had gone missing a couple of months ago, probably borrowed by Alfie to do god knows what at night in his bedroom. They'd also emulated the style of the US shows more than the UK ones, two friends actively antagonising spirits, almost daring them to show themselves, aiming to get the ghosts angry and provoke a reaction, as this gave them more chance of reaching a US based audience, which gave them the opportunity to be seen by US television networks. Alfie believed implicitly that this was possible, and that even though they only had a couple of thousand subscribers, soon they'd hit the big time with something.

All they needed was a killer show, he'd continually told Simon. With Greenwich being barred to tourists at night, the idea of being able to record an overnight lockdown there was something that nobody else had really done. And, with it soon coming up to the end of April, the weather was now clement enough for it.

Simon returned to Alfie, still working on his introduction.

'Although this has been a royal park since the fourteen hundreds, this area has been a place of ritual worship, sacrifice and bloody battles for centuries before that,' Alfie said to the camera now, revelling in his role as presenter. 'Just behind me are dozens of Anglo-Saxon burial mounds, one of the largest collections in the world. But did they die peacefully or in battle, buried with the weapons they *killed* with? Come with us as we're locked down overnight in the park.'

'And cut,' Simon said, although he didn't really need to say anything, grabbing his backpack and hurrying Alfie along. 'We've got seven minutes.'

Even though the park was due to close soon it wasn't empty of people, as many tourists came to catch the sunset over London from the vantage point beside the Royal Observatory. Alfie and Simon used this to their own advantage, hurrying along Blackheath Avenue, the wide, tarmac road that had parking spaces on either side, turning right at the Pavillion Cafe, heading down the red-gravelled Great Cross Avenue before cutting across the grass, making their way to the ancient fallen tree known as *Queen Elizabeth's Oak*, and the wild undergrowth that was just past it. Simon knew that if they could hunker down there, they could wait out the police and the wardens as they did their last patrol of the night. All they had to do then was wait until it was fully dark, and emerge out from hiding, recording their pieces *guerilla-style* while alone in the park. They wouldn't even be visible as they did this, as they'd be using night vision cameras, meaning no torchlight.

They found a place to hide and, making themselves comfortable, they waited for night to fall; Simon constantly alert, watching for any last-minute park ranger checks as he listened to a podcast, and Alfie snoring beside him, headphones on, already asleep.

IT WAS CLOSE TO ELEVEN WHEN THEY FINALLY DARED TO MOVE from their hiding place, emerging back onto the path that led to the crossroads of Temple Walk and Lover's Walk. Simon started his night vision camera, aiming at Alfie who, in the night seemed to wear grey clothing, thanks to how the camera saw things through the filter.

'This is a place of great spiritual and ethereal power, and you can definitely feel it here at night,' Alfie said as he started walking backwards towards the junction. 'Queen Anne's House, at the north end of the park is the right-hand junction of two known *Ley Lines*, from which a straight line travels all the way down Blackheath Avenue, across Blackheath Common, where many died during the Cornish Rebellion, passing through All Saints Church in Blackheath, which was built with *six hundred and sixty-six pews*.'

He let the number hang in the air for a moment before continuing.

'Is this a message to the Devil? Is it a coincidence that Elizabethan Occultist John Dee would travel to the park at night, hunting a hidden occult library? And what of the folktales that talk of a mighty Celtic battle occurring here, at the base of this valley, which leads to One Tree Hill on one side, and an ancient, Megalithic stone, turned into a fountain on the other, a stone that has no reason to be here, and has possible links to another sacred stone, *Kit's Koty* in Kent?'

He'd reached the crossroads now, where a small path led to the aforementioned megalithic stone, once adapted by Victorian engineers into a drinking fountain, now nothing more than a curiosity.

'And what of the long-lost tunnels under Greenwich?' he asked the camera. 'What horrific acts occurred under this very path we walk down? Let's find out.'

He pulled out a digital recorder, holding it up to the air, pressing record.

'Is there anyone here?' he asked, pausing for a moment to allow a reply.

'What's your name?'

Another pause, and then

'How did you die?'

Alfie stopped the digital recorder, rewinding it to the start. With Simon moving closer, still filming, he held it up to the ear.

'*Is there anyone here?*' Alfie's voice could be heard, and then a slight hiss of static followed.

'Yes!' Alfie exclaimed. 'That was a definite *yes!*'

Simon wasn't sure about that, but kept quiet as they listened to the next two answers. The second had nothing but the third had a kind of stutter sound, which sounded like *stuh* to Simon.

'Stone!' Alfie almost shouted, lowering his voice as he remembered they were technically trespassing. 'Do you mean the ancient stone? Were you killed by it? Beside it?'

He'd started moving towards the stone fountain, gingerly making his way in the dark, unable to see through a camera like Simon.

'We need to grab a Mel-meter,' he said excitedly. 'Check the readings—'

'Dude, stop,' Simon spoke suddenly, his tone urgent. 'Don't move.'

'What is it?' Alfie asked as he complied with the command. Simon aimed his camera at the fountain behind his friend.

'There's something by the fountain,' he said. 'On the floor.'

Through the camera, Simon could see a figure, laying on the ground, stretched out in front of the stone itself.

'I think it's a person,' he said.

'Might be a homeless person trying to sleep,' Alfie whispered back. 'Some of them come here because it's safer than the streets.'

'No offence, mate but you would have woken them up by now,' Simon replied cautiously, moving closer, 'and we'd have seen them arrive. I think it's someone whose had a heart attack or something.'

He turned the camera away, clicking on a pen torch.

'I just want to check they're alright—'

His words died in his throat as he now stared at the body on the ground beside the megalithic stone fountain.

It was a man, lying face upwards, and placed so that his head was at the furthest point on the path. Simon knew someone had placed him, because the position was too unnatural, too straight, as if he was lying to attention, his arms to his side. He was obviously dead, his eyes open and staring through his horn-rimmed glasses, his wispy greying hair combed and positioned. He wore a tweed suit, with a white shirt, green cravat and what seemed to be a burgundy coloured waistcoat, with tan brogues completing the ensemble. The cravat was loose at the throat, and Simon thought he could see a redness around it.

'Christ,' Alfie muttered, moving closer, kneeling down to examine the body. 'He's definitely—'

'Don't touch him!' Simon hissed. 'Don't get your DNA or fingerprints on him!'

Alfie jumped back as if scalded, but it wasn't from the warning.

'Oh my God,' he said, staggering back to the edge of the

path, turning and vomiting up his hastily eaten sandwich from earlier in the evening. 'He's had his hand cut off.'

Simon leaned in and saw what Alfie had noticed, that the body's right hand, hidden from sight by the angle had been cut off and removed, with only a stump remaining, a tiny amount of dark blood having pooled around it.

'Why take a hand?' he asked, leaning closer to the throat. 'And was it taken before or after they hanged him?'

Alfie looked up. 'Hanged?'

'Yeah, look,' Simon, seemingly far more comfortable with the body than Alfie was, shone the torch beam at the body's throat. 'That's rope marks. He's been hanged.'

Alfie rose. 'This isn't just a murder,' he whispered, now backing away. 'This was a ritual. We need to get out of here.'

'What do you mean, a ritual?' Simon asked, as Alfie grabbed his backpack and hurriedly pulled it onto his shoulders.

'Taking the hand of a hanged man, it's what you do when you create a *hand of glory*,' Alfie replied. 'It's an incredibly powerful occult item. There's one in the museum in Whitby.'

Alfie was already moving quickly up Temple Walk, away from the body. 'Either way, I want nothing to do with it!'

Simon glanced back at the strange, tweed suited body that was missing a hand, and started after Alfie.

'At least you were right about one thing,' he said as they made their way towards the closest and most easily climbable gates at Maze Hill. 'All we needed was a *killer show*.'

A RITUAL FOR THE DYING

Released 15th August 2021

Order Now at Amazon:

http://mybook.to/aritualforthedying

ACKNOWLEDGEMENTS

When you write a series of books, you find that there are a ton of people out there who help you, sometimes without even realising, and so I wanted to do a little acknowledgement to some of them.

There are people I need to thank, and they know who they are. People like Andy Briggs, who started me on this path over a coffee during a pandemic to people like Barry Hutchinson, who patiently zoom-called and gave advice back in 2020, the people on various Facebook groups who encouraged me when I didn't know if I could even do this, the designers who gave advice on cover design and on book formatting all the way to my friends and family, who saw what I was doing not as mad folly, but as something good.

Also, I couldn't have done this without my growing army of ARC readers who not only show me where I falter, but also raise awareness of me in the social media world, ensuring that other people learn of my books, and editors and problem catchers like Maureen Webb, Chris Lee, Edwina Townsend, Maryam Paulsen and Jacqueline Beard MBE, the latter of whom has copyedited all six books so far (including the prequel), line by line for me, and deserves *way more* than our agreed fee.

But mainly, I tip my hat and thank you. *The reader.* Who, five books ago took a chance on an unknown author in a pile of

Kindle books, and thought you'd give them a go, and who has carried on this far with them.

I write Declan Walsh for you. He (and his team) solves crimes for you. And with luck, he'll keep on solving them for a very long time.

Jack Gatland / Tony Lee,
    London, May 2021

ABOUT THE AUTHOR

Jack Gatland is the pen name of *#1 New York Times Bestselling Author* Tony Lee, who has been writing in all media for over thirty years, including comics, graphic novels, middle grade books, audio drama, TV and film for *DC Comics, Marvel, BBC, ITV, Random House, Penguin USA, Hachette* and a ton of other publishers and broadcasters.

These have included licenses such as *Doctor Who, Spider Man, X-Men, Star Trek, Battlestar Galactica, MacGyver,* BBC's *Doctors, Wallace and Gromit* and *Shrek*, as well as work created with musicians such as *Ozzy Osbourne, Joe Satriani* and *Megadeth.*

As Tony, he's toured the world talking to reluctant readers with his 'Change The Channel' school tours, and lectures on screenwriting and comic scripting for *Raindance* in London.

An introvert West Londoner by heart, he lives with his wife Tracy and dog Fosco, just outside London.

Locations In The Book

The locations that I use in my books are real, if altered slightly for dramatic intent. Here's some more information about a few of them...

Waterstones Piccadilly is a real store, and one of the largest bookstores in London. In fact, for many years I would always take my meetings (when in town) in the fifth floor cafe area, which was an amazing, and quite place of repose, usually filled with similarly-minded writers, directors and producers, all discussing their latest work before heading two minutes up the road to BAFTA...

The Piccadilly Hyatt isn't real, but is located on the same plot of land as *The Thistle Hotel*. I needed a slightly different layout for my hotel, and so took the architecture from one of my favourite hotels, the *Hyatt Hotel* in San Diego, where I have spent many enjoyable days in during the *San Diego Comic Con* over the years.

The Baker Institute doesn't exist, but is based on a mixture of Bethlehem 'Bedlam' hospital, The Priory and Kenwood House in Hampstead. Where, funnily enough, if you walk around the gardens you can see the trickle of water that becomes the Fleet River that once flowed trough Clerkenwell.

The Boxing Club near Meath Gardens in which the finale occurs doesn't exist, and neither do the Twins - but the location used is the current **Globe Town Social Club**, within **Green Lens Studios**, a community centre formerly known as Eastbourne House, that I would pass occasionally in my 20s.

This is also possibly the last time we use the club, so it was nice to see it's been renovated, albeit fictionally!

The Old Bank of England pub is real, and the description and the history written in the book explain more than I could here, although one thing I don't mention, which is currently (as of writing) true is that in their 'sun garden' is a double decker bus that you can drink in!

Finally, **Belmarsh Prison** also exists, built in 1991 at Woolwich, in South East London. Since then it's been classed as a Category A Prison, holding prisoners from all over the United Kingdom, notable inmates including author Jeffrey Archer, Julian Assange, Charles Bronson, Ronnie Biggs and Stephen Christopher Yaxley-Lennon, better known as Tommy Robinson.

If you're interested in seeing what the *real* locations look like, I post 'behind the scenes' location images on my Instagram feed. This will continue through all the books, and I suggest you follow it.

In fact, feel free to follow me on all my social media, by clicking on the links below. They're new, but over time it can be a place where we can engage, discuss Declan and put the world to rights.

www.jackgatland.com

Subscribe to my Readers List: **www.subscribepage.com/ jackgatland**

www.facebook.com/jackgatlandbooks
www.twitter.com/jackgatlandbook
ww.instagram.com/jackgatland

Want more books by Jack Gatland? Turn the page...

THE THEFT OF A **PRICELESS** PAINTING...
A GANGSTER WITH A **CRIPPLING DEBT...**
A **BODY COUNT** RISING BY THE HOUR...

AND ELLIE RECKLESS IS CAUGHT IN THE MIDDLE.

JACK GATLAND

PAINT
— THE —
DEAD

A 'COP FOR CRIMINALS' ELLIE RECKLESS NOVEL

A NEW PROCEDURAL CRIME SERIES WITH
A TWIST - FROM THE CREATOR OF THE
BESTSELLING 'DI DECLAN WALSH' SERIES

AVAILABLE ON AMAZON / KINDLE UNLIMITED

EIGHT PEOPLE. EIGHT SECRETS.
ONE SNIPER.

THE
BOARD
ROOM

HOW FAR WOULD YOU GO TO GAIN JUSTICE?

NEW YORK TIMES #1 BESTSELLER TONY LEE WRITING AS

JACK GATLAND

A NEW STANDALONE THRILLER WITH
A TWIST - FROM THE CREATOR OF THE
BESTSELLING 'DI DECLAN WALSH' SERIES

AVAILABLE ON AMAZON / KINDLE UNLIMITED

THEY TRIED TO KILL HIM...
NOW HE'S OUT FOR **REVENGE.**

NEW YORK TIMES #1 BESTSELLER **TONY LEE** WRITING AS

JACK GATLAND

THE MURDER OF AN **MI5 AGENT**...
A BURNED SPY **ON THE RUN** FROM HIS OWN PEOPLE...
AN ENEMY OUT TO **STOP HIM** AT ANY COST...
AND A **PRESIDENT** ABOUT TO BE **ASSASSINATED**...

SLEEPING SOLDIERS

A **TOM MARLOWE** THRILLER

BOOK 1 IN A NEW SERIES OF THRILLERS IN THE STYLE OF
JASON BOURNE, JOHN MILTON OR **BURN NOTICE,** AND
SPINNING OUT OF THE **DECLAN WALSH** SERIES OF BOOKS

AVAILABLE ON AMAZON / KINDLE UNLIMITED

JACK GATLAND

THE LIONHEART CURSE

HUNT THE GREATEST TREASURES
PAY THE GREATEST PRICE

BOOK 1 IN A NEW SERIES OF ADVENTURES
IN THE STYLE OF 'THE DA VINCI CODE'
FROM THE CREATOR OF DECLAN WALSH

AVAILABLE ON AMAZON / KINDLEUNLIMITED

Printed in Great Britain
by Amazon